"I hadn't expected to see you here."

Simon's gaze moved over her in a disconcertingly thorough sweep. "But of course it's the logical place for a woman in your situation."

Annabelle narrowed her eyes. "In my situation?"

"Trying to catch a husband."

She responded with a haughty glance. "I am not trying to 'catch' anyone, Mr. Hunt."

"Casting the lure," he continued, "setting the hook, reeling in your unwary prey until he lies gasping on the deck."

Her mouth clamped into a tight line. "You may set your mind at ease, Mr. Hunt, as I have no intention of separating you from your precious freedom. You're the very last on the list."

"Ah. You've actually made a list of potential husbands?" Amusement danced in his eyes. "It's a relief that I'm not in the running, as I have resolved to avoid being padlocked into marriage at all cost. But I can't seem to stop myself from asking . . . who is at the top of the list?"

Avon Books by
Lisa Kleypas

IT HAPPENED ONE AUTUMN
SECRETS OF A SUMMER NIGHT
AGAIN THE MAGIC
WHERE'S MY HERO?
(with Kinley MacGregor and Julia Quinn)
WORTH ANY PRICE
WHEN STRANGERS MARRY
LADY SOPHIA'S LOVER
SUDDENLY YOU
WHERE DREAMS BEGIN
SOMEONE TO WATCH OVER ME
STRANGER IN MY ARMS
BECAUSE YOU'RE MINE
SOMEWHERE I'LL FIND YOU
PRINCE OF DREAMS
MIDNIGHT ANGEL
DREAMING OF YOU
THEN CAME YOU
ONLY WITH YOUR LOVE

LISA KLEYPAS

SECRETS OF A SUMMER NIGHT

AVON BOOKS
An Imprint of HarperCollinsPublishers

This is a work of fiction. Names, characters, places, and incidents are products of the author's imagination or are used fictitiously and are not to be construed as real. Any resemblance to actual events, locales, organizations, or persons, living or dead, is entirely coincidental.

AVON BOOKS
An Imprint of HarperCollins*Publishers*
10 East 53rd Street
New York, New York 10022-5299

Copyright © 2004 by Lisa Kleypas
ISBN: 0-06-009129-0
www.avonromance.com

First Avon Books paperback printing: November 2004

Avon Trademark Reg. U.S. Pat. Off. and in Other Countries, Marca Registrada, Hecho en U.S.A.
HarperCollins® is a registered trademark of HarperCollins Publishers Inc.

Printed in the U.S.A.

10 9 8 7 6 5

To Julie Murphy,
for taking care of Griffin and Lindsay
with such love, endless patience and skill . . .
for lending your many talents
to the business side of my career . . .
for being a cherished member of our family . . .
And most of all, for being you.

Love always,
L.K.

Prologue

London, 1841

Although Annabelle Peyton had been warned all her life never to take money from strangers, she made an exception one day . . . and quickly discovered why she should have heeded her mother's advice.

It was one of her brother Jeremy's rare holidays from school, and as was their habit, he and Annabelle had gone to see the latest panorama show in Leicester Square. It had taken two weeks of household economy to save the money necessary to pay for the tickets. As the only surviving offspring of the Peyton family, Annabelle and her younger brother had always been unusually close despite the ten-year difference in their ages. Childhood illnesses had taken the two infants who had been born after Annabelle, neither of them having lived to see their first birthday.

"Annabelle," Jeremy said as he returned from the panorama ticket stand, "do you have any more money?"

She shook her head and gave him a quizzical glance. "I'm afraid not. Why?"

Sighing shortly, Jeremy pushed back a swath of honey-colored hair that had fallen over his forehead. "They've doubled the price for this show—apparently it's far more expensive than their usual production."

"The advertisement in the paper said nothing about higher prices," Annabelle said indignantly. Lowering her voice, she muttered, "Hell's bells," as she opened her drawstring purse in the hopes of finding an overlooked coin.

The twelve-year-old Jeremy cast a grim glance at the huge banner that had been hung over the columned entrance of the panorama theater. . . . THE FALL OF THE ROMAN EMPIRE: A SHOW OF MAXIMUM ILLUSION WITH DIORAMIC VIEWS. Since its opening a fortnight earlier, the show had been crammed with visitors who had been impatient to experience the wonders of the Roman Empire and its tragic fall—"like going back in time"—people raved afterward. The usual sort of panorama consisted of a canvas hung in a circular room, surrounding viewers with an intricately painted scene. Sometimes music and special lighting were used to make the view even more entertaining, while a lecturer moved around the circle to describe faraway places or famous battles.

According to the *Times*, however, this new production was a "dioramic" view, which meant that the painted canvas was made of transparent oiled calico, illuminated from the front and sometimes from the back, with special filtered lights. Three hundred and fifty viewers stood on a roundabout in the center, which was operated by two men, so that the entire audience was slowly rotated during the show. The interplay of light, silvered glass, filters, and actors hired to play the part of beleaguered Romans, resulted in an effect that was labeled an "animated exhibition." From what Annabelle had read, the final climactic moments of simulated erupting volcanoes was so realistic that some of the women in the audience had screamed and fainted.

Taking the purse from Annabelle's busy hands, Jeremy pulled the drawstring and handed it back to Annabelle. "We have enough for one ticket," he said in a matter-of-fact manner. "You go inside. I didn't want to see the show anyway."

Knowing that he was lying for her benefit, Annabelle shook her head. "Absolutely not. *You* go in. I can see a panorama anytime I want—you're the one who's always away at school. And the show is only a quarter hour long. I will visit one of the nearby shops while you're inside."

"Shopping with no money?" Jeremey asked, his blue eyes frankly skeptical. "Oh, that sounds like loads of fun."

"The point of shopping is to look at things, not to buy."

Jeremy snorted. "That's something that poor people say to console themselves while they're walking along Bond Street. Besides, I'm not going to let you go anywhere alone—you'll have every male in the vicinity pouncing on you."

"Don't be silly," Annabelle muttered.

Her brother grinned suddenly. His gaze swept over her fine-boned face, her blue eyes, and the swath of pinned-up curls that gleamed brown and gold beneath the tidy brim of her hat. "Don't bother with false modesty. You're well aware of your effect on men, and, to my knowledge, you don't hesitate to make use of it."

Annabelle reacted to his teasing with a pretend-frown. "To your knowledge? Ha! What do you know of my interactions with men, when you're away at school most of the time?"

Jeremy's expression sobered. "That's going to change," he said. "I'm not going back to school this time—I can help you and Mama a damn sight more by getting a job."

Her eyes widened. "Jeremy, you'll do no such thing. It would break Mama's heart, and if Papa were alive—"

"Annabelle," he interrupted in a low voice, "we have no money. We can't even scrape up five extra shillings for a panorama ticket—"

"And a fine job you would get," Annabelle said sardonically, "with no education, and no advantageous connections. Unless you're hoping to become a street sweeper or an errand boy, you had better stay in school until you're fit for decent employment. Meanwhile, I'm going to find some rich gentleman to marry, then everything will be all right."

"A fine husband you'll catch with no dowry," Jeremy retorted.

They frowned at each other until the doors were opened and the crowd surged past them to enter the rotunda. Sliding a protective arm around Annabelle, Jeremy eased her away from the crush. "Forget the panorama," he said flatly. "We'll do something else instead—something fun that doesn't cost anything."

"Such as?"

A thoughtful moment passed. When it became apparent that neither of them could come up with a single suggestion, they both burst into laughter.

"Master Jeremy," came a deep voice from behind them.

Still smiling, Jeremy turned to face the stranger.

"Mr. Hunt," he said heartily, extending his hand. "I'm surprised that you remember me."

"So am I—you've grown a head taller since I saw you last." The man shook hands with him. "On leave from school, are you?"

"Yes, sir."

Seeing Annabelle's confusion, Jeremy murmured in her ear, while the tall stranger motioned his friends to enter the rotunda without him. "Mr. Hunt—the butcher's son," Jeremy whispered. "I've met him a time or two at the shop, when Mama sent me to fetch an order. Be nice to him—he's a capital fellow."

Bemused, Annabelle couldn't help thinking that Mr. Hunt was unusually well dressed for a butcher's son. He wore a smart black coat and the new style of more loosely tailored trousers that somehow didn't disguise the lean, powerful lines of the body beneath. Like most of the other men entering the theater, he had already removed his hat, uncovering a head of dark, slightly wavy hair. He was a tall, big-boned man who looked to be about thirty, with strong features, a long blade of a nose, a wide mouth, and eyes so black that one couldn't distinguish the irises from the pupils. His was an utterly masculine face, with a sardonic humor lurking about the eyes and mouth that owed nothing to frivolity. It was clear to even an undiscerning viewer that this man was rarely idle, his body and his nature patterned by hard work and keen ambition.

"My sister, Miss Annabelle Peyton," Jeremy said. "This is Mr. Simon Hunt."

"A pleasure," Hunt murmured, with a bow.

Even though his manner was perfectly polite, there was a glint in his eyes that imparted a strange flutter just beneath Annabelle's ribs. Without knowing why, she shrank back into the shelter of her young brother's arm even as she nodded to him. To her discomfort, she couldn't seem to tear her gaze from his. It seemed as if some subtle current of recognition had passed between them . . . not as if they had met before . . . but as if they had come close several times until finally an impatient Fate had forced their paths to intersect. A strange fancy, but one she couldn't seem to dismiss. Unnerved, she remained a helpless captive of his intent stare, until her cheeks were infused with hot, unwelcome color.

Hunt spoke to Jeremy, even as he continued to stare at Annabelle. "May I accompany you into the rotunda?"

A moment of awkward silence ensued before Jeremy replied, with studied nonchalance, "Thank you, but we've decided not to see the show."

One of Hunt's dark brows arched. "Are you certain? It promises to be a good one." His intuitive gaze moved from Annabelle's face to Jeremy's, reading the signs that betrayed their discomfort. His voice softened as he spoke to Jeremy. "No doubt there's a rule that one should never discuss these matters in front of a lady. However, I can't help wondering . . . is it possible, young Jeremy, that you were caught unaware by the increase in ticket prices? If so, I would be happy to advance you the extra coins—"

"No, thank you," Annabelle said quickly, her elbow digging hard into her brother's side.

Wincing, Jeremy stared up into the man's unreadable face. "I appreciate the offer, Mr. Hunt, but my sister is unwilling—"

"I don't want to see the show," Annabelle interrupted coolly. "I've heard that some of the effects are quite violent, and distressing to women. I would much prefer a peaceful walk in the park."

Hunt looked back at her, his deep-set eyes containing a gleam of mockery. "Are you so timid, Miss Peyton?"

Annoyed by the subtle challenge, Annabelle took Jeremy's arm and tugged insistently. "It's time to leave, Jeremy. Let us not delay Mr. Hunt any longer, as I'm certain that he wishes to see the show—"

"I'm afraid it will be quite ruined for me," Hunt assured them gravely, "if you do not attend also." He gave Jeremy an encouraging glance. "I should hate for a matter of mere shillings to deprive you and your sister of an afternoon's entertainment."

Sensing that her brother was weakening, Annabelle whispered sharply in his ear, "Don't you dare let him pay for our tickets, Jeremy!"

Ignoring her, Jeremy replied candidly to Hunt. "Sir, if I did accept your offer of a loan, I'm not certain when I would be able to reimburse you."

Annabelle closed her eyes and let out a faint, mortified groan. She tried so desperately never to let anyone know of their straitened circumstances . . . and for this man to know that every shilling was so dear was more than she could bear.

"There's no hurry," she heard Hunt say easily. "Come by my father's shop on your next visit from school and leave the money with him."

"All right then," Jeremy said with patent satisfaction, and they shook hands on the deal. "Thank you, Mr. Hunt."

"Jeremy—" Annabelle began, in a soft but murderous tone.

"Wait right there," Hunt said over his shoulder, already striding to the ticket stand.

"Jeremy, you know how wrong it is to take money from him!" Annabelle glared into her brother's unrepentant face. "Oh, how could you? It's not proper— and the thought of being indebted to that kind of man is intolerable!"

"What kind of man?" her brother countered inno-cently. "I told you, he's a capital . . . oh, I suppose you mean because he's of a lower class." A rueful smile curved his lips. "Somehow it's hard to hold that against him, especially when he's so filthy rich. And it's not as if you and I are actually members of the peerage. We're just dangling on the lower branches of the tree, which means—"

"How can a butcher's son be filthy rich?" Annabelle asked. "Unless the population of London is consuming far more beef and bacon than I'm currently aware of, there is only so much income that a butcher is able to garner."

"I never said that he worked in his father's shop," Jeremy informed her in a superior tone. "I only said that I *met* him there. He's an entrepreneur."

"You mean a financial speculator?" Annabelle frowned. In a society that considered it vulgar ever to speak or think about mercantile concerns, there was nothing more ill-bred than a man who had made a ca-reer out of investing.

"A bit more than that," her brother said. "But I suppose it doesn't matter what he does, or how much he's got, since he's born of mere peasant stock."

Hearing the criticism in her younger brother's voice, Annabelle gave him a narrow-eyed glance. "You sound positively democratic, Jeremy," she said dryly. "And you needn't carry on as if I'm being snobbish—I would object if a duke tried to give us ticket money, just as I would with a professional man."

"But not nearly as much," Jeremy said, and laughed at her expression.

Simon Hunt's return forestalled any further bicker-ing. Surveying them with alert, coffee-colored eyes, he smiled slightly. "All taken care of. Shall we go in now?"

Annabelle moved forward jerkily in response to her brother's discreet prodding. "Please do not feel obligated to accompany us, Mr. Hunt," she said, knowing that she was being ungracious, but there was something about him that sent sparks of alarm chasing along her nerves. He did not strike her as a trustworthy man . . . in fact, for all his elegant clothes and polished appearance, he didn't seem quite civilized. He was the kind of man that a well-bred woman would never want to be alone with. And her perception of him had nothing at all to do with social position—it was an innate awareness of a full-blooded physicality and a masculine temperament that was altogether alien to her. "I'm certain," she continued uneasily, "that you'll want to rejoin your companions."

Her comment was met with a lazy shrug of broad shoulders. "In this crowd, I'd never find them."

Annabelle could have argued by pointing out that as one of the tallest men in the audience, Hunt could probably locate his friends without difficulty. However, it was obvious that debating with him would be pointless. She would have to watch the panorama show with Simon Hunt at her side—she had no choice. As she saw Jeremy's excitement, however, some of Annabelle's wary resentment faded, and her voice softened as she spoke to Hunt again.

"Forgive me. I didn't mean to sound sharp. It's just that I don't like to be obligated to strangers."

Hunt shot her a perceptive glance that was disconcertingly thorough despite its briefness. "A sentiment I can easily understand," he said, guiding her through the crowd. "However, there is no obligation in this case. And we're not precisely strangers—your family has patronized my family's business for years."

They entered the large circular theater and stepped

onto a massive roundabout sided with wrought-iron rails and gates. A meticulously crafted image of an ancient Roman landscape surrounded them, with a twelve-yard gap separating the edge of the roundabout from the painting. The gap was filled with complex machinery that drew excited comments from the crowd. Once the viewers had filled the roundabout, the room darkened dramatically, eliciting gasps of excitement and anticipation. With a soft whir of machinery, and a glow of blue light shining from the back of the canvas, the landscape acquired a dimension and a sense of realism that startled Annabelle. She could almost let herself be deceived into thinking that they were standing in Rome at midday. A few actors clad in togas and sandals appeared, while a narrator began to relate the history of ancient Rome.

The diorama was even more enthralling than Annabelle had hoped it would be. However, she wasn't able to lose herself in the unfolding spectacle—she was too acutely aware of the man standing beside her. It hardly helped that he occasionally bent down to murmur some inappropriate comment in her ear, mockingly reproving her for displaying such unseemly interest in the sight of gentlemen dressed in pillowcases. No matter how sternly Annabelle tried to hold back her amusement, a few reluctant giggles escaped, earning disapproving glances from people around them. And then, naturally, Hunt chided her for laughing during such an important lecture, which made her want to giggle all the more. Jeremy seemed too absorbed in the show to notice Hunt's antics, craning his neck eagerly to discern which pieces of machinery were producing the wondrous effects.

Hunt quieted, however, after an unexpected hitch in

the roundabout's rotation caused the platform to jerk slightly. A few people were thrown off-balance, but were immediately steadied by the people around them. Surprised by the interrupted motion, Annabelle wobbled and found herself swiftly caught in a light, secure hold against Hunt's chest. He released her the instant she had regained her balance, lowering his head to ask softly if she was all right.

"Oh, yes," Annabelle said breathlessly. "I beg your pardon. Yes, I'm perfectly . . ."

She couldn't seem to finish the sentence, her voice dwindling into bewildered silence as awareness flooded her. Never in her life had she experienced this reaction to a man. Just what this immediate sense of urgency entailed, or how to satisfy it, was far beyond the scope of her limited knowledge. All she knew was that for a moment, she had desperately wanted to continue leaning on him, against a body so spare and firm as to be wholly invulnerable, providing a safe harbor as the floor shifted beneath her feet. The scent of him; clean male skin, polished leather, and the hint of starched linen, aroused all her senses with pleasurable expectation. He was completely unlike the cologned and pomaded aristocrats she had been trying to ensnare during the past two seasons.

Profoundly troubled, Annabelle stared straight ahead at the canvas, neither seeing nor caring about the fluctuations of light and color that conveyed impressions of approaching nightfall . . . the dusk of the Roman Empire. Hunt seemed similarly indifferent to the show, his head inclined toward hers, his gaze locked on her face. Though his breathing remained soft and disciplined, it seemed to her that its rhythm had changed ever so slightly.

Annabelle moistened her dry lips. "You . . . you mustn't stare at me like that."

Soft as the murmur was, he caught it. "With you here, nothing else is worth looking at."

She didn't move or speak, pretending that she hadn't heard the gentle devil-whisper, while her heart lurched in an unsteady meter, and her toes curled inside her shoes. How could this be happening in a theater full of people, with her brother right by her side? She closed her eyes briefly against a sensation of spinning that had nothing to do with the progress of the roundabout.

"Watch!" Jeremy said, nudging her eagerly. "They're about to show the volcanoes."

Suddenly the theater was plunged into utter blinding darkness, while an ominous rumbling rose from beneath the platform. There were several little screams of alarm, a scattering of laughter, and loud gasps of anticipation. Annabelle's spine went rigid as she felt the brush of a hand on her back. *His* hand, sliding with slow deliberateness up her spine . . . his scent, fresh and beguiling in her nostrils . . . and before she could make a sound, his mouth, possessing hers in a warm, softly ravishing kiss. She was too stunned to move, her hands in the air like butterflies suspended in midflight, her swaying body anchored by his light clasp on her waist, while his other hand cradled the back of her neck.

Annabelle had been kissed before, by brash young men who had stolen a quick embrace during a walk in the garden, or in a corner of the parlor when they would not be observed. But none of those brief, flirtatious encounters had been like this . . . a kiss so slow and dizzying that it filled her with delirium. Sensations rushed through her, far too strong to manage, and she quivered helplessly in his hold. Compelled by instinct, she lifted blindly into the tenderly restless caress of his lips. The pressure of his lips increased as he demanded more, rewarding her helpless response with a voluptuous exploration that set her senses on fire.

Just as she began to lose all sanity, his mouth released hers with startling suddenness, leaving her dazed. Keeping his supportive hand on the downy-soft nape of her neck, he bent his head until a rueful murmur tickled her ear. "Sorry. I couldn't resist." His touch withdrew completely, and when red-filtered light finally invaded the theater, he was gone.

"Will you look at that?" Jeremy enthused, pointing with glee at a simulated volcano in front of them, with brilliant molten rock appearing to course down its sides. "Incredible!" Noticing that Hunt was no longer there, he frowned quizzically. "Where did Mr. Hunt go? I suppose he must have seen his friends." Shrugging, Jeremy returned to his excited observation of the volcanoes, lending his exclamations to those of the awestruck audience.

Wide-eyed and completely bereft of speech, Annabelle wondered if what she thought had just happened had in fact really happened. Surely she had not been kissed in the middle of a theater by a stranger. And kissed in *that* way . . .

Well, that was what came of allowing unknown gentlemen to pay for things—it gave them the license to take advantage of you. But as to her own behavior . . . Shamed and bewildered, Annabelle struggled to understand why she had allowed Mr. Hunt to kiss her. She should have protested and pushed him away. Instead, she had stood there in a mindless daze while he—oh, the thought made her cringe. It didn't really matter how or why Simon Hunt had been able to shatter all her well-constructed defenses. The fact was, he had . . . and, therefore, he was a man to be avoided at all cost.

Chapter 1

London, 1843
The end of the season

A marriage-minded girl could overcome practically any obstacle, except the lack of a dowry.

Annabelle swung her foot impatiently beneath the frothy white mass of her skirts while she kept her expression composed. During her past three failed seasons, she had become accustomed to being a wallflower. Accustomed, but not resigned. More than once it had occurred to her that she deserved far better than to sit at the side of the room in a spindly chair. Hoping, hoping, hoping, for an invitation that would never come. And trying to pretend that she didn't care—that she was perfectly happy to be watching others dancing and being courted.

Letting out a long sigh, Annabelle fiddled with the tiny silver dance card that hung from a ribbon on her wrist. The cover slid open to reveal a book of near-translucent ivory leaves that spread out in a fan. A girl

was supposed to pencil the names of her dance partners on those delicate slips of ivory. To Annabelle, the
fan of empty cards seemed to resemble a row of teeth,
grinning at her mockingly. Snapping the silver case
shut, she glanced at the three girls who sat next to her,
all endeavoring to look similarly unconcerned with
their fates.

She knew exactly why they were there. Miss Evangeline Jenner's considerable family fortune had been
made from gambling, and her origins were common.
Moreover, Miss Jenner was painfully shy and possessed a stutter, which made the prospect of conversation a session of torture for both participants.

The other two girls, Miss Lillian Bowman, and her
younger sister Daisy, had not yet become acclimated
to England—and from the looks of things, it would
take them a long time. It was said that the Bowmans'
mother had brought the girls from New York because
they hadn't been able to get any suitable offers there.
The soap bubble heiresses, they were mockingly referred to, or occasionally, the dollar princesses. Despite their elegantly angled cheekbones and tip-tilted
dark eyes, they would find no better luck here unless
they could find an aristocratic sponsor to vouch for
them and teach them how to fit in with British society.

It occurred to Annabelle that in the past few months
of this miserable season, the four of them—herself,
Miss Jenner, and the Bowmans—had often sat together
at balls or soirees, always in the corner or against the
wall. And yet they had rarely spoken to each other,
trapped in the silent tedium of waiting. Her gaze
caught that of Lillian Bowman, whose velvety dark
eyes contained an unexpected gleam of humor.

"At least they could have made the chairs more
comfortable," Lillian murmured, "when it's obvious

that we're going to occupy them all evening."

"We should have our names engraved on them," Annabelle replied wryly. "After all the time I've spent in it, I *own* this chair."

A muffled giggle came from Evangeline Jenner, who lifted a gloved finger to push back a vivid red curl that had fallen over her forehead. The smile made her round blue eyes sparkle and her cheeks turn pink beneath a scattering of gold freckles. It seemed that a sudden sense of kinship had temporarily caused her to forget her shyness. "It m-makes no sense that you're a wallflower," she told Annabelle. "You're the most beautiful girl here—men should be f-falling all over themselves to dance with you."

Annabelle lifted her shoulder in a graceful half shrug. "No one wants to marry a girl without a dowry." It was only in the fantasy realm of novels that dukes could marry poor girls. In reality, dukes and viscounts and the like were burdened with the massive financial responsibility of maintaining large estates and extended families, and helping the tenantry. A wealthy peer needed to marry into money just as badly as a poor one did.

"No one wants to marry a *nouveau-riche* American girl, either," Lillian Bowman confided. "Our only hope of belonging anywhere is to marry a peer with a solid English title."

"But we have no sponsor," her younger sister, Daisy, added. She was a petite, rather elfin version of Lillian, with the same fair skin, heavy dark hair, and brown eyes. An impish smile touched her lips. "If you happen to know of some nice duchess who would be willing to take us under her wing, we would be much obliged."

"I don't even *want* to find a husband," Evangeline

Jenner confided. "I'm merely s-s-suffering through the season because there is nothing else for me to do. I'm too old to stay at school any longer, and my father . . ." She broke off abruptly, and sighed. "Well, I have only one more season to go, then I'll be twenty-three and a confirmed spinster. How I'm looking f-forward to it!"

"Is twenty-three the measure of spinsterhood these days?" Annabelle asked with half-feigned alarm. She rolled her eyes heavenward. "Good Lord, I had no idea that I was so far past my prime."

"How old are you?" Lillian Bowman asked curiously.

Annabelle cast a glance to the right and left, to make certain they were not being overheard. "Twenty-five next month."

The revelation earned three rather pitying glances, and Lillian replied consolingly, "You don't look a day more than twenty-one."

Annabelle clutched her fingers around her dance card until it was concealed in her gloved hand. Time was slipping away quickly, she thought. This, her fourth season, was drawing rapidly to a close. And one simply did not embark on a fifth season—it would be ludicrous. She had to catch a husband, and soon. Otherwise, they could no longer afford to keep Jeremy at school . . . and they would be forced to move from their modest terrace and find a boardinghouse to reside in. And once the downhill slide began, there was no climbing back up.

In the six years since Annabelle's father had died of a heart ailment, the family's financial resources had dwindled to nothing. They had tried to camouflage their increasingly desperate straits, pretending they had a half dozen servants instead of one overworked cook-maid and an aging footman . . . turning their faded gowns so that the underside of the fabric was facing outward . . . selling the stones in their jewelry and replacing them with paste. Annabelle was heartily tired of their constant efforts to deceive everyone, when it seemed that everyone already knew they were on the brink of disaster. Lately, Annabelle had even begun to receive discreet offers from married men, who told her meaningfully that she had only to ask for their help, and it would be given immediately. There was no need to describe the compensations that such "help" would require. Annabelle was well aware that she had the makings of a first-rate mistress.

"Miss Peyton," Lillian Bowman asked, "what kind of man would be the ideal husband for you?"

"Oh," Annabelle said with irreverent lightness, "any peer will do."

"*Any* peer?" Lillian asked skeptically. "What about good looks?"

Annabelle shrugged. "Welcome, but not necessary."

"What about passion?" Daisy inquired.

"Decidedly *un*welcome."

"Intelligence?" Evangeline suggested.

Annabelle shrugged. "Negotiable."

"Charm?" Lillian asked.

"Also negotiable."

"You don't want much," Lillian remarked dryly. "As for me, I would have to add a few conditions. My peer would have to be dark-haired and handsome, a wonderful dancer . . . and he would *never* ask permission before he kissed me."

"I want to marry a man who has read the entire collected works of Shakespeare," Daisy said. "Someone quiet and romantic—better yet if he wears spectacles—and he should like poetry and nature, and I shouldn't like him to be too experienced with women."

Her older sister lifted her eyes heavenward. "We won't be competing for the same men, apparently."

Annabelle looked at Evangeline Jenner. "What kind of husband would suit you, Miss Jenner?"

"Evie," the girl murmured, her blush deepening until it clashed with her fiery hair. She struggled with her reply, extreme bashfulness warring with a strong instinct for privacy. "I suppose . . . I would like s-s-someone who was kind and . . ." Stopping, she shook her head with a self-deprecating smile. "I don't know. Just someone who would l-love me. Really love me."

The words touched Annabelle, and filled her with sudden melancholy. Love was a luxury she had never allowed herself to hope for—a distinctly superfluous issue when her very survival was so much in question. However, she reached out and touched the girl's gloved hand with her own. "I hope you find him," she said sincerely. "Perhaps you won't have to wait for long."

"I want you to find yours first," Evie said, with a bashful smile. "I wish I could help you somehow."

"It seems that we all need help, in one form or another," Lillian commented. Her gaze slid over Annabelle with friendly speculation. "Hmm . . . I wouldn't mind making a project of you."

"What?" Annabelle arched her brows, wondering whether she ought to be amused or offended.

Lillian proceeded to explain. "There are only a few weeks left in the season, and this is your last, I assume. Practically speaking, your aspirations of marrying a man who is your social equal will vanish at the end of June."

Annabelle nodded warily.

"Then I propose—" Suddenly Lillian fell silent in midsentence.

Following the direction of her gaze, Annabelle saw

a dark figure approaching, and she groaned inwardly.

The intruder was Mr. Simon Hunt—a man whom none of them wanted anything to do with—and with good reason.

"Parenthetically," Annabelle said in a low voice, "my ideal husband would be the exact opposite of Mr. Hunt."

"What a surprise," Lillian murmured sardonically, for they all shared the sentiment.

One could forgive a man for being a climber, if he possessed a sufficient quantity of gentlemanly grace. However, Simon Hunt did not. There was no making polite conversation with a man who always said exactly what he thought, no matter how unflattering or objectionable his opinions.

Perhaps one might call Mr. Hunt good-looking. Annabelle supposed that some women might find his robust masculinity appealing—even she had to admit that there was something compelling about the sight of all that bridled power contained in a crisp formal scheme of black-and-white evening clothes. However, Simon Hunt's arguable attractions were completely overridden by the churlishness of his character. There was no sensitive aspect to his nature, no idealism or appreciation of elegance . . . he was all pounds and pence, all selfish, grasping calculation. Any other man in his situation would have had the decency to be embarrassed by his own lack of refinement—but Hunt had apparently decided to make a virtue of it. He loved to mock the rituals and graces of aristocratic civility, his cold black eyes glittering with amusement—as if he were laughing at them all.

To Annabelle's relief, Hunt had never indicated by word or gesture that he remembered that long-ago day at the panorama show when he had stolen a kiss from her in the darkness. As time had passed, she had even half convinced herself that she had imagined the whole thing. In retrospect, it didn't seem real, especially her own fervid response to an audacious stranger.

No doubt many people shared Annabelle's dislike of Simon Hunt, but to the dismay of London's upper tiers, he was there to stay. In the past few years he had become incomparably rich, having acquired majority interests in companies that manufactured agricultural equipment, ships, and locomotive engines. Despite Hunt's coarseness, he was invited to upper-class parties because he was simply too wealthy to be ignored. Hunt personified the threat that industrial enterprise posed to the British aristocracy's centuries-old entrenchment in estate farming. Therefore, the peerage regarded him with concealed hostility even as they unwillingly allowed him access to their hallowed social circles. Worse still, Hunt made no pretense at humility, but instead seemed to enjoy forcing his way into places where he wasn't wanted.

On the few occasions they had met since that day at the panorama, Annabelle had treated Simon Hunt coldly, dismissing any attempts at conversation and refusing his every invitation to dance. He always seemed amused by her disdain and stared at her with a bold appraisal that made the hairs on the back of her neck rise. She hoped that someday he would abandon all interest in her, but for the time being he remained annoyingly persistent.

Annabelle sensed the other wallflowers' relief as Hunt ignored them and turned his attention exclusively to her. "Miss Peyton," he said. His obsidian gaze seemed to miss nothing; the carefully mended sleeves of her gown, the fact that she had used a spray of pink rosebuds to conceal the frayed edge of her bodice, the paste pearls dangling from her ears. Annabelle faced him with an expression of cool defiance. The air between them seemed charged with a sense of push-and-pull, of elemental challenge, and Annabelle felt her nerves jangle unpleasantly at his nearness.

"Good evening, Mr. Hunt."

"Will you favor me with a dance?" he asked without prelude.

"No, thank you."

"Why not?"

"My feet are tired."

One of his dark brows arched. "From doing what? You've been sitting here all evening."

Annabelle held his gaze without blinking. "I have no obligation to explain myself to you, Mr. Hunt."

"One waltz shouldn't be too much for you to manage."

Despite Annabelle's efforts to stay calm, she felt a scowl tugging at the little muscles of her face. "Mr. Hunt," she said tautly, "has no one ever told you that it isn't polite to try and badger a lady into doing something that she clearly has no desire to do?"

He smiled faintly. "Miss Peyton, if I ever worried about being polite, I'd never get anything I wanted. I merely thought you would enjoy a temporary respite from being a perpetual wallflower. And if this ball follows your usual pattern, my offer to dance is likely the only one you'll get."

"Such charm," Annabelle remarked in a tone of mocking wonder. "Such artful flattery. How could I refuse?"

There was a new alertness in his eyes. "Then you'll dance with me?"

"*No*," she whispered sharply. "Now go away. Please."

Instead of slinking away in embarrassment at the rebuff, Hunt actually grinned, his teeth flashing white in his tanned face. The smile made him appear piratical. "What is the harm in one dance? I'm a fairly accomplished partner—you may even enjoy it."

"Mr. Hunt," she muttered, in rising exasperation, "the notion of being partnered with you in any way, for any purpose whatsoever, makes my blood run cold."

Leaning closer, Hunt lowered his tone so that no one else could hear. "Very well. But I'll leave you with something to consider, Miss Peyton. There may come a time when you won't have the luxury of turning down an honorable offer from someone like me . . . or even a dishonorable one."

Annabelle's eyes widened, and she felt a flush of outrage spread upward from the neckline of her bodice. Really, it was too much—having to sit against the wall all evening, then be subjected to insults from a man she despised. "Mr. Hunt, you sound like the villain in a very bad play."

That elicited another grin, and he bowed with sardonic politeness before striding away.

Rattled by the encounter, Annabelle stared after him with narrowed eyes.

The other wallflowers breathed a collective sigh of relief at his departure.

Lillian Bowman was the first to speak. "The word 'no' doesn't seem to make much of an impression on him, does it?"

"What was that last thing he said, Annabelle?" Daisy asked curiously. "The thing that made your face turn all red."

Annabelle stared down at the silver cover of her dance card, rubbing her thumb over a tiny spot of tarnish on the corner. "Mr. Hunt implied that someday my situation might become so desperate that I would consider becoming his mistress."

If she hadn't been so worried, Annabelle would have laughed at the identical looks of owlish astonishment on their faces. But instead of exclaiming in virginal outrage, or tactfully letting the matter drop, Lillian asked the one question that Annabelle wouldn't have expected. "Was he right?"

"He was right about my desperate situation," Annabelle admitted. "But not about my becoming his—or anyone's mistress. I would marry a beet farmer before I sank to that."

Lillian smiled at her, seeming to identify with the note of grim determination in Annabelle's voice. "I like you," she announced, and leaned back in her chair, crossing her legs with a negligence that was rather inappropriate for a girl in her first season.

"I like you, too," Annabelle replied automatically, prompted by good manners to reply in kind—but as the words left her mouth, she was surprised to discover that they were true.

Lillian's assessing gaze moved over her as she continued. "I should hate to see you end up trudging behind a mule and plow in a beet field—you were meant for better things than that."

"I agree," Annabelle said dryly. "What are we to do about it?"

Although the question was intended to be facetious, Lillian seemed to take it seriously. "I was getting to that. Before we were interrupted, I was about to make a proposition: We should make a pact to help each other find husbands. If the right gentlemen won't pursue us, then we'll pursue *them*. The process will be vastly more efficient if we join forces rather than forge ahead individually. We shall start with the eldest—

which appears to be you, Annabelle—and work down to the youngest."

"That hardly works out to *my* advantage," Daisy protested.

"It's only fair," Lillian informed her. "You've got more time than the rest of us."

"What kind of 'help' do you mean?" Annabelle asked.

"Whatever is required." Lillian began to scribble industriously in her dance card. "We'll supplement each other's weaknesses and give advice and assistance when needed." She glanced up with a cheerful grin. "We'll be like a Rounders team."

Annabelle regarded her skeptically. "You're referring to the game in which gentlemen take turns whacking a leather ball with a flat-sided bat?"

"Not only gentlemen," Lillian replied. "In New York, ladies may play also, as long as they don't forget themselves in the excitement."

Daisy smiled slyly. "Such as the time Lillian became so incensed by a bad call that she pulled a sanctuary post out of the ground."

"It was already loose," Lillian protested. "A loose post could have presented a danger to one of the runners."

"Particularly while you were hurling it at them," Daisy said, meeting her older sister's frown with a sweet smirk.

Smothering a laugh, Annabelle glanced from the pair of sisters to Evie's vaguely perplexed expression. She could easily read Evie's thoughts—that the American sisters were going to require a lot of training before they would attract the attention of eligible peers. Returning her attention to the Bowman sisters, she couldn't help smiling at their expectant faces. It was not at all difficult to imagine the pair flailing at balls with sticks and running around the playing field with their skirts hitched up to their knees. She wondered if all American girls possessed such a plenitude of spirit . . . no doubt the Bowmans would terrify any proper British gentleman who dared to approach them.

"Somehow I've never thought of husband-hunting as a team sport," she said.

"Well, it should be!" Lillian said emphatically. "Think of how much more effective we'll be. The only potential difficulty is if two of us take an interest in the same man . . . but that doesn't seem likely, given our respective tastes."

"Then we'll agree never to compete for the same gentleman," Annabelle said.

"And f-furthermore," Evie broke in unexpectedly, "we shall do no harm to anyone."

"Very Hippocratic," Lillian said approvingly.

"I happen to think she's right, Lillian," Daisy protested, misunderstanding. "Don't browbeat the poor girl, for heaven's sake."

Lillian scowled in sudden annoyance. "I said 'Hippocratic,' not 'hypocritical,' you dunce."

Annabelle interceded hastily, before the two began to quarrel. "Then we must all agree on the plan of action—it won't do any good for any of us to be at cross-purposes."

"And we'll tell each other everything," Daisy said with relish.

"Even i-intimate details?" Evie asked timidly.

"Oh, *especially* those!"

Lillian smiled wryly and slid an appraising glance over Annabelle's gown. "Your clothes are atrocious," she said bluntly. "I'm going to give you a few of my gowns. I've got trunks full that I've never worn, and I'll never miss them. My mother will never notice."

Annabelle shook her head immediately, at once grateful for the offer yet mortified by her conspicuous financial straits. "No, no, I couldn't accept such a gift, although you are very generous—"

"The pale blue one, with the lavender piping," Lillian murmured to Daisy, "do you remember it?"

"Oh, that would look heavenly on her," Daisy said enthusiastically. "It will suit her much better than you."

"Thanks," Lillian retorted, flashing her a comical glare.

"No, really—" Annabelle protested.

"And that green muslin with the white lace trim down the front," Lillian continued.

"I can't take your gowns, Lillian," Annabelle insisted in a low voice.

The girl looked up from her notes. "Why not?"

"For one thing, I couldn't afford to repay you. And it won't be any use. Fine feathers won't make my lack of a dowry any more appealing."

"Oh, money," Lillian said, in the careless manner that could only come from someone who had a great deal of it. "You're going to repay me by giving me something infinitely more valuable than cash. You're going to teach Daisy and me how to be . . . well, more like you. Teach us the right things to say and do—all the unspoken rules that we seem to break every minute of the day. If possible, you might even help to find us a sponsor. And then we'll be able to walk through all the doors that are currently closed to us. As for your lack of a dowry . . . you just get the man on the hook. The rest of us will help you reel him in."

Annabelle stared at her in amazement. "You're actually serious about this."

"Of course we are," Daisy replied. "What a relief it will be for us to have something to do, rather than sit against the wall like idiots! Lillian and I have been driven to near madness by the boredom of the season."

"S-So have I," Evie added.

"Well . . ." Annabelle looked from one expectant face to another, unable to keep from grinning. "If the three of you are willing, then so am I. But if we're to make a pact, shouldn't we sign it in blood or something?"

"Heavens, no," Lillian said. "I should think we can all agree to something without having to open a vein over it." She gestured with her dance card. "Now, I suppose we should make a list of the most promising candidates left after the past season. And a sadly picked-over lot they are by now. Shall we list them in order of rank? Starting with dukes?"

Annabelle shook her head. "We may as well not bother with dukes, as I'm not aware of any eligible ones who are under seventy years old and have any teeth remaining."

"So intelligence and charm are negotiable, but not teeth?" Lillian said slyly, making Annabelle laugh.

"Teeth are negotiable," Annabelle replied, "but *highly* preferred."

"All right, then," Lillian said. "Passing over the category of gummy old dukes, let's progress to earls. I know of Lord Westcliff, for one—"

"No, not Westcliff." Annabelle winced as she added, "He's a cold fish—and he has no interest in me. I practically threw myself at him when I came out four years ago, and he looked at me as if I were something that had stuck on his shoe."

"Forget Westcliff, then." Lillian raised her brows questioningly. "What about Lord St. Vincent? Young, eligible, handsome as sin—"

"It wouldn't work," Annabelle said. "No matter how compromising the situation, St. Vincent would never propose. He has compromised, seduced, and utterly ruined at least a dozen women—honor means nothing to him."

"There's the earl of Eglinton," Evie suggested hesitantly. "But he is quite p-p-portly, and at least fifty years old—"

"Put him on the list," Annabelle insisted. "I can't afford to be particular."

"There's Viscount Rosebury," Lillian remarked with a little frown. "Although he's rather an odd sort, and so . . . well, *droopy*."

"As long as he's firm in the pocketbook, he can be droopy everywhere else," Annabelle said, causing the other girls to snicker. "Write him down, too."

Ignoring the music and the couples that swirled in front of them, the four of them worked diligently on the list, occasionally making each other laugh so hard that they drew curious glances from passersby.

"Quiet," Annabelle said, making an effort to sound stern. "We don't want anyone to suspect what we're planning . . . and wallflowers aren't supposed to be laughing."

They all attempted to assume grave expressions, which set off fresh spasms of giggles. "Oh, look," Lillian gasped, regarding their ever-growing list of matrimonial prospects. "For once our dance cards are full." Considering the roster of bachelors, she pursed her lips thoughtfully. "It occurs to me that some of these gentlemen will probably be attending Westcliff's end-of-season party in Hampshire. Daisy and I have already been invited. What about you, Annabelle?"

"I'm acquainted with one of his sisters," Annabelle

said. "I think I can get her to invite me. I'll *beg*, if necessary."

"I'll put in a word for you as well," Lillian said confidently. She smiled at Evie. "And I'll have her extend an invitation to you, too."

"How fun this will be!" Daisy exclaimed. "The plan is set, then. In a fortnight we'll invade Hampshire and find a husband for Annabelle." They all reached out and clasped hands, feeling silly and giddy and more than a little encouraged. *Perhaps my luck is about to change,* Annabelle thought, and closed her eyes with a brief prayer of hope.

Chapter 2

Simon Hunt had learned at an early age that since fate had not blessed him with noble blood, wealth, or unusual gifts, he would have to wrest his fortune from an often uncharitable world. He was ten times more aggressive and ambitious than the average man. People usually found it far easier to let him have his way rather than stand against him. Although Simon was domineering, perhaps even ruthless, his sleep at night was never troubled by pangs of conscience. It was a law of nature that only the strongest survived, and the weakest had better get the hell out of the way.

His father had been a butcher, providing comfortably for a family of six and enlisting Simon as his assistant when he was old enough to wield the heavy chopping blade. Years of working in his father's shop had given Simon the massive arms and brawny shoulders of a butcher. It had always been expected that he would eventually manage the family business, but at the age of twenty-one, Simon had disappointed his father by leaving the shop in search of a different liveli-

hood. Upon investing his small accumulation of sav-
ings, Simon had quickly discovered his true talent in
life—making money.

Simon loved the language of economics, the ele-
ments of risk, the interplay of trade and industry and
politics . . . and he had realized immediately that before long the growing British railway network would
be the primary means for banks to conduct their business efficiently. The remittance of cash and securities,
the creation of fast-developing investment opportunities, would depend heavily on the service of the railroad. Following his instincts, Simon invested every
cent he had in railroad speculation, and was rewarded
with an explosion of profits that he immediately par-
layed into a diverse range of interests. Now, at thirty-
three, he owned controlling portions of three
manufacturing companies, a nine-acre foundry, and a
shipyard. He was a guest—albeit an undesired one—
in aristocratic ballrooms, and he sat shoulder to shoulder with peers on the boards of six companies.

After years of relentless work, he had gotten almost
everything he had ever wanted. However, if someone
had asked whether he was a happy man, Simon would
have snorted at the question. Happiness, that elusive
result of success, was a sure sign of complacency. By
his very nature, Simon would never be complacent, or
satisfied; nor did he want to be.

All the same . . . in the deepest, most private corner
of his neglected heart, there was one wish that Simon
could not seem to extinguish.

He shot a covert glance across the ballroom, experiencing as always the peculiar sharp pang that the sight
of Annabelle Peyton produced. With all the women
that were available to him—and there were more than
a few—no one had ever seized his attention with such

all-encompassing thoroughness. Annabelle's appeal went beyond mere physical beauty, though God knew she'd been blessed with an inequitable surplus. Were there an ounce of poetry in Simon's soul, he might have thought of dozens of rapturous phrases to describe her charms. But he was plebeian to the core, and he could not find words accurately to describe his attraction. All he knew was that sight of Annabelle in the glittering light of the chandeliers was very nearly knee-weakening.

Simon had never forgotten the first moment that he had seen her standing outside the panorama, digging through her purse with a little pucker on her forehead. The sun had picked out streaks of gold and champagne in her light brown hair and made her skin glow. There had been something so delicious . . . so touchable . . . about her, the velvety skin and shining blue eyes, and the slight frown that he had longed to soothe away.

He had been altogether certain that Annabelle would have been married by now. The evidence that the Peytons had fallen on hard times had not signified to Simon, who had assumed that any peer with his brains intact would see her worth and claim her at once. But as two years had passed, and Annabelle had remained unwed, a fragile tendril of hope had awakened inside Simon. He saw a touching valiance in her determined search for a husband, the self-possession with which she wore her increasingly threadbare gowns . . . the clear value that she placed on herself, despite her lack of a dowry. The artful way she approached the process of husband-hunting brought to mind nothing so much as a seasoned gambler playing his last few cards in a losing game. Annabelle was smart, careful, uncompromising, and still beautiful, although lately the threat of poverty had lent a certain hardness to her eyes and mouth. Selfishly, Simon was not sorry for her financial hardship—it created an opportunity that he never would have had otherwise.

The problem was that Simon had not yet figured out how to make Annabelle want him, when she was so obviously repulsed by everything he was. Simon was well aware that there were few graces to his character. Moreover, he had no ambition to become a gentleman any more than a tiger aspired to become a house cat. He was merely a man with a great deal of money and all the accompanying frustration of realizing that it could not buy the thing he most wanted.

So far, Simon's strategy had been to wait patiently, knowing that desperation would eventually drive Annabelle to do things that she had never considered doing before. Privation had a way of presenting a situation in a whole new light. Soon Annabelle's game would end. She would be faced with the choice of marrying a poor man or becoming the mistress of a wealthy one. And in the latter case, his bed would be the one she ended up in.

"A tasty little tart, isn't she?" came a comment from nearby, and Simon turned toward Henry Burdick, whose father, a viscount, was reputedly on his deathbed. Caught in the interminable wait before his father kicked off and finally yielded the title and family fortune, Burdick spent the majority of his time gambling and skirt-chasing. He followed Simon's gaze to Annabelle, who was engaged in a lively conversation with the wallflowers around her.

"I wouldn't know," Simon returned, feeling a jolt of antipathy for Burdick and all his ilk, who'd been given all manner of privileges on a silver platter since the day they were born. And usually did nothing to justify fate's imprudent generosity.

Burdick smiled, his face florid from too much

drink and rich food. "I intend to find out soon," he commented.

Burdick was hardly in the minority. No small number of men had set their sights on Annabelle, with the anticipation of a wolf pack trailing after a wounded prey. At the moment that she was at her weakest, and would offer the least resistance, one of them would move in for the kill. However, as in nature, the dominant male would always win out.

The shadow of a smile settled on Simon's hard mouth. "You surprise me," he murmured. "I would have assumed that a lady's predicament would inspire gallantry from gentlemen of your sort—and instead I find you entertaining the ill-bred notions that one would expect from *my* sort."

Burdick emitted a low laugh, missing the feral gleam in Simon's black eyes. "Lady or no, she'll have to choose one of us when her resources finally give out."

"Will none of you offer her marriage?" Simon asked idly.

"Good God, why?" Burdick licked his lips as anticipatory thoughts crossed his mind. "No need to marry the chit when she'll soon be available for the right price."

"Perhaps she has too much honor for that."

"Doubt it," the young aristocrat returned cheerfully. "Women that beautiful, and poor, can't afford honor. Besides, there is a rumor that she's already been giving over the goods to Lord Hodgeham."

"Hodgeham?" Inwardly startled, Simon kept his face expressionless. "What started that rumor?"

"Oh, Hodgeham's carriage has been seen at the mews behind the Peyton at odd hours of the night . . . and according to some of their creditors, he takes care of their bills now and then." Burdick paused and chortled. "A night between those pretty thighs is worth paying the grocer's account, wouldn't you say?"

Simon's instantaneous response was a murderous impulse to separate Burdick's head from the rest of his body. He wasn't certain how much of the cold, splintering rage was fueled by the image of Annabelle Peyton in bed with the porcine Lord Hodgeham, and how much was elicited by Burdick's snide enjoyment of gossip that was very likely untrue.

"I would say that if you're going to slander a lady's reputation," Simon said in a dangerously pleasant tone, "you had better have some hard proof of what you're saying."

"Egads, gossip doesn't require *proof*," the young man replied with a wink. "And time will soon reveal the lady's true character. Hodgeham doesn't have the means to keep a prime beauty like that—before long she'll want more than he can deliver. I predict that at the season's end, she'll sail off to the fellow with the deepest pockets."

"Which would be mine," Simon said softly.

Burdick blinked in surprise, his smile fading as he wondered if he had heard correctly. "Wha—"

"I've watched as you and the pack of idiots you run with have sniffed at her heels for two years," Simon said, his eyes narrowing. "Now you've lost your chance at her."

"Lost my . . . what do you mean by that?" Burdick asked indignantly.

"I mean that I will afflict the most acute kind of pain, mental, physical, and financial, on the first man who dares to trespass on my territory. And the next person who repeats any unsubstantiated rumors about Miss Peyton in my hearing will find it shoved right back in his throat—along with my fist." Simon's smile contained a tigerish menace as he beheld Burdick's stunned face. "Tell that to anyone who may find it of interest," he advised, and strode away from the pompous, gape-jawed little runt.

Chapter 3

*H*aving been returned to her town house by the elderly cousin who sometimes acted as her chaperone, Annabelle strode into the empty, flagstoned entrance hall. She stopped short at the sight of the hat that had been placed on the scallop-edged demilune table against the wall. It was a high-crowned gentleman's hat, gray banded with dark burgundy satin. A distinctive hat, compared to the simple black ones that most gentlemen wore. Annabelle had seen it on far too many occasions, perched on this very table like a coiled snake.

A stylish cane with a diamond-tipped handle leaned against the table. Annabelle entertained a lively desire to use the cane to bash in the crown of the hat—preferably while the owner was wearing it. Instead, she walked up the stairs with a leaden heart while a frown pinched her forehead.

As she neared the second floor where the family rooms were located, a heavyset man came to the top landing. He viewed her with an intolerable smirk, his complexion pink and moist from recent exertion, while a lopsided lock of his combed-over hair dangled like a rooster's crest.

"Lord Hodgeham," Annabelle said stiffly, swallowing against the shame and fury that had lumped in her throat. Hodgeham was one of the few people in the world whom she genuinely hated. A so-called friend of her late father's, Hodgeham paid infrequent calls to the household, but never at regular visiting hours. He came late at night, and against all dictates of decorum, he spent time alone in a private room with Annabelle's mother, Philippa. And in the days after his visits, Annabelle could hardly fail to notice that some of their most pressing bills had been mysteriously paid, and some irate creditor or another had been appeased. And Philippa was uncustomarily brittle and irritable, and disinclined to talk.

It was nearly impossible for Annabelle to believe that her mother, who had always shrunk from impropriety, would allow anyone the use of her body in return for money. Yet it was the only reasonable conclusion to draw, and it filled Annabelle with helpless shame and rage. Her anger was not directed solely at her mother— she was also furious at their situation, and herself for not yet having been able to land a husband. It had taken a long time for Annabelle to realize that, no matter how pretty and charming she was, and no matter how much interest a gentleman displayed, she was not going to get an offer. At least not a respectable one.

Since her come-out, Annabelle had gradually been forced to accept that her dreams of some handsome, cultivated suitor who would fall in love with her and make all her problems go away was a naive fantasy. That disillusionment had sunk in deeply during the prolonged disappointment that was her third season.

And now in her fourth season, the unappealing image of Annabelle-the-farmer's-wife was alarmingly close to reality.

Stone-faced, Annabelle attempted to walk past Hodgeham in silence. He stopped her with a meaty hand on her arm. Annabelle jerked back with such antipathy that the force of the movement nearly caused her to lose her balance. "Don't touch me," she said, glaring into his florid face.

Hodgeham's eyes appeared very blue against the ruddiness of his complexion. Grinning, he rested his hand on the top of the banister, preventing Annabelle from ascending to the landing. "So inhospitable," he murmured, in the incongruous tenor voice that so many tall men seemed to be afflicted with. "After the favors I have done for your family—"

"You've done no favors for us," Annabelle said tersely.

"You would have been cast into the streets long ago if not for my generosity."

"Are you suggesting that I should be grateful?" Annabelle asked, her tone saturated with loathing. "You're a filthy scavenger."

"I've taken nothing that wasn't willingly offered to me." Hodgeham reached out and touched her chin, the damp brush of his fingers making her recoil in disgust. "In truth, it's been tame sport. Your mother is too docile for my taste." He leaned closer, until the odor of his body—stale sweat liberally overlaid with cologne—filled Annabelle's nostrils with a pungent stench. "Perhaps the next time I'll try you out," he murmured.

No doubt he expected Annabelle to cry, or blush, or plead. Instead, she leveled a cold stare at him. "You vain old fool," she said evenly, "if I were to become

someone's mistress, don't you think I could get someone better than you?"

Hodgeham eventually twisted his lips into a smile
though Annabelle was pleased to see that it had taken
some effort. "It's unwise to make an enemy of me.
With a few well-placed words, I could ruin your family beyond all hope of redemption." He stared at the
frayed fabric of her bodice and smiled contemptu-
ously. "If I were you, I shouldn't be quite so disdainful, standing there in rags and paste jewels."

Annabelle flushed and knocked his hand away angrily as he reached out in an attempt to grope her
bodice. Chuckling to himself, Hodgeham descended
the stairs, while Annabelle waited in frozen silence.
After she had heard the sound of the front door open
and close, she hastened downstairs and turned the key
in the lock. Breathing hard from anxiety and lingering
outrage, she flattened her palms on the heavy oak door
and leaned her forehead against one of the panels.

"That does it," she mumbled aloud, trembling with
fury. No more Hodgeham, no more unpaid bills . . .
they had all suffered enough. She would have to find
someone to marry immediately—she would find the
best prospect she could at the Hampshire hunting
party and finally be done with it. And failing that . . .

She slid her hands slowly along the door panel, her
palms leaving streaking imprints on the grainy wood.
If she couldn't get someone to marry her, she could become some man's mistress. Athough no one seemed to
want her as a wife, there seemed to be an infinite number of gentlemen willing to keep her in sin. If she was
clever, she could earn a fortune. But she flinched at the
thought of never again being able to go out in good society . . . being scorned and ostracized and valued
only for her skills in bed. The alternative, living in vir-

tuous poverty and taking in sewing or washing, or becoming a governess, was infinitely more perilous—a young woman in that position would be at *everyone's* mercy. And the pay wouldn't be enough to sustain her mother, or Jeremy, who would also have to go in service. It didn't seem that the three of them could afford Annabelle's morality. They lived in a house of cards . . . and the merest agitation would cause it to collapse.

The following morning, Annabelle sat at the breakfast table with a porcelain cup clasped in her icy fingers. Although she had just finished her tea, the ceramic was still warm from the sturdy brew. There was a tiny chip in the glaze, and she rubbed the pad of her thumb over it repeatedly, not looking up as she heard her mother, Philippa, enter the room.

"Tea?" she asked in a careful monotone, and heard Philippa's murmured assent. Pouring another cup from the pot before her, Annabelle sweetened it with a small lump of sugar and lightened it with a liberal splash of milk.

"I don't take it with sugar any longer," Philippa said. "I've come to prefer it without."

The day when her mother stopped liking sweets was the day they began serving ice water in hell. "We can still afford sugar for your tea," Annabelle replied, stirring the cup with a few brisk swirls of her spoon. Glancing upward, she slid the cup and saucer to Philippa's place at the table. As she had expected, her mother looked sullen and haggard, with shame writhing behind her bitter facade. Once she would have found it inconceivable that her dashing, high-spirited mother—always so much prettier than anyone else's mother—could have worn such an expression. And as she stared at Philippa's taut face, Annabelle realized that her own facade was very nearly as world-weary, her mouth holding the same edge of disenchantment.

"How was the ball?" Philippa asked, holding her face close to her own tea so that the steam wafted over her face.

"The usual disaster," Annabelle said, softening the honesty of her reply with a deliberately light laugh. "The only man who asked me to dance was Mr. Hunt."

"Dear heaven," Philippa murmured, and drank a scalding mouthful of tea. "Did you accept him?"

"Of course not. There would be no purpose to it. When he looks at me, it is clear that he has anything but marriage in mind."

"Even men such as Mr. Hunt do eventually marry," Philippa countered, glancing up from her porcelain cup. "And you would be an ideal wife for him . . . you could perhaps be a softening influence, and help to ease his way into decent society—"

"Good Lord, Mama—it sounds as if you are encouraging me to accept his attentions."

"No . . ." Philippa picked up her spoon and needlessly stirred her tea. "Not if you truly find Mr. Hunt objectionable. However, if you could manage to bring him to scratch, we would all certainly be well provided for . . ."

"He is not the marrying kind, Mama. Everyone knows it. No matter what I did, I could never get a respectable offer from him." Annabelle dug through the sugar bowl with a tiny pair of tarnished silver tongs, searching for the smallest lump she could find. Extracting a morsel of raw brown sugar, she dropped it into her cup and drowned it with fresh tea.

Philippa drank her tea, her gaze carefully averted as she jumped to a new thread of conversation that

Annabelle perceived had a disagreeable connection to the last. "We haven't the means to keep Jeremy in school for his next term. I haven't paid the servants in two months. There are bills—"

"Yes, I know all of that," Annabelle said, flushing slightly with a swift burn of annoyance. "I'll find a husband, Mama. Very soon." Somehow she forced a shallow smile to her face. "How do you feel about a jaunt to Hampshire? Now that the season is coming to a close, many people will be leaving London in search of new amusements—in particular, a hunt given by Lord Westcliff at his country estate."

Philippa glanced at her with new alertness. "I wasn't aware that we had received an invitation from the earl."

"We haven't," Annabelle replied. "Yet. But we will . . . and I have a feeling that good things await us in Hampshire, Mama."

Chapter 4

Two days before Annabelle and her mother left for Hampshire, a towering stack of boxes and parcels arrived. It took the footman three trips to convey them from the entrance hall to Annabelle's room upstairs, where he piled them in a mountain beside the bed. Unwrapping them carefully, Annabelle discovered at least a half dozen gowns that had never been worn . . . taffeta silks and muslins in rich colors, and matching jackets lined in butter-soft chamois, and a ball gown made of heavy ivory silk with spills of delicate Belgium lace at the bodice and sleeves. There were also gloves, shawls, scarves, and hats, of such quality and beauty that they nearly made Annabelle want to weep. The gowns and accessories must have cost a fortune—undoubtedly nothing to the Bowman girls, but to Annabelle, the gift was overwhelming.

Picking up the note that had been delivered along with the parcels, she broke the wax seal and read the decisively scrawled lines.

From your fairy godmothers, otherwise known as Lillian and Daisy. Here's to a successful hunt in Hampshire.

P.S. You're not going to lose your nerve, are you?

She wrote back:

Dear Fairy Godmothers,

Nerve is the only thing I've got left. Thank you endlessly for the gowns. I am in ecstasy at finally being able to wear pretty clothes again. It is one of my many failings, to love beautiful things so dearly.

Your devoted Annabelle

P.S. Am returning the shoes, however, as they are far too small. And I'd always heard that American girls had large feet!

Dear Annabelle,

Is it a failing to love beautiful things? That must be an English notion, as we are certain that it has never occurred to anyone in Manhattanville. Just for that remark about feet, we're going to make you play Rounders with us in Hampshire. You will love whacking balls with sticks. There is nothing quite so satisfying.

Dear Lillian and Daisy,

I will consent to Rounders only if you can persuade Evie to join in, which I highly doubt. And though I won't know until I've tried it, I can think of lots of things more satisfying than whacking balls with sticks. Finding a husband comes to mind . . .

By the way, what does one wear to play Rounders? A walking costume?

Dear Annabelle,

We play in our knickers, of course. One can't run properly in skirts.

Dear Lillian and Daisy,

The word "knickers" is unfamiliar to me. Can you possibly be referring to undergarments? Surely you are not suggesting that we shall romp about outdoors in our drawers like savage children . . . ?

Dear Annabelle,

The word is derived from "Knickerbockers"—a level of New York society from which we are ritually excluded. In America, "drawers" belong inside a piece of furniture. And Evie says yes.

Dear Evie,

I did not trust my eyes when the Bowman sisters wrote to inform me that you have agreed to play Rounders in knickers. Have you really said so? I am hoping that you will deny it, as I had made my acceptance contingent upon yours.

Dear Annabelle,

It is my belief that this association with the Bowmans will help to cure me of my shyness. Rounders-in-knickers seems just the way to begin. Have I shocked you? I've never shocked anyone before, not even myself! I do hope that you are impressed by my willingness to jump into the spirit of things.

Dear Evie,

Impressed, amused, and somewhat apprehensive about what scrapes these Bowmans will land us in. Where, pray tell, are we to find a place where we may play Rounders-in-knickers unobserved? Yes, I am thoroughly shocked, you shameless hussy.

Dear Annabelle,

I am coming to believe that there are two kinds of people . . . those who choose to be masters of their own fate and those who wait in chairs while others dance. I would rather be one of the former than the latter. As to how and when Rounders game shall take place, I am satisfied to leave such details to the Bowmans.

> *With all fondness,*
> *Evie the hussy*

During the flurry of these and other playful notes that were sent back and forth, Annabelle began to experience something she had forgotten long ago . . . the delight of having friends. As her past friends had moved into the hallowed existence of married couples, she had been left behind. Her wallflower status, not to mention her lack of money, had created a chasm that friendship could not seem to bridge. In the past few years she had come to be increasingly self-reliant, and had even made efforts to avoid the company of the girls with whom she had once talked and giggled and shared secrets.

However, in one fell swoop she had acquired three friends with whom she had something in common, despite their radically different backgrounds. They were all young women with hopes and dreams and fears . . . each of them entirely familiar with the sight of a gentleman's polished black shoes walking by their row of chairs in search of more promising quarry. The wallflowers had nothing to lose by helping each other, and everything to gain.

"Annabelle," came her mother's voice from the doorway, as she carefully packed the boxes of new gloves into a valise, "I have a question, and you must answer it honestly."

"I am always honest with you, Mama," Annabelle replied, looking up from her task. Guilt swept over her as she beheld Philippa's lovely, careworn face. Dear God, she was tired of Philippa's guilt, and her own. She felt pity and despair for the sacrifice that her mother had made in sleeping with Lord Hodgeham. And yet, in the back of Annabelle's mind, the unseemly thought occurred to her that if Philippa had chosen to do such a thing, why couldn't she have at least set herself up properly as a real mistress instead of settling for the petty little wads of cash that Lord Hodgeham gave her?

"Where did those clothes come from?" Philippa asked, pale but earnest as she stared directly into Annabelle's eyes.

Annabelle frowned. "I've already told you, Mama—they came from Lillian Bowman. Why are you staring at me like that?"

"Did these clothes come from a man? Perhaps from Mr. Hunt?"

Annabelle's mouth fell open. "You're actually asking if I . . . with *him*? Good Lord, Mama! Even if I had the inclination, I haven't had the slightest opportunity. How in heaven's name did you come up with such an idea?"

Her mother met her gaze without blinking. "You've mentioned Mr. Hunt quite often this season. Far more than any other gentlemen. And these gowns are obviously quite costly . . ."

"They are not from him," Annabelle said firmly.

Philippa seemed to relax, but a question remained in her eyes. Unaccustomed to having anyone look at her with suspicion, Annabelle picked up a hat and set it at a smart angle over her forehead. "They're not," she repeated.

Simon Hunt's mistress . . . Turning toward the looking glass, Annabelle saw an oddly frozen expression on her face. She supposed that her mother was right—she had mentioned Hunt quite often of late. There was something about him that made thoughts of him linger in Annabelle's mind long after they had seen each other. No other man of her acquaintance possessed Hunt's charismatic, wicked appeal, nor had any man ever been so openly interested in her. And now, in the last few weeks of a failed season, she found herself contemplating things that no decent young woman should ever think about. She knew that without much effort, she could become Hunt's mistress, and all her troubles would be over. He was a wealthy man—he would give her whatever she wanted, pay her family's debts, and provide her with beautiful clothes, jewels, her own carriage, her own house . . . all that in return for sleeping with him.

The thought sent a sharp quiver through her abdomen. She tried to imagine being in bed with Simon Hunt, what things he might demand of her, his hands on her body, his mouth—

Flushing deeply, she forced the image aside and toyed with the silk rose adornments on the corded band of her hat. If she became Simon Hunt's mistress, he would own her completely, in bed and out of it, and the thought of being so completely at his mercy was appalling. A mocking voice in her head asked, "Is your honor so important to you? More important than your family's welfare? Or even your own survival?"

"Yes," Annabelle said under her breath, staring at her own pale, purposeful reflection. "Right now it is." She couldn't answer for later. But until every last hope was exhausted, she still had her self-respect . . . and she would fight to keep it.

Chapter 5

It was easy to see why the name of Hampshire was derived from the Old English word "hamm," referring to a water meadow. The county was rich with such meadows, not to mention heath and lush woodland that had once been earmarked as royal hunting grounds. With its contrast of dramatic scarps and deep green vales, and rivers flush with trout, Hampshire offered activities for every sportsman. The earl of Westcliff's estate, Stony Cross Park, was set like a jewel in a fertile river valley that scored gently through acres of forest. It seemed that there were always guests at Stony Cross Park, for Westcliff was an accomplished host as well as an avid hunter.

From all appearances, Lord Westcliff deserved his reputation of immaculate honor and high principles. He was not the sort to be involved in scandal, as he seemed to have little tolerance for the intrigues and slippery morality of London society. Instead, he spent much of his time in the country, shouldering his responsibilities and caring for his tenants. On occasion

he traveled to London to further his business interests
or involve himself in a political matter that demanded
his attention.

It was on one of these trips that Annabelle had met
the earl, when they had been introduced at a soiree.
Although he was not classically handsome, Westcliff
was not without attractions. He was only of medium
height, but he possessed the powerful form of a seasoned sportsman and an air of unmistakable virility.
All that, combined with an immense personal fortune
and one of the oldest earldoms in the peerage, made
him the most desirable matrimonial catch in England.
Naturally, Annabelle had wasted no time in beginning
a determined flirtation with him when they had first
met. However, Westcliff was inured to such attentions
from eager young women and had immediately labeled her as a husband hunter—which had stung, even
though it had been the truth.

Ever since Annabelle had been rebuffed by Westcliff,
she had made an effort to avoid him. She did happen to
like his younger sister, Lady Olivia, a softhearted girl
who was of an age with Annabelle and had been tainted
by scandal in her past. And it was thanks to Lady
Olivia's kindness that Annabelle and Evie had been invited to this party. For the next three weeks, both the
four-legged and the two-legged varieties of prey would
be under siege at Stony Cross Park.

"My lady," Annabelle exclaimed, as Lady Olivia
came to welcome them. "How kind of you to invite
us! London was positively stifling—the refreshing climate of Hampshire is precisely what we needed."

Lady Olivia smiled. Although she was a small and
rather unassuming girl with average features, she
seemed extraordinarily pretty on this occasion, her
face glowing with happiness. According to Lillian and

Daisy, Lady Olivia was betrothed to an American millionaire. *"Is it a love match?"* Annabelle had asked in her last letter to them, and Lillian had written back that it reportedly was. *"However,"* Lillian had added wryly, *"my father says that the alliance between the two families will certainly be to Lord Westcliff's financial advantage, which is why he gave his approval."* To the earl, romance was not nearly as important as practical considerations.

Bringing her mind back to the present, Annabelle smiled as Lady Olivia took her hands in a welcoming clasp. "And you are precisely what *we* needed," Lady Olivia exclaimed with a laugh. "The place is overrun with males in search of sport—I informed the earl that we simply *had* to invite some women to keep the atmosphere reasonably civilized. Come, let me accompany you to your rooms."

Picking up the skirts of the new salmon pink muslin from Lillian, Annabelle followed Lady Olivia up the front steps into the entrance hall. "How is Lord Westcliff?" Annabelle asked as they ascended one side of the grand double staircase. "In good health, I hope?"

"My brother is quite well, thank you. Although I fear he is driving himself to distraction with plans for my wedding. He insists on overseeing every detail."

"A reflection of his great affection for you, I'm certain," Philippa said.

Lady Olivia laughed wryly. "It is more a reflection of his great need to control everything within his reach. I'm afraid that it won't be easy to find a bride who will be strong-willed enough to manage him."

Catching her mother's meaningful sideways glance, Annabelle shook her head slightly. It would do no good to encourage Philippa's hopes in that direction. However . . . "I happen to know of a strong-willed and quite charming young woman who is yet unmarried," she commented. "An American, as a matter of fact."

"Are you referring to one of the Bowman sisters?" Lady Olivia asked. "I have not yet made their acquaintance, though their father has stayed at Stony Cross before."

"Both sisters are delightful in every regard," Annabelle said.

"Excellent," Lady Olivia exclaimed. "We may yet find a match for my brother."

Reaching the second floor, they paused to glance at the people milling about the entrance hall below. "I'm afraid there are not as many unmarried men here as one could wish for," Lady Olivia commented. "But there are a few . . . Lord Kendall comes to mind. If you like, I will introduce you to him when the opportunity presents itself."

"Thank you, I would enjoy that *very* much."

"I'm afraid he is somewhat reticent, though," Lady Olivia added "He may not appeal to someone as high-spirited as you, Annabelle."

"On the contrary," Annabelle said quickly, "I find reticence to be a most attractive quality in a man. Gentlemen with dignified reserve are so much more pleasant than those who are forever swaggering and boasting about themselves." *Like Simon Hunt*, she thought darkly, whose high self-opinion couldn't be more obvious.

Before Lady Olivia could reply, her gaze was caught from afar by that of a tall golden-haired gentleman who had come to stand in the entrance hall below. He stood in a cultivated slouch, resting his shoulder against a column, his hands thrust into his coat pockets. Annabelle knew instantly that he was an American. His irreverent grin and blue eyes, and the relaxed way he wore his elegant clothes, gave him away. Moreover, Lady Olivia blushed and seemed to require an extra breath or two, from the way he was looking at her. "Do pardon me," she said absently. "I . . . my fiancé . . . he seems to require me for something . . ." And she drifted away with a dreamy over-the-shoulder comment about their room being the fifth on the right. Instantly, a housemaid appeared to show them the rest of the way, and Annabelle heaved a sigh.

"There will be vicious competition for Lord Kendall," she fretted aloud. "I hope he hasn't already been taken."

"He can't be the *only* unmarried gentlemen here," Philippa remarked hopefully. "One must not forget Lord Westcliff himself."

"Don't entertain any hope in that direction," Annabelle told her wryly. "The earl was distinctly underwhelmed by me when we met."

"That was a great lapse in judgment on his part," came her mother's indignant reply.

Smiling, Annabelle reached down and squeezed Philippa's gloved hand. "Thank you, Mama. But I had better set my sights on a far more attainable target."

As guests continued to arrive, some went immediately to their rooms to refresh themselves with a midday nap, in anticipation of the supper and welcome dance that would be held later. Gossip-minded ladies congregated in the parlor and cardroom, while the gentlemen played billiards or smoked in the library. After their maid finished unpacking their clothes, Philippa decided to doze in their room. It was a small but lovely bedchamber, with flowered French paper on the walls and windows swathed in pale blue silk.

Too impatient and excited to sleep, Annabelle reflected that Evie and the Bowman sisters had probably

arrived. Even so, they would want some time to restore themselves after traveling. Rather than endure
hours of enforced inactivity, Annabelle decided to explore the grounds outside the manor. It was a warm,
sunlit day, and she craved exercise after the long carriage ride. Changing into a blue muslin day dress
shaped with rows of tiny box pleats, she left her room.

She slipped out a side entrance, passing a few servants on the way, and walked into a gentle flood of
sunlight. There was something wonderful about the
atmosphere at Stony Cross Park. One could easily
imagine it as some magical place set in some far-off
land. The surrounding forest was so deep and thick as
to be primeval in appearance, while the twelve-acre
garden behind the manor seemed too perfect to be
real. There were groves, glades, ponds, and fountains.
It was a garden of many moods, alternating tranquil-
lity with colorful tumult. A disciplined garden, every
blade of grass precisely clipped, the corners of the box
hedges trimmed to knife blade crispness.

Hatless, gloveless, and infused with a sudden sense
of optimism, Annabelle breathed deeply of the country air. She skirted the edge of the terraced gardens at
the back of the manor and followed a graveled path
set between raised beds of poppies and geraniums.
The atmosphere soon became thick with the perfume
of flowers, as the path paralleled a drystone wall covered with tumbles of pink and cream roses.

Wandering more slowly, Annabelle crossed through
an orchard of ancient pear trees, sculpted by decades
into fantastic shapes. Farther off, a canopy of silver
birch led to woodland beds that appeared to melt
seamlessly into the forest beyond. The graveled path
ended in a small circle, where a stone table had been
centered. Drawing closer, Annabelle saw the thick

stubs of two melted candles that had been burned directly on the stone surface. She smiled a bit wistfully, realizing that the privacy of the clearing must have been the perfect setting for some romantic interlude.

Inured to the dreamy atmosphere around them, a line of five fat white ducks waddled across the graveled circle, heading to a raised pool on the other side of the garden. It appeared that the ducks had been long accustomed to the multitude of visitors at Stony Cross Park, for they ignored Annabelle completely as they passed by. They quacked loudly in anticipation of reaching the artificial pond, their progress so comically animated that Annabelle couldn't help laughing.

Before her amusement had faded, she heard the crunch of a heavy footstep on the gravel. It was a man, who was evidently returning from a walk in the forest. He had lifted his head to stare at her with an arrested expression, his dark gaze meeting hers.

Annabelle froze.

Simon Hunt, she thought, shocked beyond the power of speech to see him there at Stony Cross. She had always associated him with town life—she usually saw him indoors, at night, confined by walls and windows and starched neckties. However, in these day-lit natural surroundings, he seemed a different creature altogether. His broad-shouldered build, so irreconcilable with the narrow cut of evening clothes, seemed utterly right for the rough weave of a hunting coat and the shirt that had been left open at the throat, no cravat anywhere in sight. He was darker than ususal, his skin burnished amber from a great deal of time spent out of doors. The sun glanced off his close-cropped hair, striking a rich shimmer from thick locks that were not quite black, but an intense shade of brown. His features, finely delineated by sunlight, were hard and prominent and striking. The few touches of softness in his face . . . the thick crescents of his dark lashes, the lush curve of his lower lip, were all the more intriguing for their uncompromising setting.

Hunt and Annabelle stared at each other in silent bemusement, as if someone had posed a question that neither of them knew how to answer.

The moment lengthened uncomfortably, until Simon Hunt finally spoke. "A pretty sound, that," he said softly.

Annabelle struggled to find her voice. "What is?" she asked.

"Your laughter."

Annabelle experienced a sharp little ache in her midriff that was neither pain nor pleasure. The disarming stab of sensation was unlike anything she had ever experienced before. Unconsciously she put her fingers over the spot just beneath her ribs. Hunt's gaze shot to her hand before easing slowly back up to her face. He moved nearer to the stone table, closing some of the distance between them.

"I hadn't expected to see you here." His gaze moved over her in a disconcertingly thorough sweep. "But of course, it's the logical place for a woman in your situation."

Annabelle narrowed her eyes. "In my situation?"

"Trying to catch a husband," he clarified.

She responded with a haughty glance. "I am not trying to 'catch' anyone, Mr. Hunt."

"Casting the lure," he continued, "setting the hook, reeling in your unwary prey until he lies gasping on the deck."

Her mouth clamped into a taut line. "You may set your mind at ease, Mr. Hunt, as I have no intention of separating you from your precious freedom. You're the very last on the list."

"What list?" Hunt contemplated her in the tense silence that followed, working it out for himself. "Ah. You've actually made a list of potential husbands?" Amusement danced in his eyes. "It's a relief to hear that I'm not in the running, as I have resolved to avoid being padlocked into marriage at all cost. But I can't seem to stop myself from asking . . . who is at the top of the list?"

Annabelle refused to answer. Even as she cursed her own tendency to fidget, she could not keep from reaching over to the lumpen stub of a candle and picking at it with the edges of her fingernails.

"Westcliff, probably," Hunt guessed.

Annabelle made a scornful sound, half-sitting on the table. The aged stone surface was sun-warmed and glossy-smooth. "Certainly not. I wouldn't marry the earl if he fell to his knees and begged me."

Hunt laughed richly at the blatant lie. "A pedigreed lord, with his fortune? You'd stop at nothing to get him." Casually, he sat on the opposite side of the table, and Annabelle steeled herself not to shrink from his proximity. Usually a conversation between a gentleman and a lady was underwritten by the understanding that there were certain things a gentleman would never do . . . he would not embarrass or insult her, or take advantage in any way. However, with Simon Hunt there were no such guarantees.

"Why are you here?" she asked.

"I'm a friend of Westcliff's," he said easily.

Annabelle was unable to imagine the earl claiming someone like Hunt as a friend. "Why would he associate with you? And don't try to claim that you have anything in common with him—the two of you are as different as chalk from cheese."

"As it happens, the earl and I do have some common interests. We both like to hunt, and we share a remarkable number of political beliefs. Unlike most peers, Westcliff does not allow himself to be chained by the restrictions of aristocratic life."

"Good Lord," Annabelle mocked, "you seem to view nobility as a condition of imprisonment."

"I do, as a matter of fact."

"Then I can hardly wait to incarcerate myself and dispose of the keys."

That made Hunt laugh. "You would probably do quite well as a peer's wife."

Recognizing that his tone was far from complimentary, Annabelle frowned at him. "If you dislike the peerage so much, I wonder that you spend so much time among them."

His eyes glinted wickedly. "They have their uses. And I don't dislike them—it's just that I have no desire to be one of them. In case you haven't noticed, the peerage—or at least the way of life they've known 'til now—is dying."

Annabelle reacted with a wide-eyed glance, genuinely shocked by the statement. "What do you mean?"

"Most landholding peers are losing their fortunes, seeing them divided and shrunken by ever-increasing numbers of relatives who require support . . . and then there is the transformation of the economy to contend with. The rule of the great landowner is fast coming to a end. Only men like Westcliff—who is open to new ways of doing things—will weather the change."

"With your invaluable assistance, of course," Annabelle said.

"That's right," Hunt said with such self-satisfaction that she couldn't help laughing.

"Have you ever considered making at least a pretense of humility, Mr. Hunt? Just for the sake of politeness?"

"I don't believe in false modesty."

"People might like you more if you did."

"Would you?"

Her nails dug into the soft pastel-colored wax, and she flashed Hunt a quick glance to measure the depth of mockery in his eyes. To her bewilderment, there was none. He seemed seriously interested in her answer. As he watched her intently, she felt a dismaying tide of pink creep over her face. She was not at all comfortable in this situation, conversing alone with Simon Hunt while he lounged beside her like a lazy, inquisitive pirate. Her gaze fell to the large hand he had braced on the table, the fingers long and clean and sun-browned, with nails cut so short that the crescents of white were barely visible.

" 'Like' may be going a bit far," Annabelle said, releasing her biting grip on the candle. The more she tried to control her flush, the worse it became, until it surged into her hairline. "I suppose I could tolerate your company more easily if you would try to behave like a gentleman."

"For example?"

"To begin with, the . . . the way you like to correct people . . ."

"Isn't honesty a virtue?"

"Yes . . . but it hardly makes for the best conversation!" Ignoring his low laugh, she continued. "And the way you talk so openly about money is vulgar, especially to those in higher circles. Nice people pretend that they don't care about money, or how to earn it, or invest it, or any of the other things you like to discuss."

"I've never understood why the enthusiastic pursuit of wealth should be held in such disdain."

"Perhaps because such pursuit is accompanied by so many vices . . . greed, selfishness, duplicity—"

"Those aren't my faults."

Annabelle raised her brows. "Oh?"

Smiling, Hunt shook his head slowly, the sunlight glittering on his sable locks. "If I were greedy and selfish, I would keep most of the profits from my businesses. However, my partners will tell you that they have been handsomely rewarded for their investments. And my employees are well paid by anyone's standards. As for being duplicitous—I think it's fairly obvious that I have the opposite problem. I'm truthful—which is very nearly unpardonable in civilized society."

For some reason, Annabelle could not help grinning back at the ill-bred scoundrel. She pushed away from the table and dusted her skirts. "I'm not going to waste any more of my time telling you how to be polite when it's perfectly obvious that you don't wish to be."

"Your time wasn't wasted," he said, coming around to her. "I'm going to lend some deep consideration to changing my ways."

"Don't bother," she said, the smile lingering on her lips. "You're a hopeless cause, I'm afraid. Now, if you'll excuse me, I'm going to continue my walk through the garden. Have a pleasant afternoon, Mr. Hunt."

"Let me come with you," he said softly. "You can lecture me some more. I'll even listen."

She wrinkled her nose at him impudently. "No, you won't." She started off on the gravel path, aware of his gaze on her back until she disappeared into the pear orchard.

Chapter 6

*J*ust before supper on the first evening of the party, Annabelle, Lillian, and Daisy met in the downstairs receiving room, a spacious area set with clusters of chairs and tables where many of the guests had chosen to congregate.

"I should have known that dress would look a hundred times better on you than me," Lillian Bowman said gleefully, hugging Annabelle and holding her at arm's length to gaze at her. "Oh, it's torture, being friends with someone so ravishing."

Annabelle was wearing another of her new gowns, a yellow silk with fluttering tulle skirts caught up at narrow intervals with tiny bunches of silk violets. Her hair was pinned at the back of her head in an intricately braided plait. "I have many flaws," Annabelle informed Lillian with a smile.

"Really? What are they?"

Annabelle grinned. "I'm hardly going to admit them if you haven't already noticed."

"Lillian tells everyone about her flaws," Daisy said,

her brown eyes twinkling. "She's *proud* of them."

"I do have a terrible temper," Lillian acknowledged smugly. "And I can curse like a sailor."

"Who taught you to do that?" Annabelle asked.

"My grandmother. She was a washerwoman. And my grandfather was the soap maker from whom she bought her supplies. Since she worked near the docks, most of her customers were sailors and dockers, who taught her words so vulgar that it would curl your hair ribbons to hear them."

Laughter rustled in Annabelle's chest. She was thoroughly charmed by the mischievous spirit of two girls who were unlike anyone she had ever known before. Unfortunately, it was difficult to imagine either Lillian or Daisy being happy as the wife of a peer. Most gentlemen of the aristocracy wanted to marry a girl who was serene, regal, self-effacing . . . the kind of wife whose sole purpose was to make her husband the focus of admiring attention. However, enjoying the Bowmans' company as Annabelle did, she thought it would be a pity for either of them to have to repress the innocent audacity that made them so beguiling.

Suddenly, she caught sight of Evie, who had entered the room with the reluctance of a mouse who had been thrown into a sack of cats. Evie's face relaxed as she saw Annabelle and the Bowmans. Murmuring something to her dour-looking aunt, she headed toward them with a smile.

"*Evie*," Daisy squealed in delight, beginning to rush toward the girl. Annabelle caught her gloved arm and whispered to her.

"Wait! If you draw attention to Evie, she'll probably faint from embarrassment."

Daisy stopped obediently and flashed her an unabashed grin. "You're right. I'm an absolute savage."

"I wouldn't say that, dear—" Lillian soothed.

"Thank you," Daisy said in pleased surprise.

"You're merely a quasi-savage," her older sister finished.

Biting back a laugh, Annabelle slipped her arm behind Evie's slender waist. "How lovely you look tonight," she said. Evie's hair had been piled at the crown of her head in a mass of gleaming red curls and fastened with pearl-tipped pins. The scattering of amber freckles across her nose only increased her appeal, as if nature had given in to a moment of whimsy and sprinkled a few flecks of extra sunlight over her.

Evie leaned into her partial hug as if she was seeking comfort. "Aunt F-Florence says I look like a f-flaming torch with my hair pinned up like this," she said.

Daisy scowled at the comment. "Your aunt Florence should hardly make such statements when *she* looks like a hobgoblin."

"Daisy, hush," Lillian said sternly.

Annabelle kept her gloved arm around Evie's waist, reflecting that from what little the girl had related to her, Aunt Florence appeared to take heartless delight in shredding what little confidence Evie possessed. After Evie's mother had died at a young age, the family had taken the unfortunate girl into its respectable bosom—and the ensuing years of criticism had left Evie's self-confidence decidedly battered.

Evie's smile contained a flash of amusement as she regarded the Bowman sisters. "She's not a h-hobgoblin. I've always thought of her as m-more of a troll."

Annabelle laughed in delight at the little jab. "Tell me," she said, "have any of you seen Lord Kendall yet? I was told that he is one of the very few unmarried men here—and aside from Westcliff, the only bachelor with a title."

"The competition for Kendall is going to be brutal," Lillian remarked. "Fortunately, Daisy and I have come up with just the plan to entrap an unsuspecting gentleman into marriage." She crooked her finger for them to come closer.

"I'm afraid to ask," Annabelle said, "but how?"

"You will entice him into a compromising situation, at which time the three of us will conveniently happen along and 'catch' you together. And then the gentleman will be honor-bound to ask for your hand in marriage."

"Brilliant, isn't it?" Daisy asked.

Evie looked at Annabelle dubiously. "It's rather underh-handed, isn't it?"

"There's no 'rather' about it," Annabelle replied. "But I'm afraid that I can think of nothing better, can you?"

Evie shook her head. "No," she admitted. "The question is, are we all s-so desperate to catch husbands that we'll resort to any means, be they fair or foul?"

"I am," Annabelle said without hesitation.

"So are we," Daisy said cheerfully.

Evie regarded the three of them uncertainly. "I can't toss aside *all* scruples. That is, I sh-shouldn't care to deceive a man into doing something that he—"

"Evie," Lillian interrupted impatiently, "men *expect* to be deceived in these matters. They're happiest that way. If one were straightforward with them, the whole prospect of marriage would be too alarming, and none of them would ever do it."

Annabelle regarded the American girl with mock alarm. "You're ruthless," she said.

Lillian smiled sweetly. "It's my family heritage. Bowmans are ruthless by nature. We can even be *fiendish* if the occasion calls for it."

Laughing, Annabelle returned her attention to Evie,

who wore a nonplussed frown. "Evie," she said gently, "until now, I've always tried to do things the right way. But it hasn't gotten me very far—and at this point, I am willing to try something new . . . aren't you?"

Still not seeming entirely convinced, Evie surrendered with a nod of resignation.

"That's the spirit," Annabelle said encouragingly.

As they conversed, there was a minor stir in the crowd as Lord Westcliff appeared. Seeming entirely comfortable in the position of managing things, he deftly paired gentlemen with ladies in preparation for the procession to the dining room. Although Westcliff was not the tallest man in the room, he had a magnetic presence that was impossible to ignore. Annabelle wondered why some people possessed such a quality—something unnameable that lent significance to every gesture they made and every word they spoke. Glancing at Lillian, she saw that the American girl had noticed it, too.

"There's a man who thinks well of himself," Lillian said dryly. "I wonder what—if anything—could ever set him back on his heels."

"I can't imagine," Annabelle replied. "But I would like to be there if it happens."

Evie drew closer and nudged her arm lightly. "There is Lord K-Kendall, in the corner."

"How do you know that he is Kendall?"

"Because he is surrounded by a dozen unmarried women who are circling him like sh-sharks."

"Good point," Annabelle said, staring at the young man and his milling entourage. William, Lord Kendall, seemed befuddled by the inordinate amount of female attention he was receiving. He was a fair-haired, slightly built young man, his lean face adorned by a pair of perfectly polished spectacles. The reflection of the glass lenses flashed as his perplexed gaze moved from face to face. The passionate interest being shown to a man of Kendall's timid demeanor proved that there was no aphrodisiac more effective than end-of-season bachelorhood. Whereas Kendall had been supremely uninteresting to these same girls last January, by June he had acquired an irresistible allure.

"He looks like a nice man," Annabelle said thoughtfully.

"He looks like he will spook easily," Lillian commented. "If I were you, I'd try to appear as bashful and helpless as possible when you meet him."

Annabelle gave her an ironic glance. " 'Helpless' has never been my forte. I'll try for bashful, but I can't promise anything."

"I don't foresee that you'll have any problem in diverting Kendall's interest from those girls to you," Lillian replied confidently. "After supper, when the ladies and gentlemen return here for tea and conversation, we'll find some way to introduce you."

"How should I . . ." Annabelle began, and paused as she felt a soft prickle along the nape of her neck, as if someone had drawn the fronds of a fern across her skin. Wondering what had caused it, she reached up to touch the back of her neck, and suddenly found her gaze caught by Simon Hunt's.

Hunt was standing across the room, leaning one shoulder negligently against the side of a flat pilaster, while a group of three men around him were engaged in conversation. He looked deceptively relaxed, his gaze intent, like that of a cat considering whether or not to pounce. It was clear that he had noticed her interest in Kendall.

Hell's bells, she thought in vexation, and deliberately turned her back to him. She wouldn't put it past Hunt to cause trouble for her. "Have you noticed that

Mr. Hunt is here?" Annabelle asked her friends in a low voice, and saw their eyes widen.

"*Your* Mr. Hunt?" Lillian sputtered, while Daisy whipped her head around to catch a glimpse of him.

"He's not mine!" Annabelle protested, making a comical face. "But yes, he's standing on the other side of the room. I saw him earlier today, actually. He claims to be a close friend of the earl's." She frowned and predicted darkly, "Mr. Hunt will do everything possible to wreck our plans."

"Would he really be so s-selfish as to prevent you from marrying?" Evie asked in amazement. "With the intention of making you into his . . . his . . ."

"Kept woman," Annabelle finished for her. "It's hardly outside the realm of possibility. Mr. Hunt has a reputation for stopping at nothing to get what he wants."

"That may be true," Lillian commented, her mouth firming with determination. "But he's not going to get *you*—I can promise you that."

Supper was a magnificent presentation, with gigantic silver tureens and platters carried in a ceaseless procession around the three long tables in the dining room. Annabelle could scarcely credit that the guests would dine like this every night, but the gentleman on her left—the parish vicar—assured her that this was commonplace for Westcliff's table. "The earl and his family are renowned for their balls and supper parties," he said. "Lord Westcliff is the most accomplished host of the peerage."

Annabelle was not inclined to argue. It had been a long time since she had been served such exquisite food. The lukewarm offerings at the London soirees and parties couldn't begin to compare to this feast. In the past few months the Peyton household had not been able to afford much more than bread, bacon, and soup, with the occasional helping of fried sole or stewed mutton. For once she was glad not to have been seated next to a sparkling conversationalist, as it allowed her long periods of silence during which she could eat as much as she liked. And with the servants constantly offering new and dazzling dishes for the guests to sample, no one seemed to notice the unladylike gusto of her appetite.

Hungrily she consumed a bowl of soup made with champagne and Camembert, followed by delicate veal strips coated in herb-dressed sauce, and tender vegetable marrow in cream . . . fish baked in clever little paper cases, which let out a burst of fragrant steam when opened . . . tiny buttered potatoes served on beds of watercress . . . and, most delightful of all, fruit relish served in hollowed-out orange rinds.

Annabelle was so engrossed in the meal that several minutes passed before she noticed that Simon Hunt had been seated near the head of Lord Westcliff's table. Lifting a glass of diluted wine to her lips, she glanced discreetly at him. Hunt was exquisitely dressed as usual, in a formal black coat and a rich pewter-shaded waistcoat, its silk weave gleaming with a quiet luster. His sun-darkened skin contrasted sharply with the starched white linen at his throat, the knot of his cravat as precise as a knife blade. The heavy sable locks of his hair needed an application of pomade . . . already a thick forelock had fallen over his forehead. It bothered Annabelle for some reason, that unruly lock. She wanted to push it back from his face.

It was not lost on her that the women seated on either side of Simon Hunt were competing for his attention. Annabelle had noticed on other occasions that women seemed to find Hunt quite appealing. She knew exactly why—it was his combination of sinful charm, cool intelligence, and arrant worldliness. Hunt looked like a man who had visited many women's beds and knew exactly what to do in them. Such a quality should make him less attractive, not more so. But Annabelle was discovering that there was sometimes a vast difference between what you knew was good for you, and what you actually wanted. And though she would have liked to deny it, Simon Hunt was the only man who had ever attracted her physically to this degree.

Although Annabelle had always been somewhat sheltered, she was acquainted with the basic facts of life. Her scant knowledge had been accumulated through hearing mention of things and putting two and two together. Annabelle had been kissed by a few different men who had shown fleeting interest in her during the past four years. But none of those kisses, no matter how romantic the setting, or how handsome the young man, had ever elicited the kind of response from her that Simon Hunt had.

Try as she might, Annabelle had never forgotten that long-ago moment in the panorama theater . . . the gentle, erotic pressure of his mouth on hers, the compelling pleasure of his kiss. She wished she knew why it had been so different with Hunt, but there was no one to ask. Talking to Philippa about it had been out of the question, as Annabelle had not wanted to confess that she had once accepted ticket money from a stranger. And she was hardly going to mention the incident to the other wallflowers, who clearly didn't know anything more about kissing and men than she herself did.

As Hunt's gaze suddenly locked with hers, Annabelle was perturbed by the realization that she had been staring at him. Staring, and fantasizing. Although they were sitting far apart from each other, she was aware of an immediate, electric connection between them . . . there was an arrested expression on his face, and she wondered what he saw that fascinated him so. Coloring violently, she tore her gaze away and dug her fork into a casserole of leeks and mushrooms blanketed with shavings of white truffle.

After supper, the ladies retired to the parlor for coffee and tea while the gentlemen remained at the tables for port. In the traditional style, the group would eventually reunite in the drawing room. As clusters of women laughed and chatted easily in the parlor, Annabelle sat with Evie, Lillian, and Daisy. "Have you found out anything about Lord Kendall?" she asked, hoping that one of them might have gleaned some gossip from the dinner conversation. "Is there anyone in particular whom he might have taken an interest in?"

"The field seems to be open so far," Lillian replied.

"I asked Mother what she knew about Kendall," Daisy supplied, "and she said that he has a sizable fortune and is unencumbered by debt."

"How would she know?" Annabelle asked.

"At Mother's request," Daisy explained, "our father commissioned a written report on every eligible peer in England. And she's memorized it. She says that the ideal suitor for either one of us would be a poverty-stricken duke whose title would guarantee the Bowmans' social success, while our money would ensure his cooperation in the marriage." Daisy's smile turned sardonic, and she reached over to pat her older sister's hand as she added. "They made up a rhyme about Lillian, back in New York . . . 'Marry Lillian, you'll get a million.' The saying became so popular that it was one of the reasons we had to leave for London. Our family looked like a bunch of gauche, overly ambitious idiots."

"And we're not?" Lillian asked wryly.

Daisy crossed her eyes. "I'm only fortunate that we left before they could make up a rhyme about me."

"I have," Lillian said. "Marry Daisy, and you can be lazy."

Daisy gave her a speaking glance, and her sister grinned. "Never fear," Lillian continued, "eventually we will succeed in infiltrating London society, and then we'll marry Lord Heavydebts and Lord Shallowpockets, and finally assume our places as ladies of the manor."

Annabelle shook her head with a sympathetic smile, while Evie left with a murmur, presumably to attend to her private needs. Annabelle almost felt sorry for the Bowmans, for it was becoming apparent that their chances of marrying for love were no greater than hers.

"Is it both your parents' ambition for you to marry a title?" Annabelle asked. "What is your father's opinion on the matter?"

Lillian shrugged nonchalantly. "For as long as I can remember, Father has never had an opinion about anything regarding his children. All he wants is to be left alone so he can make more money. Whenever we write him, he disregards the contents of the letter, unless we happen to be asking to draw more funds from the bank. And then he'll respond with a single line—'Permission to draw.'"

Daisy seemed to share her sister's cynical amusement. "I think Father is pleased by Mother's matchmaking, as it keeps her too busy to bother him."

"Dear me," Annabelle murmured. "And he never complains about your requests for more money?"

"Oh, never," Lillian said, and laughed at Annabelle's patent envy. "We're hideously rich, Annabelle—and I've got three older brothers, all unmarried. Would you possibly consider one of them? If you like, I'll have one shipped across the Atlantic for your inspection."

"Tempting, but no," Annabelle replied. "I don't want to live in New York. I would rather be a peer's wife."

"Is it really so wonderful, being a peer's wife?" Daisy asked plaintively. "Living in one of these drafty old houses with bad plumbing, and having to learn all the endless rules about the proper way to do *everything* . . ."

"You're no one if you're not married to a peer," Annabelle assured her. "In England, nobility is everything. It determines how others treat you, the schools your children attend, the places you're invited . . . every facet of your life."

"I don't know . . ." Daisy began, and was interrupted by Evie's precipitate return.

Although Evie displayed no obvious signs of being in a hurry, her blue eyes were lit with urgency, and excited color had gathered at the crests of her cheeks. Taking the chair she had previously occupied, she perched on the edge of the seat and leaned toward Annabelle, stammering and whispering. "I h-had to turn 'round and hurry back to tell you . . . *he's alone!*"

"Who?" Annabelle whispered back. "Who is alone?"

"Lord Kendall! I saw him at the b-b-back terrace. Just sitting there at one of the tables by himself."

Lillian frowned. "Perhaps he's waiting to meet someone. If so, it would hardly do Annabelle any good to go charging forth like a rhino in season."

"Might you be able to come up with a more flattering metaphor, dear?" Annabelle asked mildly, and Lillian flashed her a grin.

"Sorry. Just proceed with care, Annabelle."

"Point taken," Annabelle said with an answering smile, standing and straightening her skirts deftly. "I'm going to investigate the situation. Good work, Evie."

"Good luck," Evie replied, and they all crossed their fingers as they watched her leave the room.

Annabelle's heartbeat escalated as she walked through the house. She knew full well that she was treading through an intricate maze of social rules. A lady should never deliberately seek out a gentleman's company; but if they crossed paths accidentally, or happened to find themselves on the same settee or conversation chair, they could exchange a few pleasantries. They should never spend time alone unless they were riding horses or being conveyed in an open carriage. And if a girl chanced to meet a gentleman while heading out to view the gardens, she must take pains to ensure that the situation did not appear compromising in any way.

Unless, of course, she wanted to be compromised.

Drawing close to the long row of French doors that opened onto the wide flagstone terrace, Annabelle saw her quarry. As Evie had described, Lord Kendall was sitting alone at a round table, leaning back in his chair with one leg stretched carelessly before him. He seemed to be enjoying a momentary respite from the overheated atmosphere of the house.

Quietly Annabelle strode to the nearest door and slipped through it. The air was lightly scented with heather and bog myrtle, while the sounds of the river beyond the gardens provided a soothing undercurrent. Keeping her head down, Annabelle rubbed her temples with her fingers as if she were afflicted with a nagging headache. When she was ten feet away from Kendall's table, she looked up and made herself jump a little, as if she was startled to see him there.

"Oh," she said. It was not at all difficult to sound breathless. She was nervous, knowing how important it was to make the right impression on him. "I didn't realize that someone was out here . . ."

Kendall stood, his spectacles twinkling in the light of the terrace torch. His form was slim to the point of being insubstantial, his coat hanging from his padded shoulders. Despite the fact that he was approximately three inches taller than Annabelle, she would not have been surprised to learn that they were the same weight. His posture was at once diffident and oddly tense, like that of a deer poised for a sudden, bounding retreat. As she stared at him, Annabelle had to admit silently that Kendall was not the kind of man whom she would have had any natural attraction to. On the other hand, she didn't like pickled herring, either. But if she was starving and someone handed her a jar of pickled herring, she was hardly going to turn her nose up at it.

"Hullo," Kendall said, his voice cultured and soft, though a bit high-pitched. "There's no need to be alarmed. Really, I'm harmless."

"I shall reserve judgment on that," Annabelle said, smiling, then wincing as if the effort had pained her. "Forgive me for disturbing your privacy, sir. I wanted a breath of fresh air." She inhaled until her breasts pressed becomingly at the seams of her bodice. "The atmosphere inside the house was rather oppressive, wasn't it?"

Kendall approached with his hands half-raised, as if he feared she might collapse to the terrace. "May I fetch you something? A glass of water?"

"No, thank you. A few moments outside will restore me to rights." Annabelle sank gracefully into the nearest chair. "Although . . ." She paused and tried to look self-conscious. "It wouldn't do for us to be seen out here unchaperoned. Especially as we haven't even been introduced."

He made a slight bow. "Lord Kendall, at your service."

"Miss Annabelle Peyton." She glanced at the empty chair nearby. "Do have a seat, please. I promise, I shall hurry away as soon as my head clears."

Kendall obeyed cautiously. "No need for that," he said. "Stay as long as you wish."

That was encouraging. Mindful of Lillian's advice, Annabelle pondered her next remark with great care. Since Kendall was being exhaustively pursued by a score of women, she would have to distinguish herself by pretending that she was the only one who was *not* interested in him. "I can guess why you came out here alone," she said with a smile. "You must be desperate to avoid being mobbed by eager women."

Kendall threw her a glance of surprise. "As a matter of fact, yes. I must say, I have never attended a party with such excessively friendly guests."

"Wait until the end of the month," she advised. "They'll be so friendly by then that you'll need a whip and a chair to hold them off."

"You seem to be suggesting that I'm some sort of matrimonial target," he commented dryly, giving voice to the obvious.

"The only way you could be more of a target is if you drew white circles on the back of your coat," Annabelle said, making him chuckle. "May I ask what your other reasons for escaping to the terrace are, my lord?"

Kendall continued to smile, looking far more comfortable than he had at first. "I'm afraid I can't hold my liquor. There is only so much port that I am willing to drink for the sake of being social."

Annabelle had never met a man who was willing to admit such a thing. Most gentlemen equated manliness with the ability to drink a sufficient quantity of liquor to inebriate an elephant. "Does it make you ill, then?" she asked sympathetically.

"Sick as a dog. I've been told that tolerance improves with practice—but it seems a rather pointless objective. I can think of better ways to pass the time."

"Such as . . ."

Kendall contemplated the question with great care. "A walk through the countryside. A book that improves the mind." His eyes contained a sudden friendly twinkle. "A conversation with a new friend."

"I like those things, too."

"Do you?" Kendall hesitated, while the sounds of the river and the sway of the trees seemed to whisper through the air. "Perhaps you might join me on a walk tomorrow morning. I know of several excellent ones around Stony Cross."

Annabelle's sudden eagerness was difficult to contain. "I would enjoy that," she replied. "But dare I ask—what about your entourage?"

Kendall smiled, revealing a row of small, neat teeth. "I don't expect that anyone will bother us if we depart early enough."

"I happen to be an early riser," she lied. "And I love to walk."

"Six o'clock, then?"

"Six o'clock," she repeated, standing from her chair. "I must go back inside—my absence will soon be remarked on. I am feeling much better, however. Thank you for your invitation, my lord." She allowed herself to send him a little flirting grin. "And for sharing the terrace."

As she went back inside, she closed her eyes briefly and let out a sigh of relief. It had been a good introduction—and far easier than she had anticipated to attract Kendall's interest. With a bit of luck—and some help from her friends—she might be able to catch a peer; and then everything would be all right.

Chapter 7

When the after-supper visiting was concluded, most of the guests began to retire for the evening. As Annabelle walked through one of the arched entrances of the drawing room, she saw that the other wallflowers were waiting for her. Smiling at their expectant faces, she went with them to a niche where they could exchange a few private words.

"Well?" Lillian demanded.

"Mama and I are going on a walk with Lord Kendall tomorrow morning," Annabelle said.

"Alone?"

"Alone," Annabelle confirmed. "In fact, we're meeting at daybreak, to avoid being accompanied by a herd of husband hunters."

Were they in a more private setting, they might have all squealed with glee. Instead, they settled for exchanging triumphant grins, while Daisy stamped her feet in an exuberant little victory dance.

"Wh-what is he like?" Evie asked.

"Shy, but pleasant," Annabelle replied. "And he

seems to have a sense of humor, which I hadn't dared to hope for."

"All that, and teeth, too," Lillian exclaimed.

"You were right about him being spooked easily," Annabelle said. "I am certain that Kendall would not be attracted to a strong-willed woman. He's cautious and soft-spoken. I'm trying to be demure—although I should probably feel guilty for the deception."

"All women do that during courtship—and men, too, for that matter," Lillian said prosaically. "We try to conceal our defects and say the things we think the other one wants to hear. We pretend that we're always lovely and sweet-tempered and that we don't mind the other's nasty little habits. And then after the wedding, we lower the boom."

"I don't think that men have to pretend quite as much as women do, however," Annabelle replied. "If a man is portly, or has brown teeth, or is somewhat dull-witted, he's still a catch as long as he is a gentleman and has some money. But women are held to far more exacting standards."

"Which is why we're all w-wallflowers," Evie said.

"We won't be for long," Annabelle promised with a smile.

Evie's aunt Florence came from the ballroom, looking witchlike in a black dress that did not flatter her sallow complexion. There was little family resemblance between Evie, with her round face and red hair and freckled complexion, and her ill-tempered aunt, who was a dry little wisp of a woman. "Evangeline," she said sharply, throwing the group a disapproving glance as she gestured to the girl. "I've warned you not to disappear like that—I have searched everywhere for you, for at least ten minutes, and I do not recall that you asked for permission to meet with your friends.

And of all the girls for you to associate with . . ." Chattering angrily, Aunt Florence stalked toward the grand staircase, while Evie sighed and fell into step behind her. As they watched, Evie stuck her hand behind her back and waggled her fingers to wave good-bye.

"Evie says her family is very wealthy," Daisy remarked. "But she says that they're all unhappy, every last one of them. I wonder why?"

"Old money," Lillian said. "Father says there is nothing like a lifetime of affluence to make one aware of what one hasn't got." She tucked her arm into Daisy's. "Come, dear, before Mother realizes that we've disappeared." She glanced at Annabelle with an inquiring smile. "Will you come walk with us, Annabelle?"

"No, thank you. My mother will meet me at the foot of the stairs in just a moment."

"Good night, then." Lillian's dark eyes glowed as she added, "By the time we awaken tomorrow, you'll have already gone on your walk with Kendall. I'll expect a full report at breakfast."

Annabelle saluted her playfully and watched the two of them depart. She meandered slowly to the grand staircase and paused in the shadow at the base of the curving structure. It seemed that Philippa, as usual, was taking an interminable length of time to finish a conversation back in the drawing room. Annabelle didn't mind waiting, however. Her head was filled with thoughts, including conversational gambits that might amuse Kendall during their walk tomorrow and ideas of how to secure his attention to herself, in spite of the many other girls who would be pursuing him during the next few weeks.

If she was clever enough to make Lord Kendall like her, and if the wallflowers succeeded in their plan of entrapment, what would it be like to be the wife of such a man? She was instinctively certain that she could never fall in love with someone like Kendall—but she vowed that she would do everything possible to be a good wife to him. And surely in time she could come to care for him. Marriage to Kendall could be very pleasant. Life would be comfortable and secure, and she would never again have to worry about whether or not there was enough food for the table. And most importantly, Jeremy's future would be assured, and her mother would never again have to endure the foul attentions of Lord Hodgeham.

Heavy footsteps approached as someone descended the staircase. Standing at the banister, Annabelle glanced upward with a slight smile, and suddenly she froze. Incredibly, she found herself being confronted by a fleshy face surmounted by a dangling crest of iron gray hair. *Hodgeham?* But it couldn't be!

He reached the nadir of the stairs and stood before her with a nominal bow, looking unbearably smug. As Annabelle stared into Hodgeham's cold blue eyes, the food she had eaten earlier seemed to gather into a spiky ball that rolled around her stomach.

How could he be there? Why had she not seen him earlier in the day? As she thought of her mother, who was soon to meet her at this very spot, fury boiled swiftly. This grossly insolent man, who styled himself their benefactor and subjected her mother to his disgusting attentions in return for his stingy handfuls of coins, had now come to persecute them at the worst possible time. There was no firmer guarantee of torment for Philippa at this party than Hodgeham's presence. At any moment he might betray his relationship with her—he could ruin them so easily, and they had no means of keeping him silent.

"Why, Miss Peyton," Hodgeham murmured, his

chubby face turning pink with malevolent pleasure. "What a pleasant coincidence that you should be the first guest I encounter at Stony Cross Park."

Queasy chills coursed over Annabelle as she forced herself to hold his gaze. She tried to banish all emotion from her expression, but Hodgeham smiled nastily, seeming aware of the hostile fear that engulfed her. "After the rigors of the journey from London," he continued, "I elected to have supper in my room. So sorry to have missed you earlier. However, there will be many opportunities for us to visit in the coming weeks. Your charming mother is here with you, I presume?"

Annabelle would have given anything to be able to answer "no." Her heart was beating so hard that it seemed to drive the breath from her lungs . . . she fought to think and speak above the insistent hammering. "Don't go near her," she said, amazed that her voice was steady. "Don't speak to her."

"Ah, Miss Peyton, you wound me . . . I, who have been your family's only friend in those difficult times when others have deserted you."

She stared at him without blinking, without moving, as if she was face-to-face with a venomous snake that was poised to strike.

"A happy coincidence, is it not, that we find ourselves attending the same party?" Hodgeham asked. He laughed quietly, the movement causing his combed-over hair to slip in an oily banner across his low forehead. He smoothed it back with his plump palm. "Fortune has indeed smiled on me, to provide for such proximity between myself and a woman whom I esteem so highly."

"There will be no proximity between you and my mother," Annabelle said, clenching her fist hard to keep from driving it into his gloating face. "I warn you, my lord, if you bother her in any way—"

"Dear girl, did you think that I was referring to Philippa? You are too modest. I meant *you*, Annabelle. I have long admired you. Yearned, in fact, to demonstrate the nature of my feelings for you. Now it seems that fate has presented us with the perfect opportunity to become more familiar with each other."

"I would rather sleep in a pit of snakes," Annabelle replied coldly, but there was a catch in her voice, and he smiled at the sound.

"At first you will protest, of course. Girls of your sort always do. But then you'll do the sensible thing . . . the wise thing . . . and you'll see the advantages of becoming my friend. I can be a valuable friend, my dear. And if you please me, I will reward you handsomely."

Annabelle tried desperately to think of a way to destroy any hope he might have of making her his mistress. The fear that he might trespass on another man's province was likely the only thing that would keep Hodgeham away from her. Annabelle forced her lips into a scornful smile. "Does it appear that I am in need of your so-called friendship?" she asked, fingering the folds of her fine new gown. "You're mistaken. I already have a protector—a far more generous one than you. So you had better leave me—and my mother—completely alone. Or you will answer to him."

She saw the progression of emotions across Hodgeham's face, initial disbelief followed by anger, and then suspicion. "Who is he?"

"Why should I tell you?" Annabelle asked with a cool smile. "I would much rather let you wonder."

"You're lying, you devious bitch!"

"Believe what you like," she murmured.

Hodgeham's meaty hands half curled as if he was longing to seize her and shake a confession from her. Instead, he regarded her with a fury-mottled complexion. "I'm not done with you yet," he muttered, spittle flecking his fleshy lips. "Not by half." He left her with crude abruptness, too incensed to bother with a show of courtesy.

Annabelle stood without moving. Her fury faded, leaving behind a stinging anxiety that settled in her bones. Had what she told Hodgeham been enough to keep him at bay? No—it was merely a temporary solution. In the coming days he would be watching her closely, scrutinizing every word and action to ascertain whether or not she had been lying about having a protector. And there would be threats, and barbs, designed to shred her nerves. But no matter what, she could not allow him to reveal the arrangement that he had shared with her mother. It would kill Philippa, and certainly it would ruin Annabelle's chances of marriage.

Her mind swam with feverish thoughts, and she stood motionless and taut-framed, until a quiet voice nearly startled her out of her slippers.

"Interesting. What were you and Lord Hodgeham arguing about?"

Blanching, Annabelle whirled around to behold Simon Hunt, who had approached her with catlike quietness. His shoulders blocked the profusion of glittering light from the drawing room. In his utter self-possession, he seemed infinitely more threatening than Hodgeham.

"What did you hear?" Annabelle blurted out, cursing inwardly as she heard the defensiveness in her own voice.

"Nothing," he said smoothly. "I merely saw your face as the two of you talked. Obviously, you were upset about something."

"I was not upset. You misinterpreted my expression, Mr. Hunt."

He shook his head, and stunned her by reaching out with a single fingertip to touch the upper part of her arm that was not covered by her glove. "You turn splotchy when you're angry." Looking down, Annabelle saw a pale pink patch of color, a sign of her skin's wont to color unevenly during times of distress.

A quiver ran through her at that glancing brush of his fingertip, and she stepped back from him.

"Are you in trouble, Annabelle?" Hunt asked softly.

He had no right to ask something in that gentle, almost concerned manner . . . as if he was someone she could turn to for help . . . as if she could ever allow herself to do so.

"You would like that, wouldn't you?" she retorted. "Any predicament of mine would delight you to no end—then you could step in with an offer of help and take advantage of the situation."

His eyes were narrow and intent. "What kind of help do you need?"

"Nothing from you," she assured him curtly. "And don't use my first name. I'll thank you to address me properly from now on—or better yet, don't speak to me at all." Unable to bear his speculative gaze for another moment, she swept past him. "Now if you'll excuse me . . . I must go find my mother."

Lowering herself to the chair beside the vanity table, Philippa stared at Annabelle with an ashen face. Annabelle had waited until they were safely enclosed in the privacy of their room before she had told Philippa the disastrous news. It seemed to take her mother a full minute to assimilate the information that the man whom she detested and feared most was a guest at Stony Cross Park. Annabelle had half expected her mother to dissolve into tears, but Philippa surprised her by tilting her head to the side and staring into the shadowy corner of the room with an odd, weary smile. It was a smile that Annabelle had never seen on her face before, a whimsical bitterness that indicated there was never any use in trying to improve one's situation, as fate would invariably have its way.

"Shall we leave Stony Cross Park?" Annabelle murmured. "We can go back to London immediately."

The question hovered in the air for what seemed to be minutes. When Philippa responded, she sounded dazed and contemplative. "If we did that, there would be no hope at all of your marrying. No . . . our only choice is to see this through. We are going to walk with Lord Kendall tomorrow morning—I won't allow Hodgeham to ruin your chances with him."

"He will be a constant source of trouble," Annabelle said quietly. "If we don't go back to town, it will turn into a nightmare here."

Philippa turned toward her then, still smiling in that discomforting way. "My dear, if you don't find someone to marry, then when we return to London, the real nightmare will begin."

Chapter 8

*B*edeviled by worry, Annabelle slept for a total of two, perhaps three hours. When she awoke in the morning, her eyes were shadowed, and her face was pale and weary. "Hell's bells," she muttered, soaking a cloth in cold water and pressing it to her face. "This will not do. I look a hundred years old this morning."

"What did you say, dear?" came her mother's sleepy query. Philippa was standing behind her, dressed in a worn robe and threadbare slippers.

"Nothing, Mama. I was talking to myself." Annabelle scrubbed her face roughly to bring some color to her cheeks. "I didn't sleep well last night."

Coming beside Annabelle, Philippa regarded her closely. "You do look a bit tired. I'll send for some tea."

"Send for a large pot," Annabelle said. Peering closely at her red-veined eyes in the looking glass, she added, "*Two* pots."

Philippa smiled sympathetically. "What shall we wear for our walk with Lord Kendall?"

Annabelle wrung out the cloth before draping it on

the washstand. "Our older gowns, I think, as it may be rather muddy on some of the forest paths. But we can cover them with the new silk shawls from Lillian and Daisy."

After downing a cup of steaming tea and taking a few hasty bites of cold toast that a maid had brought from downstairs, Annabelle finished dressing. She studied herself critically in the looking glass. The blue silk shawl knotted over her bodice did much to conceal the worn bodice of the biscuit-colored gown beneath. And her new bonnet, also from the Bowmans, was wonderfully flattering, its periwinkle-shaded lining bringing out the blue of her eyes.

Yawning widely, Annabelle went with Philippa to the back terrace of the manor. The hour was early enough that most of the guests at Stony Cross Park were still abed. Only a few gentlemen who were bent on trout fishing had troubled themselves to arise. A small group of men ate breakfast at the outside tables, while servants awaited nearby with rods and creel baskets. The peaceful scene was undercut with an annoying clamor that was most unexpected for this hour.

"Dear heaven," she heard her mother exclaim. Following her appalled gaze, Annabelle looked toward the other end of the terrace, which had been overrun by a cacophony of frantically chattering, squealing, laughing, aggressively posturing girls. They were surrounding something that remained unseen in the middle of the tightly packed congregation. "What are they all here for?" Philippa asked in bewilderment.

Annabelle sighed and said resignedly, "An early-morning hunt, I suspect."

Philippa's jaw sagged as she stared at the clamorous group. "You don't mean to say . . . do you think that poor Lord Kendall is caught up in the midst of that?"

Annabelle nodded. "And from the looks of things, there won't be much left of him when they're finished."

"But . . . but he arranged to go walking with *you*," Philippa protested. "*Only* you, with me as the chaperone."

As a few of the girls noticed Annabelle standing on the other side of the terrace, they crowded more tightly around their prey, as if to shield him from their view. Annabelle shook her head slightly. Either Kendall had foolishly told someone of their plans, or else the marriage frenzy had reached such a pitch that he could not venture out of his room without attracting a mob of women, no matter what the hour.

"Well, don't just stand there," Philippa urged. "Go and join the group, and try to attract his attention."

Annabelle gave her a doubtful glance. "Some of those girls look feral. I should hate to get bitten."

Distracted by a muffled laugh from nearby, she turned toward the sound. As she might have expected, Simon Hunt was lounging at the terrace balcony, a china cup nearly engulfed in his broad hand as he leisurely drank coffee. He was dressed in rugged garments similar to those of the other fishermen, made of tweed and rough twill, with a worn linen shirt left open at the throat. The mocking gleam in his eyes made no secret of his interest in the situation.

Without making a conscious decision to do so, Annabelle found herself drifting nearer to him. Coming to stand a few feet away from him, she leaned both her elbows on the balcony, gazing out at the mist-shrouded morning. Hunt rested his back against it, facing the manor wall.

Feeling the need to jab at his irritating self-confidence, Annabelle murmured, "Lord Kendall and Lord Westcliff aren't the only bachelors at Stony

Cross, Mr. Hunt. One wonders why *you* are not pursued to the degree that they are."

"That's obvious," he said pleasantly, lifting the cup to his lips and draining its contents. "I'm not a peer, and I would make a devil of a husband." He gave her a shrewd sideways glance. "As for you . . . despite my sympathy for your cause, I wouldn't advise making a play for Kendall."

"My *cause?*" Annabelle repeated, taking immediate offense to the word. "What do you define as my cause, Mr. Hunt?"

"Why, yourself, of course," he said softly. "You want what is best for Annabelle Peyton. But Kendall doesn't fall in that category. A match between you and him would be a disaster."

She turned her head to stare at him with slitted eyes. "Why?"

"Because he's much too nice for you." Hunt grinned at her expression. "That wasn't meant as an insult. I wouldn't like you half so much if you were a nice woman. All the same, you're no good for Kendall—nor would he be of much use to you, ultimately. You'd run roughshod over him until his gentlemanly soul was left in a battered pile at your feet."

Annabelle itched to knock the superior smile from his face—she, who had never before contemplated inflicting physical harm to anyone. Her anger was hardly mitigated by the fact that he was right. She knew quite well that she was far too spirited for a man as docile and civilized as Kendall. But that was none of Simon Hunt's business . . . and it wasn't as if Hunt or any other man was going to offer her a better alternative!

"Mr. Hunt," she said sweetly, her gaze poisonous, "why don't you go and—"

"Miss Peyton!" A faint exclamation came from several yards away, and Annabelle saw Lord Kendall's slight form emerging from the mass of females. He looked disheveled and vaguely harassed as he pushed his way over to her. "Good morning, Miss Peyton." He paused to straighten the knot of his cravat and adjust his skewed spectacles. "It seems that we were not the only ones who had taken it in our heads to walk this morning." Giving Annabelle a sheepish glance, he asked, "Shall we make an attempt nonetheless?"

Annabelle hesitated, inwardly groaning. There was little she could accomplish on a walk with Kendall when they would be accompanied by at least two dozen women. One might as well try to have a quiet conversation in the midst of a flock of screaming magpies. On the other hand, she could not very well refuse Kendall's invitation . . . even a minor rejection could be off-putting to him, and as a result he might never ask again.

She gave him a bright smile. "I would be delighted, my lord."

"Excellent. There are some fascinating species of flora and fauna that I would like to show you. Being an amateur horticulturist, I have made a careful study of the vegetation that is native to Hampshire . . ."

His following words were drowned out as enthusiastic girls surrounded him.

"How I *love* plants," one of them gushed. "There isn't a single plant that I don't find absolutely charming."

"And the outdoors would be *so* unattractive without them," another girl enthused.

"Oh, Lord Kendall," yet another beseeched, "you simply must explain what the difference is between a flora and a fauna . . ."

The crowd of girls carried Kendall away as if he was being swept out to sea by an irresistible current. Philippa went with them gamely, determined to look out for Annabelle's interests. "My daughter was probably too modest to tell you about her keen affinity for nature . . ." she was saying to Kendall.

Kendall threw a helpless glance over his shoulder as he was nudged strongly toward the terrace steps. "Miss Peyton?"

"I'm coming," Annabelle called back, cupping her fingers on either side of her mouth to make herself heard.

His reply, if he made one, was impossible to hear.

Lazily, Simon Hunt set his empty cup on the nearest table, and murmured something to a servant who was holding his fishing gear. The servant nodded and retreated, while Hunt fell into step beside Annabelle. She stiffened as she noticed him walking side by side with her.

"What are you doing?"

Hunt shoved his hands comfortably into the pockets of his tweed fishing coat. "I'm going with you. Whatever happens at the trout stream won't be half so interesting as watching you compete for Kendall's attention. Besides, my horticultural knowledge is sadly lacking. I may learn something."

Suppressing an ill-tempered reply, Annabelle resolutely followed Kendall and his entourage. They all walked down the terrace steps and took a path that led into the forest, where towering beeches and oaks presided over thick quilts of moss, fern, and lichen. At first Annabelle ignored Simon Hunt's presence beside her, trudging stonily behind Kendall's admiring throng. Kendall was being put to great exertion, obliged to help one girl after another to step over what seemed to be minor obstacles. A fallen tree, its circumference no bigger than Annabelle's arm, became such an overwhelming impediment that they all required Kendall's assistance to step over it. Each girl became progressively more helpless until the poor fellow was practically obliged to carry the last one over the log while she squealed in pretend-dismay and locked her arms around his neck.

Walking far behind, Annabelle refused to take Simon Hunt's arm when he offered it and stepped over the log by herself. He smiled slightly as he glanced at her set profile. "I would have expected you to have made your way up to the front by now," he remarked.

She made a scornful sound. "I'm not going to waste my efforts battling with that group of feather-wits. I'll wait for a more opportune moment to make Kendall notice me."

"He's already noticed you. He'd have been blind not to. The question is why you think that you'll have any luck getting a proposal out of Kendall, when you haven't managed to bring anyone up to scratch in the two years that I've known you."

"Because I have a plan," she said crisply.

"Which is?"

She gave him a derisive glance. "As if I would tell you."

"I hope it's something conniving and underhanded," Hunt said gravely. "You don't seem to have much success with the ladylike approach."

"Only because I have no dowry," Annabelle retorted. "If I had money, I'd have been married years ago."

"I have money," he said helpfully. "How much do you want?"

Annabelle gave him a sardonic glance. "Having a fair idea of what you'd require in return, Mr. Hunt, I can safely say that I don't want a shilling from you."

"It's nice to hear that you're so discriminating about the company you keep." Hunt reached out to hold back a branch for her. "Having heard a rumor to the contrary, I'm glad it's not true."

"Rumor?" Annabelle stopped in the middle of the path and whirled to face him. "About me? What could anyone possibly say about me?"

Hunt remained silent, watching her perturbed face as she worked it out for herself.

"Discriminating . . ." she murmured. "About the company I keep? . . . Is that supposed to imply that I've had some inappropriate . . ." She stopped abruptly as the nasty, florid image of Hodgeham sprang into her brain. Hunt had to notice the swift departure of color from her cheeks and the tiny indentations that dug between her brows. Giving him a cold glance, Annabelle turned away, her footsteps measured and heavy on the foliage-padded path.

Hunt kept pace with her, while Kendall's distant voice drifted back to them, lecturing his avid listeners on the plants they passed. Rare orchids . . . celandines . . . several varieties of fungi. The speech was punctuated every few seconds with crows of wonder from his enraptured audience. ". . . these lower plants," Kendall was saying, having paused briefly to indicate a haze of moss and lichen covering a hapless oak, "are classified as bryophytes, and require wet conditions to thrive. Were they to be deprived of the woodland canopy, they would surely perish out in the open . . ."

"I've done nothing wrong," Annabelle said shortly, wondering why Hunt's opinion mattered in the least. Still, it bothered her enough to wonder who had told him the rumor—and specifically, what it had been about. Was it possible that someone had seen Hodgeham visiting her home at night? That was bad. A reputation-destroying piece of gossip like that was impossible to defend oneself against. "And I have no regrets."

"That's a pity," Hunt said easily. "Having regrets is the only sign that you've done anything interesting with your life."

"What are *your* regrets, then?"

"Oh, I don't have regrets, either." A wicked glint appeared in his dark eyes. "Not for the lack of trying, of course. I keep doing unspeakable things in the hopes that I'll be sorry for them later. But so far . . . nothing."

In spite of her inner turmoil, Annabelle couldn't help chuckling. A long branch intersected the path, and she reached out to push it aside.

"Allow me," Hunt said, moving to hold it back for her.

"Thank you." She pushed by him, glancing at Kendall and the others in the distance, and suddenly felt a stinging prickle at the inner side of her foot. "Ouch!" Stopping on the path, she hitched the hem of her skirt up to investigate the source of the discomfort.

"What is it?" Hunt was beside her immediately, one large hand grasping her elbow to secure her balance.

"There is something scratchy in my shoe."

"Let me help," he said, sinking to his haunches and taking hold of her ankle. It was the first time a man had ever touched any part of her leg, and Annabelle went scarlet.

"*Don't* touch me there," she protested in a violent whisper, nearly losing her balance as she jerked backward. Hunt didn't loosen his grip. To keep from toppling over, Annabelle was forced to hold on to his shoulder. "Mr. Hunt—"

"I see the problem," he murmured. She felt him pluck at the veil of cotton stocking that covered her leg. "You've stepped in some prickly fern." He held something up for her inspection—a sprig of pale, chafflike scales that had worked their way into the cotton weave over her instep.

Flooding with burning color, Annabelle maintained her stabilizing grasp on his shoulder. The surface of his shoulder was astonishingly hard, the plane of bone and resilient muscle unsoftened by any layer of padding in his coat. Her stunned mind was having difficulty accepting the fact that she was standing in the middle of the woods with Simon Hunt's hand on her ankle.

Seeing her mortification, Hunt grinned suddenly. "There are more bits of chaff in your stocking. Shall I remove them?"

"Be quick about it," she said in an aggrieved tone, "before Kendall turns around and sees you with your hand up my skirts."

With a muffled laugh Hunt bent to his task, deftly picking the last of the prickly scales from her stocking. While he worked, Annabelle stared at the place on the back of his neck where the obsidian locks of hair curled slightly against firm, tanned skin.

Reaching for the discarded slipper, Hunt placed it on her foot with a flourish. "My rustic Cinderella," he said, and rose to his feet. As his gaze passed over the blooming pink surface of her cheeks, friendly mockery flickered in his dark eyes. "Why did you wear such ridiculous shoes for a walk in the woods? I would have thought you'd have the good sense to put on a pair of ankle boots."

"I don't have any ankle boots," Annabelle said, annoyed by the implication that she was some feather-wit who couldn't select the appropriate footwear for a simple walk. "My old ones fell to pieces, and I couldn't afford a new pair."

Surprisingly, Hunt did not take advantage of the

opportunity to mock her further. His face became impassive as he studied her for a moment. "Let's join the others," he said eventually. "They've probably discovered a variety of moss we haven't yet seen. Or God help us, a mushroom."

The pinching tightness eased from her chest. "I'm hoping for some lichen, myself."

That elicited a faint smile, and he reached out to snap off a slender branch that protruded across the pathway. Following gamely, Annabelle picked up her skirts and tried not to think of how nice it would be to be sitting on the manor terrace with a tray of tea and biscuits before her. They reached the summit of a shallow incline and were greeted with a surprising vista of bluebells that blanketed the forest floor. It was like stumbling into a dream, the cerulean haze seeping between the trunks of oak and beech and ash. The smell of bluebells was everywhere, the perfumed air feeling heavy and rich in her lungs.

Pausing by a slender tree trunk, Annabelle curled her arm around it loosely and stared at the stands of bluebells with surprised pleasure. "Lovely," she murmured, her face gleaming in the shadow cast by the canopy of ancient, interlaced branches.

"Yes." But Hunt was looking at her, not the bluebells, and one glance at his expression caused the blood to tingle in her veins. She had seen admiration on men's faces before, and even something that she had recognized as desire, but never a look that had been this disturbingly intimate . . . as if he wanted something far more complicated than the mere use of her body.

Uneasy, she pushed away from the tree trunk and made her way to Kendall, who was talking with her mother while the group of girls had scattered to pick wanton armfuls of bluebells. Flower stems were trampled and broken as the feminine marauders gathered up their treasure.

Kendall seemed relieved by Annabelle's approach, and even more so by the good-natured smile on her face. It seemed that he had expected her to be petulant, as most women would have been when they had been invited on a walk and then been ignored in lieu of more demanding company. His gaze alighted on Simon Hunt's dark form, and his expression was leavened with a touch of uncertainty. The two men exchanged nods, Hunt looking self-assured, Kendall appearing somewhat wary. "I see that we've attracted yet more company," Kendall murmured.

Annabelle gave Kendall her most dazzling smile. "Of course we have," she said. "You're the Pied Piper, my lord. Wherever you go, people follow."

He blushed, pleased by the bit of nonsense, and murmured, "I hope that you have enjoyed the walk so far, Miss Peyton."

"Oh, I have," she assured him. "Although I will admit to having blundered into a patch of prickly fern."

Philippa gave a soft exclamation of concern. "My goodness . . . were you injured, dearest?"

"No, no, it was a trifle," Annabelle said instantly. "Just a little scratch or two. And the fault was entirely mine—I'm afraid I wore the wrong kind of shoes." She stuck out her foot to show Kendall one of her light slippers, making certain to display a few inches of trim ankle.

Kendall clicked his tongue in dismay. "Miss Peyton, you need something far sturdier than those slippers for a tromp through the forest."

"You're right, of course." Annabelle shrugged, continuing to smile. "It was silly of me not to realize that the terrain would be so rugged. I'll try to choose my steps more carefully on the way back. But the blue-bells are so heavenly that I think I would wade through a field of prickly fern to reach them."

Reaching down to a stray cluster of bluebells, Kendall broke off a sprig and tucked it into the ribbon trim of her bonnet. "They're not half so blue as your eyes," he said. His gaze dropped to her ankle, which was now covered by the hem of her skirts. "You must take my arm when we walk back, to avoid further mishap."

"Thank you, my lord." Annabelle gazed up at him admiringly. "I'm afraid that I missed some of your earlier remarks about ferns, my lord. You had mentioned something about . . . spleenwort, wasn't it? . . . and I was *thoroughly* fascinated . . ."

Kendall obligingly proceeded to explain all one would ever want to know about ferns . . . and later, when Annabelle chanced to glance back in Simon Hunt's direction, he was gone.

Chapter 9

"Are we really going to do this?" Annabelle asked somewhat plaintively, as the wallflowers strode along the forest path with baskets and hampers in hand. "I thought that all our talk of Rounders-in-knickers was merely amusing banter."

"Bowmans *never* banter about Rounders," Daisy informed her. "That would be sacrilegious."

"You like games, Annabelle," Lillian said cheerfully. "And Rounders is the best game of all."

"I like the kind that is played at a table," Annabelle retorted. "With proper clothes on."

"Clothing is vastly overrated," came Daisy's airy reply.

Annabelle was learning that the price of having friends meant that on occasion one was compelled to defer to the group's wishes even if they went against one's own inclinations. All the same, this morning Annabelle had privately attempted to sway Evie to her side, unable to fathom that the girl truly intended to strip down to her drawers out in the open. But Evie was rashly determined to fall in with the Bowmans' plans, seeming to consider it as part of a self-devised program to embolden herself. "I w-want to be more like them," she had confided to Annabelle. "They're so free and daring. They fear nothing."

Staring at the girl's eager face, Annabelle had given in with a huge sigh. "Oh, all right. As long as no one sees us, I suppose it will be fine. Though I can't think of any purpose it will serve."

"Maybe it will be f-fun?" Evie had suggested, and Annabelle had responded with a speaking glance, making her laugh.

The weather, of course, had decided to cooperate fully with the Bowmans' plans, the sky open and blue, the air stirred by a soft breeze. Laden with baskets, the four girls walked along a sunken road, past wet meadows sprinkled with red sundew blossoms and vivid purple violets.

"Keep your eye out for a wishing well," Lillian said briskly. "Then we're supposed to cross the meadow on the other side of the lane and cut through the forest. There's a dry meadow at the top of the hill. One of the servants told me that no one ever goes there."

"Naturally it would be uphill," Annabelle said without rancor. "Lillian, what does the well look like? Is it one of those little whitewashed structures with a pail and a pulley?"

"No, it's a big muddy hole in the ground."

"There it is," Daisy exclaimed, hastening to the sloshing brown hole, which was being replenished from a bank beside it. "Come, all of you, we must each make a wish. I've even got pins that we can toss in."

"How did you know to bring pins?" Lillian asked.

Daisy smiled with bright mischief. "Well, as I sat

with Mama and all the dowagers while they were sewing yesterday afternoon, I made our Rounders ball." She unearthed a leather ball from her basket and held it up proudly. "I sacrificed a new pair of kid gloves to make it—and it was no easy task, I tell you. Anyway, the old ladies were watching me stuff it with wool snippets, and when one of them could bear it no longer, she came out and asked me what in heaven's name I was making. Of course I couldn't tell them it was a Rounders ball. I'm sure Mama guessed, but she was too embarrassed to say a word. So I told the dowager that I was making a pincushion."

All the girls snickered. "She must have thought it was the ugliest pincushion in existence," Lillian remarked.

"Oh, there's no doubt of that," Daisy replied. "I think she felt quite sorry for me. She gave me some pins for it, and said something under her breath about poor bumbling American girls who have no practical skills whatsoever." Using the edge of her nail, she pried the pins out of the leather ball and gave them over.

Setting down her own basket, Annabelle held a pin between her thumb and forefinger, and closed her eyes. Whenever the opportunity presented itself, she always made the same wish . . . to marry a peer. Strangely, however, a new thought entered her head, just as she cast the pin into the well.

I wish I could fall in love.

Surprised by the wilful, wayward notion, Annabelle wondered how it was that she could have wasted a wish on something that was obviously so ill-advised.

Opening her eyes, Annabelle saw that the other wallflowers were staring into the well with great solemnity. "I made the wrong wish," she said fretfully. "Can I have another?"

"No," Lillian said in a matter-of-fact tone. "Once you've thrown in your pin, it's done."

"But I didn't mean to make that particular wish," Annabelle protested. "Something just popped into my head, and it wasn't at all what I had planned."

"Don't argue, Annabelle," Evie advised. "You d-don't want to annoy the well spirit."

"The what?"

Evie smiled at her perplexed expression. "The resident spirit of the well. He's the one to whom y-you make a petition. But if you annoy him, he may decide to demand a terrible price for granting your wish. Or he may drag you into the well with him, to live there forever as his c-consort."

Annabelle stared into the brown water. She cupped her hands around the sides of her mouth to help direct her voice. "You don't have to grant my rotten wish," she told the unseen spirit loudly. "I take it back!"

"Don't taunt him, Annabelle," Daisy exclaimed. "And for heaven's sake, step back from the edge of that well!"

"Are you superstitious?" Annabelle asked with a grin.

Daisy glowered at her. "There's a reason for superstitions, you know. At *some* point in time, *something* bad happened to *someone* who was standing right next to a well, just as you are." Closing her eyes, she concentrated intently, then tossed her own pin into the water. "There. I've made a wish for your benefit—so there's no need for you to complain about having wasted one."

"But how do you know what I wanted?"

"The wish I made is for your own good," Daisy informed her.

Annabelle groaned theatrically. "I *hate* things that are for my own good."

A good-natured squabble followed, in which each

girl made suggestions as to what would be best for the other, until finally Lillian commanded them to stop, as they were interfering with her concentration. They fell silent just long enough to allow Lillian and Evie to make their wishes, then they made their way across the meadow and through the forest. Soon they reached a lovely dry meadow, grassy and sun-drenched, with shade extending from a grove of oak at one side. The air was balmy and rarefied, and so fresh that Annabelle sighed blissfully. "This air has no substance to it," she said in mock-complaint. "No coal smoke or street dust whatsoever. Much too thin for a Londoner. I can't even feel it in my lungs."

"It's not that thin," Lillian replied. "Every now and then the breeze carries a distinct hint of *eau de* sheep."

"Really?" Annabelle sniffed experimentally. "I can't smell a thing."

"That's because you don't have a nose," Lillian replied.

"I beg your pardon?" Annabelle asked with a quizzical grin.

"Oh, you have a regular sort of nose," Lillian explained, "but I have *a nose*. I'm unusually sensitive to smell. Give me any perfume, and I can separate it into all its parts. Rather like listening to a musical chord and divining all its notes. Before we left New York, I even helped to develop a formula for scented soap, for my father's factory."

"Could you create a perfume, do you think?" Annabelle asked in fascination.

"I daresay I could create an excellent perfume," Lillian said confidently. "However, anyone in the industry would disdain it, as the phrase 'American perfume' is considered to be an oxymoron—and I'm a woman, besides, which throws the caliber of my nose very much into question."

"You mean, men have better noses than women?"

"They certainly think so," Lillian said darkly, and whipped a picnic blanket out of her basket with a flourish. "Enough about men and their protuberances. Shall we sit in the sun for a little while?"

"We'll get brown," Daisy predicted, flopping onto a corner of the blanket with a pleasured sigh. "And then Mama will have conniptions."

"What are conniptions?" Annabelle asked, entertained by the American word. She dropped to the space beside Daisy. "Do send for me if she has them— I'm curious to see what they look like."

"Mama has them all the time," Daisy assured her. "Never fear, you'll be well acquainted with conniptions before we all leave Hampshire."

"We shouldn't eat before we play," Lillian said, watching as Annabelle lifted the lid of a picnic basket.

"I'm hungry," Annabelle said wistfully, peering inside the basket, which was filled with fruit, cheese, pâté, thick cuts of bread, and several varieties of salad.

"You're always hungry," Daisy observed with a laugh. "For such a small person, you have a remarkable appetite."

"*I*, small?" Annabelle countered. "If you are one fraction of an inch above five feet tall, I'll eat that picnic basket."

"You'd better start chewing, then," Daisy said. "I'm five feet and one inch, thank you."

"Annabelle, I wouldn't gnaw on that wicker handle quite yet, if I were you," Lillian interceded with a slow smile. "Daisy stands on her toes whenever she's measured. The poor dressmaker has had to recut the hems of nearly a dozen dresses, thanks to my sister's unreasonable denial of the fact that she is short."

"I'm not short," Daisy muttered. "Short women are never mysterious, or elegant, or pursued by handsome men. And they're always treated like children. I refuse to be short."

"You're not mysterious or elegant," Evie conceded. "But you're very pr-pretty."

"And you're a dear," Daisy replied, levering upward to reach into the picnic basket. "Come, let's feed poor Annabelle—I can hear her stomach growling."

They delved into the repast enthusiastically. Afterward, they reclined lazily on the blanket and cloud-watched, and talked about everything and nothing. When their chatter died to a contented lull, a small red squirrel ventured out of the oak grove and turned to the side, watching them with one bright black eye.

"An intruder," Annabelle observed, with a delicate yawn.

Evie rolled to her stomach and tossed a bread crust in the squirrel's direction. He froze and stared at the tantalizing offering, but was too timid to advance. Evie tilted her head, her hair glittering in the sun as if it had been overlaid with a net of rubies. "Poor little thing," she said softly, casting another crust at the timid squirrel. This one landed a few inches closer, and his tail twitched eagerly. "Be brave," Evie coaxed. "Go on and take it." Smiling tolerantly, she tossed another crust, which landed a scant few inches from him. "Oh, Mr. Squirrel," Evie reproved. "You're a dreadful coward. Can't you see that no one's going to harm you?"

In a sudden burst of initiative, the squirrel seized the tidbit and scampered off with his tail quivering. Looking up with a triumphant smile, Evie saw the other wallflowers staring at her in drop-jawed silence. "Wh-what is it?" she asked, puzzled.

Annabelle was the first to speak. "Just now, when you were talking to that squirrel, you didn't stammer."

"Oh." Suddenly abashed, Evie lowered her gaze and grimaced. "I never stammer when I'm talking to children or animals. I don't know why."

They pondered the puzzling information for a moment. "I've noticed that you never seem to stammer quite as much when you're talking to me," Daisy observed.

Lillian could not seem to resist the comment. "Which category do you fall into, dear? Children, or animals?"

Daisy responded with a hand gesture that was completely unfamiliar to Annabelle.

Annabelle was about to ask Evie if she had ever consulted a doctor about her stammering, but the red-haired girl abruptly changed the subject. "Where is the R-rounders ball, Daisy? If we don't play soon, I'll fall asleep."

Realizing that Evie didn't want to discuss her stammering any longer, Annabelle seconded the request. "I suppose if we're really going to do it, now is as good a time as any."

While Daisy dug in the basket for the ball, Lillian unearthed an item from her own basket. "Look what I've brought," she said smugly.

Daisy looked up with a delighted laugh. "A real bat!" she exclaimed, regarding the flat-sided object admiringly. "And I thought we'd have to use a plain old stick. Where did you get it, Lillian?"

"I borrowed it from one of the stableboys. It seems they sneak away for Rounders whenever possible—they're quite passionate about the game."

"Who wouldn't be?" Daisy asked rhetorically, be-

ginning on the buttons of her bodice. "Gracious, the
day is warm—it will be lovely to shed all these layers."

As the Bowman sisters unfastened their gowns with
the casual manner of girls not unaccustomed to dis-
robing out in the open, Annabelle and Evie regarded
each other in a moment of uncertainty.

"I dare you," Evie murmured.

"Oh, God," Annabelle said in an aggrieved tone,
and began to unbutton her own dress. She had discovered an unexpected streak of modesty that
brought a rush of color to her face. However, she was
not going to turn coward when even timid Evie Jenner
was willing to join in the rebellion against propriety.
Pulling her arms from the sleeves of her dress, she
stood and let the heavy overlay fall in a crumpled
mound at her feet. Left in her chemise, drawers, and
corset, her feet covered only by stockings and thin
slippers, she felt a breeze waft over the perspiration-
dampened places beneath her arms, and she shivered
pleasantly.

The other girls stood and shed their own gowns,
which lay heaped on the ground like gigantic exotic
flowers.

"Catch!" Daisy said, and tossed the ball to
Annabelle, who caught it reflexively. They all walked
to the center of the meadow, pitching the ball back
and forth. Evie was the worst at throwing and catching, though it was clear that her ineptitude was caused
by inexperience rather than clumsiness. Annabelle, on
the other hand, had a younger brother who had fre-
quently turned to her as a playmate, and so the mechanics of lobbing a ball were familiar to her.

It was the oddest, lightest feeling, walking outside
with her legs unimpeded by the weight of skirts. "I
suppose this is what men feel like," Annabelle mused

aloud, "being able to stroll here and there in trousers. One could almost envy them such freedom."

"Almost?" Lillian questioned with a grin. "Without question, I *do* envy them. Wouldn't it be lovely if women could wear trousers?"

"I w-wouldn't like it at all," Evie said. "I would die of embarrassment if a man were able to see the shape of my legs and my . . ." She hesitated, clearly searching for a word to describe unmentionable parts of the female anatomy. ". . . other things," she finished lamely.

"Your chemise is in a sad state, Annabelle," came Lillian's sudden blunt observation. "I hadn't thought to give you new underwear, though I should have realized . . ."

Annabelle shrugged offhandedly. "It doesn't matter, since this is the only occasion on which anyone will see it."

Daisy glanced at her older sister. "Lillian, we're abominably shortsighted. I think poor Annabelle drew the short straw when it came to fairy godmothers."

"I haven't complained," Annabelle said, laughing. "And as far as I can tell, the four of us are all riding in the same pumpkin."

After a few more minutes of practice, and a brief discussion of the rules of Rounders, they set out empty picnic baskets in lieu of sanctuary posts, and the game began. Annabelle planted her feet squarely on a spot that had been designated as "Castle Rock."

"I'll feed the ball to her," Daisy said to her older sister, "and you catch."

"But I have a better arm than you," Lillian grumbled, taking a position behind Annabelle nevertheless.

Holding the bat over her shoulder, Annabelle swung at the ball that Daisy threw. The bat failed to connect, and whistled through the air in a neat arc. Behind her,

Lillian expertly caught the ball. "That was a good swing," Daisy encouraged. "Keep watching the ball as it comes toward you."

"I'm not accustomed to standing still while objects are being hurled at me," Annabelle said, brandishing the bat once again. "How many tries do I get?"

"In Rounders, the striker has an infinite number of swings," came Lillian's voice behind her. "Have another go, Annabelle . . . and this time, try to imagine that the ball is Mr. Hunt's nose."

Annabelle received the suggestion with relish. "I'd prefer to aim for a protuberance somewhat lower than that," she said, and swung as Daisy fed her the ball again. This time, the flat side of the bat met the ball with a solid *thwack*. Letting out a whoop of delight, Daisy went scampering after the ball, while Lillian, who had been screeching with laughter, cried out, "Run, Annabelle!"

She did so with a triumphant chortle, skirting the baskets as she rounded toward Castle Rock.

Daisy scooped up the ball and threw it to Lillian, who snatched it from the air.

"Stay at the third post, Annabelle," Lillian called. "We'll see if Evie can bring you back to Castle Rock."

Looking nervous but determined, Evie took the bat and assumed a stance at the striker's place.

"Pretend the ball is your aunt Florence," Annabelle advised, and a grin erupted on Evie's face.

Daisy pitched a slow, easy ball, while Evie flailed with the bat. She missed, and the ball landed with a neat smack in Lillian's palms. Throwing the ball back to Daisy, Lillian repositioned Evie. "Widen your stance and bend your knees a bit," she murmured. "That's a girl. Now watch the ball as it comes, and you won't miss."

Unfortunately Evie did miss, time and again, until her face was pink with frustration. "It's t-too hard," she said, her forehead puckered with worry. "Perhaps I should stop now and give someone else a turn."

"Just a few more tries," Annabelle said anxiously, determined that Evie should hit the ball at least once. "We're in no hurry."

"Don't give up!" Daisy chimed in. "It's just that you're trying too hard, Evie. Relax—and stop closing your eyes when you swing."

"You can do it," Lillian said, pushing a lock of silky dark hair away from her forehead and flexing her slim, well-toned arms. "You almost connected with the last one. Just *keep . . . watching . . . the ball.*"

Sighing in resignation, Evie dragged the bat back to Castle Rock and lifted it once more. Her blue eyes narrowed as she stared at Daisy, and she tensed in preparation for the next feed. "I'm ready."

Daisy tossed the ball gamely, and Evie swung with grim determination. A thrill of satisfaction shot through Annabelle as she saw the bat strike the ball solidly. It soared into the air, far into the oak grove. They all whooped in jubilation at the splendid strike. Shocked at what she had done, Evie began to jump in the air, squealing, "I did it! I did it!"

"Run around the baskets!" Annabelle cried, and scampered back to Castle Rock. Gleefully Evie circled the makeshift Rounders field, her garments a blur of white. When she reached Castle Rock, the girls continued to jump and scream for no reason at all, other than the fact that they were young and healthy and quite pleased with themselves.

Suddenly, Annabelle became aware of a dark figure rapidly ascending the hill. She fell abruptly silent as she ascertained that there was one—no, two—riders advancing to the dry meadow. "Someone's coming!" she said. "A pair of riders. Hurry, fetch your clothes!" Her low-voiced alarm cut through the girls' jubilation. They stared at each other with wide eyes and burst into panicked action. Shrieking, Daisy and Evie broke into a dead run toward the remains of the picnic, where they had left their dresses.

Annabelle began to follow, then stopped and turned abruptly as the riders thundered to a halt just behind her. She faced them warily, trying to assess what danger they might present. Looking up at their faces, she felt a bolt of chilling dismay as she recognized them.

Lord Westcliff . . . and even worse . . . Simon Hunt.

Chapter 10

Once Annabelle met Hunt's stunned gaze, she could not seem to look away. It was like one of those nightmares that one always awoke from with a sense of relief, knowing that something so dreadful could never really happen. Were the situation not so completely to her disadvantage, she might have enjoyed the prospect of Simon Hunt rendered absolutely speechless. At first his face was blank, as if he was having tremendous difficulty absorbing the fact that she was standing before him dressed only in a chemise, corset, and drawers. His gaze slid over her, slowly coming to rest on her flushed face.

Another moment or two of suffocated silence, and Hunt swallowed hard before speaking in a rusty-sounding voice. "I probably shouldn't ask. But what the hell are you doing?"

The words unlocked Annabelle from her paralysis. She certainly could not stand there and converse with him while she was clad in her undergarments. But her dignity—or the threads that remained of it—

demanded that she not screech idiotically and dash for
her clothes the way Evie and Daisy were doing. Settling for a compromise, she strode briskly to her discarded gown and clasped it to her front as she turned
to face Simon Hunt once more. "We're playing
Rounders," she said, her voice far higher-pitched than
usual.

Hunt glanced around the scene before settling on
her again. "Why did you—"

"One can't run properly in skirts," Annabelle interrupted. "I should think that would be obvious."

Absorbing that, Hunt averted his face swiftly, but
not before she saw the sudden flash of his grin. "Never
having tried it, I'll have to take your word on that."

Behind her, Annabelle heard Daisy say to Lillian accusingly, "I thought you said that no one ever comes to
this meadow!"

"That's what I was told," Lillian replied, her voice
muffled as she stepped into the circle of her gown and
bent to jerk it upward.

The earl, who had been mute until that point,
spoke with his gaze trained studiously on the distant
scenery. "Your information was correct, Miss Bowman," he said in a controlled manner. "This field is
usually unfrequented."

"Well, then, why are you here?" Lillian demanded
accusingly, as if she, and not Westcliff, was the owner
of the estate.

The question caused the earl's head to whip around.
He gave the American girl an incredulous glance before he dragged his gaze away once more. "Our presence here is purely coincidental," he said coldly. "I
wished to have a look at the northwest section of my
estate today." He gave the word *my* a subtle but distinct emphasis. "While Mr. Hunt and I were traveling

along the lane, we heard your screaming. We thought it best to investigate, and came with the intention of rendering aid, if necessary. Little did I realize that you would be using this field for . . . for . . ."

"Rounders-in-knickers," Lillian supplied helpfully, sliding her arms into her sleeves.

The earl seemed incapable of repeating the ridiculous phrase. He turned his horse away and spoke curtly over his shoulder. "I plan to develop a case of amnesia within the next five minutes. Before I do so, I would suggest that you refrain from any future activities involving nudity outdoors, as the next passersby who discover you may not prove to be as indifferent as Mr. Hunt and I."

Despite Annabelle's mortification, she had to repress a skeptical snort at the earl's claim of indifference on Hunt's behalf, not to mention his own. Hunt had certainly managed to get quite an eyeful of her. And though Westcliff's scrutiny had been far more subtle, it had not escaped her that he had stolen a quick but thorough glance at Lillian before he had veered his horse away. However, in light of her current state of undress, it was hardly the time to deflate Westcliff's holier-than-thou demeanor.

"Thank you, my lord," Annabelle said with a calmness that pleased her immensely. "And now, having dispensed such excellent advice, I would ask that you allow us some privacy to restore ourselves."

"With pleasure," Westcliff growled.

Before Simon Hunt departed, he could not seem to keep from looking back at Annabelle as she stood clutching her gown across her chest. Despite his apparent composure, it seemed to her that his color had heightened . . . and there was no mistaking the smoldering of his jet-black eyes. Annabelle longed for the self-possession to stare at him with cool disregard, but instead she felt flushed and disheveled and thoroughly off-balance. He seemed on the verge of saying something to her, then checked himself and muttered beneath his breath with a self-derisive smile. His horse stomped and snorted impatiently, pivoting eagerly as Hunt guided him to gallop after Westcliff, who was already halfway across the field.

Mortified, Annabelle turned to Lillian, who was blushing but admirably self-possessed. "Of all men to discover us like this," Annabelle said in disgust, "it *would* have to be those two."

"You have to admire such arrogance," Lillian commented dryly. "It must have taken years to cultivate."

"Which man are you referring to? . . . Mr. Hunt or Lord Westcliff?"

"Both. Although the earl's arrogance just may edge out Mr. Hunt's—which I call a truly impressive feat."

They stared at each other in shared disdain for their departed visitors, and suddenly Annabelle laughed irrepressibly. "They were surprised, weren't they?"

"Not nearly as surprised as we were," Lillian rejoined. "The question is, how are we to face them again?"

"How are they to face us?" Annabelle countered. "We were minding our own business—*they* were the intruders!"

"How right you . . ." Lillian began, and stopped as she became aware of a violent choking noise coming from their picnic spot. Evie was writhing on the blanket, while Daisy stood over her with arms akimbo.

Hurrying to the pair, Annabelle asked Daisy in consternation, "What is it?"

"The embarrassment was too much for her to endure," Daisy said. "It sent her into fits."

Evie rolled on the blanket, a napkin concealing her

face, while one exposed ear had turned the color of pickled beets. The more she tried to control her giggles, the worse they became, until she gasped frantically for air in between yelps. Somehow she managed to squeak out a few words. "What a s-s-smashing introduction to lawn sports!" And then she was snorting with more spasms of helpless laughter, while the other three stood over her.

Daisy threw Annabelle a significant glance. *"Those,"* she informed her, "are conniptions."

Simon and Westcliff rode away from the meadow at a fast gallop, slowing to a walk when they entered the forest and followed a trail that wound through the wooded terrain. It was a good two minutes before either of them was inclined, or indeed able, to speak. Simon's head was whirling with images of Annabelle Peyton's firm, flourishing curves clad in ancient undergarments that had shrunk from a thousand washings. It was a good thing that he and she had not found themselves alone in such a circumstance, for Simon was certain that he wouldn't have been able to leave her without doing something completely barbaric.

In Simon's entire life, he had never experienced such potent craving as he had the moment he had seen Annabelle half-undressed in the meadow. His entire body had been flooded with the urge to dismount his horse, seize Annabelle in his arms, and carry her to the nearest soft patch of grass he could find. He could not imagine a more unholy temptation than the sight of her voluptuous body, the expanse of silken skin tinted in shades of cream and pink, the sun-streaked golden brown hair. She had looked so enchantingly mortified, blushing everywhere. He wanted to remove her ragged undergarments with his teeth and fingers; and then he wanted to kiss her from head to toe, taste her in sweet, soft places that—

"No," Simon muttered, feeling his blood heat until it scalded the inside of his veins. He could not allow himself to pursue that line of thought, or his hard-thrumming desire would make the rest of the ride damned uncomfortable. When he had gotten his lust under control, Simon glanced at Westcliff, who appeared to be brooding. That was unusual for Westcliff, who was not the brooding sort.

The two men had been friends for about five years, having met at a supper given by a progressive politician with whom they were both acquainted. Westcliff's autocratic father had just died, and it had been left to Marcus, the new earl, to take charge of the family's business affairs. He had found the family finances to be superficially sound but ailing underneath, much like a patient who had contracted a terminal disease but still appeared healthy. Alarmed by the steady losses revealed by the account books, the new earl of Westcliff had recognized that drastic changes had to be made. He had resolved to avoid the fate of other peers who spent their lives presiding over an ever-shrinking family fortune. Unlike the silver-fork novels that depicted countless peers losing their wealth at the gambling tables, the reality was that modern aristocrats were generally not so reckless as they were simply inept financial managers. Conservative investments, old-fashioned views and ill-fated fiscal arrangements were slowly eroding aristocratic wealth and allowing a newly prosperous class of professional men to encroach on the higher levels of society. Any man who chose to disregard the influences of science and industrial advances on the emerging economy was sure to be abandoned in its churning wake . . .

and Westcliff had no desire to be included in that category.

When Simon and Westcliff had struck up a friendship, there had been no doubt that each man was using the other to get something he wanted. Westcliff had wanted the benefit of Simon's financial instincts, and Simon had wanted an entree into the world of the privileged class. But as they had become acquainted with each other, it became apparent that they were alike in many ways. They were both aggressive riders and huntsmen, requiring frequent strenuous physical activity as an outlet for an excess of vigor. And they were both uncompromisingly honest, although Westcliff possessed sufficient grace of manner to make his candor far more palatable. Neither man was the kind to sit for hours at a time to chat about poetry and sentimental concepts. They preferred to deal with tangible facts and issues, and, of course, they discussed current and future business ventures with keen enjoyment.

As Simon had continued to be a regular guest at Stony Cross, and a frequent visitor to Westcliff's London house, Marsden Terrace, the earl's friends had gradually come to accept him into their circle. It had been a welcome surprise for Simon to discover that he was not the only commoner whom Westcliff considered a close friend. The earl seemed to prefer the company of men whose perspectives of the world had been shaped outside the walls of noble estates. In fact, Westcliff occasionally claimed that he would like to disclaim his title, were such a thing possible, since he did not support the notion of hereditary aristocracy. Simon had no doubt that Westcliff's statements were sincere—but it had never seemed to dawn on Westcliff that aristocratic privilege, with all its power and attendant responsibilities, was an innate part of him. As the holder of the oldest and most revered earldom in England, Marcus, Lord Westcliff, had been born to serve the demands of duty and tradition. He kept his life well organized and tightly scheduled, and he was the most self-controlled man that Simon had ever known.

At the moment, the usually coolheaded earl seemed rather more perturbed than the situation warranted.

"Damn," Westcliff finally exclaimed. "I have occasional business dealings with their father. How am I supposed to face Thomas Bowman without remembering that I've seen his daughter in her underwear?"

"Daughters," Simon corrected. "They were both there."

"I only noticed the taller one."

"Lillian?"

"Yes, that one." A scowl crossed Westcliff's face. "Good God, no wonder they're all unmarried! They're heathens even by American standards. And the way that woman spoke to me, as if *I* should have been embarrassed to interrupt their pagan revelry—"

"Westcliff, you sound like a prig," Simon interrupted, amused by the earl's vehemence. "A few innocent girls scampering about in the meadow is hardly the end of civilization as we know it. And if they had been village wenches, you'd have thought nothing of it. Hell, you probably would have joined them. I've seen you do things with your paramours at parties and balls that—"

"Well, they aren't village wenches, are they? They're young ladies—or at least they're supposed to be. Why in God's name are a bunch of *wallflowers* behaving in such a way?"

Simon grinned at his friend's aggrieved tone. "My impression is that they have become allies in their unwedded state. For most of the past season they sat without speaking to each other, but it seems they've recently struck up a friendship."

"For what purpose?" the earl asked with deep suspicion.

"Perhaps they're merely trying to enjoy themselves?" Simon suggested, interested by the degree to which Westcliff had taken exception to the girls' behavior. Lillian Bowman, in particular, seemed to have bothered him profoundly. And that was unusual for the earl, who always treated women with casual ease. To Simon's knowledge, despite the numbers of women who pursued him in and out of bed, Westcliff had never lost his detachment. Until then.

"Then they should take up needlework, or do whatever it is that proper women do to enjoy themselves," the earl growled. "At least they should find a hobby that doesn't involve running naked through the countryside."

"They weren't naked," Simon pointed out. "Much to my regret."

"That comment impels me to say something," Westcliff said. "As you know, I'm not usually one to give advice when it isn't asked for—"

Simon interrupted with a bark of laughter. "Westcliff, I doubt that a day in your life has passed without you giving advice to someone about something."

"I offer advice only when it is obviously needed," the earl said with a scowl.

Simon gave him a sardonic glance. "Dispense your words of wisdom, then, as it appears that I'm going to hear them whether I wish to or not."

"It pertains to Miss Peyton. If you're wise, you'll divest yourself of all notions concerning her. She's a shallow bit of goods, and as self-absorbed as any creature I've ever met. The facade is beautiful, I'll grant

you . . . but in my judgment there's nothing beneath
to recommend it. No doubt you're thinking of taking
her as your mistress if she fails in her bid to win
Kendall. My advice is, don't. There are women who
have infinitely more to offer you."

Simon didn't reply for a moment. His sentiments regarding Annabelle Peyton were uncomfortably complex. He admired Annabelle, he liked her, and God
knew he had no right to judge her harshly for becoming another man's mistress. But all the same, the very
real possibility that she had taken Hodgeham into her
bed engendered a mixture of jealousy and anger that
surprised him.

After hearing the rumor that Lord Burdick had been
spreading, that Annabelle had become Lord Hodgeham's secret mistress, Simon hadn't been able to resist
investigating the claim. He had asked his father, who
kept meticulous account books, if anyone had ever
given him money for the Peytons' butcher bills. Sure
enough, his father had confirmed that Lord Hodgeham had occasionally settled the Peytons' account. Although that hardly was conclusive proof of anything,
it provided yet more weight to the possibility that
Annabelle had become Hodgeham's mistress. And
Annabelle's evasiveness during their conversation the
previous morning had certainly done little to contra-
dict the rumor.

Clearly the Peyton family's situation was desperate . . . but why Annabelle should have turned to a fat
old windbag like Hodgeham for help was a mystery.
On the other hand, so many of life's decisions, good
and bad, were made as a simple result of timing. Perhaps Hodgeham had managed to intervene at a moment when Annabelle's defenses were at their weakest,
and she had allowed herself to be persuaded to give the

old bastard what he wanted in return for the money she needed so badly.

She had no walking boots. *Christ.* Hodgeham's generosity must be paltry indeed, to allow for a few new gowns but no decent shoes, and undergarments that were nearly in rags. If Annabelle was to be some man's mistress, she could damn well be Simon's, and at least receive proper recompense for her favors. Obviously it was far too soon to broach the question to her. Simon would have to wait patiently while Annabelle tried to wrest a proposal from Lord Kendall. And he intended to do nothing to harm her chances. But if she failed with Kendall, Simon intended to approach her with a much better offer than her current hole-and-corner arrangement with Hodgeham.

Envisioning Annabelle stretched naked in his bed, Simon felt his lust rekindle, and he struggled to retrieve the thread of conversation. "What gave you the impression that I had any interest in Miss Peyton?" he asked in a noncommittal tone.

"The fact that you nearly fell off your horse when you saw her in her drawers."

That elicited a reluctant smile from Simon. "With a facade like that, I may not give a damn about what's beneath."

"You should," the earl said emphatically. "Miss Peyton is a selfish jade if I've ever seen one."

"Westcliff," Simon asked conversationally, "does it ever occur to you that you might occasionally be wrong? About anything?"

The earl looked perplexed by the question. "Actually, no."

Shaking his head with a rueful grin, Simon spurred his horse to a faster gait.

Chapter 11

As the girls walked back to Stony Cross Manor, Annabelle became uncomfortably aware of a twinge in her ankle. She must have turned it during the Rounders game, though she could not recall the precise moment when it had happened. Sighing heavily, she hefted the basket in her hand and lengthened her stride to keep pace with Lillian, who looked pensive. Daisy and Evie walked a few yards behind them, both of them involved in an earnest conversation.

"What are you worrying about?" Annabelle asked Lillian in a low voice.

"The earl and Mr. Hunt . . . do you think they will tell anyone about having seen us this afternoon? It would put a nasty dent in our reputations."

"I don't think Westcliff would," Annabelle said after a moment's thought. "I was inclined to believe him when he made that remark about amnesia. And he doesn't seem to be a man who is given to gossip."

"What about Mr. Hunt?"

Annabelle frowned. "I don't know. It didn't escape

me that he made no promise to remain silent. I suppose he'll keep his mouth closed if he thinks he has something to gain from it."

"You should be the one to ask him, then. As soon as you see Mr. Hunt at the ball tonight, you must go to him and make him promise not to tell anyone about our Rounders game."

Recalling the dance that would take place at the manor that evening, Annabelle groaned. She was relatively—no, positively—certain that she could not bear to face Hunt after what had happened that afternoon. On the other hand, Lillian was right—one couldn't assume that Hunt would be silent. Annabelle would have to deal with him, much as she dreaded the prospect. "Why me?" she asked, although she already knew the answer.

"Because Hunt likes you. Everyone knows that. He'll be much more inclined to do something you ask."

"He won't give something for nothing," Annabelle muttered, while the throbbing in her ankle worsened. "What if he makes some vulgar proposition to me?"

A long, apologetic pause ensued, until Lillian offered, "You may have to throw him a bone of some sort."

"What kind of a bone?" Annabelle asked suspiciously.

"Oh, just let him kiss you, if that's what it takes to keep him quiet."

Astonished that Lillian could make such a statement in so nonchalant a manner, Annabelle inhaled sharply. "Good God, Lillian! I can't do that!"

"Why not? You've kissed men before, haven't you?"

"Yes, but—"

"One pair of lips is like any other. Just make certain no one sees you and get it over with quickly. Then Mr. Hunt will be placated, and our secret will be safe."

Annabelle shook her head with a strangled laugh, while her heart began to pound painfully hard at the idea. She couldn't help but remember that long-ago secret kiss in the panorama theater, the seconds of devastating sensual upheaval that had left her shaken and speechless.

"You'll just have to make it clear that one kiss is all he may expect from you," Lillian continued, "and that it will certainly never happen again."

"Pardon me for casting aspersions on your plan . . . but it stinks like six o'clock fish. One pair of lips is *not* like any other, if they happen to be attached to Simon Hunt! And he'll never be satisfied with something as trivial as a kiss, and I couldn't offer him anything more than that."

"Do you really find Mr. Hunt so repulsive?" Lillian asked idly. "He's not bad, actually. I'd even go so far as to call him handsome."

"He's so insufferable that I've never really taken notice of his looks. But I will admit that he's . . ." Annabelle fell into a confused silence, considering the question with a new and unsettling thoroughness.

Objectively speaking—in the unlikely circumstance that one could ever be objective about Simon Hunt—he was indeed a good-looking man. The word "handsome" was usually applied to people with highly chiseled features and slender, elegant proportions. But Simon Hunt redefined the word with his bold, clean-edged countenance, his audacious black eyes, with the strong blade of a nose that could only belong to a man, and the wide mouth that was forever edged with irreverent humor. Even his unusual height and brawn seemed to suit him perfectly, as if nature had recognized that he was not a creature to be formed by half measures.

Simon Hunt had made her uneasy from the first moment they met. Although Annabelle had never seen him any way other than perfectly dressed and thoroughly self-controlled, she had always sensed that Hunt was, at best, half-tamed. Her deepest instincts had warned her that beneath his mocking facade, there was a man who was capable of an alarming depth of passion, perhaps even brutality. He was not a man who could ever be mastered.

She tried to imagine Simon Hunt's dark face over hers, the hot brand of his mouth, his arms closing around her . . . just like before, except that she would be a willing participant. He was only a man, she reminded herself nervously. And a kiss was indeed a fleeting thing. But for the moment that it lasted, she would be bound in intimacy with him. And from then on, whenever they met, Simon Hunt would gloat silently. That would be difficult to endure.

She rubbed her forehead, which was suddenly as sore as if it had been whacked with a Rounders bat. "Can't we just ignore the whole thing and just hope that he'll have the good taste to keep his mouth shut?"

"Oh, yes," Lillian said sarcastically, "Mr. Hunt has so often been linked to the phrase 'good taste.' By all means, let's just cross our fingers and wait . . . if your nerves can bear the suspense."

Massaging her temples, Annabelle made a sound of distress. "All right. I'll approach him tonight. I'll . . ." She hesitated for a long moment. "I'll even kiss him, if necessary. But I will consider this more than adequate payment for all the gowns you gave me!"

A satisfied grin curved Lillian's mouth. "I'm certain that you can come to some agreement with Mr. Hunt."

After they parted company at the manor, Annabelle went to her room for an afternoon nap, which she hoped would restore her to rights before the supper ball. Her mother was nowhere to be seen, most likely having elected to take tea with some of the other ladies in the downstairs parlor. Annabelle was thankful for her mother's absence, which allowed her to change her clothes and wash without having to answer any unwanted questions. Although Philippa was a fond and generally permissive parent, she would not have reacted well to the news that her daughter had been involved in some scrape with the Bowman sisters.

After changing into fresh undergarments, Annabelle slipped beneath the slickly ironed bed linens. To her frustration, the nagging pain of her ankle made it impossible to sleep. Feeling weary and irritable, she rang for a maid to bring a cold footbath, and she sat with her foot soaking for a good half hour. Her ankle was most definitely swollen, leading her to conclude grumpily that it had been a singularly unlucky day. Cursing as she eased a fresh stocking over the pale, puffy flesh, Annabelle dressed herself slowly. She rang for the maid once more when she needed help to tighten her corset and fasten the back of her yellow silk gown.

"Miss?" the maid murmured, her eyes squinting with concern as she glanced into Annabelle's set face. "You look a bit peaked . . . Is there aught I can bring for you? The housekeeper keeps a tonic in her closet for female ailments—"

"No, it's not that," Annabelle said with a wan smile. "It's just a twinge in my ankle."

"Some willowbark tea, then?" the girl suggested, moving behind Annabelle to button the back of the ball gown. "I'll run down and fetch it straightaways, and you can drink it while I do your hair."

"Yes, thank you." Annabelle stood still as the maid's nimble fingers fastened the gown, then she sank gratefully into the chair before the dressing table. She stared at her own strained reflection in the Queen Anne looking glass. "I can't think how I injured it. I'm never clumsy."

The maid fluffed the pale golden tulle that trimmed the sleeves of Annabelle's gown. "I'll hurry with the tea, miss. That will set you to rights."

Just as the maid left, Philippa entered the room. Smiling at the sight of her daughter dressed in the yellow ball gown, she stood behind her, and met her gaze in the looking glass. "You look lovely, darling."

"I feel wretched," Annabelle said wryly. "I turned my ankle during my walk with the wallflowers this afternoon."

"Must you refer to yourselves that way?" Philippa asked, looking perturbed. "Surely you could think of some more flattering name for your little group—"

"But it suits us," Annabelle said with a grin. "If it makes you feel better, I do say the word with a suitable touch of irony."

Philippa sighed. "I'm afraid my own store of irony is quite depleted at the moment. It isn't easy for me to watch you struggle and scheme, while other girls of your station have so much easier a time of it. Seeing you in borrowed gowns, and knowing the burdens you carry . . . I've thought a thousand times that if only your father hadn't died, and if only we had just a little money . . ."

Annabelle shrugged. "As they say, Mama . . . 'if turnips were watches, I'd have one by my side.'"

Philippa stroked her hair lightly. "Why don't you rest in our room tonight? I'll read to you, while you lie with your ankle propped up—"

"Don't tempt me," Annabelle said feelingly. "I'd like nothing better—but I can't afford to stay up here tonight. I can't miss a single opportunity to make an impression on Lord Kendall." *And negotiate with Simon Hunt,* she thought, feeling hollow with apprehension.

After drinking a large mug of willowbark tea, Annabelle was able to make her way downstairs with scarcely a wince, although the swelling of her ankle had refused to abate. She had time for a brief exchange with Lillian before the guests were led to the dining hall. A touch of sun had left Lillian's cheeks pink and glowing, her brown eyes velvety in the candlelight. "So far, Lord Westcliff has made an obvious effort to ignore the wallflowers," Lillian said with a grin. "You were right—there'll be no trouble from that quarter. Our only potential problem is Mr. Hunt."

"He won't be a problem," Annabelle said grimly. "As I promised earlier, I'll talk to him."

Lillian responded with a relieved grin. "You're a peach, Annabelle."

As they were seated at the supper table, Annabelle was disconcerted to discover that she had been located near Lord Kendall. On any other occasion, it would have been a gratifying boon, but on this particular evening, Annabelle wasn't feeling her best. She was unequal to the task of making intelligent conversation while her ankle was throbbing and her head was aching. To add to her discomfort, Simon Hunt was seated almost directly opposite her, looking maddeningly self-possessed. And making matters even worse, a sense of queasiness kept her from doing justice to the magnificent repast. Bereft of her usual healthy appetite, she found herself picking listlessly at the contents of her plate. Every time she looked up, she found Hunt's shrewd gaze on her and braced herself for some subtle taunt. Mercifully, however, the few remarks he made to her were bland and commonplace, and she was able to suffer through the meal without incident.

A tide of music began to surge from the ballroom as the supper concluded, and Annabelle was thankful that the ball would begin soon. For once she would be entirely happy to sit in the line of wallflowers and rest her feet while others danced. She supposed that she had taken too much sun earlier in the day, as she was feeling unpleasantly light-headed and sore. Lillian and Daisy, by contrast, looked as vibrant and healthy as ever. Unfortunately, poor Evie had gotten a scolding from her aunt that had left her sorely chastened. "The sun makes her freckle," Daisy told Annabelle ruefully. "Aunt Florence told Evie that after our outing she's become as spotty as a leopard, and she's to have nothing more to do with us until her complexion returns to normal."

Annabelle frowned, feeling a wave of sympathy for her friend. "Beastly Aunt Florence," she muttered. "Obviously her sole purpose in life is to make Evie miserable."

"And she's brilliant at it," Daisy agreed. Suddenly she saw something over Annabelle's shoulder that made her eyes turn as round as saucers. "Zounds! Mr. Hunt is coming this way. I am *perishing* of thirst, so I'll just visit the refreshment table, and leave the two of you to, er . . ."

"Lillian told you," Annabelle said grimly.

"Yes, and she and Evie and I are ever so grateful for the sacrifice that you're going to make on our behalf."

"Sacrifice," Annabelle repeated, not liking the sound of the word. "That's putting it a bit strongly, isn't it? As Lillian said, 'one pair of lips is like any other.'"

"That's what she told you," Daisy said impishly. "But she told me and Evie that she would die before she would ever consent to kiss a man like Mr. Hunt."

"What—" Annabelle began, but Daisy had already scuttled away, chortling.

Beginning to feel like a sacrificial virgin being tossed into the inferno, Annabelle started as she heard Simon Hunt's deep voice close to her ear. The quiet jeer of his baritone seemed to resonate all the way down her spine. "Good evening, Miss Peyton. I see you're fully clothed . . . for a change."

Gritting her teeth, Annabelle turned to face him. "I must confess, Mr. Hunt, I was amazed by your restraint during dinner. I had expected a rash of insulting comments from you, and yet you managed to behave like a gentleman for a full hour."

"It was a strain," he acknowledged gravely. "But I thought that I would leave the shocking behavior to you . . ." He paused delicately before adding, ". . . since you seem to be doing so well at it of late."

"My friends and I did nothing wrong!"

"Did I say that I disapproved of your playing Rounders in the altogether?" he asked innocently. "On the contrary—I endorse it wholeheartedly. In fact, I think you should do it every day."

"I wasn't in the 'altogether,' " Annabelle retorted in a sharp whisper. "I was wearing undergarments."

"Is that what they were?" he asked lazily.

She flushed bright red, mortified that he had noticed how ragged her underclothes were. "Have you told anyone about seeing us in the meadow?" she asked tensely.

Obviously, that was the question that he had been waiting for. A slow smile curved his lips. "Not yet."

"Are you planning to tell anyone?"

Hunt considered the question with a thoughtful expression that didn't begin to conceal his enjoyment of the situation. "Not planning to, no . . ." He shrugged regretfully. "But you know how it is. Sometimes these things have a way of slipping out during a conversation . . ."

Annabelle narrowed her eyes. "What will it take to keep you quiet?"

Hunt pretended to be shocked by her bluntness. "Miss Peyton, you should learn to handle these matters with a bit more diplomacy, don't you think? I would have assumed that a lady of your refinement would use some tact and delicacy—"

"I don't have time for diplomacy," she interrupted with a scowl. "And it's obvious that you can't be depended upon to keep silent unless you're offered some kind of bribe."

"The word 'bribe' has such negative connotations," he mused. "I prefer to call it an inducement."

"Call it what you like," she said impatiently. "Let's get on with the negotiations, shall we?"

"All right." Hunt's facade was sober, but laughter flickered in the coffee-colored depths of his eyes. "I suppose I could be persuaded to hold my silence about your scandalous cavorting, Miss Peyton. With sufficient inducement."

Annabelle fell silent, her lashes lowering as she considered what she was about to say. Once the words were out, they couldn't be taken back. Dear Lord, why had it fallen to her to buy Simon Hunt's silence regarding a silly Rounders game that she hadn't even wanted to play in the first place? "If you were a gentleman," she muttered, "this wouldn't be necessary."

A wealth of suppressed laughter made his voice husky and uneven. "No, I'm not a gentleman. But I am compelled to remind you that *I* was not the one running half-naked through the meadow this afternoon."

"Will you *hush*?" she whispered sharply. "Someone will overhear you."

Hunt watched her with fascination, his eyes dark and heathen. "Make your best offer, Miss Peyton."

Staring fixedly at a portion of the wall far beyond his shoulder, Annabelle spoke in a suffocated tone, while the rims of her ears turned so hot that her hair was nearly singed. "If you promise to keep quiet about the Rounders game . . . I'll let you kiss me."

The unaccountable silence that followed her statement was excruciating. Forcing her gaze upward, Annabelle saw that she had surprised Hunt. He was staring at her as if she had just spoken in a foreign language, and he was not quite certain of the translation.

"One kiss," Annabelle said, her nerves shredded from the tension between them. "And don't assume that because I let you do it once, that I would ever consent to it again."

Hunt replied in an unusually guarded manner, seeming to choose his words with great care. "I had assumed that you would offer to dance with me. A waltz or a quadrille."

"I had thought of that," she said. "But a kiss is more expedient, not to mention much faster than a waltz."

"Not the way I kiss."

The soft statement caused her knees to quiver. "Don't be absurd," she replied shortly. "An ordinary waltz lasts for at least three minutes. You couldn't possibly kiss someone for that long."

Hunt's voice thickened almost imperceptibly as he replied. "You know best, of course. Very well—I accept your offer. One kiss, in return for keeping your secret. I'll decide when and where it happens."

"The 'when' and 'where' will be determined by mutual agreement," Annabelle countered. "The whole point of this is to keep my reputation from being compromised—I'm hardly going to let you jeopardize it by choosing some inappropriate time or place."

Hunt smiled mockingly. "What a negotiator you are, Miss Peyton. God help us all if you have any future ambitions to take part in the business world."

"No, my sole ambition is to become Lady Kendall," Annabelle returned with poisonous sweetness. She had the satisfaction of seeing his smile fade.

"That would be a pity," he said. "For you as well as Kendall."

"Go to the devil, Mr. Hunt," she said beneath her breath, and walked away from him, ignoring the violent throb of her sprained ankle.

As she made her way to the back terrace, she became aware that the injury to her ankle had worsened, until shooting pains had traveled up to her knee. "Hell's bells," she muttered. In this condition, she was hardly going to make progress with Lord Kendall. It was not easy to be seductive when one was on the verge of shrieking in torment. Suddenly feeling exhausted and defeated, Annabelle decided that she would return to her room. Now that her business with Simon Hunt was finished, the best thing to do would be to rest her ankle and hope it would improve by morning.

With each step she took, the pain intensified until she could feel trickles of cold sweat beneath the rigid stays of her corset. She had never had an injury like this before. Not only did her leg hurt, but her head was suddenly swimming, and she ached everywhere. Abruptly, the contents of her stomach began an alarming roil. She needed air . . . she had to go outside in the cool darkness, and sit somewhere until the nausea subsided. The door to the back terrace looked dreadfully far away, and she wondered dazedly how she was going to reach it.

Fortunately, the Bowman sisters had hurried toward

her as soon as they saw that her conversation with Simon Hunt had concluded. The expectant smile on Lillian's face died away as she met Annabelle's pain-darkened gaze. "You look terrible," Lillian exclaimed. "My God, what did Mr. Hunt say to you?"

"He agreed to the kiss," Annabelle replied shortly, continuing to hobble toward the terrace. She could scarcely hear the orchestra music over the ringing in her ears.

"If the prospect of it terrifies you that much—" Lillian began.

"It's not that," Annabelle said in pained exasperation. "It's my ankle. I sprained it earlier in the day, and now I can hardly walk."

"Why didn't you mention something earlier?" Lillian demanded in instant concern. Her slender arm was unexpectedly strong as she curved it around Annabelle's back. "Daisy, go to the nearest door and hold it open while we slip outside."

The sisters helped her outside, and Annabelle wiped her gloved hand over her sweating forehead. "I think I'm going to be sick," she moaned, while her mouth watered disagreeably, and stinging gall rose in her throat. Her leg ached as if it had been crushed by a carriage wheel. "Oh, Lord, I *can't*. I can't be sick now."

"It's all right," Lillian said, guiding her inexorably toward a flower bed that lined the side of the terrace steps. "No one can see you, dear. Be as sick as you want. Daisy and I are here to take care of you."

"That's right," Daisy chimed in from behind her. "True friends never mind holding your hair back while you cast up your crumpets."

Annabelle would have laughed, had she not been overcome with a spasm of mortifying nausea. Fortunately, she had not eaten much during supper, so the process was mercifully quick. Her stomach erupted, and she had no choice but to surrender. Gasping and spitting into the flower bed, she moaned weakly. "I'm sorry. I'm so sorry, Lillian—"

"Don't be ridiculous," came the American girl's calm reply. "You'd do the same for me, wouldn't you?"

"'Course I would . . . but you would never be so silly . . ."

"You're not being silly," Lillian said gently. "You're sick. Now take my handkerchief."

Still leaning over, Annabelle received the lace-trimmed square of linen gratefully, but recoiled at the scent of perfume. "*Ugh*, I can't," she whispered. "The smell. Do you have one that isn't scented?"

"Drat," Lillian said apologetically. "Daisy, where is your handkerchief?"

"Forgot it," came the succinct reply.

"You'll have to use this one," Lillian told Annabelle. "It's all we've got."

A masculine voice entered the conversation. "Take this one."

Chapter 12

Too dizzy to notice what was happening around her, Annabelle received the clean handkerchief that was thrust in her hand. It was mercifully free of any smell except for the crisp hint of starch. After wiping her perspiring face, then her mouth, Annabelle managed to straighten and face the newcomer. Her sore stomach did a slow, agonizing revolution at the sight of Simon Hunt. It seemed that he had followed her out to the terrace just in time to witness her humiliating nausea. She wanted to die. If only she could conveniently expire right then, and forever obliterate the knowledge that Simon Hunt had seen her cast up her crumpets in the flower bed.

Hunt's face was impassive, save for the frown indentations between his brows. Quickly he reached out to steady her as she swayed before him. "In light of our recent agreement," he murmured, "this is most unflattering, Miss Peyton."

"Oh, go away," Annabelle moaned, but she found herself leaning hard against the strong support of his body as another wave of illness washed over her. She clamped the handkerchief to her mouth and breathed through her nose, and mercifully the feeling passed. But the most debilitating weakness she had ever felt swept over her, and she knew that if he had not been there, she would have crumpled to the ground. Good Lord, what was wrong with her?

Hunt immediately adjusted his hold, bracing her easily. "I thought you looked pale," he remarked, gently stroking back a lock of hair that had fallen over her damp face. "What's the matter, sweetheart? Is it just your stomach, or do you hurt somewhere else?"

Somewhere beneath the layers of misery Annabelle was startled by the endearment, not to mention the fact that a gentleman should never, ever have referred to one of a lady's internal parts. However, at the moment she was too ill to do anything but cling to his coat lapels. Concentrating on his question, she pondered the chaos inside her inhospitable body. "I hurt everywhere," she whispered. "My head, my stomach, my back . . . but most of all my ankle."

As she spoke, she noticed that her lips felt numb. She licked at them experimentally, alarmed by the lack of sensation. Had she been just a bit less disoriented, she would have noticed that Hunt was staring at her in a way that he never had before. Later, Daisy would describe in detail how protective Simon Hunt had seemed as he had stood with his arms around her. For now, however, Annabelle was too wretched to perceive anything outside her own swamping illness.

Lillian spoke briskly, moving forward to extricate Annabelle from Hunt's grasp. "Thank you for the use of your handkerchief, sir. You may leave now, as my sister and I are fully capable of taking care of Miss Peyton."

Ignoring the American girl, Hunt kept his arm

around Annabelle as he stared into her blanched face. "How did you hurt your ankle?" he asked.

"The Rounders game, I think . . ."

"I didn't see you drink anything at dinner." Hunt laid his hand across her forehead, searching for signs of fever. The gesture was astonishingly intimate and familiar. "Did you have something earlier?"

"If you mean spirits or wine, no." Annabelle's body seemed to be collapsing slowly, as if her mind had released all control over the movement of her limbs. "I drank some willowbark tea in my room."

Hunt's warm hand moved to the side of her face, conforming gently to the curve of her cheek. She was so cold, shivering inside her sweat-dampened gown, her skin covered with gooseflesh. Perceiving the inviting heat that radiated from his body, she was nearly overcome with the urge to delve into his coat like a small burrowing animal. "I'm f-freezing," she whispered, and his arm tightened reflexively around her.

"Hold on to me," he murmured, adroitly managing to shed his coat while supporting her trembling form at the same time. He wrapped her in the garment, which retained the warmth of his skin, and she responded with an inarticulate sound of gratitude.

Nettled by the sight of her friend being held by a detested adversary, Lillian spoke impatiently. "See here, Mr. Hunt, my sister and I—"

"Go find Mrs. Peyton," Hunt interrupted, in a tone that was no less authoritative for its softness. "And tell Lord Westcliff that Miss Peyton needs a doctor. He'll know whom to send for."

"What are *you* going to do?" Lillian demanded, clearly unaccustomed to being given orders in such a fashion.

Hunt's eyes narrowed as he replied. "I'm going to

carry Miss Peyton through the servants' entrance at the side of the house. Your sister will go with us to avoid any appearance of impropriety."

"That shows how little you know about propriety!" Lillian snapped.

"I'm not going to debate the matter. Try to be of some use, will you? *Go*."

After a furious, tension-fraught pause, Lillian turned and strode toward the ballroom doors.

Daisy was clearly awestruck. "I don't think anyone has ever dared to speak to my sister that way. You're the bravest man I've ever met, Mr. Hunt."

Hunt bent carefully to hook his arm beneath Annabelle's knees. He lifted her with ease, clasping a mass of shivering limbs and rustling silk skirts in his arms. Annabelle had never been carried anywhere by a man—she could not conceive that it was really happening. "I think . . . I could walk part of the way," she managed to say.

"You wouldn't make it down the terrace steps," Hunt said flatly. "Indulge me while I demonstrate the chivalrous side of my nature. Can you put your arms around my neck?"

Annabelle obeyed, grateful to have the weight taken off her burning ankle. Surrendering to the temptation to put her head on his shoulder, she curled her left arm around his neck. As he carried her down the flagstone steps of the back terrace, she could feel the facile play of muscle beneath the layers of his shirt.

"I didn't think you had a chivalrous side," she said, her teeth clicking as another chill shook her. "I th-thought you were a complete scoundrel."

"I don't know how people get such ideas about me," he replied, glancing down at her with a teasing gleam in his eyes. "I've always been tragically misunderstood."

"I still think you're a scoundrel."

Hunt grinned and shifted her more comfortably in his arms. "Obviously illness hasn't impaired your judgment."

"Why are you helping me after I just told you to go to the devil?" she whispered.

"I have a vested interest in preserving your health. I want you to be in top form when I collect on my debt."

As Hunt descended the steps with surefooted swiftness, she felt the smooth grace with which he moved— not like a dancer, but like a cat on the prowl. With their faces so close, Annabelle saw that a ruthlessly close shave had not been able to disguise the dark grain of whiskers beneath his skin. Seeking a more secure hold on him, Annabelle reached farther around his neck, until her fingertips brushed the ends of hair that curled slightly against his nape. *What a pity I'm so sick*, she thought. *If I wasn't so cold and dizzy and weak, I might actually enjoy being carried like this.*

Reaching the path that extended along the side of the manor, Hunt paused to allow Daisy to skirt around them and lead the way. "The servants' door," he reminded her, and the girl nodded.

"Yes, I know which one it is." Daisy glanced over her shoulder as she preceded them on the path. Her small face was tense with worry. "I've never heard of a sprained ankle making anyone sick to her stomach," she commented.

"I suspect this is more than a sprained ankle," Hunt replied.

"Do you think it was the willowbark tea?" Daisy asked.

"No, willowbark wouldn't cause such a reaction. I have an idea about what the problem might be, but I won't be able to confirm it until we reach Miss Peyton's room."

"How do you intend to 'confirm' your idea?" Annabelle asked warily.

"All I want to do is look at your ankle." Hunt smiled down at her. "Surely I deserve that much, after I take you up three flights of stairs."

As it turned out, the stairs were no effort for him at all. When they reached the top of the third flight, his breathing hadn't even altered. Annabelle suspected that he could have carried her ten times as far without breaking a sweat. When she said as much to him, he replied in a matter-of-fact tone. "I spent most of my youth hauling sides of beef and pork to my father's shop. Carrying you is far more enjoyable."

"How sweet," Annabelle mumbled sickly, her eyes closed. "Every woman dreams of being told that she's preferable to a dead cow."

Laughter rumbled in his chest, and he turned to avoid bumping her foot against the doorframe. Daisy opened the door for them, and stood watching anxiously as Hunt brought Annabelle to the brocade-covered bed.

"Here we are," he said, laying her down and reaching for an extra pillow to prop her to a half-sitting position.

"Thank you," she whispered, staring into the thick-lashed sable eyes above her own.

"I want to see your leg."

Her heart seemed to stop at the outrageous statement. When her pulse resumed, it was weak and far too brisk. "I would rather wait until the doctor arrives."

"I'm not asking for permission." Ignoring her protests, Hunt reached for the hem of her skirts.

"Mr. Hunt," Daisy exclaimed in outrage, hurrying

over to him. "Don't you dare! Miss Peyton is ill, and if you don't remove your hands at once—"

"Settle your feathers," Hunt replied sardonically. "I'm not going to abuse Miss Peyton's maidenly virtue. Not yet, at any rate." His gaze switched to Annabelle's pale face. "Don't move. Charming as your legs undoubtedly are, they're not going to incite me to a frenzy of—" He broke off with a sharp intake of breath as he lifted her skirts and saw her swollen ankle. "Damn. Until now I've always thought of you as a reasonably intelligent woman. Why the hell did you go downstairs in this condition?"

"Oh, Annabelle," Daisy murmured, "Your ankle looks terrible!"

"It wasn't that bad earlier," Annabelle said defensively. "It's gotten much worse in the past half hour, and—" She yelped in a mixture of pain and alarm as she felt Hunt reach farther beneath her skirts. "What are you doing? Daisy, don't let him—"

"I'm removing your stocking," Hunt said. "And I would advise Miss Bowman not to interfere."

Frowning at him, Daisy came to Annabelle's side. "I would advise *you* to proceed with caution, Mr. Hunt," she said smartly. "I am not going to stand by passively while you molest my friend."

Hunt sent her a glance of scalding mockery, while he found the ridge of Annabelle's garter and unfastened it deftly. "Miss Bowman, in a few minutes we're going to be overrun with visitors, including Mrs. Peyton, Lord Westcliff, and your hardheaded sister, followed soon thereafter by the doctor. Even I, seasoned ravisher that I am, require more time than that to molest someone." His expression changed as Annabelle gasped in pain at his gentle touch. Deftly he unrolled her stocking, his fingertips feather-light, but her skin was so sensitive that even the softest stroke caused an unbearable sting. "Hold still, sweetheart," he murmured, drawing the length of silk from her flinching leg.

Biting her lip, Annabelle watched as his dark head bent over her ankle. He turned it carefully, taking care not to touch her more than necessary. Then he went still, his dark head bent over her leg. "Just as I thought."

Leaning forward, Daisy looked at the place on her ankle that Hunt indicated. "What are those little marks?"

"Adder bite," Hunt said tersely. He rolled up his shirtsleeves, exposing muscular forearms covered with dark hair.

The two girls glanced at him in shock. "I've been bitten by a *snake*?" Annabelle asked dazedly. "But how? When? That can't be true. I would have felt something . . . wouldn't I?"

Hunt reached inside the pocket of the coat that was still wrapped around her, searching for something. "Sometimes people don't notice the moment they're bitten. The Hampshire woods are full of adders at this time of year. It probably happened during your outing this afternoon." Finding what he sought, he extracted a small folding knife and flipped it open.

Annabelle's eyes widened with alarm. "What are you doing?"

Picking up her stocking, Hunt severed it neatly in two. "Making a tourniquet."

"D-do you always carry one of those with you?" She had always thought of him as somewhat piratical, and now seeing him in his shirtsleeves with a knife in hand, the image was strongly reinforced.

Sitting beside her outstretched leg, Hunt smoothed her skirts up to her knee and fastened a length of silk above her ankle. "Nearly always," he said wryly, concentrating on his handiwork. "Being a butcher's son consigns me to a lifelong fascination with knives."

"I never thought—" Annabelle stopped and gasped in pain at the soft cinch of silk.

Hunt's gaze shot to hers, and there was a new tautness in his face. "I'm sorry," he said, carefully looping the other half of the stocking beneath her injury. He talked to distract her while he tightened the second tourniquet. "This is what comes of wearing those damned flimsy slippers outside. You must have walked right over an adder who was sunning himself . . . and when he saw one of those pretty little ankles, he decided to take a nibble." He paused, and said something beneath his breath that sounded like, "I can't say that I blame him."

Her leg pulsed and burned, causing a watery sting of response in her eyes. Fighting the mortifying threat of tears, Annabelle dug her fingers into the thick, brocaded counterpane beneath her. "Why has my ankle only started to hurt this badly now if I was bitten earlier in the day?"

"It can take several hours for the effects to set in." Hunt glanced at Daisy. "Miss Bowman, ring the servants' bell—tell them that we need some clivers steeped in boiling water. Immediately."

"What are clivers?" Daisy asked suspiciously.

"A hedgerow weed. The housekeeper has kept a dried bundle of them in her closet ever since the master gardener was bitten last year."

Daisy rushed to comply, leaving the two of them temporarily alone.

"What happened to the gardener?" Annabelle asked through chattering teeth. She was overcome with continuous shivers, as if she had been immersed in ice water. "Did he die?"

Hunt's expression did not change, but she sensed

that her question had startled him. "No," he said gently, drawing closer. "No, sweetheart . . ." Taking her trembling hand in his, he warmed her fingers in a gentle grip. "Hampshire adders don't produce enough venom to kill anything larger than a cat, or a very small dog." His gaze was caressing as he continued. "You'll be fine. Uncomfortable as hell for the next few days, but after that you'll be back to normal."

"You're not trying to be kind, are you?" she asked anxiously.

Bending over her, Hunt stroked back a few tendrils of hair that had stuck to her sweat-shimmered forehead. Despite the size of his hand, his touch was light and tender. "I never lie for the sake of kindness," he murmured, smiling. "One of my many flaws."

Having given instructions to a footman, Daisy hastened back to the bedside. Although she raised her slender dark brows at the sight of Hunt leaning over Annabelle, she forbore to comment. Instead, she asked, "Shouldn't we cut across the puncture wounds to let the poison out?"

Annabelle sent her a warning glance and croaked, "Don't give him ideas, Daisy!"

Hunt looked up briefly as he replied. "Not for an adder bite." His eyes narrowed as he returned his attention to Annabelle, noting that her breathing was rapid and shallow. "Is it difficult to breathe?"

Annabelle nodded, struggling to pull air into lungs that seemed to have shrunk to a third of their usual size. It felt as if bands were drawing more tightly around her chest with every breath she took, until her ribs threatened to crack from the pressure.

Hunt touched her face softly, his thumb passing over the dry surface of her lips. "Open your mouth." Looking beyond her parted lips, he observed, "Your tongue isn't swelling—you'll be fine. Your corset has to come off, however. Turn over."

Before Annabelle could form a reply, Daisy protested indignantly. "*I'll* help Annabelle with her corset. Leave the room, please."

"I've seen a woman's corset before," he informed her sarcastically.

Daisy rolled her eyes. "Don't be deliberately obtuse, Mr. Hunt. Obviously *you're* not the one I'm worried about. Men don't remove young ladies' corsets for any reason, unless the circumstances are life-threatening— which you have just assured us that they are not."

Hunt regarded her with a long-suffering expression. "Dammit, woman—"

"Swear all you like," Daisy said implacably. "My older sister could outcurse you ten times over." She drew herself up to her full height, though at five feet and one debatable inch, the effect was hardly impressive. "Miss Peyton's corset stays on until you leave the room."

Hunt glanced down at Annabelle, who suddenly craved air too badly to care who removed her corset, so long as it was done. "For God's sake," he said impatiently, and strode to the window, turning his back to them. "I'm not looking. *Do it.*"

Seeming to realize that it was the only concession he was prepared to make, Daisy obeyed hurriedly. She eased the coat away from Annabelle's stiff body. "I'll untie the laces in the back and slip it off beneath your gown," she murmured to Annabelle. "That way you'll remain decently covered."

Annabelle couldn't summon sufficient breath to tell her that any concerns she might have had about modesty had paled in comparison to the far more immediate problem of not being able to breathe. Wheezing harshly, she turned to her side and felt Daisy's fingers plucking at the slippery back of her ball gown. Her lungs spasmed in their frustrated attempts to pull in precious air. Letting out an anxious moan, she began to pant desperately.

Daisy let out a few choice curses. "Mr. Hunt, I'm afraid I must borrow your knife—the corset strings are knotted, and I can't—*oof!*" The last exclamation came as Hunt strode to the bed, shoved her unceremoniously aside, and set to work on the corset himself. A few judicious applications of his knife, and suddenly the obstinate garment released its punishing clasp around Annabelle's ribs.

She felt him tug the boned garment away from her body, leaving only the thin veil of her chemise between his gaze and her bare skin. In Annabelle's current condition, the exposure was of little concern. However, she knew in the back of her mind that she would later die of embarrassment.

Turning Annabelle to her back as easily if she were a rag doll, Hunt bent over her. "Don't try so hard, sweetheart." His hand flattened over the upper reach of her chest. Holding her frightened gaze intently, he rubbed in a soothing circle. "Slowly. Just relax."

Staring into the compelling dark glitter of his eyes, Annabelle tried to obey, but her throat clenched around every wheezing breath. She was going to die of suffocation, right there and then.

He wouldn't let her look away from him. "You'll be all right. Let your breath ease in and out. Slowly. That's it. Yes." Somehow the gentle weight of his hand on her chest seemed to help her, as if he had the power to will her lungs back to their normal rhythm. "You're going through the worst of it right now," he said.

"Oh, lovely," she tried to say in acerbic response, but the effort made her choke and hiccup.

"Don't try to talk—just breathe. Another long, slow one . . . another. Good girl."

As Annabelle gradually recovered her breath, the panic began to fade. He was right . . . it was easier if she didn't struggle. The sound of her fitful gasping was underlaid by the mesmerizing softness of his voice. "That's right," he murmured. "That's the way of it." His hand continued to move in a slow, easy rotation over her chest. There was nothing sexual in his touch—in fact, she might have been a child he was trying to soothe. Annabelle was amazed. Who would have ever dreamed that Simon Hunt could be so kind?

Filled with equal parts of confusion and gratitude, Annabelle fumbled for the large hand that moved so gently on her chest. She was so feeble that the gesture required all her strength. Assuming that she was trying to push him away, Hunt began to withdraw, but as he felt her fingers curl around two of his, he went very still.

"Thank you," she whispered.

The touch made Hunt tense visibly, as if the contact had sent a shock through his body. He stared not at her face but at the delicate fingers entwined with his, in the manner of a man who was trying to solve a complex puzzle. Remaining motionless, he prolonged the moment, his lashes lowering to conceal his expression.

Annabelle used her tongue to moisten her dry lips, discovering that she still couldn't feel them. "My face is numb," she said scratchily, letting go of his hand.

Hunt looked up with the wry smile of a man who had just discovered something unexpected about himself. "The clivers will help." He touched the side of her throat, his thumb gliding along the edge of her jaw in a gesture that could only be characterized as a caress. "Which reminds me—" He glanced over his shoulder as if just remembering that Daisy was in the room. "Miss Bowman, has that damned footman brought—"

"It's here," the dark-haired girl said, coming from the doorway with a tray that had just been brought up. Apparently they had both been too absorbed in each other to notice the servant's knock. "The housekeeper sent up the clivers tea, which smells ghastly, and there's also a little bottle that the footman said was 'tincture of nettle.' And it seems the doctor has just arrived and will be coming upstairs any minute—which means that you must leave, Mr. Hunt."

His jaw hardened. "Not yet."

"*Now,*" Daisy said urgently. "At least wait outside the door. For Annabelle's sake. She'll be ruined if you're seen in here."

Scowling, Hunt looked down at Annabelle. "Do you want me to go?"

She didn't, actually. In fact, she had an irrational desire to beg him to stay. Oh, what a bewildering turn of events, that she should so desire the company of a man she detested! But the past few minutes had somehow wrought a fragile connection between them, and she found herself in the odd predicament of being unable to say "yes" or "no." "I'll keep breathing," she finally whispered. "You probably should leave."

Hunt nodded. "I'll wait in the hallway," he said gruffly, standing from the bed. Motioning Daisy forward with the tray, he continued to stare at Annabelle. "Drink the clivers, no matter how it tastes. Or I'll come back in here and pour it down your throat." Retrieving his coat, he left the room.

Sighing with relief, Daisy set the tray at the bedside table. "Thank God," she said. "I wasn't certain how I was going to make him go, if he refused. Here . . . let me lift you a bit higher, and I'll push another pillow behind you." The girl elevated her deftly, demonstrating surprising competence. Taking up a huge earthenware mug filled with steaming contents, Daisy pressed the edge against her lips. "Have some of this, dear."

Annabelle swallowed the bitter brown liquid and recoiled. "*Ugh*—"

"More," Daisy said inexorably, lifting it to her mouth.

Annabelle drank again. Her face was so numb that she wasn't aware that some of the medicine had dribbled from her lips until Daisy picked up a napkin from the tray and blotted her chin. Cautiously Annabelle lifted exploratory fingertips to the frozen skin of her face. "Feels so odd," she said, her voice slurred. "No sensation in my mouth. Daisy . . . don't say that I was drooling while Mr. Hunt was here?"

"Of course not," Daisy said immediately. "I would have done something about it if you had been. A true friend doesn't let another friend drool when a man is present. Even if it's a man that one doesn't wish to attract."

Relieved, Annabelle applied herself to downing more of the clivers, which tasted rather like burned coffee. Perhaps it was wishful thinking, but she was beginning to feel the tiniest bit better.

"Lillian must have had a devil of a time finding your mother," Daisy commented. "I can't imagine what has taken them so long." She drew back a little to look at Annabelle, her brown eyes sparkling richly. "I'm actually glad, though. If they had come quickly, I would have missed seeing Mr. Hunt's transformation from a big bad wolf into . . . well . . . a somewhat nicer wolf."

A reluctant laugh gurgled in Annabelle's throat. "Quite something, isn't he?"

"Yes, indeed. Arrogant and oh-so-masterful. Like a figure from one of those torrid novels that Mama is forever ripping from my hands. It's a good thing that I was here, or he probably would have stripped you right down to your unmentionables." She continued to chatter as she helped Annabelle to drink more of the clivers, and blotted her chin once more. "You know, I never thought I would say this, but Mr. Hunt isn't quite as terrible as I thought."

Annabelle twisted her lips experimentally as a modicum of sensation returned, making them prickle. "He has his uses, it seems. But . . . don't expect that the transformation is permanent."

Chapter 13

Barely two minutes had passed before Simon saw the group he had earlier predicted, consisting of the doctor, Lord Westcliff, Mrs. Peyton, and Lillian Bowman. Leaning his shoulders back against the wall, Simon gave them a speculative stare. Privately, he was amused by the palpable dislike between Westcliff and Miss Bowman, whose obvious mutual animosity betrayed the fact that words had been exchanged.

The doctor was a venerable old man who had attended Westcliff and his relatives, the Marsdens, for nearly three decades. Glancing at Simon with keen eyes set deeply in an age-furrowed face, he spoke with unflappable calmness. "Mr. Hunt, I am told that you assisted the young lady to her room?"

Simon brusquely described Annabelle's condition and symptoms to the doctor, choosing to omit that he, and not Daisy, had been the one to discover the puncture marks on Annabelle's ankle. Mrs. Peyton listened in white-faced distress. Frowning, Lord Westcliff bent to murmur to Mrs. Peyton, who nodded and thanked him distractedly. Simon guessed that Westcliff had promised that the best care possible would be provided until her daughter had recovered fully.

"Of course I won't be able to confirm Mr. Hunt's opinion until I examine the young lady," the doctor remarked. "However, it may be advisable to begin brewing some clivers right away, in the event that the illness was indeed caused by adder bite—"

"She's already drinking some," Simon interrupted. "I sent for it about a quarter hour ago."

The doctor regarded him with the special vexation reserved for those who undertook to make a diagnosis without benefit of a medical degree. "Clivers is a potent drug, Mr. Hunt, and possibly injurious in the event that a patient is *not* suffering from snake venom. You should have waited for a doctor's opinion before administering it."

"The symptoms of adder bite are unmistakable," Simon replied impatiently, wishing the man would cease tarrying in the hallway and go do his job. "And I wanted to alleviate Miss Peyton's discomfort as quickly as possible."

The old man's wiry gray brows descended low over his eyes. "You're quite certain of your own judgment," came the peppery observation.

"Yes," Simon replied, without blinking.

Suddenly the earl let out a muffled chuckle and settled a hand on the doctor's shoulder. "I'm afraid that we'll be forced to stand out here indefinitely, sir, if you attempt to convince my friend that he's wrong about anything. 'Opinionated' is the mildest of adjectives one could apply to Mr. Hunt. I assure you, your energies are far better directed toward caring for Miss Peyton."

"Perhaps so," the doctor returned testily. "Although one suspects that my presence is superfluous in light of Mr. Hunt's expert diagnosis." With that sarcastic comment, the old man entered the room, followed by Mrs. Peyton and Lillian Bowman.

Left alone in the hallway with Westcliff, Simon rolled his eyes. "Bilious old bastard," he muttered. "Could you have sent for someone a bit more decrepit, Westcliff? I doubt he can see or hear well enough to make his own damned diagnosis."

The earl arched one black brow as he regarded Simon with amused condescension. "He's the best doctor in Hampshire. Come downstairs, Hunt. We'll have a brandy."

Simon glanced at the closed door. "Later."

Westcliff replied in a light, far-too-pleasant tone. "Ah, forgive me. Of course you'll want to wait by the door like a stray dog hoping for kitchen scraps. I'll be in my study—do be a good lad and run down to tell me if there's any news."

Rankled, Simon flashed him a cold glare and pushed away from the wall. "All right," he growled, "I'll come."

The earl responded with a satisfied nod. "The doctor will deliver a report to me after he's finished with Miss Peyton."

As Simon accompanied Westcliff to the great staircase, he reflected moodily on his own behavior of the past few minutes. It was a new experience, being driven by his emotions rather than his intellect, and he didn't like it. That didn't seem to matter, however. At the first realization that Annabelle was ill, he had felt his chest turn painfully hollow, as if his heart had been seized for ransom. There had been no question in his mind that he would do whatever was necessary to make her safe and comfortable. And in the moments when Annabelle had struggled to breathe, staring at him with eyes bright with pain and fear, he would have done anything for her. Anything.

God help him if Annabelle ever came to realize the power she had over him . . . a power that posed a perilous threat to pride and self-control. He wanted to possess every part of her body and soul, in every imaginable cast of intimacy. The ever-increasing depth of his passion for her shocked him. And no one of his acquaintance, least of all Westcliff, would understand. Westcliff had always kept his own emotions and desires firmly in check, displaying contempt for those who made fools of themselves for the sake of love.

Not that this was love . . . Simon was not about to go *that* far. And yet it was far more than ordinary desire. It required nothing less than outright ownership.

Forcing his features into a blank mask, Simon followed Westcliff into his study.

It was a small, austere room, fitted with gleaming oak paneling and ornamented only by a row of stained-glass windows on one side. With its hard angles and unforgiving furniture, the study was not a comfortable room. However, it was a thoroughly masculine place, where one could smoke, drink, and talk frankly. Lowering himself to one of the hard chairs positioned by the desk, Simon accepted a brandy from Westcliff and downed it without tasting it. He held out the snifter and nodded in wordless thanks as the earl replenished it.

Before Westcliff could launch into an unwanted diatribe regarding Annabelle, Simon sought to distract him. "You don't seem to rub on well with Miss Bowman," he remarked.

As a diversionary tactic, the mention of Lillian Bowman was supremely effective. Westcliff responded with a surly grunt. "The ill-mannered brat dared to imply that Miss Peyton's mishap was my fault," he said, pouring a brandy for himself.

Simon raised his brows. "How could it be your fault?"

"Miss Bowman seems to think that, as their host, it was my responsibility to ensure that my estate wasn't 'overrun with a plague of poisonous vipers,' as she put it."

"How did you reply?"

"I pointed out to Miss Bowman that the guests who choose to remain clothed when they venture out of doors don't usually seem to get bitten by adders."

Simon couldn't help grinning at that. "Miss Bowman is merely concerned for her friend."

Westcliff nodded in grim agreement. "She can't afford to lose one of them, as she undoubtedly has so few."

Smiling, Simon stared into the depths of his brandy. "What a difficult evening you've had," he heard Westcliff remark sardonically. "First you were compelled to carry Miss Peyton's nubile young body all the way to her bedroom . . . then you had to examine her injured leg. How terribly inconvenient for you."

Simon's smile faded. "I didn't say that I had examined her leg."

The earl regarded him shrewdly. "You didn't have to. I know you too well to presume that you would overlook such an opportunity."

"I'll admit that I looked at her ankle. And I also cut her corset strings when it became apparent that she couldn't breathe." Simon's gaze dared the earl to object.

"Helpful lad," Westcliff murmured.

Simon scowled. "Difficult as it may be for you to believe, I receive no lascivious pleasure from the sight of a woman in pain."

Leaning back in his chair, Westcliff regarded him

with a cool speculation that raised Simon's hackles. "I hope you're not fool enough to fall in love with such a creature. You know my opinion of Miss Peyton—"

"Yes, you've aired it repeatedly."

"And furthermore," the earl continued, "I would hate to see one of the few men of good sense I know to turn into one of those prattling fools who run about pollenating the atmosphere with maudlin sentiment—"

"I'm not in love."

"You're in *something*," Westcliff insisted. "In all the years I've known you, I've never seen you look so mawkish as you did outside her bedroom door."

"I was displaying simple compassion for a fellow human being."

The earl snorted. "Whose drawers you're itching to get into."

The blunt accuracy of the observation caused Simon to smile reluctantly. "It was an itch two years ago," he admitted. "Now it's a full-scale pandemic."

Letting out a sighing groan, Westcliff rubbed the narrow bridge of his nose with his thumb and forefinger. "There is nothing I hate worse than watching a friend charge blindly into disaster. Your weakness, Hunt, is your inability to resist a challenge. Even when the challenge is unworthy of you."

"I like a challenge." Simon swirled the brandy in his snifter. "But that has nothing to do with my interest in her."

"Good God," the earl muttered, "either drink the brandy or stop playing with it. You'll bruise the liquor by swishing it around like that."

Simon sent him a darkly amused glance. "How, exactly, does one 'bruise' a glass of brandy? No, don't tell me—my provincial brain couldn't begin to grasp the concept." Obediently, he took a swallow and set the glass aside. "Now, what were we talking about . . . ? Oh yes, my weakness. Before we discuss that any more, I want you to admit that, at one time in your life or another, you've given greater shrift to desire than to common sense. Because if you haven't, there's no use in talking to you any further about this."

"Of course I have. Every man over the age of twelve has. But the purpose of the higher intellect is to prevent us from repeatedly making such mistakes—"

"Well, there's my problem," Simon said reasonably. "I don't bother with a higher intellect. I've done quite well with just my lower one."

The earl's jaw hardened. "There's a reason that Miss Peyton and her carnivorous friends are all unwed, Hunt. *They're trouble.* If the events of today haven't made that clear, then there's no hope for you."

As Simon Hunt had predicted, Annabelle was in considerable discomfort for the next few days. She had become wretchedly familiar with the flavor of clivers tea, which the doctor had prescribed to be taken every four hours for the first day, and every six hours for the next. Although she could tell that the medicine was helping to reduce the symptoms of the adder venom, it set her stomach in constant revolt. She was exhausted, and yet she couldn't seem to sleep well, and although she longed for something to alleviate her boredom, she couldn't seem to focus on anything for more than a few minutes at a time.

Her friends did their best to cheer and entertain her, for which Annabelle was acutely grateful. Evie sat at her bedside and read aloud from a lurid novel purloined from the estate library. Daisy and Lillian came to deliver the latest gossip, and made her laugh with their mischievous imitations of various guests. At her insistence, they dutifully reported who seemed to be winning the race for Kendall's attentions. One in particular, a tall, slender, fair-haired girl named Lady Constance Darrowby, had captured his interest.

"She looks to be a very cold sort, if you ask me," Daisy said frankly. "She has a mouth that reminds one of a drawstring purse, and a terribly annoying habit of giggling behind her palm, as if it's unladylike to be caught laughing in public."

"She must have bad teeth," Lillian said hopefully.

"I think she's quite dull," Daisy continued. "I can't imagine what she has to say that Kendall would find of such interest."

"Daisy," Lillian said, "we're talking about a man whose idea of high entertainment is to look at *plants*. His threshold of boredom is obviously limitless."

"At the picnic after the water party today," Daisy told Annabelle, "I thought for a supremely satisfying moment that I had caught Lady Constance in a compromising position with one of the guests. She disappeared for a few minutes with a gentleman who was *not* Lord Kendall."

"Who was it?" Annabelle asked.

"Mr. Benjamin Muxlow—a local gentleman farmer. You know, the salt-of-the-earth sort who's got some decent acreage and a handful of servants and is looking for a wife who will bear him eight or nine children and mend his shirt cuffs and make him pig's-blood-pudding at slaughtertime—"

"Daisy," Lillian interrupted, noticing that Annabelle had suddenly turned green, "try to be a bit less revolting, will you?" She smiled at Annabelle apologetically. "Sorry, dear. But you must admit that the English are willing to eat things that make Americans flee the table with screams of horror."

"Anyway," Daisy continued with exaggerated patience, "Lady Constance vanished after having been seen in the company of Mr. Muxlow, and naturally I went looking for them in the hopes of seeing something that would discredit her, thereby causing Lord Kendall to lose all interest. You can imagine my pleasure at discovering the two of them behind a tree with their heads close together."

"Were they kissing?" Annabelle asked.

"No, drat it. Muxlow was helping Lady Constance to replace a baby robin that had fallen from its nest."

"Oh." Annabelle felt her shoulders slump as she added grumpily, "How sweet of her." She knew that part of her despondency was caused by the effects of the snake venom, not to mention its unpalatable antidote. However, knowing the cause of her low spirits did nothing to improve them.

Seeing her dejection, Lillian picked up a tarnished silver-backed hairbrush. "Forget about Lady Constance and Lord Kendall for now," she said. "Let me braid your hair—you'll feel much better when it's off your face."

"Where is my looking glass?" Annabelle asked, moving forward to allow Lillian to sit behind her.

"Can't find it," came the girl's calm reply.

It had not escaped Annabelle's notice that the looking glass had conveniently disappeared. She knew that her illness had ravaged her looks, leaving her hair dull and her skin drained of its usual healthy color. In addition, her ever-present nausea had kept her from eating, and her arms looked far too thin as they rested limply on the counterpane.

In the evening, as she lay in her sickbed, the sounds of music and dancing floated through her open bedroom window from the ballroom below. Envisioning Lady Constance waltzing in Lord Kendall's arms,

Annabelle shifted restlessly amid the bedclothes, concluding morosely that her chances of marrying had all but vanished. "I hate adders," she grumbled, watching her mother straighten the collection of articles on the beside table . . . medicine-sticky spoons, bottles, handkerchiefs, a hairbrush, and hairpins. "I hate being sick, and I hate walking through the forest, and most of all I hate Rounders-in-knickers!"

"What did you say, dearest?" Philippa asked, pausing in the act of setting a few empty glasses on a tray.

Annabelle shook her head, suddenly overcome with melancholy. "I . . . oh, nothing, Mama. I've been thinking—I want to go back to London in a day or two, when I'm fit to travel. There's no use in staying here. Lady Constance is as good as Lady Kendall now, and I don't look or feel well enough to attract anyone else, and besides—"

"I wouldn't give up all hope just yet," Philippa said, setting down the tray. She leaned over Annabelle and stroked her brow with a soft, motherly hand. "No betrothal has been announced—and Lord Kendall has been asking after you quite often. And don't forget that enormous bouquet of bluebells that he brought for you. Picked by his own hands, he told me."

Wearily Annabelle glanced at the huge arrangement in the corner, its perfume hanging thickly in the air. "Mama, I've been meaning to ask . . . could you get rid of it? It's lovely, and I did appreciate the gesture . . . but the smell . . ."

"Oh, I didn't think of that," Philippa said immediately. Hurrying to the corner, she picked up the vase of nodding blue flowers and carried them to the door. "I'll set them out in the hall, and I'll ask a housemaid to take them away . . ." Her voice trailed away as she busied herself for a few moments.

Picking up a stray hairpin, Annabelle toyed with the crimped wire and frowned. Kendall's bouquet had been one of many, actually. The news of her illness had prompted a great deal of friendly sympathy from the guests at Stony Cross Manor. Even Lord Westcliff had sent up an arrangement of hothouse roses on behalf of himself and the Marsdens. The proliferation of flowers in vases had given the room a funereal appearance. Oddly, there had been nothing from Simon Hunt . . . not a single note or flower stem. After his solicitous behavior two nights ago, she would have expected *something*. Some small indication of concern . . . but the thought occurred to her that perhaps Hunt had decided that she was an absurd and troublesome creature, no longer worthy of his attention. If so, she should be grateful that she would never again be plagued by him.

Instead, Annabelle felt a stinging pressure behind her nose and the threat of unwanted tears in her eyes. She didn't understand herself. She could not identify the emotion that moved beneath the mass of hopelessness. But she seemed to be filled with a craving for an indescribable something . . . if only she knew what it was. If only—"

"Well, this is odd." Philippa sounded thoroughly perplexed as she reentered the room. "I found these just inside the door. Someone has set them there without a note, and no word to anyone. And they're completely new, by the looks of them. Do you think that they are from one of your friends? It must be. Such an eccentric gift could only have come from the American girls."

Raising herself up on a pillow, Annabelle found a pair of objects deposited in her lap, and she regarded the offering with blank surprise. It was a pair of ankle boots, tied together with a dapper red bow. The leather was buttery-soft, dyed a fashionable bronze, and polished until it shone like glass. With low stacked-leather heels and tightly stitched soles, the ankle boots were sensible but stylish. They were ornamented with a delicate embroidered design of leaves that extended across the toes. Staring at the boots, Annabelle felt a sudden laugh rise in her throat.

"They must be from the Bowmans," she said . . . but she knew better.

The boots were a gift from Simon Hunt, who was fully aware that a gentleman should never give an article of clothing to a lady. She should return them at once, she thought, even as she found herself clutching the boots tightly. Only Simon Hunt could manage to give her something so pragmatic and yet so inappropriately personal.

Smiling, she untied the red bow and held one of the boots up. It was surprisingly light, and she knew at a glance that it would fit her perfectly. But how had Hunt known what size to request, and where had he gotten the boots? Slowly she traced a finger across the tiny, exquisite stitches that joined the sole to the gleaming bronze upper.

"How attractive they are," Philippa remarked. "Almost too nice for walking through the muddy countryside."

Annabelle lifted the boot to her nose, inhaling the clean, earthy scent of polished leather. She ran a fingertip around the softly buffed edge of the upper, then held it back to examine it as if it were a priceless sculpture. "I've had quite enough of walking through the countryside," she said with a smile. "These boots will stay on nicely graveled garden paths."

Regarding her fondly, Philippa reached down to smooth Annabelle's hair. "I wouldn't have thought that a new pair of shoes would animate your spirits like this—but I'm awfully glad of it. Shall I send for a tray of soup and toast, dear? You must try to eat something before your next dose of clivers."

Annabelle made a face. "Yes, I'll have soup."

Nodding in satisfaction, Philippa reached for the ankle boots. "I'll just remove these from your lap and set them in the armoire—"

"Not yet," Annabelle murmured, clasping one of the boots possessively.

Philippa smiled as she went to ring the servants' bell.

As Annabelle leaned back and ran her fingertips over the silky leather, she felt a weight from her chest seem to ease. No doubt it was a sign that the venom's effects were fading . . . but that didn't explain why she suddenly felt so relieved and peaceful.

She would have to thank Simon Hunt, of course, and tell him that his gift was unseemly. And if he acknowledged that he had indeed been the one who had bestowed the boots, then Annabelle would have to return them. Something like a book of verse, or a tin of toffee, or a bouquet of flowers would have been far more appropriate. But no gift had ever touched her as this one had.

Annabelle kept the ankle boots with her all evening, despite her mother's warning that it was bad luck to set footwear on the bed. As she eventually dropped off to sleep, with the orchestra music still washing lightly through the window, she consented to set the boots on the bedside table. When she awoke in the morning, the sight of them made her smile.

Chapter 14

On the third morning after the adder bite, Annabelle finally felt well enough to get out of bed. To her relief, the majority of the guests had gone to a party that was being held at a neighboring estate, which left Stony Cross Manor quiet and largely empty. After consulting with the housekeeper, Philippa settled Annabelle in a private upstairs parlor that overlooked the garden. It was a lovely room, with walls that had been covered with flowered blue paper and hung with cheerful portraits of children and animals. According to the housekeeper, the parlor was usually reserved only for the Marsdens' use, but Lord Westcliff himself had offered the room for Annabelle's comfort.

After tucking a lap blanket around Annabelle's knees, Philippa set a cup of clivers tea on a table beside her. "You must drink this," she said firmly, in response to Annabelle's grimace. "It's for your own good."

"There's no need for you to stay in the parlor and watch over me, Mama," Annabelle said. "I will be quite happy to relax here, while you go have a stroll or chat with one of your friends."

"Are you certain?" Philippa asked.

"Absolutely certain." Annabelle picked up the clivers tea and took a sip. "I'm drinking my medicine . . . see? Do go, Mama, and don't give me another thought."

"Very well," Philippa said reluctantly. "Just for a little while. The housekeeper said for you to ring the bell on the table, if you want a servant. And remember to drink every drop of that tea."

"I will," Annabelle promised, pasting a wide smile on her face. She retained the smile until Phillippa had left the room. The moment that her mother was out of sight, Annabelle leaned over the back of the settee and carefully poured the contents of the cup out the open window.

Sighing with satisfaction, Annabelle curled into the corner of the settee. Now and then a household noise would interrupt the placid silence: the clatter of a dish, the murmur of the housekeeper's voice, the sound of a broom being employed to sweep the hallway carpet. Resting her arm on the windowsill, Annabelle leaned forward into a shaft of sunlight, letting the brilliance bathe her face. She closed her eyes and listened to the drone of bees as they moved lazily among the flowering bursts of deep pink hydrangea and delicate tendrils of sweet pea that wound through the basket-bed borders. Although she was still very weak, it was pleasant to sit in warm lethargy, half-drowsing like a cat.

She was slow to respond when she heard a sound from the doorway . . . a single light rap, as if the visitor was reluctant to disrupt her reverie with a loud knock. Blinking her sun-dazzled eyes, Annabelle remained sitting with her legs tucked beneath her. The mass of light speckles gradually faded from her vision, and she found herself staring at Simon Hunt's dark, lean form. He had leaned part of his weight on the doorjamb, bracing a shoulder against it in an unself-consciously rakish pose. His head was slightly tilted as he considered her with an unfathomable expression.

Annabelle's pulse escalated to a mad clatter. As usual, Hunt was dressed impeccably, but the gentle-manly attire did nothing to disguise the virile energy that seemed to emanate from him. She recalled the hardness of his arms and chest as he had carried her, the touch of his hands on her body . . . oh, she would never be able to look at him again without remembering!

"You look like a butterfly that's just flown in from the garden," Hunt said softly.

He must be mocking her, Annabelle thought, perfectly aware of her own sickroom pallor. Self-consciously she raised a hand to her hair, pushing back the untidy locks. "What are you doing here?" she asked. "Shouldn't you be at the neighbor's party?"

She had not meant to sound so abrupt and unwelcoming, but her usual facility with words had deserted her. As she stared at him, she couldn't help thinking of how he had rubbed her chest with his hand. The recollection caused the stinging heat of embarrassment to cover her skin.

Hunt replied in a gently caustic tone. "I have business to conduct with one of my managers, who is due to arrive from London later this morning. Unlike the silk-stockinged gentlemen whose pedigrees you so admire, I have things to consider other than where I should settle my picnic blanket today." Pushing away from the doorframe, Hunt ventured farther into the room, his gaze frankly assessing. "Still weak? That will improve soon. How is your ankle? Lift your skirts—I think I should take another look."

Annabelle regarded him with alarm for a fraction of a second, then began to laugh as she saw the glint in his eyes. The audacious remark somehow eased her embarrassment and caused her to relax. "That is very kind," she said dryly. "But there's no need. My ankle is much better, thank you."

Hunt smiled as he approached her. "I'll have you know that my offer was made in a spirit of purest altruism. I would had taken no illicit pleasure at the sight of your exposed leg. Well, perhaps a small thrill, but I would have concealed it fairly well." Grasping the back of a side chair with one hand, he moved it easily to the settee and sat close to her. Annabelle was impressed by the way he had lifted the sturdy piece of carved mahogany furniture as if it were feather-light. She threw a quick glance at the empty doorway. As long as the door wasn't closed, it was acceptable for her to sit in the parlor with Hunt. And her mother would eventually come to look in on her. Before that happened, however, Annabelle decided to bring up the subject of the boots.

"Mr. Hunt," she said carefully, "there is something I must ask you . . ."

"Yes?"

His eyes were definitely his most attractive feature, Annabelle thought distractedly. Vibrant and full of life, they made her wonder why people generally preferred blue eyes to dark ones. No shade of blue could ever convey the simmering intelligence that lurked in the depths of Simon Hunt's sable eyes.

Try as she might, Annabelle could think of no subtle way to ask him. After grappling silently with a variety of phrases, she finally settled for a blunt question. "Were you responsible for the boots?"

His expression gave nothing away. "Boots? I'm afraid I don't take your meaning, Miss Peyton. Are you speaking in metaphor, or are we talking about actual footwear?"

"Ankle boots," Annabelle said, staring at him with open suspicion. "A new pair that was left inside the door of my room yesterday."

"Delighted as I am to discuss any part of your wardrobe, Miss Peyton, I'm afraid I know nothing about a pair of boots. However, I am relieved that you have managed to acquire some. Unless, of course, you wished to continue acting as a strolling buffet to the wildlife of Hampshire."

Annabelle regarded him for a long moment. Despite his denial, there was something lurking behind his neutral facade . . . some playful spark in his eyes . . . "Then you deny having given the boots to me?"

"Most emphatically I deny it."

"But I wonder . . . if someone wished to have a pair of boots made up for a lady without her knowledge . . . how would he be able to learn the precise size of her feet?"

"That would be a relatively simple task . . ." he mused. "I imagine that some enterprising person would simply ask a housemaid to trace the soles of the lady's discarded slippers. Then he could take the pattern to the local cobbler. And make it worth the cobbler's while to delay his other work in favor of crafting the new shoes immediately."

"That is quite a lot of trouble for someone to go through," Annabelle murmured.

Hunt's gaze was lit with sudden mischief. "Rather less trouble than having to haul an injured woman up three flights of stairs every time she goes out walking in her slippers."

Annabelle realized that he would never admit to giving her the boots—which would allow her to keep them, but would also ensure that she would never be able to thank him. And she knew he had—she could see it in his face.

"Mr. Hunt," she said earnestly, "I . . . I wish . . ." She paused, unable to find words, and stared helplessly at him.

Taking pity on her, Hunt stood and went to the side of the room, picking up a small circular game table. It was only about two feet in diameter, constructed with a clever mechanism to allow a player to flip the top from a chessboard to a draughtsboard. "Do you play?" he asked casually, setting the table in front of her.

"Draughts? Yes, occasionally—"

"No, not draughts. Chess."

Annabelle shook her head, shrinking back into the corner of the settee. "No, I've never played chess. And I don't wish to sound uncooperative, but . . . the way I feel at present, I have no desire to try something as difficult as—"

"It's time for you to learn, then," Hunt said, heading to a niche of shelves to retrieve a polished burlwood box. "It's been said that you can never really know someone until you play chess with him."

Annabelle watched him cautiously, feeling nervous at the prospect of being alone with him . . . and yet she was thoroughly beguiled by his deliberate gentleness. It seemed almost as if he were trying to coax her to trust him. There was a softness in his manner that seemed utterly at odds with the cynical rake she had always known him to be.

"Do you believe that?" she asked.

"Of course not." Hunt brought the box to the table and opened it to reveal a set of onyx and ivory chessmen, carved in scrupulous detail. He slid her a provocative glance. "The truth is, you can never really know a man until you've loaned him money. And you can never know a woman until you've slept in her bed."

He said it deliberately, of course, to shock her. And he succeeded, although Annabelle did her best to conceal it. "Mr. Hunt," she said, frowning into his smiling eyes, "if you continue to make vulgar remarks, I will be forced to ask you to leave the parlor."

"Forgive me." His instant contrition didn't fool her in the least. "It's just that I can't resist the opportunity to make you blush. I've never known a woman to do it as often as you do."

The bloom that had begun at her throat flamed up to her hairline. "I *never* blush. It's only around you that I—" Breaking off, she stared at him with an indignant frown that made him laugh.

"I'll behave for now," he said. "Don't tell me to leave."

She stared at him indecisively, passing an unsteady hand over her forehead, and the sign of her physical frailty caused him to speak even more gently. "It's all right," he murmured. "Let me stay, Annabelle."

Blinking, she responded with a wobbly nod and subsided against the cushions of the settee while Hunt set the board methodically. His touch on the pieces was surprisingly light and deft, considering the size of his hands. Potentially ruthless hands, she thought . . . tanned and masculine, with a light dusting of black hair on the backs.

Half-standing over her as Hunt was, Annabelle became aware of the intriguing scent of him, the whisper of starch and shaving soap overlaying the fragrance of clean male skin . . . and there was something more elusive . . . some sweet tang to his breath, as if he had recently eaten pears, or perhaps a slice of pineapple. As she looked up at him, she realized that with very little

effort he could have bent down and kissed her. The
thought caused her to tremble. She actually wanted to
feel his mouth on hers, to inhale the ephemeral touch
of sweetness on his breath. She wanted him to hold her
again.

The realization caused her eyes to widen. Her sudden
stillness communicated swiftly to Hunt. His attention
swerved from the chessboard to her upturned face, and
whatever he saw in her expression caused his breath to
catch. Neither of them moved. Annabelle could only
wait in silence, her fingertips curling into the upholstery
of the settee as she wondered what he might do next.

Hunt broke the tension with a long breath, and
spoke in a softly abraded voice. "No . . . you're not
well enough yet."

It was difficult to hear the words above the thunder
of her heartbeat. "Wh-what?" she asked faintly.

Seeming unable to help himself, Hunt brushed a little
curling wisp of hair back from her temple. The stroking fingertip burned her silken skin, leaving a glow of
sensation in its wake. "I know what you're thinking.
And believe me, I'm tempted. But you're still too
weak—and my self-control is in short supply today."

"If you're implying that I—"

"I never waste time with implications," he murmured, resuming his careful placement of the chess
pieces. "Obviously, you want me to kiss you. And I'll
be happy to oblige, when the time is right. But not yet."

"Mr. Hunt, you are the most—"

"Yes, I know," he said with a grin. "You may as
well spare yourself the effort of hurling adjectives at
me, as I've heard them all before." Lowering himself
to the chair, Hunt pressed a chess piece into her palm.
The carved onyx was heavy and cool, its slick surface
warming slowly to the touch.

"It's not adjectives that I want to hurl at you," Annabelle said. "A sharp object or two would suffice."

A deep laugh stirred in his chest, and his thumb brushed over the backs of her fingers before he withdrew his hand. She felt the rasp of a callus on his thumb, the sensation not unlike the tingling scrape of a cat's tongue. Bemused by her own response to him, Annabelle looked down at the chess piece in her hand.

"That is the queen—the most powerful piece on the board. She can move in any direction, and go as far as she wishes."

There was nothing overtly suggestive in his manner of speaking . . . but when he spoke softly, as he was doing at that moment, there was a husky depth in his voice that made her toes curl inside her slippers.

"More powerful than the king?" she asked.

"Yes. The king can only move one square at a time. But the king is the most important piece."

"Why is he more important than the queen if he's not the most powerful?"

"Because once he is captured, the game is over." Reaching for the piece he had given her, Hunt exchanged it for a pawn. His fingers brushed over hers, lingering in a brief but unmistakable caress. Although Annabelle knew that she should disallow the outrageous familiarity, she found herself watching in a near daze, her knuckles whitening as she held the carved ivory in far too tight a grip. Hunt's voice was low and velvety as he continued. "This is the pawn, which moves one square at a time. It can't move backward or sideways, unless it is taking another piece. Most novice players like to move a lot of their pawns in the beginning, to control a larger area on the chessboard. But it's a better strategy to make good use of your other pieces . . ."

As Hunt continued to explain each chess piece and its uses, he pressed them into her palm one at a time. Annabelle was mesmerized by the hypnotic brushes of his hands, her senses lilting in anticipation. Her usual defenses seemed to have been pulverized like grain beneath a mill wheel. Something had happened to her, or Hunt, or perhaps to both of them, allowing them to interact with an ease that had not existed before. She did not want to invite him closer . . . nothing good could possibly come of it . . . and yet she couldn't help but enjoy his nearness.

Hunt coaxed her into a game, waiting patiently as she considered each possible move, readily offering advice when she asked for it. His manner was so charming and playfully distracting that she almost didn't care who won. Almost. When she slid her piece into a position that attacked not one but two of his pieces, Hunt glanced at her with an approving grin. "That's called a pin-and-fork strategy. As I suspected, you have a natural instinct for chess."

"Now you have no choice, other than to retreat," Annabelle said triumphantly.

"Not yet." He moved another piece in another area on the board, instantly threatening her queen.

Puzzling over the strategy, Annabelle realized that he had just put *her* in the position of having to retreat.

"That's not fair," she protested, and he chuckled.

Lacing her fingers together, Annabelle leaned her chin on her hands and contemplated the board. A full minute passed as she debated various strategies, but nothing seemed appropriate. "I don't know what to do," she finally admitted. Raising her eyes to his, she found that he was staring at her in an odd way, his gaze caressing and concerned. It unraveled her, that look, and she swallowed hard against a sensation of thick sweetness, like honey coating her throat.

"I've tired you," Hunt murmured.

"No, I'm fine—"

"We'll continue the game later. You'll see your next move more clearly when you've rested."

"I don't want to stop," she said, annoyed by his refusal. "Besides, neither of us will remember how the pieces are arranged."

"I will." Ignoring her protests, Hunt stood and moved the table aside, out of her reach. "You need a nap. Do you require some help to return upstairs, or—"

"Mr. Hunt, I'm *not* going back to my room," she said stubbornly. "I'm sick of it. In fact, I would rather sleep in the hallway than—"

"All right," Hunt murmured with a smile, resuming his seat. "Calm yourself. Far be it from me to make you do something that you don't want to do." He laced his fingers together and leaned back in a deceptively casual pose, his gaze narrowing on her. "Tomorrow the guests will be back at the manor in full force," he remarked. "I suppose you'll resume your pursuit of Kendall soon?"

"Probably," Annabelle admitted, covering her mouth as an insistent yawn stretched her lips.

"You don't want him," Hunt said softly.

"Oh, yes I do." Annabelle paused dreamily, half propping her head on her curled arm. "And . . . although you have been very kind to me, Mr. Hunt . . . I'm afraid that I can't let that change my plans."

He stared at her in the same relaxed but engrossed way he had regarded the chessboard. "I'm not going to change my plans, either, sweetheart."

If Annabelle hadn't been so tired, she would have objected to the endearment. Instead she pondered his words sleepily. His plans . . . "Which are to try and stop me from catching Lord Kendall," she said.

"They go somewhat beyond that," he replied, amusement lurking in one corner of his mouth.

"What do you mean?"

"I'm hardly going to reveal my strategy. Clearly I need every advantage I can get. The next move is yours, Miss Peyton. Just remember that I'll be watching you."

Annabelle knew that the warning should have alarmed her. But she was filled with overwhelming weariness, and she closed her eyes for a few seconds. The soothing moisture beneath her lids eased the scratchy feeling that heralded an overpowering need to sleep. She opened her heavy eyes with infinite reluctance, and Hunt's image blurred before her. It was too bad that they had to be adversaries, she thought wearily. She wasn't aware that she had spoken the words aloud until he replied in a gentle tone.

"I've never been your adversary."

"Then you're my friend?" she mumbled skeptically, surrendering to the temptation to close her eyes once more. This time sleep pulled her into its welcoming embrace, so quickly that she barely had time to register the fact that Hunt had pulled the lap blanket up to her shoulders.

"No, sweetheart," he whispered. "I'm not your friend . . ."

She napped lightly, awakening long enough to ascertain that she was alone in the private parlor, then dozing off again in the gentle sunshine. As her body relaxed into deeper slumber, she found herself in a brilliantly colored dream, in which all her senses were heightened and her body felt as buoyant as if she was floating in a warm ocean. Slowly the shapes materialized around her . . .

She wandered through an unfamiliar house, a glittering mansion where daylight streamed through tall windows. The rooms were empty, no guests or servants anywhere in sight. Music from some unseen source filtered through the air, a sad and unearthly melody that infused her with yearning. Walking alone, she found a spacious marble-columned room with no ceiling . . . it was open to the sky, lightly shaded by drifting cloud fleece overhead. The parquet floor beneath her feet was made of huge white-and-black squares that looked like a chessboard, with life-sized stone statues poised on some of the squares.

Moving among them curiously, Annabelle turned in slow circles to view their gleaming sculpted faces. Wishing for someone to talk to, some warm human hand to cling to, she walked across the giant chessboard, searching blindly through the crowd of immobile figures . . . until she saw a dark form leaning indolently against a white marble column. Her heart began to hammer, and her steps slowed as she was filled with a rush of excitement that heated her skin and made her pulse beat in urgent rhythm.

It was Simon Hunt, walking toward her with a slight smile on his face. He caught her before she could retreat, and bent to whisper in her ear.

"Will you dance with me now?"

"I can't," she said breathlessly, struggling in his tightening embrace.

"Yes, you can," he urged gently, his mouth hot and tender as it moved across her face. "Put your arms around me . . ."

As she writhed in his embrace, he laughed softly and kissed her until she was limp and helpless against him. "Queen is now subject to capture," he murmured,

*drawing back to stare at her with deviltry in his eyes.
"You're in danger, Annabelle . . ."*

*She was suddenly released, and she turned to flee
from him, stumbling against the statues in her haste.
He followed in slow pursuit, his low laugh echoing in
her ears. He stayed close behind her, deliberately pro-
longing the chase, until she was hot and exhausted
and robbed of breath. Capturing her at last, he drew
her back against him, and pulled her down to the
floor. His dark head blotted out the sky as he covered
her with his body, and the music was drowned out by
the thunder of her own heartbeat. "Annabelle," he
whispered, "Annabelle . . ."*

She awakened, her eyes widening in her sleep-
flushed face as she sensed that someone was with her.

"Annabelle," she heard again . . . but it was not the
husky, caressing baritone of her dream.

Chapter 15

As Annabelle looked up, she saw Lord Hodgeham standing over her. She struggled to a sitting position and inched backward, comprehending that this was not an imaginary figure, but an all-too-real one. Rendered speechless with surprise, she shrank from him as he reached out with a heavy hand and flicked the lace trim at the front of her day gown.

"I heard about your illness," Hodgeham said, his gaze heavy-lidded as he glanced over her half-reclining form. "How sorry I was to learn that you had suffered such an affliction. But it appears there was no permanent harm done. You seem . . ." He paused and moistened his plump lips, ". . . as exquisite as ever . . . though perhaps a bit pale."

"How . . . how did you find me here?" Annabelle asked. "This is the Marsdens' private parlor. Surely no one gave you leave—"

"I made a servant tell me," came Hodgeham's smug reply.

"Get out," Annabelle snapped. "Or I'll scream that you're assaulting me."

Hodgeham chortled richly. "You can't afford a scandal, my dear. Your interest in Lord Kendall is obvious to everyone. And we both know that one hint of disgrace attached to your name would completely ruin your chances with him." He grinned at her silence, revealing a mouthful of crooked yellow teeth. "That's better. My poor, pretty Annabelle . . . I know what will restore a blush to those pale cheeks." Reaching into his coat pocket, he extracted a large gold coin and waved it in front of her tantalizingly. "A token to express my sympathy for your ordeal."

Annabelle's breath came in an outraged hiss as Hodgeham leaned very close, the coin clutched between his fat fingers as he attempted to tuck it into the bodice of her dress. She knocked his hand away with a stiff, jerking movement. Although she was still feeble, the gesture was enough to send the coin flying from his hand. It fell to the carpeted floor with a solid thud.

"Leave me alone," she said fiercely.

"Haughty bitch. You needn't try to pretend that you're any better than your mother."

"You swine—" Cursing her own lack of strength, Annabelle struck out at him feebly as he bent over her, her body racked with chills of horror. "No," she said through gritted teeth, covering her face with her arms. She resisted fiercely as he grasped her wrists. "No—"

A clatter from the doorway caused Hodgeham to straighten in surprise. Shaking from head to toe, Annabelle looked in the direction of the noise and saw her mother standing there with a lunch tray. Silverware had tumbled from the edge of the tray as Philippa realized what was happening.

Philippa shook her head as if finding it impossible to

believe that Hodgeham was there. "You dare to approach my daughter . . ." she began in a thick voice. Scarlet with rage, she went to settle the tray on a nearby table, then spoke to Hodgeham with quiet wrath. "My daughter is ill, my lord. I will not allow her health to be compromised—you will come with me *now,* and we will discuss this in some other place."

"Discussion isn't what I want," Hodgeham said.

Annabelle saw a quick succession of emotions cross her mother's face: disgust, resentment, hatred, fear. And finally . . . resignation. "Come away from my daughter, then," she said coldly.

"No," Annabelle croaked in protest, realizing that Philippa intended to go somewhere alone with him. "Mama, stay with me."

"Everything will be fine." Philippa didn't look at her, but kept her emotionless gaze on Hodgeham's ruddy countenance. "I've brought you a lunch tray, dearest. Try to eat something—"

"*No.*" Disbelieving, despairing, Annabelle watched her mother calmly precede Hodgeham from the room. "Mama, don't go with him!" But Philippa left as if she had not heard.

Annabelle was not aware of how many minutes passed as she stared blankly at the empty doorway. There was no thought in her mind of touching the lunch tray. The tang of vegetable broth that flavored the air made her feel nauseous. Bleakly, Annabelle wondered how this hellish affair had ever started, if Hodgeham had forced himself on her mother, or if it had initially been a matter of mutual consent. No matter how it had begun, it had now turned into a travesty. Hodgeham was a monster, and Philippa was trying to pacify him to keep him from ruining them.

Weary and miserable, trying not to think of what

might be occurring between her mother and Hodgeham at that very moment, Annabelle levered herself off the settee. She winced at the protesting ache of her muscles. Her head hurt, and she was dizzy, and she wanted to go to her room. Walking like an old woman, she made her way to the bellpull and tugged. After what seemed an interminable length of time, there was still no response. With the guests gone, most the staff had been allowed their day off, and maids were in short supply.

Scrubbing her fingers distractedly through the limp locks of her hair, Annabelle assessed the situation. Although her legs were weak, they felt serviceable. That morning her mother had helped her to walk the length of two hallways from their room to the Marsdens' upstairs parlor. Now, however, she was fairly certain that she could manage the short journey on her own.

Ignoring the brilliant sparks that danced across her vision like fireflies, Annabelle left the room with short, careful steps. She stayed close to the wall in case she needed to avail herself of its support. How odd it was, she thought grimly, that even this minor exertion should cause her to pant as if she had just run for miles. Infuriated with her own weakness, she wondered ruefully if she shouldn't have drunk that last cup of clivers after all. Concentrating on setting one foot in front of the other, she made slow progress along the first hallway, until she was nearly at the corner that led to the east wing of the estate, where her room was located. She stopped as she heard quiet voices coming from another direction.

Hell's bells. It would be mortifying to be seen by anyone while she was in this condition. Praying that the voices belonged to a pair of servants, Annabelle leaned her weight against the wall and stood without moving. A few strands of hair stuck to her clammy forehead and cheeks.

Two men crossed the passageway before her, so involved in their conversation that it seemed they wouldn't notice her. Relieved, Annabelle thought that she managed to escape detection.

But she was not that fortunate. One of the men happened to glance in her direction, and his attention was immediately rivetted. As he approached her, Annabelle recognized the masculine grace of his long strides even before she saw his face clearly.

It seemed that she was destined to be forever making herself an exhibition in front of Simon Hunt. Sighing, Annabelle pushed away from the wall and tried to appear composed, even with her legs trembling beneath her. "Good afternoon, Mr. Hunt—"

"What are you doing?" Hunt interrupted as he reached her. He sounded annoyed, but as Annabelle looked up at his face, she saw the concern in his gaze. "Why are you standing alone in the hallway?"

"I'm going to my room." Annabelle started a little as he slid his arms around her, one at her shoulders, the other at her waist. "Mr. Hunt, there's no need—"

"You're as weak as a kitten," he said flatly. "You know better than to go anywhere by yourself in this condition."

"There wasn't anyone to help me," Annabelle replied irritably. Her head swam, and she found herself against him, letting him support some of her weight. His chest was wonderfully solid and hard, the fabric of his coat silky-cool against her cheek.

"Where is your mother?" Hunt persisted, smoothing back a tangled lock of her hair. "Tell me, and I'll—"

"No!" Annabelle glanced up at him with instant alarm, her slender fingers biting into his coat sleeves.

Dear God, the last thing she needed was for Hunt to instigate a search for Philippa when she was probably in some damnably compromising situation with Hodgeham at that very moment. "Don't look for her," she said sharply. "I . . . I don't need anyone. I can reach my room by myself, if you'll just let go of me. I don't want—"

"All right," Hunt murmured, his arm remaining firmly around her. "Hush, I won't look for her. Hush." His hand continued to smooth her hair in gentle, repeated motions.

She wilted against him, trying to catch her breath. "Simon," she whispered, vaguely surprised that she had just used his first name, for she had never used it even in the privacy of her thoughts. Moistening her dry lips, she tried once more, and to her astonishment, she did it again. "Simon . . ."

"Yes?" A new tension had entered his long, hard body, and at the same time, his hand moved over the shape of her skull in the softest caress possible.

"Please . . . take me to my room."

Hunt tilted her head back gently and regarded her with a sudden faint smile playing on his lips. "Sweetheart, I would take you to Timbuktu if you asked."

By that time, the other man in the hallway had reached them, and Annabelle was dismayed, though not surprised, to see that it was Lord Westcliff.

The earl glanced at her with cold disapproval, as if he suspected that she had somehow arranged this situation as an intentional inconvenience.

"Miss Peyton," he said crisply, "I assure you, there was no need for you to make your way through the hall unescorted. If there was no one available to help you, you had only to ring for a servant."

"I did, my lord," Annabelle said defensively, trying

to push away from Hunt, who wouldn't let her. "I rang the bellpull and waited for at least a quarter hour, and no one came."

Westcliff's regarded her with obvious skepticism. "Impossible. My servants always come when they're summoned."

"Well, today seems to be an exception," Annabelle snapped. "Perhaps the bellpull is broken. Or perhaps your servants—"

"Easy," Hunt murmured, pressing her head back to his chest. Although Annabelle couldn't see his face, she heard the note of quiet warning in his voice as he spoke to Westcliff. "We'll continue our discussion later. Right now I intend to escort Miss Peyton to her room."

"That is not a wise idea, in my opinion," the earl said.

"I'm glad I didn't ask for it, then," Simon returned pleasantly.

There was the sound of the earl's taut sigh, and Annabelle was vaguely aware of his carpet-muffled footsteps as he walked away from them.

Hunt bent his head, his breath warming the tip of her ear, as he inquired, "Now . . . would you care to explain what is going on?"

All her veins seemed to dilate, bringing a flush of pleasure to her cool skin. Hunt's nearness filled her with equal amounts of delight and yearning. As he held her, she couldn't help remembering her dream, the erotic illusion of his body pressing over hers. This was all so terribly wrong, that she should revel silently in being held by him . . . even knowing that she would get nothing from him but temporary pleasure followed by everlasting dishonor. She managed to shake her head in answer to his question, her cheek rubbing against the lapel of his coat.

"I didn't think so," Hunt said wryly. He released

her experimentally, assessed her unsteady balance
with a narrow-eyed glance, and bent to lift her in his
arms. Annabelle surrendered with an inarticulate murmur and linked her arms around his neck. As Hunt
carried her along the hallway, he spoke in a quiet
voice. "I might be able to help, if you would tell me
the problem."

Annabelle considered that for a moment. The only
thing that would come from confiding her woes to Simon Hunt was an almost certain offer to support her
as his mistress. And she hated the part of herself that
was tempted by the idea. "Why should you wish to involve yourself in my problems?" she asked.

"Do I have to have an ulterior motive for wanting to
help you?"

"Yes," she replied darkly, causing him to chuckle.

He set her carefully down at the threshold of her
room. "Can you reach the bed by yourself, or shall I
tuck you in?"

Though his voice was lightly teasing, Annabelle suspected that with very little encouragement, he would
do just that. She shook her head hastily. "No. I'm fine,
please don't come in." She put a palm to his chest to
keep him from entering the room. Frail though her
hand was, it was enough to stop him.

"All right." Hunt looked down at her, his gaze searching. "I'll see that a maid is sent up to attend you. Though
I suspect that Westcliff is already making inquiries."

"I did ring for a maid," Annabelle insisted, embarrassed by the peevish note in her own voice. "Obviously, the earl doesn't believe me, but—"

"I believe you." With great care, Hunt removed her
hand from his chest, briefly holding her slender fingers
in his before letting go. "Westcliff isn't quite the ogre

he seems. You have to be acquainted with him for some time before you appreciate his finer qualities."

"If you say so," Annabelle said doubtfully, and heaved a sigh as she stepped back into the stale, darkened sickroom. "Thank you, Mr. Hunt." Wondering anxiously when Philippa would return, she glanced at the empty room, then turned back to Hunt.

His penetrating gaze seemed to unearth every emotion beneath her strained facade, and she sensed the multitude of questions that hovered on his lips. However, all he said was, "You need to rest."

"I've done nothing *but* rest. I'm going mad from boredom . . . but the thought of actually doing anything makes me exhausted." Lowering her head, Annabelle stared at the few inches of floor between their feet with morose concentration, before asking cautiously, "I suppose you have no interest in continuing the chess game later this evening?"

A short silence, and then Hunt replied in a softly mocking drawl. "Why, Miss Peyton . . . I'm overwhelmed by the thought that you might have a desire for my company."

Annabelle couldn't bring herself to look at him, her face covered with an awkward blush, as she muttered, "I'd keep company with the devil himself, if only to have something to do besides stay in bed."

Laughing quietly, he reached out to tuck a lock of hair behind her ear. "We'll see," he murmured. "Perhaps I'll come by your room later."

And with that, he gave her a deft, shallow bow and left, walking down the hallway with his usual self-assured stride.

Too late, Annabelle recalled something about a musical evening that had been planned for the guests while they enjoyed a buffet supper. Certainly Simon Hunt would prefer to keep company with the guests downstairs rather than play a rudimentary game of chess with a sickly, unkempt, cross-tempered girl. She cringed, wishing that she could withdraw the spontaneous invitation . . . oh, how pitifully desperate she must have appeared! Clapping a hand to her forehead, Annabelle trudged into her room and let herself collapse stiffly onto the unmade bed like a tree that had just been chopped down.

Within five minutes, there was a knock at the door, and a pair of chastened-looking maids entered the room. "We came to tidy up, miss," one of them ventured, "The master sent us—'e said we must 'elp you with anyfing you need."

"Thank you," Annabelle said, hoping that Lord Westcliff had not been too severe on the girls. Retreating to a chair, she watched the whirlwind of activity that ensued. With almost magical speed, the young housemaids changed the bed linens, opened the window to admit fresh air, cleaned and dusted the furniture, and brought in a portable bath that they proceeded to fill with hot water. One of the girls helped Annabelle to remove her clothes, while the other brought in a length of folded toweling and a bucket of warm rinse water for her hair. Shivering in comfort, Annabelle stepped into the mahogany-rimmed folding tub.

"Take my arm, please, miss," the younger of the two said, extending her forearm for Annabelle to take hold of. "Yer not quite steady on yer feet, looks like."

Annabelle obeyed and sank down into the water, and let go of the girl's muscular arm. "What is your name?" she asked, lowering her shoulders until they were submerged beneath the steaming surface of the water.

"Meggie, miss."

"Meggie, I believe I dropped a gold sovereign on the floor of the family's private parlor—will you try to find it for me?"

The girl gave her a perplexed glance, clearly wondering why Annabelle had left a valuable coin on the floor and what would transpire if she couldn't find it. "Yes, miss." She bobbed an uneasy curtsey and rushed from the room. Dunking her head beneath the water, Annabelle sat up with a streaming face and hair and wiped her eyes as the other maid bent to rub a cake of soap over her head. "It feels nice to be clean," Annabelle murmured, sitting still beneath the girl's ministrations.

"Me ma allus says 'tisn't good to bathe when yer ill," the maid told her dubiously.

"I'll take my chances," Annabelle replied, gratefully tilting her head back as the maid poured the rinse water over her soapy hair. Wiping her eyes once more, Annabelle saw that Meggie had returned.

"I found it, miss," Meggie exclaimed breathlessly, extending the coin in her hand. It was possible that she had never held a sovereign before, since the average housemaid earned approximately eight shillings a month. "Where shall I put it?"

"You may divide it between the two of you," Annabelle said.

The housemaids stared at her, dumbfounded. "Oh, thank you, miss!" they both exclaimed, eyes wide and mouths open in amazement.

Grimly aware of the hypocrisy of giving away money from Lord Hodgeham, when the Peyton household had benefited from his questionable patronage for more than a year, Annabelle lowered her head, embarrassed by their gratitude. Seeing her discomfort, the two hastened to help her from the tub, drying her hair and shivering body, and helping her to don a fresh gown.

Refreshed but tired after the bath, Annabelle got into bed and lay between the soft, smooth bed linens. She dozed while the maids removed the bath, only hazily aware when they tiptoed from the room. It was early evening when she awoke, blinking as her mother lit a lamp on the table.

"Mama," she said groggily, dazed with sleepiness. Remembering the earlier encounter with Hodgeham, she shook herself awake. "Are you all right? Did he—"

"I don't wish to discuss it," Philippa said softly, her delicate profile gilded by the lamplight. She wore a numb, blank look, her forehead lightly scored with tense furrows. "Yes, I am quite all right, dearest."

Annabelle nodded briefly, abashed and despondent, and aware of a pervasive feeling of shame. She sat up, her back feeling as if her spine had been replaced by an iron poker. Aside from the stiffness of her unused muscles, however, she felt much stronger, and for the first time in two days her stomach was aching with real hunger. Slipping from the bed, she went to the vanity table and picked up a hairbrush, dragging it through her hair. "Mama," she said hesitantly, "I need a change of scene. Perhaps I will go back to the Marsden parlor and ring for a supper tray, and dine in there."

Philippa appeared to have only half heard the words. "Yes," she said absently, "that seems a fine idea. Shall I go with you?"

"No, thank you . . . I'm feeling quite well, and it isn't far. I'll go by myself. You probably want some privacy after . . ." Annabelle paused uncomfortably and set down the brush. "I'll be back in a little while."

With a low murmur, Philippa sat in the chair by the hearth, and Annabelle sensed that she was relieved by the prospect of being alone. After braiding her hair into a long rope that lay over her shoulder, Annabelle left the room, quietly closing the door behind her.

As she went out into the hall, she heard the subtle rumble of the guests who were enjoying the supper buffet in the drawing room. Music overlaid the blend of conversation and laughter—a string quartet with an accompanying piano. Pausing to listen, Annabelle was astonished to realize that it was the same sad, beautiful melody that she had heard in her dream. She closed her eyes and listened intently, while her throat tightened with a wistful ache. The music filled her with the kind of longing that she should not have allowed herself to feel. *Good God*, she thought, *I'm becoming maudlin in my illness—I have to get some control over myself.* Opening her eyes, she started to walk again, only to narrowly miss plowing into someone who had approached from the opposite direction.

Her heart seemed to expand painfully as she looked up at Simon Hunt, who was dressed in a formal scheme of black and white, a lazy smile curving his wide mouth. His deep voice sent a shiver down her spine. "Where do you think you're going?"

So he had come for her, in spite of the elegant crowd that he should have been mingling with downstairs. Aware that the sudden weakness in her knees had nothing to do with her illness, Annabelle toyed nervously with the end of her braid. "To have a supper tray in the parlor."

Taking her elbow, Hunt turned and guided her along the hallway, keeping his steps slow to accommodate hers. "You don't want a supper tray in the parlor," he informed her.

"I don't?"

He shook his head. "I have a surprise for you. Come, it's not far." As she went with him willingly,

Hunt slid an assessing gaze over her. "Your balance has improved since this afternoon. How are you feeling?"

"Much better," Annabelle replied, and flushed as her stomach growled audibly. "A bit hungry, actually."

Hunt grinned and brought her to a partially opened door. Leading her over the threshold, he brought her into a small, lovely room with rosewood-paneled walls hung with tapestries, and furniture upholstered in amber velvet. The room's most distinctive feature, however, was the window on the inside wall, which opened out onto the drawing room two stories below. This place was perfectly concealed from the view of the guests below, while music floated clearly through the wide opening. Annabelle's round-eyed gaze moved to a small table that was covered with silver-domed plates.

"I had the devil of a time trying to decide what would tempt your appetite," Hunt said. "So I told the kitchen staff to include some of everything."

Overwhelmed, and unable to think of a time that any man had gone to such lengths for her enjoyment, Annabelle suddenly found it difficult to speak. She swallowed hard and looked everywhere but at his face. "This is lovely. I . . . I didn't know this room was here."

"Few people do. The countess sometimes sits here when she is too infirm to go downstairs." Hunt moved closer to her and slid his long fingers beneath her chin, coaxing her to meet his gaze. "Will you have dinner with me?"

Annabelle's pulse throbbed so rapidly that she was certain he could feel it against his fingers. "I have no chaperone," she half whispered.

Hunt smiled at that, his hand dropping from her chin. "You couldn't be safer. I'm hardly going to seduce you while you're obviously too weak to defend yourself."

"That's very gentlemanly of you."

"I'll seduce you when you're feeling better."

Biting back a smile, Annabelle raised a fine brow, and said, "You're very sure of yourself. Should you have said you're going to *try* to seduce me?"

" 'Never anticipate failure'—that's what my father always tells me." Sliding a strong arm around her back, Hunt guided her to one of the chairs. "Will you have some wine?"

"I shouldn't," Annabelle said wistfully, sinking into the deeply upholstered chair. "It would probably go straight to my head."

Hunt poured a glass and gave it to her, smiling with a wicked charm that Lucifer himself would have tried to emulate. "Go on," he murmured. "I'll take care of you if you get a bit tipsy."

Sipping the smooth, soft vintage, Annabelle sent him a wry glance. "I wonder how often a lady's downfall began with that exact promise from you . . ."

"I have yet to cause a lady's downfall," Hunt said, lifting the covers from the dishes and setting them aside. "I usually pursue them after they've already fallen."

"Have there been many fallen ladies in your past?" Annabelle couldn't keep from asking.

"I've had my fair share," Hunt replied, looking neither apologetic nor boastful as he met her gaze directly. "Though lately my energies have been absorbed by a different pastime."

"Which is?"

"I'm overseeing the development of a locomotive works that Westcliff and I have invested in."

"Really?" Annabelle stared at him with kindling interest. "I've never been on a train before. What is it like?"

Hunt grinned, suddenly looking boyish in his barely suppressed enthusiasm. "Fast. Exciting. The average speed of a passenger locomotive is about fifty miles an hour, but Consolidated is building a six-coupled express engine design that should go up to seventy."

"Seventy miles an hour?" Annabelle repeated, unable to imagine hurtling forward at such speed. "Wouldn't that be uncomfortable for the passengers?"

The question made him smile. "Once the train reaches its traveling speed, you don't feel the momentum."

"What are the passenger cars like on the inside?"

"Not especially luxurious," Hunt admitted, pouring more wine into his own glass. "I wouldn't recommend traveling in anything other than a private car—especially for someone like you."

"Someone like me?" Annabelle gave him a chiding smile. "If you're implying that I'm spoiled, I assure you that I am not."

"You should be." His warm gaze slid over her pink-tinted face and slender upper body, then sought hers again. There was a note in his voice that gently robbed her of breath. "You could do with a bit of spoiling."

Annabelle inhaled deeply, trying to restore the natural rhythm of her lungs. Desperately, she hoped that he wouldn't touch her, that he would keep his promise not to seduce her. Because if he did . . . God help her . . . she wasn't certain that she would be able to resist him.

"Consolidated is the name of your company?" she asked shakily, trying to retrieve the thread of conversation.

Hunt nodded. "It's the British partner of Shaw Foundries."

"Which belongs to Lady Olivia's fiancé, Mr. Shaw?"

"Exactly. Shaw is helping us to adapt to the American system of engine building, which is far more efficient and productive than the British method."

"I've always heard that British-made machinery is the best in the world," Annabelle commented.

"Arguable. But even so, it's seldom standardized. No two locomotives built in Britain are exactly alike, which slows production considerably and makes repairs difficult. However, if we could follow the American example and produce uniform cast-molded parts, using standard gauges and templates, we can build an engine in a matter of weeks rather than months, and perform repairs with lightning speed."

As they conversed, Annabelle watched Hunt with fascination, having never seen a man talk this way about his profession. In her experience, work was not something that men usually liked to discuss, as the very concept of laboring for one's living was a distinct hallmark of the lower classes. If an upper-class gentleman was obliged to have a profession, he tried to be very discreet about it and pretend that most of his time was spent in leisure activities. But Simon Hunt made no effort to conceal his enjoyment of his work—and for some reason Annabelle found that strangely attractive.

At her urging, Hunt described the business further, telling her all about his negotiations for the purchase of a railway-owned foundry, which was being converted to the new American-inspired system. Two of the nine buildings on the five-acre site had already been transformed into a foundry that produced standardized bolts, pistons, rods, and valves. These, along with some parts that had been imported from Shaw Foundries in New York, were being assembled into a series of four-coupled and six-coupled engines that would be sold throughout Europe.

"How often do you visit the site?" Annabelle asked, taking a bite of pheasant cutlet dressed with a creamy watercress sauce.

"Daily, when I'm in town." Hunt contemplated the contents of his wineglass with a slight frown. "I've stayed away for too long, actually—I'll have to go to London soon, to check on progress."

The idea that he would soon leave Hampshire should have made Annabelle glad. Simon Hunt was a distraction that she could ill afford, and it would be far easier to focus her attentions on Lord Kendall when Hunt had quit the estate altogether. However, she felt strangely hollow, realizing how much she enjoyed his company and how lifeless Stony Cross Park would seem once he had gone.

"Will you come back before the party ends?" she asked, devoting great concentration to mincing a morsel of pheasant with her knife.

"That depends."

"On what?"

His voice was very soft. "On whether I have sufficient reason to return."

Annabelle did not look at him. Rather, she lapsed into a restless silence and turned her unseeing gaze to the window aperture, through which the luxuriant melody of Schubert's *Rosamunde* poured.

Eventually there came a discreet rap at the door, and a footman came in to remove the plates. Keeping her face averted, Annabelle wondered if the news that she had dined in private with Simon Hunt would soon be spread through the servants' hall. However, after the footman left, Hunt spoke reassuringly, seeming to have read her thoughts. "He won't say a word to anyone. Westcliff recommended him for his ability to keep his mouth shut about confidential matters."

Annabelle gave him a worried glance. "Then . . . the earl knows that you and I are . . . but I am certain that he must not approve!"

"I've done many things Westcliff doesn't approve of," Simon returned evenly. "And I don't always approve of his decisions. However, in the interest of maintaining a profitable friendship, we don't generally cross each other." Standing, he rested his palms on the table and leaned forward, his shadow covering her. "What about a game of chess? I had a board brought up . . . just in case."

Annabelle nodded. As she stared into his warm black eyes, she reflected that this was perhaps the first evening of her adult life in which she was wholly happy to be exactly where she was. With this man. She felt the most intense curiosity about him, a real need to discover the thoughts and feelings buried beneath his exterior.

"Where did you learn to play chess?" she asked, watching the movements of his hands as he set the pieces in their previous formations.

"From my father."

"Your *father?*"

One corner of his mouth lifted in mocking half smile. "Can't a butcher play chess?"

"Of course, I . . ." Annabelle felt a hot blush sweep over her face. She was mortified by her tactlessness. "I'm sorry."

Hunt's slight smile lingered as he studied her. "You seem to have a mistaken impression of my family. The Hunts are solidly middle-class. My brothers and sisters and I all attended school. Now my father employs my brothers, who also live over the shop. And in the evenings they often play chess."

Relaxing at the absence of censure in his voice, Annabelle picked up a pawn and rolled it between her fingers. "Why didn't you choose to work for your father, as your brothers did?"

"I was a stubborn hellion in my youth," Hunt admitted with a grin. "Whenever my father told me to do something, I always tried to prove him wrong."

"And what was his response?" Annabelle asked, her eyes twinkling.

"At first he tried to be patient with me. When that didn't work, he took the opposite tack." Hunt winced in reminiscence, smiling ruefully. "Trust me, you never want to be thrashed by a butcher—their arms are like tree trunks."

"I can imagine," Annabelle murmured, stealing a circumspect glance at the wide expanse of his shoulders and remembering the brawny hardness of his muscles. "Your family must be very proud of your success."

"Perhaps." Hunt gave a noncommittal shrug. "Unfortunately, it seems that my ambition has served to distance us. My parents won't allow me to buy them a house in the West End; nor do they understand why I should choose to live there. Nor does my investing strike them as a suitable profession. They would be happier if I turned to something more . . . tangible."

Annabelle regarded him intently, understanding what had remained unspoken in the spare explanation. She had always known that Simon Hunt didn't belong in the upper-class circles in which he often moved. However, until this moment it had not occurred to her that he was similarly out of place in the world that he had left behind. She wondered if he was occasionally lonely, or if he kept himself far too busy to acknowledge it. "I can think of few things more tangible than a five-ton locomotive engine," she remarked, in response to his last comment.

He laughed, and reached for the pawn in her hand. But somehow Annabelle couldn't seem to let go of the ivory piece, and their fingers tangled and held, while their gazes locked intimately. She was shocked by the radiant warmth that flooded from her hand to her shoulder, then diffused through her entire body. It was like being drunk on sunlight, heat spilling in streams of sensation, and along with the pleasure came the sudden, alarming pressure behind her eyes that heralded tears.

Bewildered, Annabelle jerked her hand back from his, the pawn clattering to the floor. "I'm sorry," she said with an unsteady laugh, suddenly afraid of what might happen if she stayed alone with him any longer. She stood clumsily and moved away from the table. "I-I've just realized that I'm very tired . . . the wine seems to have affected me after all. I should go back to my room. I think there is still ample time for you to socialize with everyone downstairs, so your evening hasn't been entirely wasted. Thank you for the dinner, and the music, and—"

"Annabelle." Hunt moved with swift grace, coming to stand before her with his hands at her waist. He looked down at her, an inquiring frown tugging at his dark brows. "You're not afraid of me, are you?" he murmured.

She shook her head dumbly.

"Then why the sudden rush to leave?"

There were infinite ways she could have replied, but at the moment she could summon no subtlety, wit, or any manner of verbal agility. She could only answer with the bluntness of a mallet strike. "I . . . don't want this."

"This?"

"I'm not going to become your mistress." She hesitated, and said in a whisper, "I can do better."

Hunt considered the bald statement with great care, his steadying hands remaining at her waist. "Do you mean that you can find someone to marry," he finally asked, "or is it that you intend to become the mistress of an aristocrat?"

"It doesn't matter, does it?" Annabelle muttered, pushing away from the support of his hands. "Neither scenario involves you."

Although she refused to look at him, she felt his gaze on her, and she shivered as the glow of warmth faded completely from her body. "I'll take you back to your room," Hunt said, without emotion, and he accompanied her to the door.

Chapter 16

When Annabelle rejoined the guests the next morning, she was heartened to discover that her encounter with the adder had earned a great deal of sympathy from everyone, including Lord Kendall. Exhibiting a great degree of sensitivity and concern, Kendall sat with Annabelle at a late-morning breakfast held al fresco on the back terrace. He insisted on holding her plate at the buffet table while she selected various morsels, and he made certain that a servant refilled her water glass as soon as it was empty. He also insisted on doing the same for Lady Constance Darrowby, who had joined them at the table.

Recalling the wallflowers' comments about Lady Constance, Annabelle assessed the competition. Kendall seemed more than a little interested in the girl, who was quiet and serenely aloof. She was also elegantly thin, in the style that had currently become quite fashionable. And Daisy had been right—Lady Constance did indeed have a mouth like a drawstring purse, constantly tightening into little cooing *o's* whenever Kendall shared a piece of horticultural information with her.

"How dreadful it must have been," Lady Constance remarked to Annabelle, upon hearing the story of the adder. "It's a wonder that you didn't die." Despite the angelic cast of her expression, a cool glitter in her pale blue eyes made Annabelle aware that the girl wouldn't have been all that displeased if she had.

"I'm quite well now," Annabelle said, turning to smile at Kendall. "And more than ready for another outing in the woods."

"I shouldn't exert myself too soon, if I were you, Miss Peyton," Lady Constance said with delicate concern. "You still don't seem to have fully recovered. But I am certain that the pastiness of your complexion will probably improve in a few days."

Annabelle maintained her smile, refusing to show how the comment had rankled . . . though she was strongly tempted to make an observation about the blemish on Lady Constance's forehead.

"Do excuse me," Lady Constance murmured, standing from the table. "I see some fresh strawberries. I shall return momentarily."

"Take your time," Annabelle advised sweetly. "We'll hardly notice your absence."

Together, Annabelle and Kendall watched Lady Constance glide toward the buffet table, where it so happened that Mr. Benjamin Muxlow was also refilling his plate. Politely, Muxlow stood back from the large bowl of strawberries and held Lady Constance's plate as she ladled a few choice berries on it. The air between them bespoke nothing more than cordial friendliness . . . but Annabelle happened to remember the story that Daisy had told her the day before yesterday.

And then she thought of it—the perfect way to eliminate Lady Constance as a contender. Before she allowed herself to consider the consequences, moral implications, or any other inconvenient notions, she leaned closer to Lord Kendall. "The two of them are quite good at concealing the true state of affairs, aren't they?" she murmured, casting a sly glance at Lady Constance and Muxlow. "But of course, it would hardly serve either of them if it became generally known . . ." She paused and looked into Lord Kendall's puzzled gaze with a trace of pretended discomfort. "Oh, I'm sorry. I assumed that you must have already heard . . ."

Kendall's face was suddenly wreathed in a frown. "Heard what?" he asked, giving the pair a wary glance.

"Well, I'm not one to spread gossip . . . but I was told by a reliable source that on the day of the water party, at the picnic on the riverbank . . . Miss Hunt and Mr. Muxlow were caught in a *terribly* compromising situation. The two of them were behind a tree, and . . ." Annabelle stopped with a carefully manufactured expression of dismay. "I shouldn't have said anything. And it's possible that there has been some misunderstanding. One never knows, does one?"

Applying herself to sipping daintily from her teacup, Annabelle shot an assessing glance over the rim. She read Kendall's emotions easily: He did not want to believe that Lady Constance could have been caught in an indiscretion. The thought of it was enough to appall him. However, being a true gentleman, Kendall would be loath to investigate the situation. He would never dare to ask Lady Constance if she had indeed been compromised by Muxlow. Instead, he would remain silent on the matter, and try to ignore his own suspicions . . . and the unanswered questions would fester.

* * *

"Annabelle, you sh-shouldn't have," Evie murmured later that afternoon when Annabelle confessed what she had done. The four friends sat in Evie's bedroom, where the girl sat with her face covered in a thick application of white cream that was supposed to get rid of freckles. Staring at Annabelle from beneath the heavy layer of bleaching unguent, Evie tried to continue, but it was clear that her powers of speech—which were not all that extensive to begin with—had been obliterated by disapproval.

"It was a brilliant strategy," Lillian declared, picking up a nail file from the vanity where she sat. Whether she actually approved of Annabelle's actions was not clear, but it was obvious that she would remain loyal to the end. "Annabelle didn't actually *lie*, you see. She merely repeated a rumor that had been told to her, and she made it clear that it was just that—a rumor. What Kendall chooses to make of it is up to him."

"But Annabelle didn't tell him that she knows for a fact that the rumor is unf-founded," Evie argued.

Lillian concentrated on filing her nail to a perfect oval. "Still, she didn't lie."

Feeling defensive and guilty, Annabelle looked at Daisy. "Well, what do you think?"

The younger Bowman sister, who had been repeatedly tossing the Rounders ball from one hand to the other, gave Annabelle an astute look as she replied. "I think that sometimes not giving someone all the information is nearly the same as a lie. You've started on a slippery path, dear. Beware your next step."

Lillian scowled in annoyance. "Oh, do stop talking like a sideshow fortune-teller, Daisy. Once Annabelle gets what she wants, it won't matter how she accomplished it. Results are everything. And Evie—no ethical hairsplitting. You agreed to help us manipulate

Lord Kendall into a compromising situation—how is that any worse than Annabelle repeating an unfounded rumor?"

"We all promised not to hurt anyone," Evie said with great dignity, taking a small towel and wiping thick streaks of cream from her face.

"Lady Constance hasn't been hurt," Lillian insisted. "She's not in love with him. It is quite obvious that she wants Kendall only because he's an end-of-the-season bachelor, and she's unmarried. Heavens, Evie, you've got to harden yourself. Is Lady Constance any worse off than we are? Look at us—four wallflowers who've got nothing to show for their efforts so far, except freckles, an adder bite, and the humiliation of having exposed our knickers to Lord Westcliff."

Annabelle, who had been sitting on the edge of the mattress, let herself fall back to the center of the four-poster bed. She stared at the striped canopy overhead, feeling guilty. Oh, how she wished that she could be more like Lillian, who believed that the end justified the means! She promised herself that she would be strictly honorable in the future.

But . . . as Lillian had pointed out, Lord Kendall could either believe or disregard the rumor at will. He was a grown man who could make decisions for himself. All Annabelle had done was to sow the seeds—it was Kendall's choice either to nurture them, or let them lie fallow.

In the evening, Annabelle dressed in an ice pink gown made of countless floating layers of transparent silk gauze. The waist was tightly cinched with a reinforced silk belt adorned with a huge white rose. Her skirts made a soft swishing sound as she walked, and she fluffed out the top layers, feeling like a princess. Too impatient to wait for Philippa, who was taking forever to dress, Annabelle left the room early, in the hopes of seeing her friends. With any luck, she might even encounter Lord Kendall and find some excuse to slip away with him for a few moments.

Favoring her ankle slightly, Annabelle walked along the hallway that led to the grand staircase. On impulse, she stopped at the Marsden private parlor, the door of which had been left ajar, and she entered it cautiously. The parlor was unlit, but surplus light from the hallway was sufficient to illuminate the shadowy outlines of the chess table in the corner. Drawn to the board, she saw with a flicker of pleasure that her game with Simon Hunt had been restored. Why had he taken the time to arrange the pieces as if they were still in play? Did he expect her to make another move?

Don't touch anything, she told herself . . . but the temptation was too great to resist. She squinted in concentration, assessing the situation with a fresh eye. Hunt's knight was in the perfect position to capture her queen, which meant that she would either have to move the piece or defend it. Suddenly she saw best how to protect her threatened queen—she slid a nearby rook forward to capture Hunt's knight, thereby eliminating it from the board altogether. Smiling in satisfaction, she set the captured piece to the side and left the room.

Descending the grand staircase, she crossed through the entrance hall and walked along another hallway toward a circuit of public rooms. The carpet beneath her feet muffled all sound . . . but suddenly she sensed that someone was behind her. She felt a frisson of warning across her exposed upper back. Glancing over her shoulder, she saw that Lord Hodgeham was following her, moving with surprising swiftness for such a stocky man. His heavy fingers hooked into the back of her silk belt, forcing her to stop or risk the possibility of having the fragile band snap in two.

It was a sign of how arrogant Hodgeham had become that he would accost her in a place where they could so easily be seen. Gasping in outrage, Annabelle spun to face him. She was confronted by the sight of his portly torso crammed into tight evening clothes, while the oily scent of his cologned hair assaulted her nostrils. "Lovely creature," Hodgeham muttered, his breath pungent with the scent of brandy. "Recovering nicely, I see. I think perhaps we should resume our conversation of yesterday, before I was so pleasantly diverted by your mother."

"You revolting—" Annabelle began in fury, but he interrupted the flow of words by clamping his fingers on either side of her jaw and squeezing hard.

"I'll tell Kendall everything," he said, his bulbous lips very close to hers. "With sufficient embellishment to ensure that he will look upon you and your family with the purest disgust." His ponderous body pressed hers against the wall, nearly squeezing the breath from her. "Unless," he said, his sour respirations striking her face, "you decide to accommodate me in the same manner that your mother has."

"Then go and tell Kendall," Annabelle said, her eyes blazing with hatred. "Tell him everything and be done with it. I'd rather starve in the gutter than 'accommodate' a repulsive swine like you."

Hodgeham stared at her in incredulous fury. "You'll regret it," he said, flecks of spittle gleaming on his lips.

She smiled with cold contempt. "I don't think so."

Before Hodgeham let go of her, Annabelle caught a movement out of the corner of her vision. Turning her head to the side, she saw someone walking toward them—a man who was moving with the stealthy strides of a stalking panther. It must have appeared to him that she and Hodgeham had been caught in an amorous embrace.

"Release me," she hissed to Hodgeham, and shoved hard at his bulky girth. He stepped back, finally allowing her to take a full breath, and shot her a glance of malevolent promise before walking in the opposite direction of the approaching man.

Rattled, Annabelle stared into the face of Simon Hunt as he took her by the shoulders. He was watching Hodgeham hurry away, with a hard, almost bloodthirsty gaze that made her blood turn cold. Then he looked down at her in a way that caused her breath to catch. Until that moment she had never seen Simon Hunt without his usual nonchalance. No matter how she had insulted or cut or spurned him, he had always reacted with predictable jeering self-assurance. But it seemed that she had finally done something that had provoked genuine fury. He looked ready to strangle her.

"Were you following me?" she asked with forced calmness, wondering how he had managed to appear at that particular moment.

"I saw you walk through the entrance hall," he said, "and Hodgeham trailing after you. I followed because I wanted to find out what was going on between the two of you."

Her gaze turned defiant. "And have you found out?"

"I don't know," came his dangerously soft reply. "Tell me, Annabelle—when you said that you could do better, was this what you had in mind? Servicing that idiotic lump of lard on the sly, in return for the pitiful recompense he gives you? I wouldn't have believed you to be that much of a fool."

"You sodding hypocrite," Annabelle whispered furiously. "You're angry with me for being his mistress and not yours—well, you tell *me* something—why does it matter to whom I sell my body?"

"Because you don't want him," Hunt said through his teeth. "And you don't want Kendall. You want me."

Annabelle did not understand the seething tangle of emotions inside herself, or why this confrontation had begun to fill her with a strange, terrible exhilaration. She wanted to hit him, throw herself on him, provoke him until the last few fragments of his self-control were smashed to powder. "Let me guess—you're prepared to offer me a more profitable version of the same arrangement that I supposedly have with Hodgeham?" She laughed scornfully as she saw the answer on his face. "The answer is no. *No.* So once and for all, leave me alone—"

She stopped as she heard the chatter of more people coming along the hallway. Exasperated and desperate, she whirled around to find a door that she could slip through, to keep from being seen alone with Hunt. Catching her in one arm, Hunt hauled her inside the closest room and shut the door smartly.

Registering the shape of the piano and the clutter of music stands, Annabelle jerked away from Hunt. He reached out to steady a flimsy music stand that had nearly been overturned by the brush of her skirts. "If you can stand to be Hodgeham's mistress," Hunt muttered, following as she retreated farther into the music room, "God knows you can stand to be mine. You could say that you're not attracted to me, but we both know that you'd be lying. Tell me your price, Annabelle. Any sum you'd care to name. Do you want a house of your own? A yacht? Done. Let's get this over with—I've had enough of waiting for you."

"How romantic," Annabelle said with an unsteady laugh. "My God. Your proposition is somewhat lacking in subtlety, Mr. Hunt. And you're wrong in your assumption that my only option is to be someone's mistress. I can get Lord Kendall to marry me."

His eyes were as dark as volcanic glass. "Marriage to him would turn into a living hell for you. He'll never love you. He'll never even know you."

"I don't want love," she said, stricken by his words. "I just want—" She paused as a sudden pain centered in her chest, in a ball of unendurable coldness. Staring up into his unreadable face she tried again. "I just want—"

There was a sound at the door. The knob began to turn. Startled, Annabelle realized that someone was about to enter the room—and then all hope of marrying Kendall would vanish like so much dust in the wind. Reacting instinctively, she seized Hunt's arm and dragged him with her toward an alcove by the window, framed by paneled curtains that had been hung on a brass rod. The only thing in the alcove was a window seat upholstered in velvet, with a few books stacked carelessly on one side. Jerking the curtain shut, Annabelle flung herself on Hunt and clapped her hand over his mouth, just as someone . . . or several someones . . . entered the music room. She could hear the muffled sounds of masculine voices, and some banging and clanking that perplexed her until she heard the plucking of out-of-tune violin strings. Oh, God. The musicians had come there to tune their instruments before the ball began. In all likelihood she was just about to be compromised in front of an entire orchestra.

There was just enough light spilling over the top of the curtain to cast a faint glow over their features—enough for Annabelle to see the evil smile that had suddenly appeared in Simon Hunt's eyes. One word or sound from him in these incriminating circumstances, and she was done for. Her hand pressed harder over his mouth, her eyes only inches from his as she pinned him with a gaze that threatened murder.

The musicians' voices mingled with the sound of instruments being tuned, drawn-out notes being held until they joined in harmony, dissonance being disciplined into order. Wondering if they would be caught, Annabelle stared blindly at the curtains, willing them to remain closed. She felt the touch of Hunt's breath against the edge of her hand and realized that his jaw had gone taut. Glancing at him, she saw that the malicious amusement had vanished from his gaze, replaced by a look that was far more alarming. She froze, her heart beginning to hammer so heavily that it hurt, and she stared at him with widening eyes as his free hand lifted slowly. Her fingers were still clamped over his mouth . . . he began to pry at them delicately, one by one, starting with the smallest, while his breath fanned in quickening surges against the side of her hand. Her head moved in a stiff little shake, and she strained away from him, even as his arm tightened around her waist. She was utterly trapped . . . helpless to prevent Simon Hunt from doing whatever he wanted.

The last finger was pulled away, and Hunt pushed her hand down and gripped the back of her neck. Her fingers fluttered against his sleeves, her upper body arching slightly as his grasp on her nape tightened. He was not hurting her, but he had made it impossible for her to move or struggle. As his head lowered, her lips parted with a silent gasp, and her mind went dark.

His mouth was on hers, gentle but sure as he coaxed a response from her. She was filled with instant fever, burning everywhere, helpless against the onslaught of a desire like nothing she had ever known before. The

memory of their one kiss was nothing compared to
this . . . perhaps because he was no longer a stranger
to her. She wanted him with a desperation that frightened her. The pressure of his lips floated lightly over
hers, straying briefly to her chin, her cheek, leaving
trails of soft fire wherever they ventured, before he returned to her mouth with more explicit pressure. She
felt the tip of his tongue against hers, the silken touch
so unexpected that she would have recoiled had he not
been holding her so tightly.

The elegant cacophony of the musicians jangled in
her ears, reminding her of the imminent possibility of
discovery. She forced herself to relax against Hunt, her
body shaking. For the next few minutes, she would let
him do anything to her, anything, just so long as he
didn't betray their presence. Hunt tasted her again,
searching with subtle strokes of his tongue. She was
shocked by the intimate exploration, and even more
by the unspeakable sensations that shot through the
vulnerable places of her body. Delicious weakness
overtook her, and she wobbled in his hold, her hands
groping for his neck, his hair, the locks thick and silky
against her fingers. The tentative inquiry of her hands
caused him to draw an out-of-rhythm breath, as if her
touch had affected him intensely. He slid one hand up
to the side of her face, cradling her cheek as he pulled
back just enough to nibble and tease, catching gently
at her upper lip, then the lower one, lavishing her with
feathery brushes of warmth. Compulsively, she ex-
erted shaky pressure behind his neck, urging him back
down to her, and when his mouth took hers in another
penetrating kiss, she nearly moaned aloud. Before the
sound could escape her dilated throat, she tore her
mouth away and buried her face against his shoulder.

She felt the quick rise and fall of his deep-vaulted

chest, and the hot rush of his breath against her hair. Grasping the mass of pinned-up curls at the back of her head, he pulled her head back to expose her throat. The burning path of his lips began at the tiny hollow just beneath her right ear, awakening exquisitely sensitive nerves as he traced the line of a delicate vein with his tongue. His fingers slid over the top of her shoulder, his thumb finding the wing of her collarbone, his open hand exploring the fragile architecture of her body. Nuzzling the side of her throat, he found a place that made her shiver, and he lingered there until she felt another moan threatening to break from her kiss-dampened lips.

Pushing at him frantically, she managed to divert him for all of three seconds, after which he sought her mouth with another hungering kiss. His palm brushed over the silk that covered her breast, once, twice, thrice. With each slow pass, the heat of his skin sank through the veil of fabric. As her nipple tingled and budded, he stroked it tenderly with the backs of his fingers until it tightened even more. The increasing pressure of his kiss forced her head back in a position of surrender, opening her to the lazy caress of his tongue, the artful investigation of his hands. This wasn't supposed to happen, her nerves shattering with pleasure, her body consumed with sensual heat.

He made her forget everything in those silent, febrile moments—she lost awareness of time, of where they were, and even who she was. All she knew was that she needed him closer, deeper, tighter . . . his skin, his hard flesh, his mouth wandering in heated trails over her body. She gripped at his shirt until it loosened from his trousers, clutching handfuls of the starched white linen in desperate need of the warm skin beneath. He seemed to understand that she had no experience at controlling this level of desire—his kisses became soothing, his hands beginning to move over her back in calming strokes. However, the more he tried to ease her craving, the worse it became, her mouth moving frantically beneath his, her body twisting in an anxious rhythm.

He finally resorted to taking his mouth away and holding her in a crushing embrace, his lips buried against the flushed curve of her neck and shoulder. Annabelle was absurdly grateful for the brutality of his grip, his arms forming heavy bands of muscle that helped to contain her violent trembling. They stood like that for what seemed an eternity, until Annabelle became hazily aware that the room was silent. Sometime during the past few minutes, the musicians had finished their preparations and left. Lifting his head, Hunt slowly reached for the edge of a curtain panel and moved it an inch to the side. Seeing that the music room was empty once more, he returned his attention to Annabelle, using the tip of his thumb to brush back a lock of glinting hair that had fallen over her ear.

"They're gone," came his rasping whisper.

Too stunned to think coherently, Annabelle looked at him without speaking. His fingertips traced the hot surface of her cheek, the swollen cushion of her lips. With something like despair, she felt the skyrocketing response of her unappeased body, the renewed vigor of her pulse, the wash of pleasure that slipped over her skin. That was the time to pull away from him, or her disappearance would soon be remarked on. To her shame, she remained still, her body hungrily absorbing sensations as Hunt continued to caress her. His hand moved to the back of her gown, and she felt the deft workings of his fingers, even as he bent and kissed her mouth again. This time she could no longer hold back the sounds; the small sobs that broke from her throat, the whimper of relief as the tight bodice of her gown was loosened. The cut of the neckline had made it impossible for her to wear a corset with cups—instead she had worn an under-the-bust style that had left her breasts unconfined beneath her chemise.

Continuing to kiss her, Hunt drew her down with him to the upholstered window seat. He cradled her in his lap, his fingers smoothing the sagging bodice downward, and he made a sound of pleasure against her mouth as he discovered the fullness of her breasts. Suddenly frightened by the realization of what she was allowing, Annabelle pushed weakly at his wrist. He lifted her body higher and pressed his mouth to the center of her chest, where her heart thumped in a hard, regular rhythm. His supportive arms maintained the arch of her back as his lips slid downward to investigate the plump rise of her breast. At the touch of his passion-heated breath on her nipple, she stopped straining and went still, her hand balling into fists against his shoulders. He took her into his mouth, his tongue brushing gently until the peak was wet and tender-hard, and her veins were filled with simmering honey. He whispered reassurances as his hand smoothed over her breast, his thumb rubbing the glaze of moisture into her glowing skin. Murmuring incoherently, she circled her arms around his taut neck, and gasped as his mouth closed over her other nipple and tugged gently.

A new urgency crept through her, something that drew shuddering moans from her chest, and made her body tighten rhythmically in his lap. Hunt was tormented by the same compelling need—she could feel the violence of his heartbeat and the strain of his lungs as they labored with each breath. But he seemed far more able to bridle his passion than she, the move-

ments of his hands and mouth remaining careful and
controlled. She thrashed in the densely layered silk of
her gown, her fingers clawing at the sleeves of his coat
and waistcoat—too many clothes, everywhere, and she
was going mad with the need to feel his skin on hers.

"Easy, sweetheart," he whispered against her
cheek. "Relax. No, lie still in my arms . . ." But she
couldn't make her body obey, couldn't seem to stop
the writhing of her hips and the shivering pleas that
came from her kiss-bruised mouth.

Hunt continued to murmur softly as he held her,
brushing his lips over her face, his fingers massaging
the delicate hollows where her pulse beat frantically.
She felt him adjusting her clothes, gently lifting her as
if she were a doll, fastening the back of her gown. At
one point he even gave a soft, shaky laugh, as if bemused by his own actions. Later, she would come to
reflect that he had seemed just as dazed as she was; but
right then, in the flush of frustrated longing, she could
not unravel her tangled thoughts. As the desire ebbed
from her body, it left behind a sickening residue of
shame.

Struggling from his lap, Annabelle faced away from
him, her legs quivering. She could summon only two
words to break the heavy silence. Without looking at
him, she said hoarsely, "Never again." Pushing
through the paneled curtains, she left the room as
quickly as she was able and bolted down the hallway.

Chapter 17

After Annabelle had fled the music room, Simon had remained there for at least a half hour, fighting to settle his roaring passion, letting the fire in his blood cool. He straightened his clothes and raked a hand through his hair, moodily contemplating his next move. "Annabelle," he muttered, more troubled and confused than he had ever been in his life. The fact that he had been brought to this state by a woman was infuriating. He, who was known as a crafty and disciplined negotiator, had made the clumsiest possible offer for her, and he had been roundly rejected. Deservedly so. He should never have tried to force her to name a price before she had even admitted that she wanted him. But the suspicion that she might be sleeping with Hodgeham . . . *Hodgeham,* of all men, had nearly driven Simon mad with jealousy, and all his usual skills had deserted him.

Remembering how it had felt to kiss her, to finally caress the warm, supple silk of her skin, Simon felt passion threatening to boil up inside him once again.

With all his experience, he had thought he was familiar with every physical sensation imaginable. But he had just forcibly been made aware that sleeping with Annabelle would be a different matter altogether. The experience would involve his emotions as well as his body . . . emotions so alarming that he could not yet bring himself to examine them.

The attraction between them had become dangerous—no less so for him than it was for her. And it was clear that Simon needed to gain some perspective on the situation. At the moment, however, he wasn't thinking too well.

Leaving the music room with a muttered curse, he straightened the knot of his black silk necktie. Tension strung through his limbs, shortening his usual long stride and making him feel predatory and volatile as he walked toward the ballroom. The prospect of another social evening was nearly maddening. His tolerance for extended parties had never been high—he was not a man who enjoyed hours of indolent chatter and idle amusements. He would have been long gone, had it not been for Annabelle's presence at Stony Cross.

Brooding, he went into the ballroom and glanced speculatively over the crowd. He immediately caught sight of Annabelle, occupying a chair in the corner with Lord Kendall at her side. Kendall was openly infatuated with her, his enraptured gaze making no secret of his interest. Annabelle looked subdued and flushed, seeming to have trouble meeting Kendall's admiring gaze. She spoke very little and sat with her hands tightly knotted in her lap. Simon's eyes narrowed as he watched her. Ironically, now when Annabelle was feeling diminished and uncertain, Kendall's attraction to her had finally taken root. It would be a nasty surprise for Kendall later, if

Annabelle did get him on the string, to find out that his wife was not the timid ingenue that she seemed. She was a woman of spirit and passion, a decidedly ambitious creature who needed a partner of equal strength. Kendall would never be able to manage her. He was too much of a gentleman for Annabelle—too mild and moderate, and too intelligent in the wrong ways. Annabelle would never respect him, nor would she take any pleasure in his virtues. She would come to despise him for the very things she should have admired . . . and Kendall would shrink from the qualities in Annabelle that Simon would have relished.

Dragging his gaze away from the pair, Simon made his way to the other side of the room, where Westcliff and a few other friends were talking. Turning toward him, the earl murmured, "Enjoying yourself?"

"Not particularly." Simon shoved his hands into his coat pockets and glanced around the ballroom with simmering impatience. "I've stayed long enough in Hampshire—I need to return to London, to see what is happening at the foundry."

"What of Miss Peyton?" came the soft-voiced question.

Simon considered that for a moment. "I think," he said slowly, "that I'm going to wait and see what comes of her pursuit of Kendall." He looked at Westcliff with a questioning arch of his brow.

The earl responded with a brief nod. "When will you depart?"

"Early in the morning." Simon could not repress a long, taut sigh.

Westcliff smiled wryly. "The situation will untangle itself," he said in a prosaic manner. "Go to London, and come back when your head is clear."

*   *   *

Annabelle could not seem to shake the melancholy that clung to her like a mantle of ice. Sleep had been elusive, and she had hardly been able to eat a bite of the sumptuous breakfast that had been served downstairs. Lord Kendall had regarded her wan countenance and her quietness as lingering effects of her recent illness, and he had plied her with sympathy and solace until she had wanted to shove him away in irritation. Her friends, too, were being similarly annoying in their niceness, and for the first time Annabelle took no enjoyment in their cheerful banter. She tried to identify the moment when her spirits had turned so sour, and realized that it had been the moment when she had learned from Lady Olivia that Simon Hunt had left Stony Cross.

"Mr. Hunt has gone to London on business," Lady Olivia had said lightly. "He never stays long at these parties—the wonder is that he didn't leave sooner than this. No dust settles on that one, to be certain . . ."

When someone had questioned why Mr. Hunt's departure had been so precipitate, Lady Olivia had smiled and shook her head. "Oh, Hunt comes and goes at will, rather like a tomcat. His departures are always abrupt, as he seems to dislike good-byes of any kind."

Hunt had left without one word to Annabelle, and as a result, she was left feeling abandoned and anxious. Thoughts of the previous night—oh, hideous evening!—kept playing relentlessly in her mind. After the events in the music room, she had been disoriented, so thoroughly occupied with thoughts of Hunt that she couldn't seem to focus on the here and now. She had kept her gaze down so that she wouldn't catch an unexpected glimpse of him, and she had prayed silently that he wouldn't approach her. Mercifully he had kept his distance, while Lord Kendall had planted himself firmly at her side. Kendall had spent the rest of the night talking to her about subjects she didn't understand and couldn't have cared less about. She had encouraged him with innocuous murmurs and half-hearted smiles, and had thought dimly that she should be ecstatic about the attention he was paying to her. Instead, she had only wished that he would go away.

Her subdued manner at breakfast seemed to attract Kendall all the more. Assuming that her docile facade was an act, Lillian Bowman had surreptitiously whispered near her ear, "Good job, Annabelle. He's eating out of your hand."

Excusing herself from the breakfast table on the pretext of needing to rest, Annabelle wandered alone through the manor, until she reached the blue parlor. The chess table lured her, and she approached it slowly, wondering if a housemaid had finally replaced the pieces in the box, or if someone had interfered with the game. No, it was exactly as she had left it . . . with one minor change. Simon Hunt had moved a pawn into a defensive position, which allowed her the opportunity either to shore up her own defense, or move aggressively to pursue his queen. It was not a move that she would have expected of him. She would have thought he would attempt something more ambitious. More contentious. Studying the board, she strove to understand his strategy. Had his move been made out of indecision, or carelessness? Or was there some hidden purpose she could not discern?

Annabelle reached for one of her pieces, hesitated, and withdrew her hand. It was just a game, she told herself. She was ascribing far too much importance to every move, as if some momentous prize hung in the balance. Nevertheless, she reconsidered her decision carefully before reaching out once again. She slid her queen forward and captured the pawn, experiencing a

thrill of satisfaction as the pieces clicked together,
ivory on onyx. Clasping the pawn in her palm, she
tested the weight of it before setting it carefully beside
the board.

As the week unfolded, it turned out that the one moment at the chessboard had been Annabelle's solitary
flicker of enjoyment. She had never felt this way before . . . not happy, nor sad, nor even worry-bitten
about the future. She was simply numb, her senses and
emotions dulled until she began to think she might
never care about anything again. The sense of detachment was so thorough that she sometimes had the
sense of standing outside herself, watching a mechani-
cal doll move stiffly through each day.

Lord Kendall partnered Annabelle with increasing
frequency . . . they danced together at a ball, sat side
by side at a musical evening, and walked through the
garden with Philippa meandering at a discreet distance
behind them. Kendall was pleasant, respectful, and
quietly charming. He was so tolerant, in fact, that
Annabelle began to think that when she and the wallflowers sprung their final trap on him, he might not
even resent it so terribly, being forced to marry a girl
he had inadvertently compromised. He would get used
to it eventually, and, being a philosophical man, he
would find some way to accept the situation.

As for Hodgeham, it was clear that Philippa was
managing to keep him away from Annabelle. Moreover, Philippa had somehow convinced him not to
carry out his threat to expose their secret to Lord
Kendall, though she would not discuss the details of
the conversation. Concerned about the effect that such
constant distress must be having on her mother,
Annabelle tentatively brought up the possibility of

leaving Stony Cross Park. However, Philippa would not hear of it. "I will manage Hodgeham," she said firmly. "You just continue on with Lord Kendall. It is clear to everyone that Kendall is taken with you."

If only Annabelle could obliterate the memory of the music room alcove from her mind . . . she dreamed of it with startling clarity and awoke in stewing torment, with the sheets tangled around her legs and her skin burning fever-hot. She was bedeviled by thoughts of Simon Hunt, the memory of his scent and warmth and his provoking kisses . . . the hardness of the body beneath the elegant black evening suit.

Despite the wallflowers' promise to tell each other everything about their romantic adventures, Annabelle could not bring herself to confide in any of them. What had happened with Hunt had been too private and too personal. It was not something to be scrutinized by eager friends who knew no more about men than she did. And had she tried to explain the experience to them, she knew they would not have understood. There were no words to describe such soul-stealing intimacy and the devastating confusion that had followed.

How in God's name could she feel this way about a man she had always despised? For two years she had dreaded seeing him at social events—she had considered him to be the most unpleasant companion imaginable. And now . . . and now . . .

Shoving aside the unwanted thoughts, Annabelle retreated to the Marsden parlor one day, hoping to divert her churning mind with some reading material. Under her arm, she carried a heavy tome inscribed with gilded letters on the front: *Royal Horticultural Society—Findings and Conclusions of Reports Submitted by Our Respected Members in the Year 1843*. The book was as heavy as an anvil, and Annabelle

wondered grimly how anyone could find so much to
say about plants. Setting the book on a small table,
Annabelle began to lower herself to the settee by the
window, when something about the chessboard in the
corner caught her attention. Was it her imagination,
or . . .

Eyes narrowing in curiosity, Annabelle strode to the
table and stared at the configuration of chessmen,
which had remained undisturbed all week long.
Yes . . . something was different. She had used her
queen to capture Simon's pawn. Now her queen had
been taken from the board, and set precisely to the side.

He's come back, she thought with a sudden blaze of
feeling that went all through her body. She felt certain
that Simon Hunt was the only one who would have
touched the chessboard. He was there, at Stony Cross.
Her face turned paper white except for the flags of
heat that scorched the crests of her cheeks. Realizing
that her reaction was all out of proportion, she struggled to calm herself. His return meant nothing—she
did not want him, could not have him, and must avoid
him at all cost. Closing her eyes, she breathed deeply
and concentrated on governing her pulse, willing her
rampaging heart to slow its recalcitrant beat.

When she had finally regained herself, she looked
down at the chessboard, trying to understand his last
move. How had he taken her queen? Rapidly she calculated the previous locations of the pieces. Then she
realized . . . he had lured her forward with the defensive pawn, positioning her perfectly for capture by his
rook. And with her queen having been eliminated, her
king was threatened and . . .

He had put her in check.

He had tricked her with that humble pawn, and she
was in jeopardy. Letting out an incredulous laugh,

Annabelle turned from the chess table and paced around the room. Defense strategies filled her head, and she tried to decide on the one he wouldn't expect. Obeying her instinct, she turned and headed back to the chessboard, smiling as she wondered what Hunt's reaction would be, once he discovered her counter-move. As her hand hovered over the board, however, the flood of warm excitement died away completely, and her face turned to stone. What was she doing? Continuing this game, maintaining even this fragile communication with him, was pointless. No . . . it was dangerous. There was no choice to be made between safety and disaster.

Annabelle's hand trembled a little as she reached for one chess piece after another, arranging them neatly in the box, methodically packing the game away. "I resign," she said aloud, her throat painfully tight. "I resign." She swallowed against the painful lump that the words engendered. She wasn't fool enough to allow herself to want something . . . someone . . . who was so obviously wrong for her. When the chess box was closed, she backed away from the table and stood looking at it for a moment. She felt faded and abruptly weary, but resolute.

Tonight. Her ambiguous courtship with Lord Kendall would have to be resolved this evening. The party was almost over, and now that Simon Hunt had returned, she couldn't afford to risk having everything ruined by another complication with him. Squaring her shoulder, she went to tell Lillian, and together they would come up with a plan. The evening would end with her betrothal to Lord Kendall.

Chapter 18

"The trick is all in the timing," Lillian said, her brown eyes gleaming with enjoyment. Surely no military officer had ever conducted a campaign with more determination than Lillian Bowman currently displayed. The four wallflowers sat together on the back terrace with glasses of cool, pulpy lemonade, giving every appearance of indolence, while in reality they were carefully plotting the evening to come.

"I'll suggest a nice before-supper walk through the garden to awaken our appetites," Lillian said to Annabelle, "and Daisy and Evie will agree, and we'll bring our mother and Aunt Florence and anyone else we happen to be talking with—and hopefully by the time we reach the clearing on the other side of the pear orchard, you will be seen *in flagrante delicto* with Lord Kendall."

"What is *flagrante delicto?*" Daisy asked. "It sounds illegal."

"I don't know, precisely," Lillian admitted. "I read

it in a novel . . . but I'm sure it's just the thing to get a girl compromised."

Annabelle responded with a halfhearted laugh, wishing that she could feel even a modicum of the Bowmans' enjoyment of the situation. A fortnight ago, she would have been beside herself with glee. But somehow it felt all wrong. There was no pleasurable anticipation in the prospect of *finally* prying a proposal out of a peer. No sense of excitement or relief, or anything remotely positive. It felt like an unpleasant duty that had to be done. She concealed her apprehensiveness while the Bowman sisters plotted and calculated with the expertise of seasoned conspirators.

However, it seemed that Evie, who was more observant than the rest of them put together, perceived the true emotions behind Annabelle's facade. "Is this what you w-want, Annabelle?" she asked softly, her blue eyes filled with concern. "You don't have to do this, you know. We'll find another suitor for you, if you don't want Kendall."

"There's no time to find another one," Annabelle whispered back. "No . . . it must be Kendall, and it has to be tonight, before . . ."

"Before?" Evie repeated, tilting her head as she regarded Annabelle with soft perplexity. The sun illuminated her scattered freckles, making them glint like gold dust on her velvety skin. "Before what?"

As Annabelle kept silent, Evie lowered her head and drew a fingertip along the edge of her glass, collecting fragments of sweetened pulp that had clung to the rim. The Bowman sisters were talking animatedly, debating the question of whether or not the pear orchard was the best place to waylay Kendall. Just as Annabelle thought that Evie would abandon the side conversation, the girl murmured softly, "Have you heard, Annabelle, that Mr. Hunt returned to Stony Cross late last night?"

"How do you know that?"

"Someone told my aunt."

Meeting Evie's perceptive gaze, Annabelle couldn't help thinking that woe befall anyone who ever made the mistake of underestimating Evangeline Jenner. "No, I hadn't heard," she murmured.

Tilting the glass of lemonade slightly, Evie stared into the depths of sugar-clouded liquid. "I wonder that he never took you up on your offer of a kiss," she said slowly. "After all the interest that he's sh-shown to you in the past . . ."

Their gazes met, and Annabelle felt her face redden. Her eyes implored Evie to say no more, and she shook her head quickly.

Understanding passed like a shadow over Evie's face. "Annabelle," she said slowly, "would you mind awfully if I didn't come along with the others to catch you with Lord Kendall tonight? There will be m-more than enough people to witness it. No doubt Lillian will bring an entire crowd of unsuspecting witnesses. I would be s-superfluous."

"Of course I wouldn't mind," Annabelle said, and asked with a sheepish smile, "Ethical reservations, Evie?"

"Oh, no, I'm not being hypocritical. I'm quite ready to admit guilt by association . . . and wh-whether or not I come to the garden tonight, I'm part of the group. It's just that . . ." She paused and continued quite softly. "I don't th-think you want Lord Kendall. Not as a man—not for what he truly is. And now after having come to know you a little better, I . . . I don't believe that marriage to him will make you happy."

"But it will," Annabelle argued, her tone sharpening until it had caught the Bowmans' attention. They stopped chattering and stared at her curiously. "No one could possibly come closer to my ideal than Lord Kendall."

"He's perfect for you," Lillian agreed firmly. "I hope you're not trying to sow seeds of doubt, Evie—it's far too late for that. We're hardly going to jettison a perfectly good plan now, when we've almost achieved victory."

Evie shook her head instantly, seeming to shrink in her chair. "No, no . . . I wasn't tr-trying to . . ." Her voice faded to a mumble, and she threw Annabelle an apologetic glance.

"Of course she wasn't," Annabelle said in Evie's defense, summoning a reckless smile. "Let's go over the plan once more, Lillian."

Lord Kendall reacted with amused complacency when Annabelle Peyton urged him to slip away with her for an early-evening walk through the garden. The air was soft with twilight, settling damply over the estate with no breeze to stir the thick atmosphere. With most of the guests dressing for dinner, or idling and fanning themselves in the card room and parlor, the outside grounds were mostly unoccupied. No man could be unaware of what a girl wanted when she suggested an unchaperoned walk in such circumstances. Apparently not adverse to the prospect of a stolen kiss or two, Kendall allowed Annabelle to coax him along the side of the terraced gardens and behind the drystone wall covered with climbing roses.

"I rather think we should have enlisted a chaperone," he said with a slight smile. "This is decidedly improper, Miss Peyton."

Annabelle flashed him a smile. "Steal away with me just for a moment," she urged. "No one will notice."

As he went with her willingly, Annabelle became aware of the growing weight of guilt that seemed to press on her from all sides. She felt as if she was leading a lamb to the slaughter. Kendall was a nice man—he didn't deserve to be tricked into a forced marriage. If only she had more time, she might have been able to let things progress naturally and pry a genuine proposal out of him. But this was the last weekend of the party, and it was imperative that she bring him up to scratch now. If she could just get this part of her plan over with, things would be so much easier from then on. *Annabelle, Lady Kendall* she reminded herself grimly. Annabelle, Lady Kendall...she could see herself as a respectable young matron who lived in the peaceful world of Hampshire society, taking occasional trips to London, welcoming her brother home from school on the holidays. Annabelle, Lady Kendall would have a half dozen fair-haired children, some of them endearingly fitted with spectacles like their father. And Annabelle, Lady Kendall would be a devoted wife who would spend the rest of her days trying to atone for the way she had deceived her husband into marrying her.

They reached the clearing beyond the pear orchard, where a stone table had been set in a graveled circle. Coming to a stop, Kendal looked down at Annabelle, who had leaned back against the edge of the stone table in a studied pose. He dared to touch a stray curl that had fallen to her shoulder, admiring the glints of gold in the pale brown strands. "Miss Peyton," he murmured, "by now it must be evident to you that I've developed a decided preference for your company."

Annabelle's heart had begun to hammer high in her

throat, until she thought she might choke on it. "I . . . I have found great pleasure in our conversations and walks together," she managed to say.

"How lovely you are," Kendall whispered, drawing closer to her. "I've never seen eyes so blue."

A month ago, Annabelle would have been over-joyed for this to happen. Kendall was a nice man, not to mention attractive, young, and wealthy, and *ti-tled* . . . oh, what the devil was wrong with her? Her entire being was suffused with reluctance as he bent over her flushing, tightening face. Agitated, bewildered, she tried to hold still for him. Before their lips could meet, however, she wrenched away with a muffled gasp and turned away from him.

Silence descended in the clearing.

"Have I frightened you?" came Kendall's inquiry. His manner was gentle and quiet . . . so different from Simon Hunt's arrogance.

"No . . . it's not that. It's just . . . I can't do this." Annabelle rubbed her suddenly aching forehead, her shoulders stiff amid the florid puffs of her peach silk gown. When she spoke again, her voice was heavy with defeat and self-disgust. "Forgive me, my lord. You are one of the nicest gentlemen I've ever had the privilege of knowing. Which is exactly why I must leave you now. It's not right for me to encourage your interest when nothing could come of it."

"Why do you think that?" he asked, openly confused.

"You don't really know me," Annabelle said with a bitter smile. "Take my word for it, we're an ill-matched pair. No matter how I tried, I wouldn't be able to keep from trampling you eventually—and you would be too much of a gentleman to object, and we would both be miserable."

"Miss Peyton," he murmured, trying to make sense of her outburst, "I can't begin to understand—"

"I'm not certain that I understand it, either. But I am sorry. I wish the best for you, my lord. And I wish . . ." Her breath came in irregular spurts, and she laughed suddenly. "Wishes are dangerous things, aren't they," she murmured, and left the clearing quickly.

Chapter 19

Railing at herself, Annabelle strode along the path that led back to the house. She couldn't believe it. Right when everything she wanted had been within her grasp, she had thrown it all away. "Stupid," she muttered to herself beneath her breath. "Stupid, stupid . . ." She couldn't begin to imagine what she should tell her friends after they arrived at the clearing only to find it empty. Perhaps Lord Kendall would remain where she had left him, looking like a horse whose feed bag had been yanked from his jaws before he had the chance to eat.

Annabelle vowed that she would not ask the other wallflowers to help her find another potential husband—not when she had just thrown away the opportunity that had been handed to her. She deserved whatever happened to her now. Her pace increased to a near run as she headed to her room. She was so intent on her frantic retreat that she nearly plowed into a man who was walking slowly along the path behind the drystone wall. Stopping suddenly, she murmured

"I beg your pardon," and would have rushed around him. However, his distinctive height and the sight of the large, tanned hands withdrawing from his coat pockets immediately betrayed his identity. Stunned, she staggered backward as Simon Hunt looked at her.

They regarded each other with identical blank stares. Having just run from Lord Kendall, Annabelle could hardly fail to note the differences between them. Hunt looked positively swarthy in the gathering dusk, big and potently masculine, with the eyes of a pirate and the casually ruthless air of a pagan king. He was no less arrogant than he had ever been . . . no tamer, no more refined . . . and yet somehow he had become the object of such all-consuming desire that Annabelle was certain she had lost her mind. The air around them felt charged, crackling with passion and conflict.

"What is it?" Hunt asked without preliminaries, his eyes narrowing at the sight of her tumult.

The task of distilling her emotions into a few coherent sentences was impossible. Nevertheless, Annabelle tried. "You left Stony Cross without a word to me."

His gaze was as hard and cold as ebony. "You put away the chess game."

"I . . ." She looked away from him, biting her lip. "I couldn't afford distractions."

"No one's distracting you now. You want Kendall?—Have at him."

"Oh, thank you," she said sarcastically. "It's so kind of you to step aside gracefully, now that you've ruined everything."

He glanced at her alertly. "Why do you say that?"

Annabelle felt absurdly cold in the swaddling of summer-warm evening air. A fine trembling began in her bones and rose upward through her skin. "The ankle boots I received when I was ill," she said recklessly, "the ones I'm wearing right now—they were from you, weren't they?"

"Does it matter?"

"*Admit it*," she insisted.

"Yes, they were from me," he said curtly. "What of it?"

"I was with Lord Kendall just a minute or two ago, and everything was going according to plan, and he was just about to . . . but I *couldn't*. I couldn't let him kiss me while I was wearing these blasted boots. No doubt he thinks that I'm deranged, after the way I left him. But you were right after all . . . he's far too nice for me. And it would have been a terrible match." She paused to inhale raggedly as she saw the sudden blaze in Hunt's eyes. His body was predatory in its alert stillness.

"So," he said softly, "now that you've thrown Kendall aside, what are your plans? Going back to Hodgeham?"

Goaded by the jeering question, Annabelle scowled. "If I do, it's no business of yours." She spun on her heel and began to walk away from him.

Hunt reached her in two strides. He whirled her around to face him, his hands closing around her upper arms. Giving her a soft shake, he bent his mouth to her ear. "No more games," he said. "Tell me what you want. Now, before I lose what's left of my patience."

The smell of him, soapy and fresh and wonderfully male, made Annabelle dizzy. She wanted to crawl inside his clothes . . . she wanted him to kiss her until she fainted. She wanted the despicable, arrogant, mesmerizing, devilishly handsome Simon Hunt. But oh, he would be merciless. Her threatened pride asserted itself, clotting in her throat until she could hardly speak. "I can't," she said gruffly.

Drawing his head back, Hunt gazed down at her, his

eyes glinting with wicked amusement. "You can have whatever you want, Annabelle . . . but only if you can bring yourself to ask for it."

"You're determined to humble me completely, aren't you? You won't allow me to retain one particle of dignity—"

"I, humble *you?*" He raised one brow in a sardonic slant. "After two years of receiving cuts and slights every time I asked you to dance—"

"Oh, all right," she said balefully, beginning to shake all over. "I'll admit it—I want you. There, are you satisfied? I want *you.*"

"In what capacity? Lover, or husband?"

Annabelle stared at him in shock. "What?"

His arms slid around her, holding her quivering frame securely against his. He said nothing, only watched her intently as she tried to grasp the implications of the question.

"But you're not the marrying kind," she managed to say weakly.

He touched her ear, his fingertip tracing the fragile outer curve. "I've discovered that I am when it comes to you."

The subtle caress set fire to her blood, making it difficult to think. "We would probably kill each other within the first month."

"Probably," Hunt conceded, his smiling mouth brushing over her temple. The warmth of his lips sent a rush of dizzying pleasure through her. "But marry me anyway, Annabelle. As I see things, it would solve most of your problems . . . and more than a few of mine." His big hand slid gently down her spine, calming her tremors. "Let me spoil you," he whispered. "Let me take care of you. You've never had anyone to lean on, have you? I've got strong shoulders,

Annabelle." A deep laugh rumbled in his chest. "And I may possibly be the only man of your acquaintance who'll be able to afford you."

She was too stunned to respond to the gibe. "But why?" she asked, as his hand traveled up to her unprotected nape. She gasped as his fingertip dipped softly into the shallow depression at the base of her skull. "Why offer to marry me when you might have me as your mistress?"

He nuzzled her throat gently. "Because I realized during the past few days that I can't leave doubt in anyone's mind about to whom you belong. Especially not yours."

Annabelle closed her eyes, her senses flooded with euphoria as his mouth wandered slowly up to her dry, parted lips. His hands and arms compressed her willing flesh into his demanding hardness. If there was mastery in the way he held her, there was also reverence, his fingertips discovering the most sensitive places on her exposed skin and teasing in whisper-light strokes. She let him coax her lips open, and she moaned at the gentle probe of his tongue. He ravished her with tender kisses that assuaged her need, yet made her desperately aware of empty places that longed to be filled. As Hunt felt the urgent quiver of her flesh against his, he soothed her with a long caress of his mouth, while his arms supported her body. Cradling her blood-hot cheek in his hand, he drew his thumb across the satin veneer of her lips. "Give me your answer," he whispered.

The warmth of his hand sent fine shivers across her skin, and she nestled her cheek deeper into his palm. "Yes," she said breathlessly.

Hunt's eyes gleamed with triumph. He tilted her head back and kissed her again, stealing deeper and deeper tastes. His palms clamped gently on either side of her head, altering the angle between them until their mouths fit together perfectly. The rhythm of her breath became capricious, and she was suddenly light-headed from the inrush of too much oxygen. Reaching for him, she clutched at the support of his hard-muscled body, her fingers digging into the broadcloth of his coat. Without breaking the kiss, Hunt helped her to hold on to him, reaching for her hand to draw it around his neck. When he was satisfied that her balance had been secured, he moved his hand to her corseted waist and applied light pressure to bring her body closer to his. He kissed her with rising urgency, until the potent influence of his mouth had reduced her to sensual delirium.

Eventually he took his mouth away and hushed her as she moaned in protest, telling her in a low murmur that they had company. Sleepy-eyed and bewildered, Annabelle peered out from the circle of his arms. They were confronted by a group of witnesses who could hardly avoid the sight of a couple embracing in the middle of the path by the drystone wall. Lillian . . . Daisy . . . their mother . . . Lady Olivia and her handsome American fiancé, Mr. Shaw . . . and, finally, none other than Lord Westcliff. "Oh, God," Annabelle said feelingly, and turned her face against Hunt's shoulder, as if closing her eyes would make them all disappear.

Her ear tingled as Hunt bent to murmur to her, his voice threaded with amusement. "Checkmate."

Lillian was the first to speak. "What in the world is going on, Annabelle?"

Cringing, Annabelle forced herself to meet her friend's gaze. "I couldn't go through with it," she said sheepishly. "I'm so sorry—the plan was such a good one, and you did your part beautifully—"

"And it would have been a great success if you hadn't been *kissing the wrong man*," Lillian exclaimed. "What in God's name happened? Why aren't you in the pear orchard with Lord Kendall?"

It was hardly the sort of thing that one wanted to articulate in front of a crowd. Annabelle hesitated and looked up at Hunt, who was watching her with a mocking smile, seeming fascinated to hear what explanation she might offer.

In the lengthening silence, Lord Westcliff appeared to have put two and two together, and he looked from Annabelle to Lillian with obvious disgust. "So this is why you were so insistent upon a walk. You two made an arrangement to trap Kendall!"

"I was part of it, too," Daisy asserted, determined to share in the blame.

Westcliff didn't appear to hear the comment, his gaze locked on Lillian's unrepentant face. "Good God—is there *nothing* you won't stoop to?"

"If there is," Lillian replied smartly, "I haven't discovered it yet."

Had her own circumstances not been quite so mortifying, Annabelle would have dissolved into laughter at the earl's expression.

Frowning, Lillian returned her attention to Annabelle. "It may not be too late to salvage things," she said. "We'll make everyone here promise to hold their tongues about having seen you and Mr. Hunt together. Without any witnesses, it hasn't happened."

Lord Westcliff considered the words with a scowl. "Much as I despise the prospect of agreeing with Miss Bowman," he said darkly, "I have to concur. The best thing for all concerned is for us to ignore this incident. Miss Peyton and Mr. Hunt have not been seen, and, therefore, no one has been compromised, which means that there will be no consequences to this unfortunate situation."

"Oh, yes, she *has* been compromised," Hunt said in sudden grim determination. "By me. And I don't want to avoid the consequences, Westcliff. I—"

"Yes, you do," the earl assured him authoritatively. "I'll be damned if I'll allow you to ruin your life over this creature, Hunt."

"Ruin his life?" Lillian repeated indignantly. "Mr. Hunt couldn't do better than to marry a girl like Annabelle! How dare you insinuate that she isn't good enough for him, when obviously he's the one who—"

"No," Annabelle interrupted anxiously. "Please, Lillian—"

"Excuse us," Mr. Shaw murmured with impeccable politeness, doing a poor job of concealing a grin. He pulled Lady Olivia's hand through the crook of his arm and executed a graceful bow in no particular direction. "I believe that my fiancée and I will excuse ourselves from the proceedings, being somewhat *de trop*. I think I can safely speak for the both of us when I say that we intend to be as deaf, dumb, and blind as a trio of Hong Tze monkeys." His blue eyes sparkled with good-natured humor. "We'll leave the rest of you to decide just what has been seen and heard tonight . . . or not. Come, darling." Drawing Lady Olivia away with him, he escorted her back toward the manor.

The earl turned to the Bowmans' mother, a tall woman with a narrow, foxlike face. She had worked her expression into one of righteous indignation, but had held her tongue out of a desire not to miss anything. As Daisy later explained ruefully, Mrs. Bowman never had her conniptions in the middle of an act, preferring to save them for intermission.

"Mrs. Bowman," Westcliff asked, "may I prevail on you to maintain your silence regarding this matter?"

Had the earl, or any other titled man within reach,

asked the ambitious Mrs. Bowman to jump headfirst into the flower bed for his amusement, she would have done so with a perfect somersault. "Oh, of course, my lord—I would *never* spread such distasteful gossip. My daughters are such sheltered innocents—it grieves me to see what their association with this . . . this unscrupulous girl has brought them to. I'm certain that a gentleman of your discernment can see that my two angels are completely blameless in this situation, having been led astray by the scheming young woman they sought to befriend."

Casting a skeptical glance at the two "angels," Westcliff replied coldly. "Quite."

Hunt, who had retained a possessive arm around Annabelle's waist, surveyed the lot of them coolly. "Do as you please. Miss Peyton is going to be compromised tonight, one way or another." He began to pull her along the path with him. "Come."

"Where are we going?" Annabelle asked, resisting his hold on her wrist.

"To the house. If they're not willing to be witnesses, then it seems I'll have to debauch you in front of someone else."

"Wait!" Annabelle squeaked. "I've already agreed to marry you! Why must I be compromised again?"

Hunt ignored the combined protests of Westcliff and the Bowmans as he replied succinctly. "Insurance."

Annabelle braced her heels, refusing to budge as he pulled at her arm. "You have no need of insurance! Do you think I would break my promise to you?"

"In a word, yes." Calmly, Hunt began to drag her along the path. "Now, where should we go? The entrance hall, I think. Plenty of people to witness you being ravished there. Or maybe the card room—"

"Simon," Annabelle protested, as she was hauled unceremoniously in his wake. "*Simon—*"

Her use of his name caused Hunt to stop suddenly, turning to look down at her with a curious half smile. "Yes, sweet?"

"For God's sake," Westcliff muttered, "let's save this for amateur theatrical night, shall we? If you're so bloody bent on having her, Hunt, then you may as well spare us all any further exhibitions. I'll gladly bear witness from here to London about your fiancée's besmirched honor, if only to have some peace around here. Just don't ask me to stand up with you at the wedding, as I have no desire to be a hypocrite."

"No, just an ass," came Lillian's murmur.

Low-spoken as the words were, it appeared that Westcliff had heard. His dark head whipped around, and he met Lillian's deliberately innocent expression with a threatening scowl. "As for you—"

"We're all agreed, then," Simon interrupted, preventing what surely would have evolved into a prolonged argument. He glanced at Annabelle with purely male satisfaction. "You've been compromised. Now let's go find your mother."

The earl shook his head, exhibiting a degree of frosty offense that could only be achieved by an aristocrat whose wishes had just been gainsaid. "I've never heard of a man being so eager to confess to the parent of a girl he's just ruined," he said sourly.

Chapter 20

*P*hilippa's reaction to the news was one of astonishing calmness. As the three of them sat in the Marsdens' private parlor, and Simon relayed the news of their betrothal, and the reason for it, Philippa's face turned white, but she made no sound. In the brief silence that followed Simon's spare recitation, Philippa regarded Simon with an unblinking stare, and spoke carefully. "As Annabelle has no father to protect her, Mr. Hunt, it falls to me to ask for certain reassurances from you. Every mother wishes for her daughter to be treated with respect and kindness . . . and you must agree that the circumstances . . ."

"I understand," Simon said. Struck by his soberness, Annabelle watched him intently, while he focused his attention completely on Philippa. "I give you my word that your daughter will have no cause for complaint."

A flicker of wariness crossed Philippa's face, and Annabelle chewed her inner lip, knowing what was coming next. "I suspect you are already aware, Mr.

Hunt," her mother murmured, "that Annabelle has no dowry."

"Yes," Simon replied matter-of-factly.

"And it makes no difference to you," Philippa said with a questioning lilt in her voice.

"None whatsoever. I am fortunate in being able to set aside financial considerations in the matter of choosing a wife. I don't give a damn if Annabelle comes to me without a shilling to her name. Moreover, I intend to make things easier for your family—assuming debts, taking care of bills and creditors, school tuition and the like—whatever is required to see that you're comfortably settled."

Annabelle saw Philippa's hands tighten in her lap until her fingers were white, and an unfathomable tremor of what could have been excitement, relief, embarrassment, or some combination of the three, shook her voice. "Thank you, Mr. Hunt. You understand, if Mr. Peyton was still with us, things would be much different—"

"Yes, of course."

There was a contemplative silence before Philippa murmured, "Of course, without a dowry, Annabelle will have no source of pin money . . ."

"I'll open an account for her at Barings," Hunt said equably. "We'll start it at, say, five thousand pounds? . . . and I'll refresh the balance from time to time as necessary. Of course, I'll be responsible for the maintenance of a carriage and horses . . . clothes . . . jewelry . . . and Annabelle may have credit at every shop in London."

Philippa's reaction to the news was lost on Annabelle, whose mind spun like a top. The thought of having five thousand pounds at her disposal . . . a fortune . . . it scarcely seemed real. Her amazement was tinged with a tingle of anticipation. After years of deprivation, she would be able to go to the best modistes, and buy a horse for Jeremy, and refurbish her family's home with the most luxurious furniture and fittings. However, this blunt discussion of money coming on the heels of a marriage proposal gave Annabelle the disquieting feeling of having sold herself for profit. Glancing cautiously at Simon, she saw that a familiar taunting gleam had entered his eyes. He understood her far too well, she thought, while unwanted heat climbed up her cheeks.

Annabelle kept silent as the conversation touched upon lawyers, contracts, and stipulations, discovering that her mother had the persistence of a bull terrier when it came to marriage negotiations. The businesslike discussion was hardly the stuff of high romance. Furthermore, it did not escape Annabelle that Philippa had not asked Hunt if he loved Annabelle, nor had he claimed to.

After Simon Hunt had left, Annabelle followed her mother to their room, where they would undoubtedly talk some more. Worried by Philippa's unnatural quietness, Annabelle closed the door and considered what to say to her, wondering if she had reservations about the prospect of Simon Hunt as a son-in-law.

As soon as they were alone, Philippa went to the window and looked outside at the evening sky, then covered her eyes with one hand. Alarmed, Annabelle heard the sound of a muffled sob. "Mama . . ." she said hesitantly as she stared at her mother's rigid back, "I'm sorry, I—"

"Thank God," Philippa murmured unsteadily, not seeming to hear her. "Thank God."

Despite Lord Westcliff's vow that he would not stand up with Simon at the wedding, he came to London in a fortnight to attend the ceremony. Grim-faced but polite, he even offered to give Annabelle away, assum-

ing the place of her deceased father. She was strongly
tempted to turn him down, but the offer had made
Philippa so happy that Annabelle was forced to accept. And she even took a certain spiteful pleasure in
obliging the earl to take a significant part in a ceremony that he so obviously opposed. Only Westcliff's
loyalty to Hunt had brought him to London, revealing
a bond of friendship between the two men that was far
stronger than Annabelle would have guessed.

Lillian, Daisy, and their mother were also present at
the private church ceremony, their presence made possible only by Lord Westcliff's presence. Mrs. Bowman
would never have allowed her daughters to attend the
wedding of a girl who was marrying outside the peerage
and was a bad influence to boot. However, any opportunity to be in the proximity of the most eligible bachelor
in England was to be seized on. The fact that Westcliff
was completely indifferent to her younger daughter, and
actively disdainful of the elder, was a minor hindrance
that Mrs. Bowman was certain could be overcome.

Evie, unfortunately, had been forbidden to attend
by her aunt Florence and the rest of her mother's family. Instead, she had sent Annabelle a long, affectionate letter, and a Sèvres china tea service painted with
pink-and-gold flowers as a wedding gift. The rest of
the small congregation consisted of Hunt's parents
and siblings, who were more or less what Annabelle
had expected. His mother was coarse-faced and stout
of build, a genial woman who seemed inclined to
think well of Annabelle until something happened to
persuade her otherwise. His father was a big, angular
man who did not smile once through the ceremony,
though the deep laugh lines at the corners of his eyes
indicated that he was a man of pleasant disposition.
Neither of the parents was particularly handsome, but

they had produced five striking children, all tall and black-haired.

If only Jeremy could have attended the wedding . . . but he was still at school, and she and Philippa had decided that it would be best for him to finish the term and come to London when Hunt and Annabelle had returned from their honeymoon. Annabelle wasn't quite certain what Jeremy's reaction would be to the prospect of having Simon Hunt as a brother-in-law. Although Jeremy had seemed to like him, Jeremy had long been accustomed to being the only male in the family. There was every chance that he would chafe at any restrictions that Hunt might impose on him. For that matter, Annabelle herself wasn't terribly fond of the prospect of kowtowing to the wishes of a man whom, in all honesty, she didn't know that well.

That fact was forcibly brought home to Annabelle on her wedding night, as she waited for her new husband in a room at the Rutledge Hotel. Having assumed that Hunt resided at a private terrace house like many bachelors, Annabelle had been more than a little surprised to discover that he lived in a suite of hotel rooms.

"Why not?" Hunt had asked a few days earlier, amused by her open perplexity.

"Well . . . living in a hotel affords one so little privacy . . ."

"I beg to differ. I'm able to come and go as I please, without a horde of servants to gossip over my every habit and gesture. From what I've seen, life in a well-run hotel is far preferable to taking up residence in a drafty town mansion."

"Yes, but a man of your position must have enough servants to demonstrate his success to others—"

"Forgive me," Hunt had said, "but I always thought one hired servants if they were actually needed to work. The benefit of displaying employees as stylish accessories has always escaped me until now."

"They're hardly slave labor, Simon!"

"At the rate most servants are paid, that's an arguable point."

"We will need to hire a great deal of help if we're ever to live in a proper house," Annabelle had said pertly. "Unless you plan to have me on my hands and knees, scrubbing the floors and cleaning the grates?"

The suggestion had caused Hunt's coffee black eyes to glint with a wicked humor that escaped her. "I plan to have you on your hands and knees, my sweet, but I can guarantee that you won't be scrubbing." He had laughed softly as he saw her bewilderment. Gathering her close, he had crushed a brief kiss to her lips.

She had strained a little in his embrace. "Simon . . . do let go . . . my mother won't approve if she sees us like this—"

"Oh? I could do whatever I want with you now, and she wouldn't offer a single objection."

Frowning, Annabelle had wedged her arms between them. "Oh, you arrogant—no, I mean it, Simon! I want this settled . . . must we live in a hotel forever, or will you buy a house for us?"

Stealing another quick kiss, he had laughed at her expression. "I'll buy any house you like, sweet. Better yet, I'll build you a new one, as I've gotten rather accustomed to the comforts of good lighting and modern plumbing."

Annabelle had stopped squirming. "Really? Where?"

"I suspect we could get a fair amount of acreage near Bloomsbury, or Knightsbridge—"

"What about Mayfair?"

Simon had smiled as if he had been expecting such a suggestion. "Don't tell me you want to live in some overbuilt square like Grosvenor or St. James, staring out the window at pompous aristocrats waddling through their little iron-fenced yards—"

"Oh, yes, that would be *perfect*," she had enthused, making him laugh.

"All right, we'll get something in Mayfair, God help me. And you can hire as many servants as you want. Notice that I didn't say 'need,' as that seems to be completely beside the point. In the meantime, do you think you could tolerate a few months at the Rutledge?"

Recalling the conversation, Annabelle investigated their large suite of rooms, all luxuriously appointed in velvet and leather and gleaming mahogany. She had to admit, the Rutledge certainly changed one's perceptions about what a hotel could be. It was said that the mysterious owner, Mr. Harry Rutledge, aspired to create the most elegant and modern hotel in Europe, combining Continental style with American innovations. The Rutledge was a massive building located in the theater district, occupying five blocks between the Capitol Theater and the Embankment. Features such as fireproof construction, food service lifts, and a private bathroom for every suite, not to mention a renowned restaurant, had made the Rutledge a favorite haunt of wealthy Americans and Europeans. To Annabelle's delight, the Bowmans occupied five of the hotel's one hundred luxury suites, which meant that she, Lillian, and Daisy would have frequent opportunities to see each other after she returned from the honeymoon.

Having never traveled outside of England in her life, Annabelle had been excited to discover that Simon intended to take her to Paris for a fortnight. Supplied with a list of dressmakers, milliners, and perfumers from the Bowmans, who had once visited Paris with their mother, Annabelle eagerly anticipated her first glimpse of the City of Light. However, before their departure on the morrow, there was still the wedding night to get through.

Dressed in a nightgown trimmed with lavish falls of white lace from the bodice and sleeves, Annabelle paced restlessly around the suite. She sat beside the bed and picked up a hairbrush from the night table. Methodically, she began to brush her hair as she wondered if all brides felt this apprehensive, uncertain as to whether the next few hours were something to dread or enjoy. At that moment, the key turned in the door, and Simon's dark, lean form entered the private suite.

A nervous thrill went down Annabelle's spine, and she forced herself to continue brushing her hair with calm strokes, though her grip was too tight on the handle, and her fingers were shaking. Simon's gaze wandered over the drifts of lace and muslin that covered her body. Still dressed in his formal black wedding suit, he approached her slowly and came to stand before her as she remained sitting in the chair. To her surprise, he lowered to his knees to bring their faces level, his thighs bracketing her slender calves. A large hand lifted to the shimmering fall of her hair, and he combed his fingers through it, watching with fascination as the golden brown strands slipped across his knuckles.

Although Simon was immaculately dressed, there were signs of dishevelment that lured her attention . . . the short forelocks of his hair falling over his forehead, the loosened knot of his ice gray silk cravat. Dropping the brush to the floor, Annabelle used her fingers to smooth his hair in a tentative stroke. The sable filaments were thick and gleaming, springing willfully against her fingertips. Simon held still for her as she untied the cravat, the heavy silk saturated with the warmth of his skin. His eyes contained an expression that caused a ticklish sensation in the pit of her stomach.

"Every time I see you," he murmured, "I think you couldn't possibly become any more beautiful—and you always prove me wrong."

Letting the cravat hang on either side of his neck, Annabelle smiled at the compliment. She jumped a little in her seat as she felt his hand close around hers. His mouth curved slightly as he gave her a quizzical glance. "You're nervous?"

Annabelle nodded, her fingers unresisting in his as he held and chafed them gently. Simon spoke quietly, seeming to choose his words with unusual care. "Sweetheart . . . I assume that your experiences with Lord Hodgeham were not pleasant. But I hope you'll trust me when I say that it doesn't have to be like that. Whatever your fears are—"

"Simon," she interrupted with an apprehensive croak, and cleared her throat. "That is very kind of you. A-And the fact that you are prepared to be so understanding about it . . . well . . . I appreciate that. But . . . I'm afraid I wasn't entirely forthcoming about my relationship with Hodgeham." Seeing his sudden curious stillness, and the way his expression had been wiped clean of emotion, Annabelle took a deep, steadying breath. "The truth is, Hodgeham did indeed come to our house some evenings, and he did pay some of our bills in return for . . . for . . ." Pausing, she felt her throat contract until it was hard to force the words through. "But . . . I wasn't actually the one that he was visiting."

Simon's dark eyes widened slightly. "What?"

"I never slept with him," she admitted. "His arrangement was with my mother."

He stared at her, dumbfounded. "Holy hell," he breathed.

"It started a year ago," she said, her voice edged with defensiveness. "Our circumstances were desperate. We had endless bills and no means to pay them. The income from my mother's jointure had dwindled because it had been invested badly. Lord Hodgeham had been sniffing at my mother's heels for some time . . . I don't know precisely when his evening visits began . . . but I saw his hat and cane in the entrance hall at odd hours, and the debts eased a little. I realized what was happening, but I never said anything about it. And I should have." She sighed and rubbed her temples. "At the party, Hodgeham made it clear that he had tired of my mother and wanted me to take her place. He threatened to expose the whole secret . . . 'with embellishments,' he said . . . and we would be ruined. I refused him, but somehow my mother managed to keep him quiet."

"Why did you let me think that *you* were sleeping with him?"

Annabelle shrugged uncomfortably. "You just assumed so . . . and there didn't seem to be any reason to correct you, as I certainly never thought that we would end up like this. And then you proposed to me anyway, which led me to conclude that it wasn't especially important to you whether or not I was a virgin."

"It wasn't," Simon murmured, his voice sounding strange. "I wanted you regardless. But now that I . . ." He broke off and shook his head in amazement. "Annabelle—just to be clear—are you saying that you've never been to bed with a man before?"

She tugged at her hands, for his grip had become crushingly tight. "Well . . . yes."

"Yes, you have, or no, you haven't?"

"I have never slept with anyone," Annabelle said

precisely, and gave him a questioning glance. "Are you annoyed because I didn't tell you earlier? I'm sorry. But it's not the sort of thing one can just blurt out over tea, or in the entrance hall . . . 'Here's your hat, and by the way, I'm a virgin'—"

"I'm not annoyed." Simon's gaze traveled over her pensively. "I'm just wondering what the hell to do with you now."

"The same thing you were going to do before I told you?" she asked hopefully.

Simon stood and pulled her to her feet and embraced her rather gingerly, as if he feared she might shatter with too much pressure. He pressed his face into the shining fall of her hair and breathed deeply. "Believe me, I'll get around to it," he said, sounding bemused. "But first it seems there are a few things I need to ask you."

Annabelle pushed her arms inside the front of his coat and slid them around his hard, sleek torso. The heat of his body had permeated the thin fabric of his shirt, and she shivered pleasantly as she delved into the male-scented warmth of his embrace. "Yes?" she prompted.

Until that moment she had never witnessed Simon being less than fully articulate . . . but he spoke with exceptional hesitancy, as if this was a kind of discussion he'd never been obliged to have before. "Do you know what to expect? Do you have all the . . . er, necessary information?"

"I think so," Annabelle replied, smiling at the interesting discovery that his heart was beating very fast against her cheek. "My mother and I had a talk just a little while ago—after which I was strongly tempted to ask for an annulment."

Suddenly, he gave a muffled laugh. "I'd better claim my husbandly rights without delay, then." Taking her fingers in his hot, light grip, he lifted them to his mouth. The touch of his breath was like steam. "What did she tell you?" he murmured against her fingertips.

"After imparting the basic facts, she said that I should let you do as you wished and try not to complain if I didn't like something. And she suggested that if it becomes too unpleasant, I should turn my mind to thoughts of that enormous bank account that you opened for me."

Annabelle regretted the words as soon as they left her lips, expecting that Simon might be offended by such candor. But he had begun to laugh huskily.

"That's a refreshing change from thinking of England." He drew his head back to look at her. "Shall I woo you with whispers of balance transfers and rates of interest, then?"

Turning her hand in his, Annabelle let her fingertips graze the surface of his lips, lingering at the velvety edge, then drifting down to the masculine scrape of his chin. "That won't be necessary. Just say the usual things."

"No . . . the usual things won't do for you." Simon tucked a loose lock of hair behind her ear and cupped her cheek in his palm as he leaned forward. His mouth teased hers into yielding openness, while his hands found the outline of her body within the ample billows of lace. With no corset to constrict her ribs, she could feel his touch through the thin veil of her gown. The stroke of his hands along her unbound sides caused her to quiver, the tips of her breasts turning exquisitely sensitive. His palm traveled slowly over her front, finding the pliant weight of one breast, and he made a gentle cup of his fingers, lifting the vulnerable flesh. Her breath halted momentarily as his thumb nudged her nipple into delicately aching distension.

"It's usually painful for a woman, the first time," he murmured.

"Yes, I know."

"I don't want to hurt you."

The admission touched and surprised her. "My mother says it doesn't last for long," she said.

"The pain?"

"No, the rest of it," she said, and for some reason that made him laugh again.

"Annabelle . . ." His mouth drifted along her throat. "I've wanted you since the first moment I saw you standing outside that panorama, digging for coins in your purse. I couldn't take my eyes from you. I could hardly believe you were real."

"You stared at me for the entire show," she said, gasping a little as he nibbled at the silken lobe of her ear. "I doubt you learned a single thing about the fall of the Roman Empire."

"I learned that you have the softest lips I've ever kissed."

"You have a novel way of introducing yourself."

"I couldn't help it." His hand skimmed gently up and down her side. "Standing next to you in the darkness was the most unholy temptation I'd ever experienced. All I could think about was how adorable you were and how much I wanted you. When the lights went out completely, I couldn't stand it any longer." A note of masculine smugness entered his voice as he added, "And you didn't push me away."

"I was too surprised!"

"That was the reason you didn't object?"

"No," Annabelle admitted, tilting her face so that her cheek brushed against his. "I liked your kiss. You know that I did."

He smiled at that. "I had hoped it wasn't all one-sided." He looked into her eyes, their faces so close that their noses were nearly touching. "Come to bed with me," he whispered, a nearly imperceptible question in his voice.

She nodded with a shaky sigh and let him lead her to the large four-poster bed, covered with a counterpane made of heavy quilted burgundy silk. Drawing back the covers, Simon lifted Annabelle onto the slick-pressed linens, and she slid over to make room for him. He stood by the bed, watching her face as he removed the rest of his formal clothes. The contrast between the neatly tailored garments, so eminently civilized, and the raw masculine power of the body beneath, was disconcerting. As Annabelle had expected, he possessed an unusually muscular torso, his back and shoulders rippling, his stomach tightly corrugated. His swarthy skin was tinted amber-gold in the lamplight, the surface of his shoulders gleaming as rich and taut as freshly cast metal. Even the dark fleece that covered his chest could not soften the powerful vaulting of flesh and bone. Annabelle doubted that a healthier, more vigorous-looking man could be found anywhere. Perhaps he didn't match the fashionable ideal of a pale, slender-framed aristocrat . . . but Annabelle thought he was altogether splendid.

Pangs of excited apprehension went through her stomach as he joined her on the bed. "Simon," she said, breathing fast as he took her into his arms, "my mother didn't tell me if . . . if tonight there was something that I should do for you . . ."

His hand began to play in her hair, his fingers drifting over her scalp in a way that sent hot tingles down her spine. "You don't have to do anything tonight. Just let me hold you . . . touch you . . . discover some of the things that please you . . ."

His hand found the placket of mother-of-pearl buttons at the back of her gown. Annabelle closed her eyes as she felt the frothy mass of ruffled lace loosening over her shoulders. "Do you remember that night in the music room?" she whispered, gasping as she felt him ease the gown from her breasts. "When you kissed me in the alcove?"

"Every blistering second," he whispered back, pulling her arms from the billowing sleeves. "Why do you mention it?"

"I couldn't stop thinking about it," she confessed. She wriggled to help him strip the gown away from her body, a blush covering every inch of exposed skin.

"Neither could I," he admitted. His hand slid over her breast, cupping the cool roundness until the peak was rosy and hard in his palm. "We seem to be a flammable combination—even more so than I had expected."

"It's not always like this, then?" she asked, letting her fingers explore the deep groove of his spine and the tough-knit muscle on either side of it.

Her touch, simple as it was, disrupted the rhythm of his breath as he leaned over her. "No," he murmured, resting one long leg against the seam of her tightly cinched thighs. "Hardly ever."

"Why—" she began to question him, but stopped with a faint moan as he traced the satiny undercurve of her breast with the edge of his thumb. Containing her narrow rib cage in his hands, he bent over her chest. His lips were hot and light as they opened gently over a tightly budded nipple. She let out a gasping cry at the tender tugs of his mouth, his tongue flicking her sensitive flesh until she could no longer remain still beneath him. Her legs parted involuntarily, and immediately he filled the space with his own hair-roughened thigh. As his hands and mouth wandered slowly over her body, Annabelle lifted her hands to his head, letting the thick waves slip through her fingers as she had so often longed to do. He kissed the fragile skin of her

wrists, and the insides of her elbows, and the shallow
depressions between her ribs, leaving no part of her
unexplored. She let him do as he wished, quivering as
she felt the prickle of his night beard contrasting with
the silky wet heat of his mouth. But when he reached
her navel, and she felt the slick point of his tongue enter the little hollow, she rolled away from him with a
shocked inhalation. "No . . . Simon, I . . . *please* . . ."

Immediately he levered upward to gather her in his
arms, smiling into her scarlet face. "Too much?" he
asked huskily. "I'm sorry—for a moment I forgot that
it's new to you. Here, let me hold you. You're not
frightened, are you?"

Before she could answer, his mouth had settled on
hers, dragging gently back and forth. The hair on his
chest abraded her breasts like coarse velvet, her nipples rubbing against him with each breath she took.
Her throat vibrated with low sounds, evincing the
pleasure that had escaped her crumbling restraint. She
gasped sharply as his fingers drifted over her stomach
and his knee intruded more deeply between hers.
Widening the angle between her thighs, he slipped his
fingers into the soft feminine curls, exploring her
swollen flesh. He parted her, found the silken peak
that throbbed at his touch, and stroked just above it
with sweet, dancing lightness.

She gasped against his mouth, her flesh heating into
melting pliancy. A passion-blush covered her skin,
dappling the paleness with rosy stains. Simon sought
the opening of her body, his gentle fingertip insinuating
carefully into the fluid-drenched suppleness. Her heart
pounded, and all her limbs stiffened against the height-
ening pleasure. Rolling away from him with a muffled
exclamation, she stared at Simon with wide eyes.

He lay on his side, raised on one elbow, his dark hair disheveled and his gaze bright with passion and subtle amusement. It seemed as if he understood what had begun to happen inside her and was fascinated by her innocent consternation. "Don't go anywhere," he murmured, smiling. "You don't want to miss the best part." Slowly, he pulled her back beneath him, arranging her body with caressing hands. "Sweetheart, I won't hurt you," he whispered against her cheek. "Let me pleasure you . . . let me inside you . . ."

He continued to murmur to her, while he kissed and caressed his way stealthily down her body. By the time his dark head reached the shadowy ingress between her thighs, Annabelle was moaning repeatedly. His mouth found her, nuzzling past delicately crinkled hair and tiny silken ruffles of pink flesh, his tongue gliding over her in curling strokes. She shrank from him bashfully, but he gripped her hips in his hands and explored her mercilessly, the tip of his tongue gliding over every tender fold and crevice. The sight of his dark head between her thighs was a visceral jolt to her senses. The room around them blurred, and she felt as if she was floating amid layers of shadow and candlelight, conscious of nothing but exquisite, twisting rapture. She could hide nothing from him, could do nothing except surrender to the demanding mouth that solicited unholy delight from her awakening flesh. He centered on the peak of her sex, licking softly, steadily, until it finally became too much to endure, and she felt her hips rise of their own accord, quivering against his mouth, heat jetting through her pleasure-racked limbs.

Giving her sated flesh a last savoring lick, Simon worked his way back up her body. Her thighs were limp as he pushed them wide apart, the head of his shaft nudging against her. Looking down into her dazed face, Simon smoothed her hair back from her forehead.

Her lips curved in a wobbly smile as she glanced up at him. "I forgot all about my bank account," she said, and he laughed softly.

His thumb brushed over the edge of her forehead, where fine skin blended into flossy hair. "Poor Annabelle . . ." The pressure between her legs increased, delivering the first intimation of pain. "I'm afraid the next part won't be nearly as enjoyable. For you, at any rate."

"I don't mind . . . I . . . I'm just so glad that it's you."

No doubt it was an odd thing for a bride to say on her wedding night, but it brought a smile to his lips. He lowered his head and began to whisper in her ear, even as he tightened his hips to breach her untried flesh. She forced herself to hold still despite the instinct to writhe away from the intrusion. "Sweetheart . . ." His breath became ragged, and as he paused inside her, he seemed to struggle for self-control. "Yes, that's it . . . just a little more . . ." He moved in another careful advance, and hesitated again. "A little more . . ." He deepened his entry in lingering degrees, carefully courting her body into accepting him. "More . . ."

"How much more?" she gasped. He was too hard, the pressure too intense, and she wondered anxiously how this could ever be anything but uncomfortable.

Simon gritted his teeth at the effort it took to hold still. "I'm about halfway there," he finally managed, an apologetic note in his voice.

"*Half*—" Annabelle began to protest with a shaky laugh, and winced as he pushed again. "Oh, this is impossible, I can't, I can't—"

But he kept impelling himself deeper, trying to soothe her pain with his mouth and hands. Gradually it became easier, the pain fading into a mild, prolonged burn. A long sigh escaped her as she felt her body yielding, her virginal flesh conceding to the inevitability of his possession. Simon's back was a mass of tightly cobbled muscle, his belly as hard as carved rosewood. Holding himself deep inside her, he groaned, while a shiver ran across his shoulders. "You're so tight," he said hoarsely.

"I-I'm sorry—"

"No, no," he managed. "Don't be sorry. My God." His voice was slurred, as if he was drunk on pleasure.

They studied each other, one gaze sated, the other brilliant with yearning. A sense of wonder crept over Annabelle as she realized how thoroughly he had controverted her expectations. She had been so certain that Simon would use this opportunity to prove himself her master . . . and instead he had come to her with infinite patience. Filled with gratitude, she wrapped her arms around his neck. She kissed him and let her tongue enter his mouth, and she drew her hands down his back, until her palms reached the hard contours of his buttocks. She stroked him in shy encouragement, urging him to sink deeper inside her. The caress seemed to eradicate the remainder of his self-control. With a growl of hunger, he pushed rhythmically inside her, shaking with the effort to be gentle. The force of his release caused him to shiver hard, his teeth gritting as sensation culminated in blinding rapture. Burying his face in the filtering strands of her hair, he soaked in her honey-slick warmth. A long time passed before the iron-hard tension left his muscles, and he let out a slow breath. As he withdrew carefully from Annabelle's body, she winced at the intimate soreness. Perceiving her discomfort, he caressed her hip in gentle consolation.

"I may never leave this bed again," he muttered, cuddling her in the crook of his arm.

"Oh, yes you will," Annabelle said, half-drowsing. "You're going to take me to Paris tomorrow. I won't be deprived of the honeymoon you promised."

Nuzzling into her tangled curls, Simon replied with the trace of a smile in his voice. "No, sweet wife . . . you won't be deprived in any way."

Chapter 21

During the two weeks of their honeymoon, Annabelle discovered that she was not nearly as worldly as she had considered herself to be. With a mixture of naïveté and British arrogance, she had always thought of London as the center of all culture and knowledge, but Paris was a revelation. The city was astonishingly modern, making London look like a dowdy country cousin. And yet for all its intellectual and social advancements, the streets of Paris were nearly medieval in appearance; dark, narrow and crooked as they twined through arrondissements of artfully shaped buildings. It was a messy, delightful assault to the senses, with architecture that ranged from the gothic spires of ancient churches to the solid grandeur of the Arc de Triomphe.

Their hotel, the *Coeur de Paris*, was located on the left bank of the Seine, between a dazzling array of shops on rue de Montparnasse and the covered markets of Saint-Germain-des-Pres, where exotic produce and fabrics and laces and art and perfume were displayed in bewildering varieties. The *Coeur de Paris* was a palace, with suites of rooms that had been designed for sensual pleasure. The bathing room, for example—the *salle de bain*, it was called—had been fitted with a rosy marble floor and Italian tiled walls, and a gilded rococo settee where the bather rested after the exertions of washing. There was not one but two porcelain tubs, each with its own boiler and cold water tank. The tubs were surmounted with a painted oval landscape on the ceiling, designed to entertain the bather as he or she relaxed. Having been brought up with the British view of a bath as a matter of hygiene to be conducted with expediency, Annabelle was amused by the notion that the act of bathing should be a decadent entertainment.

To Annabelle's delight, a man and a woman could share a table in a public restaurant without having to request a private dining room. She had never had such delicious food . . . tender cockerel that had been simmered with tiny onions in red wine . . . duck confit expertly roasted until it was melting-soft beneath crisp oiled skin . . . rascasse fish served in thick truffled sauce . . . then, of course, there were the desserts . . . thick slices of cake soaked in liqueur and heaped with meringue, and puddings layered with nuts and glacéed fruit. As Simon witnessed Annabelle's agonized choice of what to order for dessert each night, he assured her gravely that generals had gone to war with far less deliberation than she gave to the choice between the pear tart or the vanilla soufflé.

One night Simon took her to a ballet with scandalously underdressed dancers, and the next, a comedy with lewd jokes that needed no translation. They also attended balls and soirees given by acquaintances of Simon's. Some were French citizens, while others were tourists and émigrés from Britain, America, and Italy. A few were stockholders or board members of companies that he had part ownership in, while others had been involved with his shipping or railway enterprises. "How do you know so many people?" Annabelle had asked Simon in bewilderment, when he was hailed by several strangers at the first party they attended.

Simon had laughed and gently mocked that one would think that she had never realized that there was a world outside of the British aristocracy. And the truth was, she hadn't. She had never thought to look outside the narrow confines of that rarefied society until now. These men, like Simon, were elite in a purely economic sense, actively engaged in building fortunes, many of them literally owning entire towns that had been built around rapidly expanding industries. They possessed mines, plantations, mills, warehouses, stores, and factories; and it seemed that their interests were seldom confined to just one country. While their wives shopped and had gowns made by Parisian dressmakers, the men lounged in cafes or private salons for endless discussions of business and politics. Many of them smoked tobacco in tiny paper tubes called cigarettes, a fashion that had started among Egyptian soldiers and had spread rapidly across the Continent. At dinner, they spoke of things that had never been mentioned in front of Annabelle before, events that she had never heard of and had surely not been reported in the papers.

Annabelle realized that when her husband spoke, the other men paid keen attention to his opinions and sought his advice on a variety of matters. Perhaps Simon was someone of little consequence in the view of the British aristocracy, but it was clear that he wielded considerable influence outside of it. Now she understood why Lord Westcliff held him in such high esteem. The fact was, Simon was a powerful man in his own right. Seeing the respect that others paid him, and noticing the coquettish excitement that he inspired in other women, Annabelle began to see her husband in an altered light. She even began to feel somewhat possessive of him—of Simon!—and found herself beginning to simmer with jealousy when a woman seated next to him at supper tried to monopolize his attention, or when another lady declared flirtatiously that Simon was obligated to partner her for a waltz.

At the first ball they attended, Annabelle stood in an anterior parlor with a group of sophisticated young matrons, one of them the wife of an American munitions maker, the other two Frenchwomen whose husbands were art dealers. Awkwardly fielding their questions about Simon and reluctant to admit how little she still knew about her husband, Annabelle was somewhat relieved when the subject of their conversation appeared to claim her for a dance. Impeccably dressed in a black evening suit, Simon exchanged polite greetings with the laughing, blushing women, and turned to Annabelle. Their gazes locked, while a lovely melody began to play from the nearby ballroom. Annabelle recognized the music . . . a popular waltz in London, which was so haunting and sweet that the wallflowers had agreed that it was literally torture to sit still in a chair while it was being played.

Simon extended his arm, and Annabelle took it, remembering the countless times in the past that she had spurned his invitations to dance. Reflecting that Simon had finally gotten his way, Annabelle smiled. "Do you always succeed at getting what you want?" she asked.

"Sometimes it takes longer than I would prefer," he said. As they entered the ballroom, he put his hand on Annabelle's waist and guided her to the edge of the swirling mass of dancers.

She experienced a pang of giddy nervousness, as if they were about to share something far more significant than a mere dance. "This is my favorite waltz," she told him, moving into his arms.

"I know. That's why I requested it."

"How did you know?" she asked with an incredulous laugh. "I suppose one of the Bowman sisters told you?"

Simon shook his head, while his gloved fingers curved around hers. "On more than one occasion, I saw your face when they played it. You always looked ready to fly out of your chair."

Annabelle's lips parted in surprise, and she stared up at him with a wondering gaze. How could he have noticed something so subtle? She had always been so dismissive of him, and yet he had noticed her reaction to a particular piece of music and remembered it. The realization brought the sting of tears to her eyes, and she looked away immediately, fighting to bring the sudden baffling swell of emotion under control.

Simon drew her into the current of waltzing couples, his arms strong, the hand at her back offering firm pressure and guidance. It was so easy to follow him, to let her body relax into the rhythm he established while her skirts swept across the gleaming floor and whipped lightly around his legs. The enchanting melody seemed to penetrate every part of her, dissolving the ache in her throat and filling her with unruly delight.

Simon, for his part, was not above a sense of triumph as he guided Annabelle across the floor. Finally, after two years of pursuit, he was having his long-sought waltz with her. And more satisfying still, Annabelle would still be his after the waltz . . . he would take her back to the hotel, and undress her, and make love to her until dawn.

Her body was pliant in his arms, her gloved hand

light on his shoulder. Few women had ever followed his lead with such fluid ease, as if she knew what direction he would take her in before he even knew it himself. The result was a physical harmony that enabled them to move swiftly across the room like a bird in flight.

Simon had not been surprised by the reactions from his acquaintances upon meeting his new bride—the congratulatory words and subtly covetous gazes, and the sly murmurs of a few men who said they did not envy him the burden of having such a beautiful wife. Lately Annabelle had become even lovelier, if possible, the strain leaving her face after many nights of dreamless slumber. In bed she was affectionate and even frolicsome—the previous night she had climbed over him with the grace of a sportive seal, scattering kisses over his chest and shoulders. He had not expected that of her, having known beautiful women in the past who invariably lay back passively to be worshiped. Instead, Annabelle had teased and caressed him until he'd finally had enough. He had rolled on top of her while she giggled and protested that she wasn't yet finished with him. "I'll finish you," he had growled in mock-threat, and thrust inside her until she was moaning with pleasure.

Simon had no illusions that their relationship would be continually harmonious—they were both too independent and strong by nature to avoid the occasional clashes. Having relinquished her chance to marry a peer, Annabelle had closed the door on the kind of life she had always dreamed of, and instead would have to adjust to a far different existence. With the exception of Westcliff and two or three other wellborn friends, Simon had relatively little interaction with the aristocracy. His world consisted mainly of professional men like him, unrefined and happily driven to the endeavor of making money. This crowd of industrialists could not have been more different than the cultivated class Annabelle had always been familiar with. They talked too loudly, socialized too often and too long, and had no respect for tradition or manners. Simon was not entirely certain how Annabelle would accommodate such people, but she seemed game to try. He understood and appreciated her efforts more than she could have known.

He was well aware that scenes like the one she had endured two evenings ago would have reduced any other sheltered young woman to embarrassed tears, and yet Annabelle had handled it with relative poise. They had attended a soiree given by a wealthy French architect and his wife, a rather chaotic affair with flowing wine and too many guests, resulting in an atmosphere of raucous immoderation. Having left Annabelle at a table of acquaintances for just a few minutes, Simon had returned from a private conversation with the host to discover that his flustered wife had been cornered by two men who were drawing cards to see who would have the privilege of drinking champagne from her shoe.

Although the game was being played in a spirit of fun, it had been clear that the rivals for Annabelle's favor were deriving a great amount of enjoyment from her discomfort. There was nothing more pleasurable to those of jaded disposition than assaulting someone's modesty, especially when their victim was an obvious innocent. Although Annabelle had been trying to make light of it, the brazen game had distressed her, and the smile on her face had been entirely false. Standing from her seat, she had cast a quick glance around the room in search of sanctuary. ❧

Maintaining a bland social facade, Simon had reached the table and slid a reassuring hand over Annabelle's stiff back, his thumb stroking over the ridge at the exposed top of her spine. He had felt her relax slightly, and the hectic color had eased from her face as she looked up at him. "They're quarreling over who will drink pink champagne from my shoe," she had told him breathlessly. "I did *not* suggest it, and I don't know how—"

"Well, that's a problem easily solved," Simon had interrupted matter-of-factly. He had been well aware that a crowd was gathering, eager to see if he would lose his temper over the men's audacious advances toward his wife. Gently but firmly, he had guided Annabelle back into her chair. "Have a seat, sweetheart."

"But I don't want—" she had begun uneasily, and gasped as Simon sank to his haunches before her. Reaching beneath the hem of her skirts, he removed both her beaded satin slippers. "Simon!" Her eyes had been round with astonishment.

Standing, Simon had handed a slipper to each rival with a flourish. "You may have the shoes, gentlemen— just so long as you're both aware that their contents belong to me." Picking up his barefoot wife, he had carried her from the room, while the crowd reacted with laughter and applause. On the way out, they had passed the waiter who had been sent to fetch the bottle of champagne. "We'll take that," Simon told the dumbfounded waiter, who had handed the heavy chilled bottle to Annabelle.

Simon had carried Annabelle out to the carriage, while she clutched the bottle in one hand and curled her free arm around his neck. "You're going to cost me a fortune in footwear," he told her.

Laughter had shimmered in her eyes. "I have some more shoes back at the hotel," she told him cheerfully. "Are you planning to drink champagne from one of them?"

"No, my love. I'm going to drink it from you."

She had shot him a startled glance, and as understanding dawned, she had pressed her face against his shoulder, her ear turning crimson.

Recalling the episode, and the pleasurable hours that had followed, Simon looked down at the woman in his arms. The glittering light of eight chandeliers was reflected in her upturned eyes, filling them with tiny sparks that made the blue irises look like a starry summer midnight. She was staring at him with an intensity that she had never shown before, as if she yearned for something she might never have. The look disquieted him, eliciting a powerful need to satisfy her in any way possible. Whatever she might have asked him for in that moment, he would have given without a qualm.

No doubt they presented a hazard to every other couple there, as the room had become dreamily unfocused, and Simon couldn't bring himself to give a damn about which direction they were going. They danced until people remarked dryly that it was rather gauche for a husband and wife to display such exclusivity at a ball, and that soon after the honeymoon they would tire of each other's company. Simon only grinned at such comments, and bent to whisper in Annabelle's ear. "Are you sorry now that you never danced with me?"

"No," she whispered back. "If I hadn't been a challenge, you would have lost interest."

Letting out a low laugh, Simon hooked his arm around her waist and led her to the side of the room. "That would never happen. Everything you do or say interests me."

"Really," she said skeptically. "What about Lord Westcliff's claim that I'm shallow and self-absorbed?"

As she faced him, Simon braced one hand on the wall near her head and leaned over her protectively. His voice was very soft. "He doesn't know you."

"And you do?"

"Yes, I know you." He reached out to finger a tendril of damp hair that clung to her neck. "You guard yourself carefully. You don't like to depend on anyone. You're determined and strong-willed, and you're decided in your opinions. Not to mention stubborn. But never self-absorbed. And anyone with your intelligence could never be called shallow." He let his finger stray into the wisps of hair behind her ear. A teasing glint entered his eyes as he added, "You're also delightfully easy to seduce."

With an outraged laugh, Annabelle lifted a fist as if to pummel him. "Only for you."

Chuckling, he grasped her fist in his large hand, and kissed the points of her knuckles. "Now that you're my wife, Westcliff knows better than ever to utter another word of objection to you or the marriage. If he did, I would end the friendship without a second thought."

"Oh, but I would never want that, I . . ." She looked at him in sudden bemusement. "You would do that for me?"

Simon traced a vein of golden hair that ran through the honey brown locks. "There is nothing I wouldn't do for you." The vow was sincere. Simon was not a man given to half measures. In return for Annabelle's commitment to him, she would have his unequivocal loyalty and support.

Annabelle was unaccountably quiet for a long time after that, leading Simon to conclude that she was tired. But when they returned to their room at the *Coeur de Paris* that evening, she gave herself to him with a new fervor, trying to express with her body what she could not say in words.

Chapter 22

As he had promised, Simon was a generous husband, paying for a lavish quantity of French-made gowns and accessories that would be sent to London when they were finished. When he took Annabelle to a jeweler's shop one afternoon and told her to pick out anything she liked, she could only shake her head helplessly at the array of diamonds, sapphires, and emeralds spread on black velvet. After years of wearing paste stones and thrice-turned gowns, the habits of economy were slow to die.

"Is there nothing you like?" Simon prodded, lifting a necklace made of white and yellow diamonds strung together like strands of little flowers. He held it against her bare throat, admiring the glitter of diamonds against her fine skin. "What about this?"

"There are earrings to match, madame," the jeweler said eagerly, "*et aussi* a bracelet that would accompany the piece quite well."

"It's beautiful," Annabelle replied. "It's just that . . . well, it seems so odd to walk into a shop and buy a necklace as casually as if it were a tin of sweets."

Slightly perplexed by her diffidence, Simon regarded her intently, while the jeweler tactfully retreated to the back of the shop. Gently Simon laid the necklace back in its bed of velvet and took Annabelle's hand in his. His thumb caressed the backs of her fingers. "What is it, sweet? There are other jewelers if this one's wares are not to your taste—"

"Oh, it's not that! I suppose I'm so accustomed to *not* buying things, that it's rather difficult to adjust to the fact that I can now."

"I have every expectation that you'll be able to overcome that problem," Simon replied dryly. "In the meanwhile, I'm tired of seeing you in paste jewels. If you can't bring yourself to choose something, then allow me." He proceeded to select two pairs of diamond earrings, the flowered necklace, a bracelet, two long ropes of pearls, and a ring with a five-carat pear-shaped diamond. Unnerved by such extravagance, Annabelle had offered a few halfhearted protests, until Simon laughed and told her that the more she objected, the more he was going to buy. She promptly closed her mouth and watched with wide eyes as the jewelry was purchased and placed in a velvet-lined mahogany trunk with a little handle on top. Everything except the ring, which Simon slid onto her finger, ascertained that it was too loose, and gave it back to the jeweler.

"What about my ring?" Annabelle asked, holding the mahogany box with both hands as they left the shop. "Are we just going to leave it there?"

Amused, Simon arched his brow as he glanced down at her. "He's going to resize the band and send it to the hotel later."

"But what if it gets lost?"

"What happened to your objections? In the shop, you behaved as if you didn't even want it."

"Yes, but now it's *mine*," she said worriedly, causing him to roar with laughter.

To her relief, the ring was safely delivered to the hotel that evening, in a little velvet-lined box. While Simon gave a coin to the man who had brought it, Annabelle hurriedly emerged from her bath, dried herself, and donned a fresh white nightgown. Closing the door, Simon turned to discover that his wife was standing right behind him, her face lit with the anticipation of a child on Christmas morning. He couldn't help smiling at her expression, seeing that her efforts to be ladylike were fast being demolished in a rush of excitement. The ring glittered and flashed as he took it from the box and reached for Annabelle's hand. He slid the ring onto her fourth finger, fitting it snugly against the simple gold band he had given her on their wedding day.

Together they admired the sight of the diamond on her hand, until Annabelle threw her arms around him with an exclamation of delight. Before he could respond, she broke away and did a little dance of glee in her bare feet. "It's so lovely—look how it sparkles! Simon, do go away—I'm well aware of how horridly mercenary I must appear. Never mind, I *am* mercenary, and you may as well know it. Oh, I do love this ring!"

Enjoying her excitement, Simon caught her slender body against his. "I'm not about to go away," he informed her. "This is my opportunity to reap the benefits of your gratitude."

Enthusiastically, Annabelle tugged his head down and crushed her mouth against his. "And so you shall." She pressed another ardent kiss to his lips. "Now."

He chuckled at her full-bodied assault. "No doubt I

should say that seeing your enjoyment is repayment
enough. On the other hand, if you insist—"

"I do! I do insist." Striding away from him,
Annabelle went to the bed, clambered onto the mattress, and dramatically flung herself backward until
she landed spread-eagle on the counterpane. Simon
followed her into the room, fascinated by her antics.
This was an Annabelle he had not seen before, droll
and enchantingly capricious. As he approached the
bed, she lifted her head and encouraged, "I'm all
yours. Start reaping your rewards."

Deftly he stripped off his jacket and removed his
necktie, more than ready to oblige her. Annabelle
hoisted herself to a sitting position to watch him. Her
legs remained spread beneath the veil of her nightgown, her hair falling in a silky tumble over her shoulders. "Simon . . . you should know that I would go to
bed with you even without this ring."

"You're too kind," he replied dryly, stepping from
his trousers. "A husband always likes to hear that he is
valued for more than his financial merit."

Her gaze slid along his lean body. "Of all your mer-
its, Simon, the financial one is probably the least."

"Probably?" Walking to the edge of the bed, Simon
picked up one of her bare feet and pressed his mouth
to her tender instep. "Don't you mean 'definitely'?"

She fell back, gasping at the warm stroke of his
tongue, while the hem of her gown slid to the tops of her
thighs. "Oh . . . yes, definitely. Most definitely . . ."

Her body was damp and sweet from her recent
bath, retaining the crisp scent of soap and the heady
influence of rose oil. Aroused by the sight of her pink,
fragrant skin, Simon kissed and nibbled his way to her
ankle, then to her knee. At first Annabelle giggled and
writhed beneath the ministrations of his mouth, but

when he moved to her other leg, she quieted, her breath coming in slow, deep surges. He knelt between her parted thighs, inching her gown upward and kissing every newly exposed inch of flesh, until he had reached the thatch of glinting curls. After letting his chin barely graze the springy softness, he continued his journey upward, while she made a feeble sound of protest. Intoxicated by the velvety texture of her skin, he kissed her waist and each tender projection of her ribs, making his way to the place on her chest where her heart pounded beneath his lips.

Annabelle made a pleading sound and took hold of his hand, trying to bring it between her thighs. Resisting with a quiet laugh, Simon pinned both of her wrists over her head and settled his mouth on hers. He sensed her surprise at being restrained, and the response that followed, her eyes closing and her breath striking his cheek in a faster rhythm. Maintaining the secure grip on her wrists with one hand, he slid his free hand along the front of her body, his fingertips circling the peaks of her breasts. His own body was hard and hot with arousal, his muscles tight with coiling need. In all his experience with lovemaking, he had never known such feverish absorption, all connection to the world outside completely severed so that he was occupied only with Annabelle . . . her delight fueling his . . . her quivering responses intensifying his own desire. Her mouth opened beneath his in trembling welcome, moans slipping from her throat as his penetrating kisses became more aggressively penetrating. He touched the crevice between her legs, loving the silky moisture of her flesh. Her body undulated upward, her hips tilting toward his hand, while her imprisoned wrists flexed in his grasp. Every writhing movement communicated her need to be taken and filled, and his body hardened to an exquisite degree as primitive hunger rushed through him.

Slowly he entered her with one finger, and she moaned against his mouth. Perceiving the increased pliancy of her flesh, he added another finger, caressing gently until she was swollen with arousal. As soon as he freed her mouth, she begged incoherently, "Simon, please . . . please, I need you . . ." She trembled all over as he withdrew his fingers. "No, Simon—"

"Shhh . . ." He grasped her knees and carefully pulled her across the bed. "It's all right," he whispered. "I'll take care of you . . . let me love you this way . . ." Bringing her hips to the edge of the mattress, he eased her over, until her pale buttocks were turned upward. He stood on the floor, positioning himself between her thighs, the rigid head of his cock slipping easily into the slick entrance of her body. Grasping her hips firmly, he entered her in a long glide, not stopping until he was fully embedded. A flare of heat covered his entire body, as if he had stepped before an open furnace, and his groin tightened with an ache of lust that was nearly too acute to bear. He breathed in sharp pants, fighting to control the intensity of his desire before he unraveled completely. Annabelle lay passive and still on the mattress except for the clenching of her fingers against the counterpane. Afraid that he was causing her pain, Simon somehow managed to restrain his savage need long enough to bend over, and murmur hoarsely, "Sweetheart . . . am I hurting you?" The movement impelled him even deeper inside her, and she whimpered. "Tell me, and I'll stop."

She was slow to respond, as if it took her several seconds to comprehend the question, and when she replied, her voice was thick with pleasure. "No, don't stop."

He remained hunched over her, moving in deep-seated nudges that caused her inner muscles to flex greedily around his hardness. His hands covered hers, fingers wrapping around her fists . . . a position that overpowered her completely, and yet he was not forcing his own rhythm on her. Rather, he was moving in response to the demands of her body, thrusting in complement to the pulsing grasp of her flesh . . . each time she tightened helplessly, he pushed farther, using himself to stroke and caress the depths of her. She hovered on the edge of a nerve-shattering release, and yet she couldn't quite reach it, her breath coming in long gasps, her bottom pressing hard against his loins. "Simon . . ."

He reached beneath her, easily finding the place where she was stretched to accommodate him, and the tender hood above. Using his fingertip, he spread the warm moisture of her body over the engorged nub and manipulated it delicately, circling and stroking, varying his rhythms until he found one that made her cry out as she clamped tightly around him. She groaned as he thrust and stroked in tireless counterpoint, her back arched in ecstasy. The lush twisting and gripping of her body became too much for his overstimulated senses . . . he gasped with his own climax, tunneling inside the sweetness of her flesh as relief roared through him in uncontrollable bursts.

The worst moment of their honeymoon came on the morning that Annabelle cheerfully told Simon that she thought the old saying was true—that marriage was the highest state of friendship. She had meant to please him, but Simon had reacted with bewildering hostility. Recognizing the well-known quote from Samuel Richardson, Simon had commented tersely that he hoped her literary taste improved, so as to spare him having to hear cheap philosophy garnered from novels. Stung, Annabelle had reacted with cold silence, unable to understand why her comment had provoked him so.

Simon stayed away for the entire morning and part of the afternoon, returning to find Annabelle playing cards with some other matrons in one of the hotel salons. Approaching the back of her chair, he rested his fingertips on the curve of her shoulder. She felt his touch through the corded silk of her dress, the sensation wrapping delicately around her nerves. Strongly tempted to prolong her wounded resentment, Annabelle thought briefly of shrugging off his hand. Instead, she told herself that it would cost her nothing to show him a little tolerance. Summoning a smile, Annabelle glanced up at him over her shoulder. "Good afternoon, Mr. Hunt," she murmured, referring to him in the formal way that most married couples adopted in public. "I hope that you enjoyed your outing." Impishly she showed him her cards. "Look at the hand I've been dealt. Do you have any helpful advice?"

Sliding his hands along the sides of her chair, Simon bent his dark head to murmur in her ear. "Yes—finish your game quickly."

Conscious of the other women's interested gazes, Annabelle kept her face expressionless, even though she felt warmth creeping up from her neckline. "Why?" she asked, while his mouth remained near her ear.

"Because I'm going to make love to you in precisely five minutes," he whispered back. "Wherever we happen to be . . . here . . . in our suite . . . or on the stairs. So if you would like some privacy, I suggest that you lose the game with all expediency."

He wouldn't, Annabelle thought, her heartbeat quickening with alarm. On the other hand, knowing Simon, there was a possibility . . .

With that thought in mind, Annabelle laid out a

card with trembling fingers. The next player took a torturously long time to play one of her cards, and the next woman paused for a humorous exchange with her own husband, who had just come to the table. Aware of an accumulating mist of sweat on her bosom and brow, Annabelle considered ways to bow out of the game. The voice of reason calmed her, as she reflected that no matter how audacious Simon was, he wouldn't actually ravish his wife on the hotel staircase. However, the voice of reason was abruptly strangled as Simon leisurely consulted his watch.

"You have three minutes," came his soft murmur in her ear.

Somewhere in the midst of her agitation, Annabelle felt a shameful throb of sensation between her thighs, her body keenly attuned to the smoky promise in his voice. Pressing her legs together tightly, she waited with forced composure for her turn, even as her heart pounded in frantic drives. The players conversed lazily, fanning themselves and sending a waiter for another pitcher of iced lemonade. At last it was Annabelle's turn, and she threw out her highest face card and drew another. Relief stabbed through her as she saw that her new card was worthless, and she cast down her hand. "I'm afraid I'm out," she said, making an effort to keep from sounding breathless. "What a lovely game it was—thank you, I must go—"

"Do stay for the next round," one of the ladies urged, and the others added their own entreaties.

"Yes, do!"

"At least have a glass of wine while we finish this hand—"

"Thank you, but—" Annabelle stood and gasped slightly as she felt the gentle pressure of Simon's hand on her back. Her nipples tightened inside her gown.

"I'm simply exhausted from all the dancing last night," she improvised. "I must have some rest before we attend the theater this evening."

Followed by a chorus of farewells, and a few knowing glances, Annabelle attempted a dignified exit from the salon. As soon as they reached the winding staircase that led to the upper floors, Annabelle heaved a sigh of relief, and cast her husband a reproving glance. "If you were trying to embarrass me, you succeeded quite—what are you doing?" Her gown had become loose across her shoulders, and she realized with a little shock of amazement that he had unfastened some of her buttons. "Simon," she hissed, "don't you dare! No, stop that!" She hurried away from him, but he kept pace with her easily.

"You have one minute left."

"Don't be silly," she said shortly. "We can't possibly reach the suite in less than a minute, and you wouldn't—" She broke off with a squeak as she felt him pluck at another button, and turned to swat at his marauding hands. Her gaze caught his, and she realized incredulously that he had every intention of carrying out his threat. "Simon, *no*."

"Yes." His eyes were filled with tigerish playfulness, and the look on his face was one that she had become entirely familiar with by now.

Hiking up her skirts, Annabelle turned to rush up the stairs, her breath coming in pants of panicked laughter. "You're impossible! Leave me alone. You're—oh, if anyone sees us like this, I'll never forgive you!"

Simon followed without apparent hurry—but then, he didn't have masses of skirts and binding underclothes to hamper him. She reached the top landing and rounded the corner, her knees aching as her legs pumped in a desperate ascent, stair after stair.

Her skirts felt weighted, and her lungs were close to bursting. Oh, damn him for doing this to her—and damn herself for the airless giggles that kept slipping from her throat.

"Thirty seconds," she heard behind her, and she wheezed as she arrived at the top of the second flight. Three long hallways before she reached their suite— and not nearly enough time. Clutching at the sagging front of her dress, she looked up and down the hallways that extended from the landing. She rushed toward the first door she could find, which opened into a small, unlit closet. The scent of starched linen billowed outward, and shelves of neatly stacked bed linens and toweling were just visible in the light from the hallway.

"Keep going," Simon murmured, crowding her into the closet and closing the door.

Annabelle was immediately engulfed in darkness. Laughter swelled in her chest, and she shoved ineffectually at the hands that reached for her. It seemed that her husband had suddenly developed more arms than an octopus, unfastening her clothes and peeling them away much faster than she could move to defend herself. "What if you've locked us in here?" she asked, as her dress dropped to the floor.

"I'll break the door down," he replied, tugging at the tapes of her drawers. "Afterward."

"If one of the maids finds us, we'll be thrown out of the hotel."

"Believe me, the maids have seen far worse than this." Her dress was crushed beneath Simon's feet as he shoved Annabelle's drawers to her ankles.

She made a few more halfhearted protests, until Simon reached between her thighs and discovered the evidence of her arousal, after which further remonstrations seemed rather pointless. Her mouth opened to his kiss, eagerly returning the rough, stroking pressure of his lips. The plush entrance of her body stretched easily to take him, and a whimper slipped from her throat as she felt his fingers there, spreading her so that every rolling thrust of his hips gently abraded the sensitive peak of her sex.

They struggled to press closer, their bodies flexing, fusing, each kiss a searching invasion that aroused her further. Her corset was too tight, but there was unexpected delight in the constriction, as if extra sensation had been detoured to the lower half of her body and trapped in pleasure-swollen tissues. Her fingers clawed uselessly at his clothes as her desire escalated to near madness. Simon invaded her in deep lunges, his rhythm insistent, until rapture shot and echoed through both of them, and their lungs pulled in drafts of air laden with the scent of clean, pressed linen, and their entwined limbs tightened as if to trap the sensation between them.

"Damn," Simon muttered a few minutes later, when he was able to catch his breath.

"What?" Annabelle whispered, her head resting heavily against his coat lapel.

"For the rest of my life, the smell of starch is going to make me hard."

"That's your problem," she replied with a languid smile, and inhaled as she felt his body, still joined with hers, nudge upward.

"Yours, too," he told her, just before his mouth found hers in the darkness.

Chapter 23

Soon after Simon and Annabelle's return to England, they were confronted with the inevitable interaction of two families that could not have been more different. Simon's mother, Bertha, demanded that they come to dinner so that they all could become better acquainted, as they had not been able to do before the wedding. Although Simon had warned Annabelle what to expect, and she in turn had endeavored to prepare her mother and brother, she suspected that the encounter would produce, at best, mixed results.

Thankfully Jeremy was happily reconciled to the fact that Simon Hunt was now his brother-in-law. Having grown tall and lanky in the past few months, he stood over Annabelle as he embraced her in the parlor of their home. His golden brown hair had lightened considerably from all the time he had spent out of doors, and his blue eyes were bright and smiling in his sun-browned face. "I couldn't believe my eyes when I read Mama's letter saying that you were going to marry Simon Hunt," he told her. "After all the things you've said about him during the past two years—"

"Jeremy," Annabelle scolded. "Don't you dare repeat any of that!"

Laughing, Jeremy continued to keep an arm around her while he extended his hand to Simon. "Congratulations, sir." As they shook hands, he continued mischievously, "Actually, I wasn't a bit surprised. My sister complained about you so often and for so long that I knew she entertained a strong feeling for you."

Simon's warm gaze fell on his scowling wife. "I can't imagine what she found to complain about," he said blandly.

"I believe she said—" Jeremy began, and gave an exaggerated wince as Annabelle shoved her elbow against his ribs. "All right, I'll be quiet," he said, holding up his hands defensively and laughing as he staggered back from her. "I was just having a little polite parlor conversation with my new brother-in-law."

" 'Polite parlor conversation' entails talking about the weather, or asking after someone's health," Annabelle informed him. "*Not* revealing potentially embarrassing remarks that one's sister made in confidence."

Sliding an arm around Annabelle's waist, Simon pulled her back against his chest and lowered his head to murmur in her ear, "I have a fair idea of what you said. After all, you were willing enough to tell me face-to-face."

Hearing the note of amusement in his voice, Annabelle relaxed against him.

Having never seen his sister interact so comfortably with a man, and noticing the changes in her, Jeremy smiled. "I would say that marriage seems to agree with you, Annabelle."

Just then Philippa entered the room, and she rushed

to her daughter with a glad cry. "Darling, I have missed you so!" She embraced her daughter tightly, then turned to Simon with a brilliant smile. "Dear Mr. Hunt, welcome home. Did you enjoy Paris?"

"Beyond telling," Simon replied pleasantly, bending to kiss her proffered cheek. He did not look at Annabelle as he added, "I especially enjoyed the champagne."

"Why, of course," Philippa replied, "I'm certain that anyone who . . . Annabelle, dear, what are you doing?"

"Just opening the window," Annabelle said in a strangled voice, her face having turned the color of pickled beets at Simon's remark, as she remembered the evening when he had put a glass of champagne to especially creative use. "It's terribly warm in here—why on earth are the windows closed at this time of year?" Keeping her face averted, she struggled with the latch until Jeremy came to help her.

While Simon and Philippa conversed, Jeremy pushed the paned glass open and grinned as Annabelle turned her overheated cheeks toward the cooling breeze. "It must have been quite a honeymoon," he murmured with a swift grin.

"You're not supposed to know about such things," Annabelle whispered.

Jeremy let out an amused snort. "I'm fourteen, Annabelle, not four." His head leaned closer to hers. "So . . . why did you marry Mr. Hunt? Mama says it's because he compromised you, but knowing you, there's more to the story than that. One thing is certain—you wouldn't let yourself be compromised unless you wanted to be." The glint of humor left his eyes, and he asked more soberly, "Was it because of his money? I've seen the household accounts—obviously we hadn't two shillings to rub together."

"It wasn't entirely the money." Annabelle had never

been anything but completely frank with her brother, but it was difficult to admit the truth, even to herself. "I fell ill at Stony Cross, and Mr. Hunt was unexpectedly kind to me. And then when I began to soften toward him, I discovered that he and I have a sort of . . . well, affinity . . ."

"Intellectual or physical?" Jeremy's smile returned as he read the answer in her eyes. "Both? That's good. Tell me, are you in—"

"What are you two whispering about?" Philippa asked with a laugh, gesturing for them to come away from the window.

"I was begging my sister not to browbeat her new husband," Jeremy replied, and Annabelle rolled her eyes.

"Thank you," Simon told him gravely. "As you can imagine, it takes a great deal of fortitude to stand up to such a wife, but so far I've managed—" He stopped with a grin as he saw Annabelle's threatening glance. "I can see that your brother and I would do well to share our manly confidences outside, while you tell your mother all about Paris. Jeremy—would you care for a ride in my phaeton?"

Her brother needed no further urging. "Let me find my hat and coat—"

"Don't bother with a hat," Simon advised laconically. "You wouldn't be able to keep it on your head for more than a minute."

"Mr. Hunt," Annabelle called after them, "if you maim or kill my brother, you won't get any supper."

Simon called out something indistinct over his shoulder, and the pair of them disappeared into the entrance hall.

"Phaetons are too light and swift, and they overturn

so easily," Philippa said with a frown of worry. "I do hope that Mr. Hunt is an accomplished driver."

"Exceedingly," Annabelle said with a reassuring smile. "He drove us from the hotel at such a controlled pace that I would have thought we were riding in a heavy old family barouche. I promise you, Jeremy couldn't be in safer hands."

For the next hour, the two women sat in the parlor and shared a pot of tea as they discussed everything that had happened during the last fortnight. As Annabelle had expected, Philippa did not ask any questions about the more intimate aspects of the honeymoon, forbearing to intrude on the couple's privacy. However, she was keenly interested in Annabelle's account of the many foreigners they had met, and the parties they had attended. The crowd of wealthy industrialists was unfamiliar to Philippa, and she listened intently as Annabelle endeavored to describe them to her.

"One sees more and more of such people coming to England," Philippa remarked, "to match their wealth with titles."

"Like the Bowmans," Annabelle said.

"Yes. It seems that with each season, we are being infiltrated with increasing numbers of Americans—and heaven knows, it's already hard enough to catch a peer. We certainly don't need an excess of competition. I will be pleased when all this entrepreneurial fervor has finally settled, and things go back to the way they were."

Annabelle smiled ruefully as she wondered how to explain to her mother that from all she had seen and heard, the process of industrial expansion was only just beginning . . . and that things would never go back to the way they were. Annabelle had just begun to gain a small understanding of the transformation that the railroads and propeller-driven ships and mech-anized factories would effect in England and the rest of the world. Those were the subjects that Simon and his acquaintances had discussed at dinner instead of upper-class pursuits like hunting and country parties.

"Tell me, are you getting on well with Mr. Hunt?" Philippa asked. "It would certainly seem so."

"Oh, yes. Though I will say that Mr. Hunt is not like any man that you or I have ever known before. The gen-tlemen that we're accustomed to . . . his mind works differently than theirs. He . . . he is a progressive . . ."

"Oh, dear heavens," Philippa said in vague distaste. "Do you mean politically?"

"No . . ." Annabelle paused and made a comical face as she reflected that she didn't even know what party her husband subscribed to. "Actually, having heard some of his views, I wouldn't doubt that he is a Whig, or even a liberal—"

"Dear me. Perhaps in time you can persuade him to go in the other direction."

That made Annabelle laugh. "I doubt that. But it doesn't really matter, because . . . Mama, I am actu-ally beginning to believe that someday the opinions of these entrepreneurs and mercantilists will carry more weight than those of the peerage. Their financial influ-ence alone—"

"Annabelle," Philippa interrupted gently, "I think it is a wonderful thing that you wish to be supportive of your husband. But a man in trade will never be as influential as a peer. Not in England, certainly."

Suddenly their conversation was interrupted by Je-remy's bursting entrance into the parlor. He looked disheveled and wild-eyed.

"Jeremy?" Annabelle exclaimed in worry, jumping to her feet. "What happened? Where is Mr. Hunt?"

"Walking the horses around the square to cool them." He shook his head and spoke breathlessly. "The man is a lunatic. We nearly overturned at least three times, we came close to killing a half dozen people, and I was jolted until the entire lower half of my body is black-and-blue. If I'd had the breath to spare, I would have started praying, as we were clearly going to die. Hunt has the meanest horses I've ever set eyes on, and he let out curses so foul that just one of them would have gotten me expelled from school for good—"

"Jeremy," Annabelle began apologetically, aghast that Simon would have treated her brother so terribly. "I'm so—"

"It was without doubt the *best* afternoon of *my entire life!*" Jeremy continued jubilantly. "I begged Hunt to take me out again tomorrow, and he said that he would if he had the time—Oh, what a *ripper* he is, Annabelle! I'm off to get some water—I've got a half inch of dust lining my throat." He rushed off with adolescent glee, while his mother and sister stared after him, openmouthed.

Later that evening Simon took Annabelle, Jeremy, and their mother to the residence over the butcher shop, where his parents still lived. Consisting of three main rooms and a narrow staircase leading to a third-floor loft, the place was small but well-appointed. Even so, Annabelle could read the perplexed disapproval on her mother's face, for Philippa could not understand why the Hunts did not choose to live in a handsome town house or terrace. The more Annabelle had tried to explain that the Hunts felt no shame about their profession, and had no wish to escape the stigma of belonging to the working class, the more confused Philippa had become. Suspecting with annoyance that her mother was being deliberately obtuse, Annabelle had abandoned all attempts to discuss Simon's family and had privately enjoined Jeremy to keep Philippa from saying anything disdainful in front of them.

"I'll try," Jeremy had said doubtfully. "But you know that Mama has never rubbed on well with people who are different from us."

Annabelle had sighed in exasperation. "Heaven forbid that we should spend an evening with people who are not exactly the same as ourselves. We might learn something. Or worse, we might even enjoy it . . . oh, the shame!"

A curious smile touched her brother's lips. "Don't be too severe on her, Annabelle. It wasn't so long ago that you had the same disdain for those on the lower rungs."

"I did not! I . . ." Annabelle had paused with a ferocious scowl, then sighed. "You're right, I did. Though now I can't see why. There's no dishonor in work, is there? Certainly it's more admirable than idleness."

Jeremy had continued to smile. "You've changed," was his only comment, and Annabelle had replied ruefully.

"Perhaps that's not a bad thing."

Now, as they ascended the narrow stairs that led up from the butcher shop to the Hunts' private rooms, Annabelle was aware of the subtle restraint in Simon's manner, the only sign of the uncertainty that he must be feeling. No doubt he was concerned about how she and his family would "rub on," as Jeremy had put it. Determined to make a success of the evening, Annabelle pasted a confident smile on her face, not flinching even as she heard the commotion in the Hunt residence . . . a cacophony of adult voices, childrens' squeals, and thumps that sounded like furniture being overturned.

"Dear me," Philippa exclaimed. "That sounds like . . . like . . ."

"A brawl?" Simon supplied helpfully. "It could be. In my family, it's not always easy to distinguish parlor conversation from a rope-ring exchange."

As they entered the main room, Annabelle tried to sort through the mass of faces . . . there was Simon's older sister, Sally, the married mother of a half dozen children who were currently stampeding like Pamplona bulls through the little circuit of rooms . . . Sally's husband and Simon's parents and three younger brothers, and a younger sister named Meredith, whose dark serenity was oddly jarring in all the tumult. From what Simon had told Annabelle, he had a special fondness for Meredith, who was quite different from her rough-and-tumble siblings, being shy and bookish.

The children crowded around Simon, who displayed a surprising facility with them, tossing them easily into the air and managing to simultaneously inspect a newly lost tooth and apply a handkerchief to a runny nose. The first few minutes of welcome were confusing ones, with rounds of shouted introductions, and children scattering back and forth, and the yowling indignation of a hearthside cat who had just been nipped by an inquisitive puppy. Annabelle had every expectation that things would calm down after that, but in truth, the general upheaval continued all through the evening. She had brief glimpses of her mother's frozen smile, and Jeremy's relaxed enjoyment, and Simon's amused exasperation as his efforts to settle the bedlam met with poor results.

Simon's father, Thomas, was a huge, imposing man with features that could easily have lent themselves to intimidating austerity. Occasionally his face and eyes were softened with a smile that was not quite as charismatic as Simon's but possessed its own quiet appeal. Annabelle managed to have a friendly exchange with him as she was seated beside him at dinner. Unfortunately, it appeared that the two mothers were not communicating well. The cause did not seem to be dislike so much as a complete inability to relate to one another. Their lives, the accumulation of experiences that had formed them and shaped their views, could not have been more opposed.

Dinner consisted of thick cuts of well-cooked beefsteak, sided by pudding and the barest spoonful of vegetables. Suppressing a wistful sigh as she thought of the cuisine they had enjoyed in France, Annabelle worked diligently on the heavy slab of beef.

Before long, Meredith engaged her with a friendly comment. "Annabelle, you must tell us more about Paris. My mother and I will soon be touring the Continent for the very first time."

"How wonderful," Annabelle exclaimed. "When will you depart?"

"In a week, actually. We'll be gone for at least a month and a half, starting at Calais and finishing with Rome . . ."

The conversation about travel continued until the meal was concluded, and a cook-maid came to clear the plates while the family retired to the parlor for tea and sweets. To the children's delight, Jeremy sat with them on the floor near the hearth, playing jackstraws and helping to restrain the puppy. Annabelle sat nearby, watching their antics while she conversed with Simon's older sister. She couldn't help but notice that Simon had disappeared with his mother, whom she guessed had many questions for her oldest son about his precipitate wedding and the state of his marriage.

"Oh, blast," came Jeremy's exclamation. "The puppy's made a puddle on the hearth."

"Someone please find the maid and tell her," Sally

said, while the children laughed uproariously at the ill-mannered puppy.

Since Annabelle was sitting closest to the door, she jumped up at once. Entering the next room, Annabelle discovered the cook-maid still clearing away the remnants of dinner. After Annabelle informed her of the small mishap, the girl swiftly went to the parlor with a handful of rags. Annabelle would have followed her, but she heard the sounds of conversation coming from the nearby kitchen, and she paused as she heard Bertha's low, disapproving voice.

". . . and does she love you, Simon?"

Annabelle froze where she stood, listening intently to Simon's reply. "People marry for many reasons other than that."

"She doesn't, then," came Bertha's flat statement. "I can't say as I'm surprised. Women like that never—"

"Have a care," Simon murmured. "You're speaking of my wife."

"She makes a pretty ornament for your arm," Bertha persisted, "when you go among higher-ups. But would she have married you without your money? Would she stay by you in times of trouble or want? If only you had given a second glance to one of the girls I tried to match you with. That Molly Havelock, or Peg Larcher . . . good, sturdy girls who would be true helpmates . . ."

Annabelle could bear to hear no more. Controlling her expression, she slipped back into the noise and light of the parlor. *Well, that's what comes of eavesdropping,* she told herself ruefully, wondering if Bertha's opinion of her could sink much lower. The criticism hurt . . . but Annabelle had to acknowledge that there was no overwhelming reason for Simon's family, or his mother, to like her. In fact, Annabelle realized that in all her pondering over the benefits of marrying Simon, it had never occurred to her to question what she could give him in return.

Troubled, she wondered if she should say anything to Simon about what she had overheard and immediately decided against it. Broaching the subject would only force him to offer reassurance, or perhaps apologize for his mother, neither of which was necessary. She knew that it would take time for her to prove her worth to Simon, and his family . . . and perhaps even to herself.

Much later in the evening, when Annabelle and Simon had returned to the Rutledge, Simon took her shoulders in his hands and regarded her with a slight smile. "Thank you," he said.

"For what?"

"For being so agreeable to my family." Pulling her forward, he pressed his mouth to the top of her head. "And for choosing to overlook the fact that they're so different from you."

Annabelle flushed with pleasure at his praise, suddenly feeling much better. "I enjoyed the evening," she lied, and Simon grinned.

"You don't have to go that far."

"Oh, perhaps there was a moment or two, when your father was discussing animal entrails . . . or when your sister talked about what the baby did in his bathwater . . . but on the whole, they were very, very . . ."

"Noisy?" Simon suggested, his eyes glinting with sudden laughter.

"I was going to say 'nice.'"

Simon slid his hands over her back, massaging the tense places beneath her shoulder blades. "You're taking to this wife-of-a-commoner business fairly well, all things considered."

"It's not so bad, really," Annabelle mused. She ran a light, flirtatious hand along the front of his body, and gave him a teasing glance. "I can overlook quite a lot, in return for this . . . impressive . . . well-endowed . . ."

"Bank account?"

Annabelle smiled and slipped her fingers into the waist of his trousers. "Not the bank account," she whispered, just before his mouth closed over hers.

The following day, Annabelle was thrilled to be reunited with Lillian and Daisy, whose suite was in the same wing of the Rutledge as her own. Squealing and laughing as they embraced, the three of them made far too much noise, until Mrs. Bowman sent a maid to tell them to be quiet.

"I want to see Evie," Annabelle complained, locking arms with Daisy as they went to the suite's receiving room. "How is she faring?"

"She got into dreadful trouble a fortnight ago for trying to see her father," Daisy replied with a sigh. "His condition has worsened, and he's bedridden now. But Evie was caught sneaking out of the house, and now she's being kept in seclusion by Aunt Florence and the rest of the family."

"For how long?"

"Indefinitely," came the discouraging reply.

"Oh, those odious people," Annabelle muttered. "I wish we could go and rescue Evie."

"Wouldn't that be fun?" Daisy mused, instantly taken with the idea. "We should kidnap her. We'll bring a ladder and set it beneath her window, and—"

"Aunt Florence would set the dogs on us," Lillian said darkly. "They have two huge mastiffs that wander the grounds at night."

"We'll toss them some drugged meat," Daisy countered. "And then while they're sleeping—"

"Oh, plague take your harebrained plans," Lillian exclaimed. "I want to hear about Annabelle's honeymoon."

Two pair of dark brown eyes regarded Annabelle with unmaidenly interest. "Well?" Lillian asked. "What was it like? Was it as painful as they say?"

"Out with it, Annabelle," Daisy urged. "Remember, we promised to tell each other everything!"

Annabelle grinned, rather enjoying the position of being knowledgeable about something that was still so much a mystery to them. "Well, at certain moments it was rather uncomfortable," she admitted. "But Simon was very kind, and . . . attentive . . . and although I have no prior experience for comparison, I can't imagine that any man could be a more wonderful lover."

"What do you mean?" Lillian asked.

A warm shade of pink stained Annabelle's cheeks. Hesitating, she searched for the words to explain something that suddenly seemed impossible to describe. One might detail the mechanics of it, but that would hardly convey the tenderness of such a private experience. "The intimacy of it is far beyond what you could ever imagine . . . at first you want to die of embarrassment, but then there are moments when it feels so wonderful that you forget to be self-conscious, and the only thing that matters is being close to him."

There was a short silence as the sisters contemplated her words.

"How long does it take?" Daisy ventured.

Annabelle's blush deepened. "Sometimes only a few minutes . . . sometimes a few hours."

"*A few hours?*" both of them repeated at once, looking amazed.

Lillian wrinkled her nose in distaste. "My God, that sounds horrid."

Annabelle laughed at her expression. "It's not at all horrid. It's lovely, actually."

Lillian shook her head. "I'm going to figure out a way to make my husband get it over with quickly. There are far better things to do than spend hours in bed doing *that*."

Annabelle grinned. "Speaking of the mysterious gentleman who will someday be your husband . . . we should begin planning the strategy for our next campaign. The season won't begin until January, which leaves us several months to prepare."

"Daisy and I need an aristocratic sponsor," Lillian said with a sigh. "Not to mention some etiquette lessons. And unfortunately, Annabelle, since you've married a commoner, you've got no real social influence, and we're no farther along than when we started." Hastily she added, "No offense meant, dear."

"None taken," Annabelle replied mildly. "However, Simon does have some friends in the peerage—Lord Westcliff in particular."

"Oh, no," Lillian said firmly. "I want nothing to do with him."

"Why not?"

Lillian raised her brows as if surprised by the need to explain. "Because he's the most insufferable man I've ever encountered?"

"But Westcliff is very highly placed," Annabelle wheedled. "And he is Simon's best friend. I have no great liking for him myself, but he could be a useful ally. They say that Westcliff's title is the oldest one in England. Blood doesn't get any bluer than his."

"And well he knows it," Lillian said sourly. "Despite all his populist talk, one can see that he's inwardly thrilled to be a peer with lots of minions he can order about."

"I wonder why Westcliff hasn't married yet," Daisy mused. "Despite his flaws, one has to admit that he is a whale-sized catch."

"I'll be thrilled when someone harpoons him," Lillian muttered, making the other two laugh.

Although London was largely emptied of "good society" during the warmest of the summer months, town life was by no means completely stagnant. Until Parliament adjourned on the twelfth of August, coinciding with the opening of grouse season, the occasional presence of titled gentlemen was still required during afternoon sessions. While the men attended Parliament or went to their clubs, their wives went shopping, paid calls on their friends, and wrote letters. In the evenings, they attended dinners, soirees, and balls that usually lasted until two or three o'clock in the morning. Such was the schedule of an aristocrat, or even those in what were considered aristocratic professions, such as clergymen, naval officers, or physicians.

To Annabelle's chagrin, it quickly became evident that her husband, despite his wealth and undeniable success, was not in a remotely aristocratic profession. Therefore, they were sometimes excluded from the elegant upper-class events she longed to be part of. Only when a peer was financially obligated to Simon in some way, or if he was a close friend of Lord Westcliff, did he invite the Hunts to his home. Annabelle received very few calls from the young aristocratic matrons who had formerly been her friends, and although she was never turned away when she visited, she was hardly encouraged to return. The boundaries of class and social position were impossible to traverse. Even a viscount's wife who had become impoverished from her husband's gambling habits and spendthrift ways, and therefore was living in a shabby home with only two servants to attend her, seemed determined to maintain her superiority over Annabelle. After all, her husband, despite his shortcomings, was a peer, and Simon Hunt was distastefully mercantile.

Fuming over her cool reception from the viscount's wife, Annabelle went to Lillian and Daisy, to rant about the accumulation of snubs and set-downs she had received. They were both amused and sympathetic as they listened to her passionate complaints. "You should have seen her parlor!" Annabelle said, striding back and forth before the sisters, who were occupying the settee in their receiving room. "Everything was dusty and threadbare, and there were wine stains all over the carpet, and all she could do was look down her nose at me and pity me for having married down. *Down*, she said, when everyone knows that her husband is a foolish sodden drunkard who throws every last shilling onto the hazard table! He may be a viscount, but he isn't fit to lick Simon's boots, and I had the greatest difficulty in refraining from telling her so."

"Why did you refrain?" Lillian inquired idly. "I would have told her exactly what I thought of her silly snobbery."

"Because one gains nothing by trying to argue with such people." Annabelle scowled. "If Simon saved a dozen people from drowning, he would never be regarded with the same admiration as some fat old peer who sat by and watched without lifting a finger to help."

Daisy raised her brows slightly. "Are you sorry that you didn't marry a peer?"

"No," Annabelle said instantly, and ducked her head in sudden shame. "But I suppose . . . I suppose there are moments that I can't help wishing that Simon was a peer."

Lillian regarded her with a touch of concern. "If you could go back and change things, would you choose Lord Kendall over Mr. Hunt?"

"Good Lord, *no*." Sighing, Annabelle sank down onto a needlepoint stool, the skirts of her silk dress, green with tiny printed flowers, billowing around her. "I don't regret my choice. But I do regret not being able to go to the Wymarks' ball. Or the soiree at Gilbreath House. Or any of the other events that people of good society attend. Instead, Mr. Hunt and I most often go to parties given by a far different crowd."

"What sort of crowd?" Daisy asked.

As Annabelle hesitated, Lillian answered in a voice laden with wry amusement. "I would guess that Annabelle is referring to the climbers. All the people with new money and lower-class values and vulgar manners. In other words, our sort."

"No," Annabelle said instantly, and both sisters laughed.

"Yes," Lillian said gently. "You've married into our world, dear, and you don't belong there any more than we will belong in the peerage, if we ever manage to get titled husbands. The truth is, I couldn't care less about mingling with the Wymarks or the Gilbreaths, who are all deadly dull and intolerably full of themselves."

Annabelle regarded her with a thoughtful frown, suddenly seeing her situation from a new vantage point. "I've never questioned whether they were dull," she murmured. "I suppose I've always wanted to ascend to the top of the ladder without ever wondering if I would like the view. But now the question is immaterial, of course. And I must find a way to adapt to a different life than the one I thought I wanted." Resting her elbows on her knees, Annabelle propped her chin on her hands and added ruefully, "I'll know that I've succeeded when it no longer hurts to be snubbed by some whey-faced wife of a viscount."

Ironically, the Hunts were invited that same week to a ball given by Lord Hardcastle, who was privately indebted to Simon for advising him on how to restructure the family's dwindling balance of investments and assets. It was a large and well-attended event, and despite Annabelle's new resolution not to care about going to balls given by the upper class, she couldn't help but be excited. Dressed in a lemon-ice satin ball gown, her hair dressed in ringlets caught up with yellow silk cording, Annabelle entered the ballroom on Simon's arm. The ballroom, lined with white marble columns, was bathed in the sparkling glow of eight chandeliers, the air perfumed from the massive arrangements of roses and peonies. Accepting a glass of iced champagne, Annabelle eagerly mixed with friends and acquaintances, and basked in the serene elegance of the affair. These were the people she had always understood and tried to emulate—civilized, beautifully mannered, knowledgeable about music and art and literature. These gentlemen would never dream of discussing politics or business matters in front of a lady, and any of them would have chosen to be shot rather than mention the cost of things or speculate openly about what someone else was worth.

She danced often, with Simon and with other men, laughing and chatting in a relaxed manner and skillfully deflecting the compliments that were showered on her. Midway through the evening, she spied Simon across the room as he stood conversing with friends, and she experienced a sudden urge to go to him. Managing to detach herself from a pair of persistent young men, she skirted the side of the ballroom, where the space behind the columns provided a shadowy corridor. Between the columns, settees and small groupings of chairs provided spaces for guests to relax and talk. She passed behind a group of dowagers . . . then a group of disconsolate wallflowers, who provoked a sympathetic smile from her. As she crossed in back of a pair of women, however, a few overheard words caused her to pause, while her presence was screened by a heavy cluster of palms.

". . . don't know why they had to be invited tonight," one of them was saying angrily. Annabelle recognized the voice as one belonging to a former friend, now Lady Wells-Troughton, who had spoken to her only a few minutes earlier with brittle congeniality. "How smug she is, flaunting that vulgar diamond on her finger and that ill-bred husband, with no trace of shame whatsoever!"

"She won't be smug forever," came her friend's reply. "She doesn't yet seem to have realized that they are invited only to the homes of those who are financially obligated to him. Or those who are friends of Westcliff, of course."

"Westcliff is a significant ally," Lady Wells-Troughton admitted. "But his favor can only get them so far. The fact is, they should have the good taste not to push their way into places where they don't belong. She married a commoner, and therefore she should mix with commoners. Though I suppose she thinks of herself as too good for them . . ."

Feeling sick and hollow, Annabelle backed away unseen from the pair of chatting women and headed to the corner of the ballroom. *I really have to cure this habit of eavesdropping,* she thought with ironic humor, remembering the evening she had heard the comments that Bertha Hunt had made about her. *I always seem to overhear such unflattering things about myself.*

It did not surprise her that there was gossip about her and Simon—what had startled her was the viciousness of the women's tone. It was difficult to fathom what could cause such antipathy . . . except, perhaps, envy. Annabelle had acquired a handsome, virile, and wealthy husband, whereas Lady Wells-Troughton had married a peer at least thirty years older than she, who had all the charisma of a potted plant. It followed that Lady Wells-Troughton and her contemporaries would be fiercely determined to protect the one superiority they possessed . . . their membership in the aristocracy.

Annabelle recalled Philippa's comment, *"A man in trade will never be as influential as a peer . . ."* But it seemed to her that the peerage was afraid of the growing power of industrialists like Simon. Very few of them would be as clever as Lord Westcliff in realizing that they had to do far more than cling to the ancient privileges of land ownership to maintain their power. Stepping through a pair of columns, Annabelle glanced around the room at the aristocratic crowd . . . so prideful, so embedded in their traditional ways of thinking and behaving . . . so determined to ignore that the world around them was beginning to change. She still found their company to be infinitely more soothing than the raw, often callow conduct of Simon's professional friends. However, she no longer regarded them with awe or yearning. In fact—

Her thoughts were interrupted as a gentleman approached her, bearing two glasses of iced champagne. He was balding and portly, the folds of his neck bulging over the edge of his silk necktie. Annabelle groaned inwardly as she recognized him—Lord Wells-Troughton, the husband of the woman who resented her so deeply. From the way his avid gaze dropped to the shape of her breasts covered by pale satin, it appeared that he did not share his wife's wish that Annabelle had abstained from the ball.

Wells-Troughton, whose penchant for extramarital affairs was well-known, had approached Annabelle a year earlier, hinting strongly that he would be willing to help her with her financial difficulties, in exchange for her companionship. The fact that she had turned him away had not seemed to dampen his interest. Neither had the news of her marriage. For aristocrats like Wells-Troughton, marriage was not a detriment to an affair—if anything, it was an encouragement. "Never bed the unwed" was a common sentiment in the peerage . . . and love affairs were a privilege that was often enjoyed by married lords and ladies. Nothing was so attractive to a peer as another man's young wife.

"Mrs. Hunt," Wells-Troughton said jovially, handing her a glass of champagne, which she accepted with a cool smile of thanks. "You are as fair as a summer rose this evening."

"Thank you, my lord," Annabelle said demurely.

"To what shall we attribute your obvious glow of contentment, my dear?"

"To my recent marriage, sir."

Wells-Troughton chuckled. "Ah, I remember well those early days of marriage. Enjoy the pleasure while it lasts, for it is all too fleeting."

"Perhaps for some. For others it may last a lifetime."

"My dear, how delightfully naive." He gave her a knowing smirk, his gaze falling to her breasts again. "But I will not disabuse you of such romantic notions, as they will fade in due time."

"I doubt that," Annabelle said, causing him to chortle.

"Is Hunt proving a satisfactory husband, then?"

"In every regard," she assured him.

"Come, I shall be your confidant, and we'll find some favorable corner to talk in. I know of several."

"No doubt you do," Annabelle replied lightly, "but I have no need of a confidant, my lord."

"I insist on stealing you away for just a moment." Wells-Troughton settled a meaty hand at the small of her back. "You won't be so silly as to make a fuss, will you?"

Knowing that her only defense was to make light of his persistence, Annabelle smiled and turned away from him, sipping her champagne with studied insouciance. "I don't dare go anywhere with you, my lord. I'm afraid my husband possesses a rather jealous temperament."

She jumped a little as she heard Simon's voice from behind her. "With good reason, it seems." Although he spoke quietly, there was a biting note in his tone that alarmed Annabelle. She stared at him in silent entreaty, begging him not to make a scene. Lord Wells-Troughton was irritating but harmless, and Simon would make them all into objects of ridicule if he overreacted to the situation.

"Hunt," the heavyset peer murmured, grinning with an utter lack of shame. "You are a fortunate man to be in possession of such a delectable prize."

"Yes, I am." Simon's gaze was openly murderous. "And if you ever approach her again—"

"Darling," Annabelle interrupted with a whimsical smile, "I adore your primitive moods. But let's save this one for after the ball."

Simon didn't reply, glaring at Wells-Troughton until his simmering menace attracted the attention of people standing nearby. "Stay the hell away from my wife," he said softly, causing the other man to blanch.

"Good evening, my lord," Annabelle said, draining

the rest of her glass and giving him a bright, artificial smile. "Thank you for the champagne."

"A pleasure, Mrs. Hunt," came Wells-Troughton's disgruntled reply, and he hastily took his leave.

Pink with embarrassment, Annabelle avoided the curious stares of the other guests as she left the ballroom with Simon at her heels. Finding her way to an outside balcony, she set her glass down, and let a gentle breeze cool her burning cheeks.

"What did he say to you?" Simon demanded roughly, looming over her.

"Nothing of importance."

"He made an advance to you—anyone could see that."

"It meant nothing to him, or to anyone else here. That's how they all are—you know quite well these matters are never taken seriously. To them fidelity is just a . . . a middle-class prejudice. And if a man approaches another's wife as Lord Wells-Troughton did, no one attaches any importance to it—"

"I attach importance to it when my wife is the one being approached."

"For you to react so belligerently will make us both objects of mockery—and besides, it hardly demonstrates any faith in my fidelity."

"You just said that your kind doesn't believe in fidelity."

"They're *not* my kind," Annabelle snapped, losing her temper. "Not since I married you, at any rate! I don't know where I belong now—not with those people, and not with yours, either."

His expression did not change, but she sensed that she had hurt him. Instantly contrite, she sighed and rubbed her forehead. "Simon, I did not mean to imply—"

"It's all right," he said gruffly. "Let's go back inside."

"But I want to explain—"

"You don't need to explain."

"Simon . . ." She winced and closed her mouth as he took her back to the ballroom, wishing with all her heart that she could take back her impulsive words.

Chapter 24

As Annabelle had feared, the impetuous accusation she had made at the Hardcastle ball had created a small but undeniable distance between her and her husband. She longed to apologize and explain that she did not blame him for anything. However, her efforts to tell him that she had no regrets about having married him were quietly but firmly rebuffed. Simon, who was always willing to discuss any subject, had drawn the line at this matter. Unwittingly, she had struck at him with the delicate accuracy of a stiletto, and his reaction betrayed a certain guilt at having removed her from the upper-class world that she had once dreamed of occupying.

To Annabelle's relief, their relationship quickly returned to the way it had been before, their interactions playful, challenging, and even affectionate. Still, she was troubled by the awareness that things were not completely the same. There were moments when Simon was slightly guarded with her, for now they both knew that she had the power to hurt him. It seemed

LISA KLEYPAS

that he would allow her to come only so close, protecting himself by preserving a last crucial distance between them. He would, however, give her unqualified help and support when she needed him . . . and he proved that on the night that trouble came from an unexpected quarter.

Simon had come home at an unusually late hour, having spent all day at the Consolidated Locomotive works. Strongly scented of coal smoke, oil, and metal after spending a day at the site, he returned to the Rutledge with his clothes decidedly the worse for wear.

"What have you been doing?" Annabelle exclaimed, both amused and alarmed by his appearance.

"Walking through the foundry," Simon replied, stripping off his waistcoat and shirt as soon as he crossed the threshold of their bedroom.

Annabelle threw him a skeptical glance. "You did more than merely 'walk.' What are those stains on your clothes? You look as if you were trying to build the locomotive by yourself."

"There was a moment when some extra help was required." An expanse of well-honed muscle was revealed as Simon dropped his shirt to the floor. He seemed to be in an exceptionally good mood. Being a supremely physical man, Simon enjoyed exerting himself, especially when there was some risk involved.

Frowning, Annabelle went to draw a bath for him in the nearby bathing room, and returned to find her husband clad in his linens. There was a fist-sized bruise on his leg, and a red scorch mark on his wrist, causing her to exclaim anxiously, "You've been hurt! What happened?"

Simon looked momentarily puzzled by her concern, and by the way she flew to him. "It's nothing," he said, reaching out to catch her waist.

Pushing his hands away, Annabelle sank to her knees to inspect the bruise on his leg. "What caused this?" she demanded, skimming the edge of it with her fingertip. "It happened in the foundry, didn't it? Simon Hunt, I want you to stay away from that place! All those boilers and cranes and vats . . . the next time you'll probably be crushed or boiled or punched full of holes—"

"Annabelle . . ." Simon's voice was edged with amusement. Bending to grasp her elbows, he pulled her to her feet. "I can't talk to you when you're kneeling in front of me like that. Not coherently, at any rate. I can explain exactly what—" He broke off, his dark eyes flickering strangely as he saw her expression. "You're upset, aren't you?"

"Any wife would be, if her husband came home in this condition!"

Simon slid his hand behind her neck and squeezed lightly. "You're reacting a bit strongly to a bruise and a slight burn, aren't you?"

Annabelle scowled. "First tell me what happened, then I'll decide how to react."

"Four men were trying to pull a metal plate out of a furnace with long-handled pincers. They had to carry it to a frame where it could be rolled and pressed. The metal plate turned out to be a bit heavier than they expected, and when it became clear that they were about to drop the damned thing, I picked up another pair of pincers and went to help."

"Why couldn't one of the other foundrymen do it?"

"I happened to be standing closest to the furnace." Simon shrugged in an effort to make light of the episode. "I got the bruise when I knocked my knee against the frame before we managed to lower the plate—and the burn happened when someone else's

pincers brushed against my arm. But no harm done. I
heal quickly."

"Oh, that was all?" she asked. "You were only lifting hundreds of pounds of red-hot iron in your shirtsleeves?—how silly of me to be concerned."

Simon lowered his head until his lips brushed her
cheek. "You don't have to worry about me."

"Someone needs to." Annabelle was keenly aware of
the strength and solidity of his body, standing so close
to hers. His big-boned frame was formed with power
and masculine grace. But Simon wasn't invulnerable, or
indestructible. He was only human, and the dawning realization of how important his safety had become to her
was nothing short of alarming. Twisting away from
him, Annabelle went to check the accumulating bathwater, saying over her shoulder, "You smell like a train."

"With an extended smokestack," he rejoined, following at her heels.

Annabelle snorted derisively. "If you're trying to be
amusing, don't bother. I'm furious with you."

"Why?" Simon murmured, catching her from behind. "Because I got hurt? Trust me, all your favorite
parts are still working." He kissed the side of her neck.

Annabelle stiffened her spine, resisting the embrace.
"I couldn't care less if you jumped headfirst into a vat
of melted iron, if you're so silly as to go into the
foundry with no protective clothing and—"

"Hell-broth." Simon nuzzled into the delicate wisps
of her hairline, while one hand coasted upward to find
her breast.

"What?" Annabelle asked, wondering if he had just
spouted some new profanity.

"Hell-broth . . . that's what they call the melted
iron." His fingers circled the reinforced shape of her
breast, molded artificially high and stiff within the

frame of her corset. "Good God, what do you have on under this dress?"

"My new steam-molded corset." The fashionable garment, imported from New York, had been heavily starched and pressed onto a metal form, giving it more stiffness and structure than the conventionally designed corset.

"I don't like it. I can't feel your breasts."

"You're not supposed to," Annabelle said with exaggerated patience, rolling her eyes as he brought his hands up to her chest and squeezed experimentally. "Simon . . . your bath . . ."

"What idiot invented corsets in the first place?" he asked grumpily, letting go of her.

"An Englishman, of course."

"It would be." He followed her as she went to shut the valves in the bathing room.

"My dressmaker told me that corsets used to be kirtles, which were worn as a mark of servitude."

"Why are you so willing to wear a mark of servitude?"

"Because everyone else does, and if I didn't, my waist would look as big as a cow's by comparison."

"Vanity, thy name is woman," he quoted, dropping his linens to pad across the tiled floor.

"And I suppose men wear neckties because they are so excessively comfortable?" Annabelle asked sweetly, watching her husband step into the tub.

"I wear neckties because if I didn't, people would think I was even more uncivilized than they already do." Lowering himself with care, for the tub had not been designed for a man of his proportions, Simon let out a hiss of comfort as the hot water lapped around his middle.

Coming to stand beside him, Annabelle ran her fingers over his thick hair, and murmured, "They don't know the half of it. Here—don't lower your arm into the water. I'll help you to wash."

As she lathered him, Annabelle took a pleasurable inventory of her husband's long, well-exercised body. Slowly her hands coasted over hard planes of muscle, some places ropy and delineated, others smooth and solid. Sensual creature that he was, Simon made no effort to conceal his pleasure, watching her lazily through half-closed eyes. His breath quickened, though it was still measured, and his muscles turned iron-hard at the stroke of her fingertips.

The silence in the tiled room was broken only by the sluice of water and the sounds of their breathing. Dreamily, Annabelle tunneled her fingers through the soapy mat of hair on his chest, recalling the feel of it on her breasts as his body moved over hers. "Simon," she whispered.

His lashes lifted, and his dark eyes stared into hers. One large hand slid over hers, pressing it to the taut contours of his chest. "Yes?"

"If anything ever happened to you, I . . ." She paused as she heard the sound of vigorous knocking at the door of the suite. Her reverie was broken by the intrusive sound. "Hmm . . . who could that be?"

The interruption caused annoyance to cross Simon's features. "Did you send for something?"

Shaking her head, Annabelle rose to her feet and reached for a length of toweling to dry her hands.

"Ignore it."

Annabelle smiled wryly as the rapping became more insistent. "I don't think our visitor will give up that easily. I suppose I'll have to go see who it is." She left the bathing room and closed the door gently, allowing Simon to finish his bath in privacy.

Striding to the entrance of the suite, Annabelle

opened the door. "Jeremy!" Her pleasure at her brother's unexpected visit vanished quickly as she saw his expression. His young face was pale and set, and his mouth was clamped in a grim line. He was hatless and coatless, and his hair was in wild disarray. "Jeremy, is something wrong?" she asked, welcoming him into the suite.

"You could say that."

Reading the barely suppressed panic in his gaze, she stared at him with increasing concern. "Tell me what's happened."

Jeremy raked a hand through his hair, causing the thick golden brown strands to stand on end. "The fact is—" He paused with a dumbfounded expression, as if he couldn't believe what he was about to say.

"The fact is *what?*" Annabelle demanded.

"The fact is . . . our mother just stabbed someone."

Annabelle regarded her brother with blank-faced confusion. Gradually a scowl spread across her features. "Jeremy," she said sternly, "this is the most distasteful prank you've ever—"

"It's not a prank! I wish to hell it was."

Annabelle made no effort to hide her skepticism. "Whom is she supposed to have stabbed?"

"Lord Hodgeham. One of Papa's old friends—do you remember him?"

Suddenly, the color drained from Annabelle's face, and a shock of horror went through her. "Yes," she heard herself whisper. "I remember him."

"Apparently he came to the house this evening while I was out with friends—I returned home early— and when I crossed the threshold, I saw blood on the entrance floor."

Annabelle shook her head slightly, trying to take in the words.

"I followed the trail into the parlor," Jeremy continued, "where the cook-maid was in hysterics, and the footman was trying to clean a puddle of blood from the carpet, while Mama stood there like a statue, not saying a word. There was a pair of bloody scissors on the table—the ones she uses for needlework. From what I could get out of the servants, Hodgeham went into the parlor with Mama, there were sounds of an argument, then Hodgeham came staggering out with his hands clasping his chest."

Annabelle's mind began to work at twice its usual speed, her thoughts racing madly. She and Philippa had always hidden the truth from Jeremy, who had been away at school whenever Hodgeham had called. As far as Annabelle knew, Jeremy had never been aware that Hodgeham had visited the house. He would be devastated if he realized that some of the money that had paid his school bills had been given in exchange for . . . no, he must not find out. She would have to make up some explanation. Later. The most important thing for now was to protect Philippa.

"Where is Hodgeham now?" Annabelle asked. "How severely was he injured?"

"I have no idea. It seems that he went to the back entrance where his carriage was waiting, and his own footman and driver carried him away." Jeremy shook his head wildly. "I don't know where Mama stabbed him, or how many times, or even why. She won't say—just looks at me as if she can't remember her own name."

"Where is she now? Don't say you just left her at home by herself?"

"I told the footman to watch her every minute, and not to let her—" Jeremy broke off and directed a wary glance to a point beyond Annabelle's shoulder.

"Hello, Mr. Hunt. I'm sorry to interrupt your evening, but I've come because—"

"Yes, I heard. Your voice carried to the next room." Simon stood there calmly tucking the tail of a fresh shirt into his trousers, his gaze alert as he stared at Jeremy.

Turning, Annabelle went cold at the sight of her husband. There were times when she forgot how intimidating Simon could be, but at the moment, with his pitiless eyes and complete lack of expression, he looked as ruthless as a killer-for-hire.

"Why did Hodgeham come to the house at such an hour?" Jeremy wondered aloud, his young face fraught with worry. "And why the hell did Mama receive him? And what would have provoked her like that? He must have tricked her somehow. He must have said something about Papa . . . or maybe even made an advance to her, the filthy bastard."

In the tension-riddled silence that followed Jeremy's innocent speculations, Annabelle opened her mouth to say something, and Simon shook his head slightly, silencing her. He turned his attention fully to Jeremy, his voice cool and quiet. "Jeremy, run to the stables at the back of the hotel and have my carriage hitched to a team. And tell them to saddle my horse. After that, go home to collect the carpet and bloodstained clothes and take them to the locomotive works—the first building on the lot. Mention my name, and the manager won't ask questions. There is a furnace—"

"Yes," Jeremy said, understanding immediately. "I'll burn everything."

Simon gave him a short nod, and the boy strode to the door without another word.

As Jeremy left the hotel suite, Annabelle turned toward her husband. "Simon, I . . . I want to go to my mother—"

"You can go with Jeremy."

"I don't know what's to be done about Lord Hodgeham . . ."

"I'll find him," Simon said grimly. "Just pray that his wound is superficial. If he dies, it will be a hell of a lot more difficult to cover up this mess."

Annabelle nodded, biting her lip before she said, "I thought we were finally rid of Hodgeham. I never dreamed that he would dare bother my mother again, after I married you. It seems that nothing will stop him."

He took her shoulders in his hands, and said, with almost frightening softness, "I'll stop him. You can rest assured about that."

She regarded him with a worried frown. "What are you planning to—"

"We'll talk later. Right now, go fetch your cloak."

"Yes, Simon," she whispered, and sped to her armoire.

When Annabelle and Jeremy arrived at their mother's house, they found Philippa sitting on the stairs, a glass of spirits clutched in her hands. She looked small and almost childlike, and Annabelle's heart twisted in her chest as she stared at her mother's downbent head. "Mama," she murmured, sitting on the step beside her. She laid an arm over her mother's rounded back. Meanwhile, Jeremy assumed a businesslike manner as he enjoined the footman to help him roll up the parlor carpet and convey it to the carriage outside. In the midst of her worry, Annabelle could not help reflecting that he was handling the situation extraordinarily well for a boy of fourteen.

Philippa's head lifted, and she regarded Annabelle with a haunted gaze. "I'm so sorry,"

"No, don't be—"

"Just when I thought everything was finally all

right, Hodgeham came here . . . he said that he wanted to continue visiting me, and if I didn't agree, he would tell everyone about the arrangement we'd had. He said he would ruin all of us and make me a figure of public scorn. I cried and pleaded, and he *laughed* . . . then, when he put his hands on me, I felt something give way inside. I saw the scissors nearby, and I couldn't keep from picking them up, and . . . I tried to kill him. I hope I did. I don't care what happens to me now—"

"Hush, Mama," Annabelle murmured, putting an arm around her shoulders. "No one could blame you for your actions—Lord Hodgeham was a monster, and—"

"Was?" Philippa asked numbly. "Does that mean he's dead?"

"I don't know. But everything will be fine regardless—Jeremy and I are here, and Mr. Hunt will not let anything happen to you."

"Mama," Jeremy called, hefting one end of the rolled-up carpet as he and the footman carried it toward the back entrance of the house, "do you know where the scissors are?" The question was asked in such a casual manner that one might have thought he needed them to cut a package string.

"The cook-maid has them, I think," Philippa replied. "She's trying to clean them."

"All right, I'll get them from her." As they progressed down the hall, Jeremy called over his shoulder, "Have a glance over your clothes, will you? Anything with a speck of blood on it has to go."

"Yes, dear."

Listening to the pair of them, Annabelle couldn't help wondering how it was that she and her family were having a casual Thursday night conversation about disposing of murder evidence. And to think that she had felt the slightest bit of superiority over Simon's family . . . she cringed at the thought.

Two hours later, Philippa had finished her drink and was safely tucked into bed; Simon and Jeremy arrived at the town house within minutes of each other. They conferred briefly in the entrance hall. As Annabelle came downstairs, she paused midflight as she saw Simon enfold her brother in a quick, one-armed hug, and tousle his already disheveled hair. The fatherly gesture seemed to reassure Jeremy immensely, and a weary grin came to his face. Annabelle froze as she watched the two of them.

How surprising that Jeremy had accepted Simon so easily, when Annabelle had expected him to rebel against Simon's authority. It gave her a strange feeling to witness the bond that had formed instantly between them, especially knowing that Jeremy's trust was not easily won. She hadn't thought until now what a relief it must be for her brother to have someone strong to lean on, someone who could provide solutions to problems that he was still too young to handle by himself. The yellow light from the entrance hall lamp slid over the clipped dark layers of Simon's hair and gleamed over the high planes of his cheekbones as he looked up at her.

Battening a perplexing swell of emotions, Annabelle descended the rest of the way, and asked, "Did you find Hodgeham? And if so—"

"Yes, I found him." Reaching for the cloak draped over the banister, Simon draped it over her shoulders. "Come, I'll tell you everything on the way home."

Annabelle turned toward her brother. "Jeremy, will you be all right if we leave?"

"I have the situation well in hand," the boy replied with manly confidence.

Simon's eyes glinted with amusement as he fitted

his hand behind Annabelle's waist. "Let's go," he murmured.

Once they were in the carriage, Annabelle pelted Simon with questions until he placed his hand over her mouth. "I'll tell you if you can bring yourself to be quiet for a minute or two," he said. She nodded behind his hand, and he grinned, leaning forward to replace his fingers with his mouth. After stealing a quick kiss, he settled back in his seat, his expression turning serious. "I found Hodgeham at his home, being attended by his family physician. And it was a good thing I appeared when I did, as they had already summoned a constable and were waiting for his arrival."

"How did you convince the servants to let you past the front door?"

"I shoved my way into the house and demanded to be taken to Hodgeham immediately. There was so much confusion that no one dared refuse me. I had a footman show me to the upstairs bedroom, where the doctor was stitching Hodgeham's wound." Dark humor infused his expression. "Of course, I could have found the room merely by following the bastard's screams and howls."

"Good," Annabelle said in vehement satisfaction. "Whatever pain Lord Hodgeham is suffering isn't nearly great enough, in my opinion. What was his condition, and what did he say when you appeared in his room?"

One side of Simon's mouth curled in disgust. "It was a shoulder wound—a small one, at that. And most of what he said is better left unrepeated. After letting him rant for a few minutes, I told the doctor to wait in the next room while I had a private talk with Hodgeham. I told him that I was quite sorry to learn of his severe digestive upset—a comment that confused him until I explained that it would be in his best interest to describe his malady to friends and family as a stomach ailment rather than a stab wound."

"And if he didn't?" Annabelle asked with a faint smile.

"If he didn't, then I made it clear that I would carve him up like a side of Yorkshire gammon. And if I ever learned of the slightest rumor that would tarnish your mother's reputation, or that of the family, I would lay the blame at his door, after which there wouldn't be enough of his remains left for a decent burial. By the time I finished with Hodgeham, he was too terrified to breathe. Believe me, he will never approach your mother again. As for the doctor, I compensated him for his visit and persuaded him to banish the episode from his mind. I would have left then, but I had to wait for the constable."

"And what did you tell the constable?"

"I told him there had been a mistake, and he wasn't needed after all. And for his trouble, I told him to go to the Brown Bear tavern after his shift and order as many rounds of ale as he wanted on my credit."

"Thank God." Relieved beyond measure, Annabelle snuggled next to him. She sighed against his shoulder. "What about Jeremy? What will we tell him?"

"It isn't necessary for him to know the truth—it would only hurt and confuse him. As far as I'm concerned, Philippa overreacted to Hodgeham's advances and forgot herself in the moment." Simon caressed the edge of her jaw with the tip of his thumb. "I do have a suggestion, to which I would like you to lend some serious thought."

Wondering if this "suggestion" was going to be a thinly veiled command, Annabelle looked at him suspiciously. "Oh?"

"I think it would be for the best if Philippa put

some distance between herself and London—and Hodgeham—until the dust settles."

"How much distance? And where would she go?"

"She can join my mother and sister on their tour of the Continent. They're leaving in just a few days—"

"That is the worst idea I've ever heard," Annabelle exclaimed. "I want her to stay right here, where Jeremy and I can look after her. Second, I can guarantee that *your* mother and sister would be none too pleased—"

"We'll send Jeremy along. He has enough time before his next school term, and he'll be an excellent escort for all three of them."

"Poor Jeremy . . ." Annabelle tried to envision him escorting the trio of women across Europe. "I wouldn't wish such a fate on my worst enemy."

Simon grinned. "He'll probably learn a great deal about women."

"And none of it pleasant," she retorted. "Why do you think it is necessary to whisk my mother away from London? Does Lord Hodgeham still pose some kind of danger?"

"No," he murmured, gently angling her face upward. "I told you, he'll never dare to approach Philippa again. However, if it turns out that there is any lingering trouble with Hodgeham, I'd prefer to handle it while she is away. Moreover, Jeremy said that she doesn't seem quite herself. Understandable, given the circumstances. A few weeks of touring should make her feel better."

As Annabelle considered the idea, she had to admit that there was some sense in it. It had been a long time since Philippa had gone on any kind of holiday. And if Jeremy went with her, perhaps even the company of the Hunts could be tolerated. As for what Philippa would want . . . she seemed too numb to make any decisions. It seemed likely that she would agree to any plans that Annabelle and Jeremy made. "Simon . . ." she asked slowly, "are you asking for my opinion, or telling me what you've already decided?"

Simon's gaze swept her face in clever assessment. "Which would be more likely to induce you to agree?" He laughed softly as he read the answer in her expression. "Very well . . . I'm asking."

Annabelle smiled wryly and snuggled back into the crook of his shoulder. "Then if Jeremy agrees . . . so will I."

Chapter 25

Annabelle had not asked Simon how Bertha and Meredith Hunt had received the news of their additional traveling companions, and she had certainly not been eager to hear the answer. All that mattered was that Philippa would be far away from London and all reminders of Lord Hodgeham. Annabelle hoped that when her mother returned, she would be refreshed and at ease, and ready to make a new beginning. The trip might even hold some enjoyment for Jeremy, who was looking forward to seeing some of the foreign places he had learned about at school.

With less than a week before their departure, Annabelle threw herself into the project of packing for her mother and brother, trying to anticipate their needs for a six-week journey. Openly amused by the quantity of supplies that Annabelle had purchased for them, Simon remarked that one would think her family was forging through regions of unexplored wilderness rather than lodging in a succession of inns and pensiones.

"Foreign travel can be uncomfortable at times,"

Annabelle replied, busily stuffing tins of tea and biscuits into a leather satchel. A stack of boxes and parcels towered beside their bed, where she was sorting various articles into organized piles. Among other things, she had collected compounds from the apothecary shop, a pair of down pillows and extra linens, a box of reading material, and a collection of packaged edibles. Holding up a glass jar of preserves, she examined it critically. "The food is different on the Continent—"

"Yes," Simon said gravely. "Unlike ours, it's been known to have flavor."

"And the climate can be unseasonable."

"Blue sky and sunshine? Oh, they'll want to avoid that at all cost."

She responded to his mockery with an arch glance. "Surely you must have better things to do, other than to watch me open boxes."

"Not when you're doing it in the bedroom."

Straightening, Annabelle folded her arms across her chest and regarded him with flirtatious challenge. "I'm afraid you'll have to control your baser urges, Mr. Hunt. Perhaps you hadn't noticed, but the honeymoon has ended."

"The honeymoon doesn't end until I say so," Simon informed her, reaching out to snatch her before she could evade him. He crushed her lips with a dominating kiss and tossed her onto the bed. "Which means there's no hope for you."

Giggling, Annabelle flailed in the tangle of her skirts until she found herself pinned on the mattress with his body lying over hers. "I have more packing to do," she protested, as he settled between her thighs. "Simon—"

"Did I ever happen to mention that I can unfasten buttons with my teeth?"

A breathless laugh escaped her, and she squirmed as

his head lowered to the front of her bodice. "That's not a very practical skill, is it?"

"It's useful in certain situations. Let me show you . . ."

Very little packing was done for the rest of the day.

Eventually, however, Annabelle found herself standing at the door of her family's town house, watching as her mother and brother left in a carriage bound for Dover, where they would meet with the Hunts and cross to Calais.

Simon stood with her, his hand resting comfortingly on her back as the carriage rounded the corner and headed along the main thoroughfare. She waved forlornly after them, wondering how they would manage without her.

Drawing her into the house, Simon closed the door. "This is for the best," he assured her.

"For them or for us?"

"For all parties concerned." Smiling slightly, he turned her to face him. "I predict the next few weeks will pass quickly. And in the meantime you're going to be very busy, Mrs. Hunt. To start with, this morning we're going to meet with an architect about the house plans, then you'll have to decide between two lots that our agent has found in Mayfair."

Annabelle dropped her head on his chest. "Thank God. I've begun to despair of ever leaving the Rutledge. Not that I haven't enjoyed it, mind you, but every woman wants a home of her own, and . . ." She paused as she felt him playing with her pinned-up hair. "Simon," she warned, "don't pull out my pins. It's too much trouble to put my hair back up, and . . ." She sighed and frowned at him as she felt her coiffure loosening and heard the *plink* of crimped wire pins hitting the floor.

"I can't help it." His fingers worked greedily in her unraveling braid. "You have such beautiful hair." He brought a handful of the slippery silk to his face and rubbed his cheek against it. "It's so soft. And it smells like flowers. How do you make it smell this good?"

"Soap," Annabelle replied dryly, hiding a smile against his chest. "Bowman's soap, actually. Daisy gave some to me—their father sends cases from New York."

"Mmmn. No wonder he's a millionaire. Every woman should smell like this." He strained her hair through his fingers and bent to nuzzle her throat. "Where else do you use it?" he whispered.

"I would invite you to find out," she said, "but we're going to meet with the architect, remember?"

"He can wait."

"So can you," Annabelle said severely, though a laugh was working upward in her throat. "Good Lord, Simon, it's not as if you've been deprived. I've expended a great deal of effort to satisfy—"

He fitted his mouth to hers in a kiss so warm and coaxing that every rational thought vanished from her mind. Fisting his large hands in her hair, he urged her back against the wall of the entrance hall and entered her with his tongue, feasting leisurely until Annabelle was light-headed and dizzy, her fingers clutching the fabric of his coat sleeves. Gradually his mouth shifted away from hers, and he bit softly at the delicate silk of her throat. He murmured things that shocked her, expressing himself not in flowery phrases, but with the raw simplicity of a man whose lust for her knew no limits. "I have no self-control where you're concerned. Every minute that I'm not with you, all I can think about is being inside you. I hate everything that keeps you separate from me."

He reached behind her to pull hard at the back of

her dress, and she gasped as she felt the plackets of buttons give way, bits of carved ivory scattering everywhere. Smothering the sound with his mouth, Simon tugged the dress from her arms and deliberately stepped on the hem of her gown. The much-abused garment ripped and dropped to the floor. He pulled her against his body, grasping her wrist and guiding it to his loins. Annabelle inhaled deeply as her fingers molded over the heavy breadth of his erection, and her eyes half closed. "I want to make you scream and claw and faint in my arms," he whispered, his masculine bristle scraping against her skin. "I need to touch you everywhere, inside and outside, as far as I can reach—" He broke off and seized her lips with insistent pressure, suddenly reckless in his desire, as if the taste of her was an exotic stimulant that drove him to frenzy. She was vaguely aware of him fumbling in the pocket of his coat, and then something nicking at the knots of her corset . . . he had cut them with his knife, she realized, feeling the confining stays release their squeezing pressure around her ribs and waist.

Comprehending that she was about to be ravished in the entrance of her family home, Annabelle stumbled back from him, smiling and shivering. Even in his moments of highest arousal, Simon had always seemed to be governing himself, placing careful restraints on his passion. She had never feared that he would be less than gentle with her . . . until now. He looked almost savage, his face darkened with an unfamiliar flush. Her heart began to beat in painful thumps, and she moistened her dry lips. The nervous flick of her tongue drew his attention sharply, and he stared at her mouth with startling intensity.

"My bedroom . . ." she managed to say, turning toward the stairs. She began to ascend the flight with

quivery legs. After the first few steps, she felt Simon
come up behind her swiftly, catching and turning her
in his muscular arms. Before she could make a sound,
he lifted her and carried her up the rest of the stairs
with almost frightening ease.

He took her to the bedroom, where the sight of his
dark form was startling among the pale, timeworn ruffles and tattered lace and the framed needlework sam-
plers that had been sewn by her own childish hands.
Undressing her roughly, Simon laid her among the bed
linens, which were smooth and slightly stale from having gone unused for so long. His clothes quickly joined
hers on the floor, then his body slid over hers. She countered his urgency with unequivocal willingness, her
arms spreading to hold him, her legs parting easily at his
slightest touch. He thrust into her, filling her with a low,
thick slide, and she gasped and strained with the effort to
accommodate him. Once he had joined her, he became
gentler, his urgency transforming into ravaging intensity. It seemed that every part of him had been designed
to pleasure her, the satin reaches of hard muscle, the
thick fleece that rubbed gently over the tips of her
breasts, the scent and taste that drugged her senses.

Overwhelmed by the devastating intimacy, Annabelle
felt tears come to her eyes, and Simon comforted her
with soft murmurs even as he pushed deeper, longer,
taking more of her than she thought was possible to
give. His mouth brushed over hers, absorbing her er-
ratic breaths, as he moved in lush, gauging thrusts that
caused all her muscles to tighten and strain. She
sobbed against his lips, begging wordlessly for him to
relieve her. Relenting at last, he quickened his pace and
drove her to a piercing climax, their joining raw and
exalted and astonishing in its potency.

Minutes later, as Annabelle lay bonelessly over his

body, her cheek nestled on his shoulder, she tried to sort through the bewilderment of her senses. She had never been so satiated, every nerve glazed with pleasure. And yet she had perceived something new in their lovemaking . . . an unattained height that loomed even beyond what they had just experienced . . . some unrealized possibility that hovered just out of reach. A feeling . . . a wish . . . a tantalizing something that had no name. Closing her eyes, Annabelle basked in the closeness of their bodies, while the elusive promise haunted the air like some benevolent spirit.

Increasingly curious about the project that demanded so much of her husband's attention, Annabelle asked Simon if she could visit the locomotive works, only to meet with refusals, diversions, and assorted tactics to keep her from going to the site. Realizing that for some reason Simon did not want to take her to the place, she became increasingly determined. "Just a short visit," she insisted one evening. "All I want is one glimpse of it. I won't touch anything. For heaven's sake, after listening to you discuss the locomotive works so often, aren't I entitled to see it?

"It's too dangerous," Simon replied flatly. "A woman has no business going into a place full of heavy machinery and thousand-pound vats of boiling hell-broth—"

"You've been telling me for weeks how safe it is, and how there is absolutely no reason for me to worry when you go there . . . and now you're saying that it's dangerous?"

Realizing his tactical error, Simon scowled. "The fact that it's safe for me doesn't mean that it's safe for you."

"Why not?"

"Because you're a woman."

Boiling like one of the aforementioned vats of hell-broth, Annabelle regarded him through slitted eyes. "I'll reply to that in a moment," she muttered, "if I can manage to conquer the urge to crown you with the nearest heavy object."

Simon paced around the parlor, frustration evident in every taut line of his body. He stopped before the settee on which she reposed and towered over her. "Annabelle," he said gruffly, "visiting the foundry is like looking through the doors of hell. The place is as safe as we can make it, but even so, it's a noisy, rough, dirty business. And yes, there is always a chance of danger, and you . . ." He stopped and dragged his fingers through his hair, and looked around impatiently, as if it was suddenly difficult for him to meet her gaze. With an effort, he forced himself to continue. "You're too important for me to risk your safety in any way. It's my responsibility to protect you."

Annabelle's eyes widened. She was touched and more than a little surprised by his admission that she was important to him. As they stared at each other, she was conscious of a peculiar tension . . . not unpleasant, but disquieting nonetheless. Leaning the side of her head against her hand, she studied him intently. "You're entirely welcome to protect me," she murmured. "However, I don't want to be locked in an ivory tower." Sensing his inner struggle, she continued reasonably. "I want to know more about what you do during the hours that you're away from me. I want to see the place that is so important to you. Please."

Simon brooded silently for a moment. When he replied, there was an unmistakable thread of surliness in his tone. "All right. Since it's obvious that I'll have no peace otherwise, I'll take you there tomorrow. But don't blame me when you're disappointed. I warned you what to expect."

"Thank you," Annabelle said in satisfaction, giving him a sunny smile that dimmed somewhat at his next words.

"Fortunately, Westcliff will be visiting the foundry tomorrow as well. It will be a good opportunity for the two of you to become better acquainted."

"How nice," Annabelle said in a brittle attempt at pleasantness, fighting the temptation to glower at the news. She had still not forgiven the earl for his cutting remarks about her and his prediction that marriage to her would ruin Simon's life. However, if Simon thought that the prospect of being in the company of a pompous ass like Westcliff would dissuade her, he was mistaken. Pasting a thin smile on her face, she spent the rest of the evening thinking what a pity it was that a wife could not choose her husband's friends for him.

Late the next morning, Simon took Annabelle to the nine-acre site of the Consolidated Locomotive works. The rows of cavernous buildings were fitted with myriads of jutting smokestacks, spewing out smoke that drifted over truck yards and intersecting walkways. The scale of the locomotive works was even larger than Annabelle had expected, housing equipment so mammoth in scale that she was nearly rendered speechless at the sight. The first place they visited was the assembly shop, where nine locomotive engines were in various stages of production. The company's goal was to produce fifteen engines the first year and double that the next. Upon learning that the cash outlay for the locomotive works was, on average, a million pounds a *week*, with a capitalization of twice that amount, Annabelle stared at her husband with slack-jawed astonishment. "Good Lord," she said faintly. "How rich *are* you?"

Simon's dark eyes danced with sudden laughter at the ill-bred question, and he bent to murmur in her ear. "Rich enough to keep you well supplied in walking boots, madam."

Next they went to the pattern shop, where drawings of parts were carefully examined and wooden prototypes constructed according to specifications. Later, as Simon explained to her, the wooden patterns would be used to make molds, into which molten iron would be poured and cooled. Fascinated, Annabelle asked a slew of questions about the casting process and how the hydrostatic riveting machines and presses worked, and why quickly cooled iron was stronger than slow-cooled.

Despite Simon's initial misgivings, he seemed to enjoy touring her through the buildings, smiling occasionally at her absorbed expression. He guided her carefully into the foundry, where she discovered that his description of it as a glimpse into hell was not the exaggeration it had seemed. It had nothing to do with the condition of the workers, who seemed to be well treated, nor was it because of the buildings, which were relatively organized. Rather, it was the nature of the work itself, a kind of coordinated bedlam in which fumes and thundering noise and the red glow of roaring furnaces provided a seething backdrop for heavily clothed workers bearing brands and mallets. Surely the devil's minions were not half so well orchestrated as they went about their labors. Moving through the labyrinth of fire and steel, the foundrymen ducked beneath massive pivoting cranes and vats of hell-broth, and paused casually to allow huge plates of metal to swing across their paths. Annabelle was aware of a few curious glances cast her way, but for the most part, the foundrymen were too intent on their work to allow for distractions.

Traveling cranes were set all through the center of

the foundry, hoisting trucks filled with pig iron, scrap iron and coke to the tops of cupola stacks more than twenty feet high. The iron mixture was loaded at the top of the cupolas, where it was melted and forced into gigantic ladles and poured into molds by additional cranes. Odors of fuel, metal, and human sweat imparted a hazy weight to the air. As Annabelle watched the melted iron being transferred from vats to molds, she drew instinctively closer to Simon.

Buffeted by the relentless shrieks and moans of bending metal, the startling hiss of steam-powered machinery, and the echoing jolts of a great hammer being operated by six men, Annabelle found herself flinching with each new assault on her ears. Instantly, she felt Simon's arm slide around her back, while he engaged in a friendly, half-shouted conversation with the flange-shop manager, Mr. Mawer.

"Have you caught sight of Lord Westcliff yet?" Simon asked. "He had planned to arrive at the foundry at noon—and I've never known him to be late before."

The middle-aged foundryman blotted his sweating face with a handkerchief as he replied. "I believe the earl is at the assembly yard, Mr. Hunt. He had a concern about the dimensions of the new cylinder castings, and he wanted to inspect them before they were bolted into place."

Simon glanced down at Annabelle. "We'll go outside," he told her. "It's too damned hot and noisy to wait for Westcliff in here."

Relieved at the prospect of escaping the relentless clamor of the foundry, Annabelle agreed immediately. Now that she had gotten a thorough look at the place, her curiosity was satisfied, and she was ready to leave—even if that mean having to spend time in the company of Lord Westcliff. As Simon paused to exchange a few last words with Mawer, she watched as a steam-powered blower was employed to force air into the large central cupola. The blast of air caused hot metal to run into carefully positioned ladles, each one containing a thousand pounds of unstable liquid.

A particularly large heap of scrap iron was dumped into the charging door at the top of the cupola . . . too large, apparently, for the foreman shouted angrily at the foundryman who had loaded the truck. Narrowing her eyes, Annabelle observed them intently. A few rough shouts of warning from the men at the top of the gallery heralded another air blast of the steam blower . . . and this time, disaster struck. Boiling iron swiftly overran the ladles and dropped in bubbling wads from the cupola, some of it catching in the traveling cranes. Simon paused in midconversation with the flange-shop manager, both of them glancing upward at the same time.

"*Jesus,*" she heard Simon say, and she had one flashing glimpse of his face before he shoved her to the ground and covered her with his own body. At the same time, two pumpkin-sized clots of hell-broth dropped into the cooling troughs below, setting off a series of instantaneous explosions.

The impact of the blasts was like a succession of full body blows. Annabelle had no breath to cry out as Simon hunched over her, his shoulders curving in a shield over her head. And then—

Silence.

At first it seemed the motion of the earth itself had been brought to a jarring halt. Disoriented, Annabelle blinked to clear her vision, and was assaulted by the harsh brilliance of fire, the looming shapes of machinery silhouetted like monsters from the illustrations of a medieval tome. Intermittent blasts of heat struck her with such force that they threatened to peel the flesh from her bones. Flurries of metal chips and filings flew through the air as if they had been shot from a gun. She was surrounded by a whirl of movement and chaos, all of it blanketed in stunning quiet. Suddenly, there was a popping sensation in her ears, and they were filled with a tinny, high-pitched tone.

She was being pulled from the floor. Simon gave a hard tug to her arms, bringing her up in one powerful motion. Helpless against the force of momentum, she landed against his chest. He was saying something to her . . . she could almost make out the sound of his voice, and she began to hear the bursts of smaller explosions and the roaring undercurrent of fire as it fed hungrily on the building. Staring at Simon's hard face, she tried to comprehend his words, but she was distracted by the sting of more hot metal chips that peppered her face and neck like a swarm of nasty biting insects. Driven by instinct rather than reason, she couldn't stop herself from swatting foolishly at the air with her hand.

Simon shoved and dragged her through the pandemonium while trying to protect her with his body. An elephantine boiler barrel rolled gently before them, placidly crushing everything in its path. Cursing, Simon jerked Annabelle backward as the object rumbled by. There were men everywhere, shoving and swarming and shouting, white-eyed with the will to survive as they headed to the entryways on both ends of the building. A new set of eruptions shook the foundry, accompanied by rough cries. It was too hot to breathe, and Annabelle wondered dazedly if they would be roasted alive before they reached the door of the foundry. "Simon," she shouted, clinging to his lean waist, "On second thought . . . I've decided that you were right."

"About what?" he asked, his gaze locked on the foundry entrance.

"This place *is* too dangerous for me!"

Simon bent and hoisted her over his shoulder, carrying her over toppled cranes and collapsed equipment, with his arm clamped tightly around her knees. Dangling helplessly, Annabelle saw bloody holes in his coat, and realized that the blast had embedded metal filings and splinters in his back as he had covered her with his body. Crossing obstacle after obstacle, Simon finally reached the triple-width doors and set Annabelle on her feet. He startled her by pushing her firmly toward someone, shouting for him to take her. Twisting, Annabelle discovered that Simon had given her over to Mr. Mawer. "Take her outside," Simon commanded hoarsely. "Don't stop until she's completely clear of the building."

"Yes, sir!" The shop manager seized Annabelle in an unbreakable hold.

As she was compelled forcibly toward the entrance, Annabelle looked back wildly at Simon. "What are you going to do?"

"I have to make certain that everyone gets out."

A thrill of horror went through her. "No! Simon, come with me—"

"I'll be out in five minutes," he said brusquely.

Annabelle's face contorted, and she felt tears of terrified fury spring to her eyes. "In five minutes the building will have burned to the ground."

"Keep going," he said to Mawer, and turned away.

"Simon!" she screeched, balking as she saw him disappear back into the foundry. The ceiling was rippling with blue flame, while the machinery in the building shrieked as it was warped by intense heat. Smoke poured from the doorways, erupting in black blossoms that contrasted weirdly with the white

clouds overhead. Annabelle quickly discovered that resisting Mawer's superior hold was useless. She drew in
deep lungfuls of outside air, coughing as her irritated
lungs tried to expel the taint of smoke. Mawer didn't
pause until he had deposited her on a graveled walk-
way, delivering a firm order to stay where she was.

"He'll come out," he told her shortly. "You stay
here and watch for him. Promise you won't move,
Mrs. Hunt—I must try and account for all my men,
and I don't need extra trouble from you."

"I won't move," Annabelle said automatically, her
gaze fixed on the foundry entrance. "Go."

"Yes, ma'am."

She was motionless as she stood on the gravel, staring
dazedly at the doorway of the foundry while a furor of
activity raged around her. Men passed her at a dead run,
while others crouched over the wounded. A few, like her,
stood as still as statues, watching the blaze with empty
gazes. The fire roared with a force that made the ground
vibrate, gaining new and angry life as it consumed the
foundry. A hand-pump engine pulled by two dozen men
rolled close to the building—it must have been kept on
the site for emergencies, as there had not been sufficient
time to send for outside help. Frantically, the men sought
to connect a leather siphon hose to an underground water cistern. Taking hold of long side handles, they began
to pump in concerted effort, producing enough pressure
in the engine's air chamber to send a stream of water a
hundred feet in the air. The effort was pitifully inconse-
quential against the magnitude of the inferno.

Each minute that Annabelle waited took the toll of
a year. She felt her lips moving, shaping silent
words . . . *Simon, come out . . . Simon, come . . .*

A half dozen forms staggered from the entrance,
their faces and clothes smoke-blackened. Annabelle's

gaze raked over the emerging men. Perceiving that her husband was not among them, she switched her attention to the hand engine. The men had directed the hose to the adjoining building, drenching it in an effort to keep the fire from spreading. Annabelle shook her head in disbelief as she realized that they had given the foundry up for lost. They were surrendering all its contents . . . including anyone who may have been trapped inside. Galvanized into action, she ran to the other side of the foundry, desperately scanning the crowd for any sign of her husband.

Catching sight of one of the shop managers, who was taking inventory of the evacuated foundrymen, Annabelle hurried to him. "Where is Mr. Hunt?" she asked sharply, having to repeat the question before she had caught his attention.

He barely spared her a glance as he replied with distracted impatience. "There was another collapse inside. Mr. Hunt was helping to free a foundryman who was pinned by debris. He hasn't been seen since."

Despite the blistering heat that radiated from the foundry, Annabelle felt cold from her skin to her bones. Her mouth trembled. "If he was able to come out," she said, "he would have by now. He needs help. Can someone go in there to find him?"

The shop manager looked at her as if she was a madwoman. "*In there?* It would be suicide." Turning away from her, he went to a man who had collapsed to the ground, and bent to shove a wadded-up coat beneath his head. When he thought to spare a glance back at the space where Annabelle had been, it was empty.

Chapter 26

*I*f anyone had noticed that a woman was plunging into the building, they did not try to stop her. Covering her mouth and nose with a handkerchief, Annabelle made her way through billows of acrid smoke that drew streams of water from her squinting eyes. The fire, which had begun at the other side of the foundry, was eating its way across the rafters in voluptuous ripples of blue and white and yellow. More frightening than the scalding heat was the noise; the growling flames, the screeches and groans of bending metal, the clangs of heavy machinery as it snapped like children's toys being crushed underfoot. Liquid metal popped and sprayed in occasional bursts of grapeshot.

Picking up her skirts in awkward bunches, Annabelle stumbled over the smoldering knee-deep rubble, calling out for Simon, her voice muted in the cacophany. Just as she despaired of finding him, she caught sight of movement in the rubble.

Crying out, she hurried to the long, fallen form. It

was Simon, alive and conscious, his leg trapped beneath the steel shaft of a fallen crane. As he saw her, his soot-smeared face contorted with horror, and he struggled to a half-sitting position. "Annabelle," he said hoarsely, pausing as he was wracked with coughing. "Dammit, *no*—get out of here! What the hell are you doing?"

She shook her head, unwilling to waste breath in arguing. The crane was too heavy for either of them to move—she had to find something . . . some makeshift lever to dislodge it. Wiping her burning eyes, she hunted through a pile of castings and broken stone and a heap of counterbalance weights. Everything was covered with layers of oil and soot that caused her feet to slip as she moved through the wreckage. A row of driving wheels rested against the shuddering wall, some of them taller than she. She made her way toward them and found a stack of axles and connecting rods as thick as her fist. Grasping one of the heavy, grease-coated rods, she tugged it from the stack and dragged it back to her husband.

One glance at Simon left no doubt that if he could have gotten his hands on her, he would have murdered her on the spot. "Annabelle," he roared, between spasms of coughing, "get out of this building *now!*"

"Not without you." She fumbled with a wooden block that had been placed at the end of a hydrostatic ram.

Twisting and tugging at his pinned leg, Simon showered her with threats and profanities while she lugged the wooden block over to him and shoved it against the crane.

"It's too heavy!" he snarled, as she struggled with the connecting rod. "You can't budge it! Get out of here. *Damn you*, Annabelle—"

Grunting with effort, she braced the rod on the wooden block and wedged the end of it beneath the crane. She pushed down, using all her weight. The crane remained solidly in place, indifferent to her efforts. With a gasp of frustration, she struggled with the lever, until the rod creaked in protest. It was no use—the crane would not move.

A loud crack went off, and iron shards flew through the air, causing her to duck and cover her head. She felt a blow against her arm, striking with enough force to send her to the ground. An aching burn penetrated her upper arm, and she glanced down to discover that a metal chip had lodged in her flesh, provoking a splash of brilliant red blood. Crawling to Simon, she felt him snatch her against his chest, shielding her until the shower of iron pellets had abated. "Simon," she panted, drawing back to look into his fume-reddened eyes, "you always carry a knife. Where is it?"

Simon went still as the import of the question struck him. For a split-second she saw him weigh the possibility, then he shook his head. "No," he rasped. "Even if you could manage to sever the leg, you couldn't drag me out of here." He shoved her away from him. "There's no time left—you have to get out of the damned foundry." As he saw the refusal on her face, his features twisted with hideous fear, not for himself but for her. "My God, Annabelle," he grated, finally reduced to begging, "don't do this. Please. If you care for me at all—" A shuddering cough tore through his body. "Go. *Go.*"

For an instant Annabelle wanted to obey him, as the desire to escape the hellish nightmare of the burning foundry nearly overwhelmed her. But as she staggered to her feet, and looked down at him, so large and yet so defenseless, she could not make herself walk away. Instead she picked up the connecting rod once more,

and hoisted it back onto the wooden block, while pain shot through her injured shoulder. Blood thundered in her ears, making it impossible to distinguish Simon's outburst from the din of the shuddering building around them. And that was likely a good thing, as he looked insane with fury. She pulled and hung on the lever, while her tortured lungs pulled in choking air and spasmed in response. The scene blurred around her, but she continued to exert her remaining strength on the iron bar, her slight weight straining to move it.

All of a sudden she felt something grasp the back of her dress. Had she any breath left to scream, she would have. Startled out of her wits, Annabelle went stiff as she was hauled backward, and her hands were pried from the bar. Choking and sobbing, she stared through smoke-blinded eyes at the lean, dark shape behind her. A cool voice reverberated in her ear. "I'll lift the crane. Go pull his leg free at my command."

She recognized his autocratic tone even before his face registered. *Westcliff*, she thought in amazement. It was indeed the earl, his white shirt torn and filthy, his features streaked with soot. Yet for all his dishevelment, he looked calm and capable as he motioned for her to go to Simon. Hefting the iron bar with ease, he deftly adjusted the lever beneath the crane shaft. Although he was only of medium height, his lean body was solid and superbly fit, conditioned by years of punishing physical exertion. As Westcliff pushed downward with a mighty shove, Annabelle heard the squeaks and groans of bending metal, and the massive crane eased upward a few crucial inches. The earl barked at Annabelle, who frantically tugged at Simon's leg, ignoring his groan of agony as he rolled from beneath the crushing object.

Lowering the crane with a massive *thud*, Westcliff

came to help Simon struggle to his feet, wedging a solid shoulder beneath his arm to support his injured side. Annabelle took the other side and winced as Simon seized her in a punishing grip. Smoke and heat overwhelmed her, making it impossible to see or breathe or think. Continuous coughing rattled her slender frame. Had she been left to her own devices, she would never have been able to find her way out of the foundry. She was hauled and pushed forward by Simon's brutal grasp, occasionally lifted from her feet as they crossed the wreckage on the ground, her shins and ankles and knees battered painfully. The torturous journey seemed to last forever, their progress incremental, while the foundry shook and roared like a beast hovering over its injured prey. Annabelle's mind swam. She fought to stay conscious, while her vision was filled with glittering sparks and an inviting darkness that loomed just beyond them.

She never remembered the moment they emerged from the foundry with smoking clothes and singed hair and heat-parched faces . . . all she could recall later was that there were countless pairs of hands reaching for her, and her aching legs were suddenly relieved of the burden of her own weight. Collapsing slowly into someone's arms, she felt herself being lifted while her lungs worked greedily to collect clean air. A dripping, brackish cloth passed over her face, and unfamiliar hands reached inside her dress to unfasten her corset. She couldn't even bring herself to care. Blanketed in an exhausted stupor, she surrendered to the rough ministrations and gulped the contents of a metal dipper that was pressed to her mouth.

When Annabelle finally came to herself, she blinked repeatedly to let the assuaging fluids spread across the stinging surface of her eyeballs. "Simon . . . ?" she

mumbled, struggling upward. She was gently subdued.

"Rest for another minute," came a gravelly voice. "Your husband is fine. A bit battered and scorched, but definitely salvageable. I don't even think his damned leg is broken."

As full awareness seeped over her, she realized in slug-gish amazement that she was half-sitting in Lord West-cliff's lap, on the ground, with her gown partly undone. Glancing up into the earl's harsh-planed face, she saw that his tanned complexion was streaked with black, and his hair was rumpled and filthy. The usually impec-cable earl looked so sympathetic and disheveled and ap-proachably human that she barely recognized him.

"Simon . . ." she whispered.

"He is being loaded into my carriage as we speak. Needless to say, he is rather impatient for you to join him. I am taking the both of you to Marsden Terrace—I've already sent for a doctor to meet us there." West-cliff shifted her a little higher in his arms. "Why did you go in after him? You could have been a very wealthy widow." The question was asked not with mockery, but with a gentle interest that confused her.

Rather than answer, Annabelle turned her attention to a bloody blotch on his shoulder. "Hold still," she murmured, using her broken fingernails to grasp the end of a needle-thin metallic shard that protruded from his shirt. She tugged it out quickly, and West-cliff's face twitched with pain.

Regarding the shard as she held it up for him to see, the earl shook his head ruefully. "God. I hadn't no-ticed that."

Enclosing the object in her fingers, Annabelle asked warily, "Why did *you* go in, my lord?"

"Having been informed that you had dashed into a burning building to fetch your husband, I thought to

offer my services . . . perhaps open a door, clear an object from your path . . . that sort of thing."

"You were rather helpful," she said, deliberately matching his bland tone, and he grinned, his teeth white in his smoke-blackened face.

Carefully, Westcliff helped her to sit up. Keeping his arm behind her back, he closed the fastenings of her dress with a deft, impersonal touch, while he contemplated the full-bore devastation of the foundy. "Only two men perished, and one still unaccounted for," he murmured. "Miraculous, considering the scope of the disaster."

"Does this mean the end of the locomotive works?"

"No, I expect that we'll rebuild as soon as possible." The earl stared kindly into her exhausted face. "Later you might describe to me what happened. For now, allow me to take you to the carriage."

Annabelle gasped a little as he stood and lifted her in his arms. "Oh—there's no need—"

"It's the least I can do." Westcliff flashed another rare smile as he carried her with facile strength. "I have some amends to make, where you're concerned."

"You mean because you now believe that I actually care about Simon, instead of having just married him for his money?"

"Something like that. It seems I was mistaken about you, Mrs. Hunt. Please accept my humble apology."

Suspecting that the earl was rarely given to making apologies of any kind, much less humble ones, Annabelle linked her arms around his neck. "I suppose I'll have to," she said grudgingly, "since you saved our lives."

He shifted her more comfortably in his arms. "Shall we cry pax, then?"

"Pax," she agreed, and coughed against his shoulder.

* * *

While the doctor visited Simon in the master bedroom of Marsden Terrace, Westcliff took Annabelle aside and personally tended to the wound in her upper arm. After tweezing out the metal chip that was half-buried in her skin, he doused the area with alcohol while Annabelle screeched in pain. He dabbed the cut with salve, bandaged it expertly, and gave her a glass of brandy to dull her discomfort. Whether he had added something to the brandy, or pure exhaustion had amplified its effects, Annabelle would never know. After downing two fingers of the dark amber liquid, she felt woozy and light-headed. Her voice was distinctly slurred as she told Westcliff that the world was fortunate that he hadn't gone into the medical profession, which he gravely acknowledged was probably true. She staggered off drunkenly to find Simon, and was firmly dissuaded by the housekeeper and a pair of housemaids, who seemed intent on washing her. Before Annabelle quite knew what had happened, she had been bathed and changed into a nightgown purloined from Westcliff's elderly mother's closet and was lying in a soft, clean bed. As soon as she closed her eyes, she sank into a helpless slumber.

To Annabelle's chagrin, she awoke quite late the next morning, struggling to gather where she was and what had happened. The moment her thoughts touched on Simon, she floundered out of bed, paying no heed to her handsome surroundings as she padded barefoot into the hall. She crossed the path of a housemaid, who looked mildly startled by the appearance of a woman with wild, unbound hair, a scratched and reddened face, and an ill-fitting nightgown . . . a woman, who, in spite of a thorough washing the night before, was still strongly scented of foundry smoke.

"Where is he?" Annabelle asked without prelude.

To the housemaid's credit, she comprehended the abrupt query and directed Annabelle to the master bedroom at the end of the hall.

Coming to the open doorway, Annabelle saw Lord Westcliff standing by the side of the huge bed, where Simon was sitting up against a stack of pillows. Simon was bare-chested, his shoulders and torso swarthy against the snowy linens that had been pulled up to his midriff. Annabelle winced as she saw the profusion of plasters affixed to his arms and chest, having some idea of the discomfort that he must have endured in having so many metal pellets removed. The two men stopped talking as soon as they became aware of her presence.

Simon's gaze locked on her face and held with unnerving intensity. An invisible swell of emotion filled the room, drowning them both in acute tension. As Annabelle stared into her husband's granite-hard face, no words seemed appropriate. If she spoke to him just then, it was either going to be puerile hyperbole or inane understatement. Absurdly grateful for Westcliff's presence as a temporary buffer, Annabelle addressed her first comment to him.

"My lord," she said, inspecting the cuts and burns on his face, "you look like the loser in a tavern brawl."

Coming forward, Westcliff took her hand and executed an impeccable bow over it. He surprised her by pressing a chivalrous kiss to the back of her wrist. "Had I ever participated in a tavern brawl, madam, I assure you that I would not have lost."

That drew a grin from Annabelle, who could not help reflecting that twenty-four hours ago, she had despised his arrogant aplomb, whereas now it seemed almost endearing. Westcliff released her hand after giving it a reassuring squeeze. "With your permission,

Mrs. Hunt, I will withdraw. No doubt you have a few things to discuss with your husband."

"Thank you, my lord."

As the earl left and closed the door, Annabelle approached the bedside. Simon looked away from her with a frown, the bold structure of his profile gilded with sunlight.

"Is your leg broken?" Annabelle asked huskily.

Simon shook his head, concentrating on the ornately flowered paper that covered the bedroom wall. He spoke in a smoke-ravaged voice. "It will be fine."

Annabelle's gaze touched on him, lingering on the heavy musculature of his arms and chest, the long fingers of his hand, the way a lock of dark hair fell over his brow. "Simon," she asked softly. "Won't you look at me?"

His eyes narrowed as he turned to pin her with a hostile stare. "I'd like to do more than look at you. I'd like to throttle you."

It would have been ingenuous for Annabelle to ask why, since she already knew. Instead, she waited with forced patience, while Simon's throat worked violently. "What you did yesterday was unforgivable," he finally muttered.

She gave him a startled glance. "What?"

"Lying there in that hell-pit, I made what I thought would be the last request of my life. And you refused."

"As things turned out, it wasn't your last request," Annabelle replied warily. "You survived, and so did I, and now everything is fine—"

"It is *not fine*," Simon snapped, his face darkening with rising fury. "For the rest of my life I will remember how it felt to know that you were going to die along with me, while I couldn't do a damned thing to

stop you." He averted his face as his breath turned harsh with unwanted emotion.

Annabelle reached for him, then checked herself, her hands suspended in the air between them. "How could you ask me to leave you there, hurt and alone? I couldn't."

"You should have done as I told you!"

Annabelle didn't flinch, understanding the fear that seethed beneath his anger. "*You* wouldn't have left had it been me on the foundry floor—"

"I knew you were going to say that," he said in savage disgust. "Of course I wouldn't have left you. I'm the man. A man is supposed to protect his wife."

"And a wife is supposed to be a helpmate," Annabelle countered.

"You were not helping me," Simon bit out. "You were putting me through agony. Dammit, Annabelle, why didn't you obey me?"

She took a deep breath before replying. "Because I love you."

Simon continued to look away from her, while the soft words sent a visible shock through him. His large hand tightened into a fist on the coverlet as his defenses began to crack visibly. "I would die a thousand times over," he said, a tremor in his voice, "to spare you the slightest harm. And the fact that you were willing to throw your life away in a completely pointless sacrifice is more than I can bear."

Annabelle's eyes stung as she stared at him, while need and inexhaustible tenderness gathered like an ache in her body. "I realized something," she said huskily, "when I was standing outside the foundry, watching it burn and knowing you were inside." She swallowed hard against the thickness in her throat. "I

would rather have died in your arms, Simon, than face a lifetime without you. All those endless years . . . all those winters, summers . . . a hundred seasons of wanting you and never having you. Growing old, while you stayed eternally young in my memories." She bit her lip and shook her head, while her eyes flooded. "I was wrong when I told you that I didn't know where I belonged. I do. With you, Simon. Nothing matters except being with you. You're stuck with me forever, and I'll *never* listen when you tell me to go." She managed a tremulous smile. "So you may as well stop complaining and resign yourself to it."

With startling suddenness, Simon turned to snatch her against him. He buried his face in the tangled skein of her hair. His voice came out in an anguished growl.

"My God, I can't stand this! I can't let you go out every day, fearing every minute that something might happen to you, knowing that every ounce of sanity I've got left is hinged on your well-being. I can't feel this way . . . it's too strong . . . oh, *hell*. I'll turn into a raving lunatic. I'll never be of use to anyone again. If I could just reduce it somehow . . . love you only half this much . . . I might be able to live with it."

Annabelle laughed shakily at his rough confession, while a hot rush of joy spilled through her. "But I want all your love," she said. As Simon drew his head back to look at her, his expression knocked the breath from her lungs. It took her several seconds to recover. "All your heart and mind," she continued with a crooked smile, and lowered her voice provocatively. "All your body, too."

Simon trembled and stared at her radiant face as if he would never be able to tear his gaze away. "That's reassuring. Since you seemed more than eager to saw off my leg with a pocketknife yesterday."

Annabelle's mouth quirked, and she stroked her fingertips over his hairy chest, playing with the glinting dark strands. "My intention was to preserve the largest possible portion of you, and get you out of that place."

"At that point I might have let you, had I thought it would work." Simon caught her hand in his, and pressed his cheek against her abraded palm. "You're a strong woman, Annabelle. Stronger than I would have believed."

"No, it's my love for you that is strong." Sliding him a glance of sparkling mischief from beneath her lashes, Annabelle murmured, "I wouldn't be able to saw off just *anyone's* leg, you know."

"If you ever risk your life again, for any reason, I'm going to strangle you. Come here." Gripping his hand behind her head, Simon pulled her forward. When their noses were nearly touching, he took a deep breath, and said, "I love you, dammit."

She brushed her lips teasingly against his. "How much?"

He made a slight sound, as if the soft kiss had affected him intensely. "Without limit. Beyond forever."

"I love you more," Annabelle said, and brought her mouth to his. She felt a surge of exquisite pleasure, accompanied by the elusive sense of completeness, of perfect fulfillment, that they had never quite reached before. She was floating in warmth, as if her soul was bathed in light. Drawing back, she saw from the stunned brilliance in Simon's gaze that he had felt it, too.

There was a new, wondering note in his voice as he said, "Kiss me again."

"No, I'll hurt you. I'm leaning on your leg."

"That's not my leg," came his roguish reply, making her laugh.

"You perverse man."

"You're so beautiful," Simon whispered. "Inside and out. Annabelle, my wife, my sweet love . . . kiss me again. And don't stop until I tell you to."

"Yes, Simon," she murmured, and cheerfully obeyed.

Epilogue

". . . No, that's not the best part," Annabelle said animatedly, waving a handful of pages in a gesture for the Bowmans to be quiet. The three women lounged in Annabelle's suite at the Rutledge, dangling their stockinged feet as they sipped glasses of sweet wine. "Let me read on . . . *'As we stopped in the Loire Valley to view a sixteenth-century chateau that is undergoing restoration, Miss Hunt made the acquaintance of an unmarried English gentleman, Mr. David Keir, who is accompanying his two younger cousins on their Grand Tour. Apparently he is an art historian, engaged in writing a scholarly work on something-or-other, and he and Miss Hunt found much to discuss. According to the mothers—from now on that is how I shall refer to Mama and Mrs. Hunt, as they are always in each other's company and appear to have divided one brain between themselves—'* "

"Good God," Lillian exclaimed with a laugh, "does your brother have to write in such long sentences?"

"Hush!" Daisy admonished. "Jeremy was about to say what the mothers think of Mr. Keir! Go on, Annabelle."

" '—they are of the unified opinion that Mr. Keir is a prepossessing and well-favored gentleman—' " Annabelle read.

"Does that mean handsome?" Daisy asked.

Annabelle grinned. "Decidedly. And Jeremy goes on to say that Mr. Keir has asked permission to write to Meredith, and he intends to call on her when she returns to London!"

"How lovely!" Daisy exclaimed, extending her glass to Lillian. "Pour me another, dear—I want to drink to Meredith's future happiness."

They all drank obligingly, and Annabelle set the letter aside with a pleased sigh. "I wish I could tell Evie."

"I miss Evie," Lillian said with a surprising wistfulness. "Perhaps soon her jailers—pardon, her family—will allow us to visit."

"I have an idea," Daisy commented. "When father comes from New York next month, we'll have to go with him for another visit to Stony Cross. Naturally, Annabelle and Mr. Hunt will be invited, because of their friendship with Lord Westcliff. Perhaps we can ask that Evie and her aunt be included, too. Then we can have an official wallflower meeting—not to mention another Rounders game."

Annabelle groaned theatrically, downing her wine in a large gulp. "God help me." Placing her glass on a nearby table, she fished in her pocket for a tiny paper packet with an object folded inside. "That reminds me—Daisy, will you do a favor for me?"

"Of course," the girl replied promptly and opened the paper. Her face wrinkled in curiosity as she saw a

needlelike piece of metal. "What in heaven's name is this?"

"I pulled that from Lord Westcliff's shoulder on the day of the foundry fire." She grinned at their appalled expressions as they saw the long iron shard. "If you wouldn't mind, take it with you to Stony Cross and toss it into the wishing well."

"What should I wish for?"

Annabelle laughed softly. "Make the same wish for poor old Westcliff that you did for me."

"Poor old Westcliff?" Lillian snorted, and regarded the two of them suspiciously. "What *was* the wish that you made for Annabelle?" she demanded of her younger sister. "You never told me."

"I never told Annabelle, either," Daisy murmured, regarding Annabelle with a curious smile. "How do you know what it was?"

Annabelle grinned back at her. "I figured it out." Curling her legs beneath her, she leaned forward and murmured, "Now, about finding a husband for Lillian . . . I have a rather interesting notion . . ."